The Trouble
with Dating Sue

A GROVER BEACH TEAM BOOK

ANNA KATMORE

GENRE: YA/CONTEMPORARY ROMANCE

This book is a work of fiction. Names, places, characters and incidents are either the product of the author's imagination or are used fictitiously. Any resemblance to actual people, living or dead, businesses, organizations, events or locales is entirely coincidental.

For Chris

He knows why.

The Trouble with Dating Sue

ANNA KATMORE

Chapter 1

LAUREN PARKER-LEE was a satanic tease. She detached her lips from mine, fastened her long black hair—which I'd just had my hands in—with a clip at the back of her head, and grinned at me. "Learn to conjugate future perfect tense and you'll get a bigger reward next time."

Dammit, she knew how to make my heart go *boom*. Or maybe it wasn't so much my heart that exploded at this incentive as my imagination. Her body was just as exotic as her Thai eyes and always a pleasure to explore. But today her lacy underwear still covered all the good parts, which meant I hadn't studied hard enough the past week. We were in the same Spanish class, both seniors at Grover Beach High, and since we'd started seeing each other for noncommittal fun under the cover of her tutoring me, my grades had shot straight up to a solid B.

I reached for Lauren's cell on the nightstand and swiped my thumb across the display. It flashed ten past four—time to run. Detangling from her mile-long legs turned out to be a tough job. When I'd finally managed, I climbed out of bed, finding my shirt and jeans on the parquet floor. Basketball practice on Monday was something I wouldn't miss—not for any of the girls I occasionally hooked up with, and not for a smoking-hot Spanish lesson with Lauren either.

"Remember that we have a test a week from Friday," she cooed, slowly sliding the dark red satin sheets over her body just far enough to touch the curve of her rack. Jeez! With my jeans pulled up halfway, I stumbled and caught myself on the backrest of the swivel chair in front of her desk. That girl knew how to tempt an eighteen-year-old for sure.

Well, two could play this game.

I buttoned my pants as I prowled back to her bed. Hands braced on the pillow at either side of her head, I leaned down so she had to roll from her side onto her back. Merely an inch separated our noses. Lauren squinted at the bright sun scratching at her window above her bed. A smirk on my lips, I drawled, "Guess that means I'll be seeing you a little more often the next two weeks." Without giving her the goodbye kiss her flirty pout demanded, I pulled my t-shirt over my head, slipped on my shoes, and was out of her room before the testosterone in my body got a chance to object.

Her voice caught up with me. "You forgot your textbook, Chris!"

Right. Rolling my eyes, I skittered to a halt in the hallway, turned around, and headed back into her room. The book lay on the desk, pretty much untouched the entire afternoon. I

ANNA KATMORE

shoved it into the duffle bag that held my jersey and shorts, gave Lauren a tight-lipped grin, and was gone the next minute.

Lauren lived so far out of town that it took me fifteen minutes to get back to Grover Beach. It was a shame when half a year before your graduation you still didn't have your own car. But Mom's black SUV was good enough for now. And hey, look at that, my brother's car was parked two spaces down in front of school.

What was Ethan doing here so late? As far as I knew, he should've been home, in his room with his lonely self. At least that's what I'd seen him doing for most of this fall. The complete opposite of me, my identical twin wasn't what one would call a social guy—at least not anymore.

Until last spring, he too had been part of the Dunkin' Sharks, our basketball team. The two of us had hung out with the rest of the gang every minute of the day. That changed when one of the guys started rumors about Ethan. Rumors of the really bad kind. At some point, it just got to be too much for Ethan to cope with. He should have shoved a fist into Will's mouth—that's what I would have done. But my brother, much to my irritation, simply quit the team instead of retaliating.

Frankly, that sucked. On the other hand, I could kind of see why he'd rather avoid a confrontation that would be happening under the header: *Dude, are you gay?*

I didn't care if he was or wasn't. Gay or straight, Ethan had been one of the best players on our team, and giving up basketball because of dickhead William Davis was a stupid thing to do. But who was I to tell Ethan how to live his life?

Abandoning thoughts of my brother altogether, I snatched the duffle bag from the passenger seat, headed into the changing room, and got ready for my favorite ninety minutes of the day.

*

"Chris!" my mom yelled through the door. "Dinner!"

I slammed my books closed and jogged down the hallway, pleased with my diligence. After basketball practice, I'd engrossed myself in Spanish and studied real hard. I had every intention of seeing Lauren after school tomorrow and getting laid for being such a good student. At the thought, my lips stretched into a grin.

As I entered the kitchen, I saw Ethan had already laid out the dishes, so I took a seat to his left at the dark, round table. We didn't have a separate dining room, our one-story house was just too small for that. But the kitchen was big enough, and even with the island unit, there was plenty of space to move.

"What've you been doing at school so late?" I asked Ethan around a mouthful of chicken salad. "Don't tell me you got in detention, because even that would have ended way before"—I glanced at my watch—"thirty minutes ago." I'd checked the time when I heard my brother parking in front of our house. Him coming home at seven in the evening was almost as spectacular as me staying home on a Friday night. Mom, on the other hand, didn't care about the reason. She was just happy to see Ethan being social again. Her beaming face said as much when she turned in my direction.

"Had something to discuss with Hunter," Ethan explained, munching on some salad. "He asked me if I was interested in playing on his soccer team."

"Oh, Ethan, how wonderful!" That was my mom being supportive, hoping Ethan would find a hobby outside his room—which, in the long run, would help him find a girlfriend, too. Of course, she hadn't been oblivious to the signs that her other son might be interested in boys more than girls, but she would never call him out on it, and neither would I. However, "a mother can hope," she'd told me once.

Deep in my gut, I had this feeling that her hope was in vain.

Subtly, I shook my head at her to tell her to drop pestering Ethan, but he replied casually as if talking about the weather, "I trained with them today and it was kinda good. It's actually a co-ed team. Didn't know Grover Beach High even had one."

Hmm. I didn't know that either. Then again, I'd never been interested in anything outside basketball activities, least of all something as boring as soccer. It would be good for Ethan to socialize a little more, however, so who cared if he played soccer, badminton, or pin the tail on the donkey? I'd be there at his first game for sure and cheer him on until my vocal cords got sore. That's a favor I'd happily return, because he and Mom had come to every one of my basketball games this season. The very last one before Christmas was this Saturday. Mom had marked the day in her calendar in the kitchen.

Frankly, I couldn't wait to kick some Clearwater High ass. They were a damn good team, but we were better. It could be an epic finish for the season.

Mom wouldn't let the topic go now that she knew there were actually girls on a team that Ethan might or might not join, but I didn't get a chance to listen to their conversation. My phone rang in my pocket. Since I'd finished my meal, I carried my plate to the sink and then answered the phone on the way back to my room.

It was a call from *Tiffany 6*. She was a blonde I hooked up with last summer. The number next to her name was an indication that I'd like to hook up with her again sometime. I saved all girls to my contacts list with a number from one to ten, which was a ranking of "doable" in my own books. Six was good. Lauren was better. She had a solid 10 next to her name. And since Tiffany wanted to go out with me on Saturday—the Saturday my final basketball game of the season took place— she lost a number in my personal ranking right this minute. If she'd known me at all, she wouldn't have suggested going out but instead would come and watch me play ball. After I hung up, I changed the 6 to a 5 and tossed my phone onto my bed. Time for more Spanish studying. Future perfect tense it was.

As I slipped into bed later that night, Spanish verbs spiraled through my brain. Honestly, studying alone wasn't half as much fun as studying with a hot Thai girl on my lap. Actually, studying alone wasn't fun, period.

I closed my eyes and tried very hard not to dream in Spanish. Whether I managed that or not, I couldn't tell, because when the alarm woke me in the morning, I didn't remember any dreams at all.

Running through my morning routine—which was a quick shower, no breakfast, hunting for some clothes to wear that my twin brother didn't own too, and begging him for a ride to school—I repeatedly went through the one line I'd learned by heart yesterday before going to sleep. I was going to find Lauren before first period, and I was going to impress her. That was my plan for today.

When Ethan let me out in front of school to find a parking spot around the corner, I ran into my friend and captain of the basketball team, Tyler Moss, who most people called T-Rex because he played one hell of an aggressive style. His girlfriend, Rebecca Evers, was with him. "Hey, Becks," I said to her and slung my arm around her shoulders in a casual greeting as I walked along with them. "Have you seen Lauren today?" The two girls were best friends, and I didn't want to wait for fourth period to see Lauren in Spanish.

Rebecca, who I knew was secretly hoping that her friend and I started dating seriously so the four of us could hang out on double dates, raised her brows, the edges of her lips curling into a smile. "Eager to see her, are we?"

"Quite," I whispered into her ear, but removed my arm from her a second later when we walked through the glass doors and entered the building.

Rebecca tossed her thick hair, blond as mine, over her shoulder and wrapped her arm around Tyler, but glanced my way. "She's got biology first period. Let's see if she's already there."

Tyler chuckled at his girlfriend's high hopes when he knew as well as I did that Lauren and I dating for real was never going to happen. We shared a quick look over Rebecca's head as she led the way to some biology classroom, but neither of us dared to pull her out of her mission.

Lauren was a bombshell, all right, and two years ago, I might have considered a relationship with someone like her for sure. I'd actually had a girlfriend before I started hooking up with random girls. But a lot has happened since, and for me to be exclusive again meant there had to be a girl who wouldn't flirt around—or worse, dump me for my best friend. I still gritted my teeth at the memory of Amanda Roseman telling me on the phone that Michael had replaced me as her boyfriend during spring break in tenth grade. I doubted there was a girl in this town who could make me fall in love again. However, if there was, I challenged fate to send her my way right this minute.

As we rounded the corner, the only girl I saw was Lauren. Apparently, fate had a screwed up sense of humor, and I silently laughed to myself, shaking my head.

We joined Lauren and the two guys she was talking to, Allen Stone and Wesley something. I wasn't really friends with Wes, but he seemed cool enough to hang out with sometimes. His elephant-like ears were the one thing I always noticed about him first. Right now, he was leaning with one shoulder against the line of lockers in front of Lauren, who had her back to me, and said something that made her laugh. He

ANNA KATMORE

straightened the moment I stepped up to them, giving my presence away to her.

Pearly white teeth appeared in a lazy smile as she turned around. "Hey there, handsome."

"Hello, beautiful." I might have placed a kiss on her mouth, too, but she'd used a shiny red lipstick this morning, which I couldn't stand. I'd kissed her with glossed lips before— and other girls too, in fact—but it always filled my mouth with a plastic taste I couldn't get rid of for hours afterward. Lauren knew that. It was the reason she never wore makeup when we met to study.

"What brings you to my biology class?" she mocked with a lifted chin and a real spark of interest in her dark eyes. "Did you miss me?"

Confidently, I placed one hand against the locker next to her head. "How about you wipe off your lips, and I'll show you just how much?"

"I thought I made myself clear yesterday." Lauren held my gaze with a taunting smirk. "That's not going to happen until you learn to conjugate future perfect tense."

That was my cue. Leaning in a little closer, I purred into her ear, "*Al final del día...yo habré quitado tus bragas.*"

Lauren sucked in a soft breath at my pledge that I would have pulled her panties down by the end of the day. "With my teeth..." I added in a dangerously low tone, enjoying the light blush my promise put on her usually pale cheeks. Catching her off guard was something that happened like twice a year and always made me feel a little more sure of myself around her.

"Ah, I see you actually took a look at your textbook for once."

"I'm up for some case studies later. What do you think?"

She gave me a cocky look. "I'll be home alone until four thirty."

Unfortunately, that collided with my plans for the afternoon. "I've got basketball practice right after school today," I told her, dropping the bedroom voice and speaking normal again. "But you can come to my place after five."

"Hey." A soft voice behind me made me turn my head before I got an answer from Lauren. Next to my right shoulder stood a girl for whom no name was in my memory. Her honey-colored hair was in a modest ponytail, and she shoved her glasses farther up her pert nose as she looked me directly in the eyes. "Expecto Patronum" stood in a Harry Potter font on her left boob, with the white outline of a bunny flashing out of a magic wand standing out against the pink of the shirt. A calculator also stuck out of her right breast pocket. She had to be one of those kids who dressed up for comic cons and calculated the three-hundredth digit of pi or something for fun. A poster child for the nerd club.

"Um, I brought you the CD," she continued, while I was still trying to figure out if I should know her. But I didn't hang out with girls from the geek squad, so who the hell was she?

The weirdest thing happened then. She offered me a CD case. What on earth was I supposed to do with that? I took a step back from Lauren and fully turned to the strange girl. Instead of taking what she held out to me, I shoved my hand into my pocket and tightly wrapped the other around the strap of my backpack. Being chatted up in the corridors of my school was normal for me—just not by strangers. I knew all of the senior girls and probably up to sixty percent of the rest. This face was new to me. My gaze roamed down her body and back up to her eyes.

My being quiet must have made her uncomfortable, because she cleared her throat. "Listen—" It was almost a croak. There was nothing left of the confidence she'd showed ten seconds ago. "I can't meet you at three today, something's come up. So maybe we can postpone the date until a little later? Would five work for you?"

Sorry, *what*?

I tried very hard to keep my composure, but a surprised laugh escaped me anyway. I certainly wasn't one to decline a date so easily, but this was ridiculous. With my arms folded, I asked, "Sweetness, what made you think you and I would be going out together?"

She gulped. Oh boy, had I embarrassed her? My friends chuckled behind me while I bit the inside of my cheek to keep a sober expression. Claimed by a nerd; it was too funny.

A moment later, the girl sucked in a breath that sounded like bravery and squared her shoulders. Was she going to summon her magic wand to blow me up now? "Obviously I got it wrong. Sorry, my bad," she stated in a wry voice. As she spun on her heel and stomped away, she flipped me the bird.

Holy cow! I didn't know if I should be offended or impressed.

There was no time to think about it because as soon as she was gone, Lauren smacked me on the chest. "What was that?" she demanded. Like the others, she had to control her giggles. "Are you dating that girl?"

If I said yes, even just to mock her, she wouldn't be coming to my place later today. Instead, I feigned being hurt by her words and clutched my chest. "Ow, you're breaking my heart, Lauren! You're the only one I'm dating tonight. I don't even know who she is." Then I wound a tendril of her straight black hair around my finger and grinned at her. "See you after five?"

Lauren looked after the stranger for a moment, then she turned back to me and cracked a smile. "Sure."

Chapter 2

MY ROOM STILL smelled of Lauren's perfume the next morning. No matter what hot memories that scent brought on, I was getting sick of the sweetness. As I came back in after a shower, I had to open both windows to get some fresh air inside. I should have done that right after she left last night.

The late November wind brought a morning chill to my room, but that was as cold as we got here in California in the winter. In a couple of hours the sun would be so strong again that a jacket wasn't even necessary. I put on a white sweatshirt and the same ragged jeans from yesterday. As I packed my school bag, Ethan knocked on my open door.

"If you want a ride, hurry up. But just so you know, I'll be training with Hunter and the guys again today, so you'll have to walk home after school," he informed me.

Soccer practice again? Did that mean he was part of Ryan Hunter's team now? Ryan was a good friend of mine, and apart from sitting behind him in trig and him being my lab partner in biology, I had already spent countless nights at his house when he gave those epic parties. Since I wouldn't see much of Ethan today—we had no classes together whatsoever—I might ask Ryan what the deal was with my brother suddenly being so interested in soccer.

"You go ahead," I told Ethan, finishing up with my school bag. "I'll borrow Mom's car."

"All right. See you later."

Grover Beach had the crime rate of a convent, yet our bungalow made it kind of easy for interested thieves to take the opportunity. From an early age, my brother and I had been drilled by Mom to close the windows when we weren't home. There was actually something very dear to me in my room that made me heed her advice extra carefully.

Backpack over one shoulder, I checked my perfectly chaotic hair in the bathroom mirror and went looking for my mother in the living room. "Morning, Mom. Do you need the car today?"

She swiped her brown hair off her forehead as she looked up from rearranging the pillows on the couch and gave me a smile. "I don't have any clients. You can use it."

Her not having any clients for an entire day was rare. She was a real estate agent and spent a lot of time on the road, meeting people in and outside town to show them pretty houses up for sale. The job didn't make her a millionaire, but it made her happy. She earned enough that we never had to worry about bills, and she didn't have to ask my dad—who'd replaced her with his secretary when Ethan and I were twelve—for support either. Only a new car for me wasn't in the cards, and since I'd refused to work like Ethan last summer, the amount in my bank account was missing a digit needed to afford a decent one.

On the plus side, Mom's black SUV was easy to handle and great for off-road trips when we went camping in the woods.

I parked the car next to Ethan's in front of school, but he'd already gone inside and none of my friends were around, so I went to first period alone. In the hallway, I bumped into Ryan. Since I'd completely forgotten to ask him about the soccer thing yesterday in trig—or biology for that matter—and my brother told me jack shit these days, I stopped him for a moment.

"Hey, what's the deal with Ethan and—?"

I didn't get to finish my question, because Ryan grabbed my collar with a mixture of hysteria and relief. "Man, you're just the one I wanted to see. Would you let me copy your trig homework? I totally forgot to do that, and Mr. Swanson's quite an ass when it comes to undone stuff."

"Sure, no problem. It wasn't that much. Come to trig early and you'll have plenty of time to do it." But Ryan not doing his homework? That was indeed a little strange. "What got you so distracted?" I asked, even though I had a good idea of the answer.

Ryan shoved a hand through his black hair and gave me a smug smile. "Lisa had free run of her house the past few days. Homework wasn't my top priority, to be honest."

"Ah, dude, you're so shitty!"

"What? Don't tell me you would've done anything less in my place."

"Probably not." We both laughed at the truth. "You owe me, though."

"Whatever you want."

I was about to tell him that our next trig assignment would be his to do, so I could get an afternoon off and copy it in the morning, when I saw her. The geek girl. She rounded the corner and came straight for us—no, straight for *me*. Her determined stride awoke the urge in me to back away a step. Yet I stood my ground, even when her nose was almost in my face. A soft coconut scent came off her skin. Utterly forgetting what I wanted to say to Hunter, I simply stared at her.

"Okay, explain," she snapped at me.

Equally surprised, Ryan turned toward to her, but her hard glare rested on me alone. What in the world did this girl want from me?

"Explain *what* exactly?" I asked in a somewhat condescending tone. But hey, she asked for it. And then something dawned on me. This feisty little thing probably had a crush on me. That was just cute. Especially when the nerdy girl had no idea how to handle her hormones at age...what? Seventeen? With a slight tilt of my head, I tried to sound flirtations, even if the geek squad wasn't—and would never be—a place I hunted in. "Sweetness, are you stalking me?"

"Oh my *God*! What's wrong with you?" she barked in all seriousness, her eyes bright with anger.

Uh-oh. Did I misread her? But there was no reason to get

loud with an audience around. "Excuse me? You're the one who keeps chatting me up."

Steam was nearly blowing out of her nose. Fascinated with the weird girl for a moment, I barely registered Hunter's chuckle. But when he said her name—Susan—I wondered where he knew her from. It took him putting an arm around her shoulders and calling her name again for her to finally notice him. Annoyed, she turned to his side and growled, "What?"

Jeez, someone was cranky this morning. Her chest rose and fell under that lemongrass-green t-shirt with her angry breaths. She might start stomping an impatient rhythm with her slender legs any moment.

Ryan grabbed her firmly by her shoulders and turned her around to face me again. "Meet Chris."

So it was introduction time. Fine with me. But all she snapped was, "Chris who?"

"Donovan," I told her, a little miffed.

"Ah, right." With her arms now folded over her chest, she staked me with a cynical look. "And you're Ethan's alter ego, or what?"

Alter ego? Was she crazy? "Brother," I answered with a sly grin, adopting the same cynical stare as her.

Susan's face turned pale. "Brother..."

Much too amused by this whole damn situation, Ryan leaned closer and whispered the word "twins" in her ear.

"Twins," geek Sue reiterated in a stunned whisper. Then she blurted again, "*Twins*?" like such a thing meant we were two horsemen of the apocalypse. What she did next was just sweet, and it coaxed a smile from me. She spun to Ryan and knocked her head against his chest, whining, "Nooo..."

Shit, was that it? She'd confused me with my brother? It had to be, and now I could hardly stand upright from rippling laughter. "So you met Ethan? Hell, now I get it."

She didn't bother talking to me again, which was a shame. Almost. In a low huff, she told Ryan, "See you later," and stalked away with her head held high. My gaze was still fixed on her. To say she'd made an impression was quite the understatement. A few steps down the hallway, she came to a sudden stop and whirled around. My laugh died in my throat, my attention wary in an instant, as she stormed toward me once more.

Without a word, she fished for something in her backpack until her hand reappeared with a pen. Next she grabbed my wrist. I was too stunned to object when she shoved up the sleeve of my sweatshirt and started writing something on my inner forearm. What the hell?

Motionless, I watched her until she lifted her head again and locked her smug gaze with mine. "Tell Ethan to call me."

I glanced down. A series of blue digits glowed on my skin. The damn little geek spun around, about to head off. However, she changed her mind without a warning and had already fetched something else from her bag when she faced me a third time. Somewhat forcefully, she shoved the CD from yesterday against my chest with another order. "Give him that and tell him thanks for the latte."

Pushy. Weird. And cryptic. The dictionary doubtlessly held a picture of her next to each of those words. Slightly out of breath and out of things to say, I blinked several times in wonder. And why the heck was Hunter so quiet? Now would be a good moment for him to shelter me from this crazy attack. If only. The moron just grinned and watched me struggle for a reply.

Oh, this girl wouldn't get the better of me. After a cough to find my voice again, I drawled the word "pleeease" with a smirk at Susan, to show her that nothing from me was free.

"Pleeease," she repeated nicely, even mirroring my smile—fake of course. I wouldn't have expected anything less. Then she headed away, for good this time. Well, she would have, if she hadn't bumped into Hunter's girlfriend. Her schoolbag slipped from her shoulder, and though she reached for it with a good reflex, she missed it and the backpack dropped to the floor. Both girls squatted down and whispered to each other. Hunter's girl cast me a quick glance. I returned it with a slight lift of the corners of my mouth, just to say hi. We hadn't yet had the pleasure of talking to each other, even though Ryan had been in a relationship with her since last summer.

When the little geek rose to her feet again, she threw one last crabby look at me over her shoulder. I didn't know why, but I couldn't seem to bring myself to be the one who looked away first.

"So you know that crazy chick?" I asked Hunter when Susan was gone and his girl came toward us, flinging her arms around his neck. She turned to me and flashed me with a smile

I'd only seen from a distance so far.

"I'm Lisa, actually, his girlfriend," she said with a funny look, holding out her hand to me. "And you must be Chris Donovan."

I let go of the laugh she stirred in me with her introduction and shook her hand. "Nice to finally meet you. But I meant *her,* in fact." I nodded in the direction geek Sue had disappeared and put her CD in my backpack to give to Ethan after school.

"Yeah, I was getting to that part," Ryan explained, rubbing his neck. "Lisa told me yesterday there was something odd going on between Ethan and Susan. Some confusion over a missed date apparently."

"Yes, your brother asked her out, but then she ran into you, and you pretty much threw her off balance," Lisa clarified.

I chuckled. "Off balance?" I'd been known to do that to girls from time to time.

"Yeah. In the absolutely worst sense of the word, you know," she muttered, clearly not impressed with my hookup successes.

Remembering my first meeting with Sue yesterday morning, when I'd had no freaking idea what the girl wanted from me, I could just picture how easily I'd rattled her. But had Ethan really asked her out? Weird. For the first time in months, I wondered if I'd been wrong about him liking guys. Was he really just shy with the chicks?

Though I was dying to hear more about this girl and my brother, the bell ringing sprang our little group apart, and I

ANNA KATMORE

made my way to history. Maybe I would get some answers from Ryan later in trig. Only, I forgot about our deal with the homework. There was no time to speak with him before the teacher came in for second period and silenced the class.

Biology then, I decided, while Mr. Swanson started writing a problem on the blackboard that we were supposed to solve by ourselves in the following fifteen minutes. It took him some time to copy everything from his notes. My mind started to wander out of class and back into the hallway where geek Sue had nearly bitten off my head this morning. Leaning back in my chair, I let go of a breath and replayed the strange encounter in my head.

Ethan's alter ego. Hah! The girl was quick with a comeback. How charming. It made her sweet somehow.

I pulled back my sleeve. The number she'd written on my skin flashed like a celeb's signature on a crazy fan's arm. My thoughts wandered off to how cold her hands had felt on my skin. Too damn cold. Tracing the numbers on my arm one by one, I frowned. Her eyes had been really sharp. I'd half expected her to vaporize me with them like Superman. As to their color, nope, I didn't remember if they were brown, green, blue, or even a glowing red.

Did Ethan really have a date with that cannonball of a geek?

That meant my first assumption hadn't been so far off after all. She might not be crushing on me in the precise sense, but she obviously found my brother quite likable. We looked exactly the same—she proved that herself by talking to the wrong twin, twice. Ergo: She found me attractive, too.

Worshipped by a geek. That one was missing on my dating record as of yet. I laughed quietly, because it was kind of cute.

A chalk piece hit me straight in the chest and landed on my desk, ripping me out of my musings. "Mr. Donovan," my trigonometry teacher said, standing in front of the class with his arms folded and his inquisitive look pinned on me. "Would you care to answer my question, since you're already using your arm as a cheat sheet?"

Question? Cheat sheet? Dammit! I swallowed, at a loss for words, looking down at Susan's number, which surely wasn't what Mr. Swanson wanted to know. Clearing my throat, I slowly pulled my sleeve back down. "I—umm..."

He cocked his head. "Can it be that you, for once, don't have an answer, Mr. Donovan?" he mocked, implying, correctly, that I was usually a little smugger than right now. Some of the kids around me snickered.

"Yeah, I'm obviously below par today," I admitted, to the amusement of my classmates, throwing a smirk his way.

"I can see that." Mr. Swanson liked me, because he was also the basketball coach and I was one of his best players. No one else would have gotten away with a sigh and a grunt in trig. He gave me one last pointed look and then turned to my neighbor, Alice. "Miss Hart, would you give us the right answer then?"

I aimed a sheepish look at her. Alice returned my glance with a smile and was soon blabbering away about Pythagoras and stuff, but I didn't listen. I caught Ryan's entertained gaze

ANNA KATMORE

on me, as he'd turned around in his chair. I gave a helpless shrug, then lowered my eyes, and started working on the problem.

Once I concentrated on the subject again and banned a pert geek from my mind, I had the answer before everyone else. The rest of the class would certainly need a few more minutes, so I leaned back in my chair and relaxed. It didn't take long for Coach Swanson to nail me with a speculative look.

"Twenty-seven," I mouthed the result. I promptly received his approving nod in return. Free to my thoughts again, I started reveling in the memories of Lauren and the things she'd done to my neck with her teeth yesterday. A pleasant shudder traveled down my spine. I was *so* up for a repeat of that.

Green!

Dammit, the geek girl's eyes were gummy-bear green.

I swallowed, dragging my hands down my face. Why the heck had my brain spit out that bit of information when I was thinking about a vixen in my bed?

Because she gave you her number, a twisted part of me pointed out. Yep, she had. The edges of my lips wanted to curve up. Girls had given me their phone numbers on countless occasions, but never like that. Much to her credit, Susan had style. If Ethan really liked her, he'd actually missed out on something this morning.

Before everyone else was done with the math problem, I pulled out my cell from my pocket and hid it under the desk. Twisting my arm so I could read the digits there, I saved the number in my contacts. There was already a Susan on the list, so I typed *Weird Geek* instead.

Because I had gym next and didn't want to look like someone had printed a barcode on my arm, I made a detour to the restrooms with Hunter on my heels. While he went to the stalls in the back to take a leak, I dropped my backpack on the tiled floor and started rubbing my arm under the faucet.

Water alone wasn't enough to get rid of the scribble. By the time Hunter returned to the sinks, I was scrubbing at the ink really hard with soap and paper towels. "What's wrong with this stuff?" I muttered. "Did she use a fricking sharpie on me?"

"Who? Miller?"

Was that her name? Susan Miller? Suddenly it seemed too innocent a name for a little beast like her. "Yeah, the girl with the charming personality," I gritted out as the skin on my arm turned a vibrant red under the remaining smudges of blue ink. Great, now I looked like an idiot who'd wiped his arm across wet ink rather than a supermarket product with a barcode. Not a hell of a lot better.

"You just got on her bad side. She can be really nice."

I made a wry face at my friend. "When she's sleeping or someone duct-tapes her mouth shut, right?"

He laughed but gave me a commiserating look for my hurting arm.

"Any idea how to get this off?" I groaned.

A shrug rolled off Hunter's shoulder. "Turpentine?"

Ah, too funny. "Don't you have an English class to go to?"

"Sure. See you after lunch." He left with an amused

chuckle.

All my fighting against this resistant ink merely led to a burning forearm, so at the point that only fine hues of blue were left, I stopped scrubbing and rushed to the gym. I didn't know if the red or the blue was now more apparent, but Justin Andrews, an old friend, was the only one to comment on it as we did a hard workout according to the lesson plan.

"Try to graffiti yourself?" he mocked.

"If only. I got badgered by a stray member of the geek squad this morning."

"By *what?*" Choking with laughter, he almost fell off the bar on which we were both doing pull-ups.

"Weird girl. Weird story. Maybe I'll tell you one day." I pulled myself up once more, chin over the bar, let out a lungful of air, and lowered myself back down. When I was done with my twenty-five reps, I hopped to the ground and wiped the sweat from my forehead with the front of my muscle shirt. If nothing else, the sweating today would take care of the remnants of geek Sue's ink on my skin.

At the teacher's whistle, the two of us moved on to the next station. Skipping rope for three solid minutes. This was pretty hard cardio, so we didn't talk during that task.

I showered quickly after gym and practically ran to Spanish class. I wanted to catch Lauren before fourth period started to ask her for an extra lesson later at her place.

Her face split with a smile when she saw me coming. She skimmed her soft, slender fingers over my temple. "Your hair is still wet. I like that."

Yes, I knew that from after-shower experiences with her, but that was not the reason I hadn't toweled it thoroughly. There just hadn't been enough time. "Say you're free this afternoon, and I'll have it wet for you again," I offered with a smirk. Then something behind Lauren's shoulder tore my attention away from her.

Twenty feet down the hall, Susan Miller slammed the iron door of her locker shut and disappeared around the corner. It was her plain ponytail and glasses set against the slender move of her hips clad in tight-ass jeans that snagged my brain into a temporary knot. Could there actually be sexy geeks? Because that girl clearly walked the border.

"Hey?" I heard Lauren's voice and felt her fingers on my chin. She turned my head back to her and waited until I looked into her dark eyes. "Are you listening?"

"Sure." I knitted my brows. "Umm...what did you say?"

Suspicious now, she looked down the hallway but of course found nothing that explained my distraction. "Are you all right, Chris?" She laughed her flirtatious laugh, though it sounded somewhat abrasive.

"Of course."

"You seemed a little sidetracked for a moment."

If we included trig in my record of mental absence today, it was not just for a moment, it seemed. "It's nothing," I lied, not intending to ruin a possible date with Lauren by mentioning another girl. "So, this afternoon?"

Head tilted to the side, she deliberately cleared her throat. "I just said I can't this afternoon. How about tomorrow?"

Tomorrow. Right. Not as good as today, but at least it was something to look forward to. "Tomorrow then."

"Chris...are you really okay?"

"Absolutely." I shook my head with a grin, mostly to forget the swaying hips of geek Sue, slung my arm around Lauren's shoulders, and steered her to our seats in the back of the classroom.

At the beginning of the lesson, Mrs. Sanchez returned our homework assignments, dropping the papers on everybody's desks. When she gave me back my homework, she nodded, positively surprised. "I knew it was a good idea to team you up with Miss Parker-Lee as your tutor," she told me with a proud smile.

I couldn't stop wondering whether her smile would waver just a tiny bit if she actually knew how much body contact was involved in that tutoring. Subtly turning my head to Lauren, I waggled my brows and knew by her suppressed giggle that she was thinking exactly the same. Yep, definitely a good idea to *team up* with her.

After Spanish was lunch. Finally. I took a relaxing breath and walked to the cafeteria to eat with my friends. A table behind the swing doors to the right was dedicated to the geek squad. Walking extra slowly, I checked them out and tried to catch what they were talking about. Their excited chatter had never made it to my attention before, mostly because nerds didn't do it for me, and now that I was actually listening in, they bored me to hell. All about Newton and theories about freezing milk. Because that was so important when you were a teenager trying to spend the undoubtedly best years of your life in an unforgettable way.

I watched them for another minute, silently munching my burger as I sat with my team around a table close to the entrance. Strangely enough, the nerd table was full, but Susan Miller wasn't with them. Maybe she was on a different schedule and her lunch break was an hour later or even earlier than mine.

The idea irritated me. I would have loved to catch a glimpse of her interacting with my brother, and lunch break was the only time of the day that Ethan and I were in the same room. Curiosity killed the cat, all right, but seeing them together could help me solve the to-be-gay-or-not-to-be-gay riddle about him.

Well, no such luck. She wasn't sitting at his table, and I didn't see her for the rest of the day either.

Since I didn't have basketball practice on Wednesdays, I went home after seventh period, changed into black sweatpants, practiced some dunking in the backyard, and started doing homework an hour later. It wasn't until I'd finished my English essay that I remembered the CD in my backpack. I hadn't even taken a closer look when Susan had given it to me, so I was curious what she wanted Ethan to listen to and rummaged around between my books to find it.

Volbeat. What the hell was that?

I put the CD into my computer. Moments later, a few rocky chords blasted from the surround sound attached. A metal band. And they were actually good. If that was geek Sue's taste in music, she had me just slightly impressed—again.

The second song hadn't finished when I heard my brother coming home from his newly found after-school activities, aka soccer practice. I paused the CD and headed out into the hallway. Leaning against the wall while he slipped out of his shoes and tossed his sweaty shirt into the laundry basket in the bathroom, I said, "Hey, E.T."

"Hi, bro," he replied with as much interest as he had in turnips. Well, he didn't yet know what stunning news awaited him.

"Who's Susan Miller?" There was just a hint of teasing in my voice.

"A girl from school."

What? That was all? No looking up, no curiosity, no emotion whatsoever? He so wasn't into this girl.

"Wow. I thought you'd have a little more to tell about her."

Now he did look at me, head cocked, interest spiked just a little. "Why? Do you know her?"

"Ran into her yesterday. And again today. Wild little thing, isn't she?"

"Maybe. I don't know her that well." He shrugged it off and that was that. Ethan actually passed me in the hall and went to his room.

"Wait!" I shouted after him. "Don't you want to know what she said?"

His look more skeptical than nonchalant this time, he turned around once more. "*Should* I want to know? Since she ran into you, I guess you're hooking up with her now."

What the hell? "No, I'm not. I thought *you* were."

The next words he mumbled so low that I couldn't be sure if I'd heard him right. "She stood me up."

"Well, she gave me her number today. Said I should pass it on to you."

There was a definite lift in his gloomy look. "Really?"

"Yep. And she gave me a CD, too."

"Cool. Can I have it?"

"Umm...in a little while. I started listening to it while you were gone, and I'd like to finish." Ethan couldn't help that. If he wanted the CD now, he would have to fight me for it, and I was simply the stronger brother. However, I wasn't a complete asshole and added with a grin, "But I'll turn up the volume extra loud so you can listen as well."

"Why did I know it would go something like that?" He laughed and went to get fresh clothes from his room to take with him to shower. When he came back, he asked, "Are you going to give me her number then?"

"I have it on my phone. I'll send it to you in a minute."

"Okay." He slammed the bathroom door in my face, and three seconds later the sound of water raining down on the tub drifted out.

I turned around, about to walk back to my room, but instead I faced a beaming, red-cheeked mom.

"Is that true?" she whispered. "Is Ethan dating a girl?"

Oh man, the *mom*ster was awake. "No, Mom, I don't think he's dating anyone. But that girl seems to be interested in him, and she told me to tell him to call her."

ANNA KATMORE

"Oh! At long last!" She clasped her fingers together, very obviously trying not to clap her hands in excitement.

"Get a grip, Mom!" I laughed, not bothering to be as quiet as her. But then I pushed her back into the kitchen, where she'd emerged from. "The girl's weird. I'm not sure you'd really want her as Ethan's girlfriend."

The edges of her mouth sank. "What do you mean 'weird'?"

"Well, I talked to her today, and she was really...unfriendly."

"Oh." She pivoted to the sink and wiped her hands on the dishtowel lying on the counter, even though her hands weren't wet. "But maybe that was just a mistake. What if he really likes her?"

"Maybe he *is* interested in her. But that doesn't mean you should get your hopes up. Don't push him, Mom," I warned. Especially since he hadn't seemed in the least concerned about Susan Miller five minutes ago.

As I opened the fridge and retrieved a can of Sprite, a random thought journeyed through my mind. Would he have been be a little more excited if I'd told him about a *guy* wanting him to call? That was probably a topic neither of us would ever stop speculating about. Not until he told us the truth about him being gay—or came home with a girl on his arm, for that matter.

I popped the cap and took a long drink, then wiped my mouth with the back of my hand. "You know how he's going to crawl back into his shell if you bring it up again." We'd had *silent Ethan* long enough after Will's accusations last spring. I really didn't want a brother who wasn't talking to anybody again. Things had just gone back to normal in the fall. Comfortable. "I want to keep happy Ethan." The brother who loved playing basketball with me in the yard, not the mulling and hiding one.

Mom needed to accept that she couldn't help him make a decision in this. Whatever that decision was going to be, she would love Ethan all the same. And if this was only about the grandchildren Mom hoped for one day, I would give her a barn full, if it made her happy. Just not before I was forty, I decided, as I abandoned the mother ship and returned to my room.

"I'm off to work in half an hour. Last-minute call from a client," her voice drifted after me. "You guys have to fend for yourselves tonight, but I'll leave you some pizza money."

"Okay!" I shouted back before closing the door. My finger on the computer mouse, I was about to restart the CD when I remembered I still had to send Ethan the nerd's number.

I flung myself into the dark purple, comfy chair in the middle of the room and scrolled through the entries on my contacts list down to *Weird Geek*. Hmm, what would Ethan talk about with this crazy little imp? I'd never actually seen him do it, so I just couldn't picture him flirting with a girl. And snappy Susan Miller could definitely do with a little flirting to loosen up.

In fact, she also deserved a little something for stamping her graffiti on my arm today and forcing me to almost scratch my skin off.

Here was her number—who said *I* couldn't use it?

I chuckled to myself and, instead of sending Ethan her number, pressed the call button.

Chapter 3

SUE'S ANXIOUS VOICE drifted through the line. "Hello?"

"Hey, sweetness," I drawled in greeting, knowing she'd recognize me straight away with that form of address. Talking to her this time would be fun, but I wanted her to know who I was and not confuse me with Ethan again.

Her disappointed groan, though, cut the fun immediately. "Why are you calling me, Chris?"

Really, it should've been obvious. "Because you gave me your number."

"I didn't give it to *you*."

"No?" I stared at the faint blue remnants of her phone number on my skin. "The handwriting on my forearm objects."

A pause, followed by a deep sigh, then she elaborated, "Fine. I didn't give it to you to *call* me." Yes, that much I'd figured, but it didn't matter. I enjoyed speaking to her. Probably more than I should. "Where's your brother?" she demanded.

"Last time I checked, he was in his room."

"Get him on the phone, please, will you?"

Nuh-uh. She wasn't getting rid of me that fast, not when I hadn't had a chance to bring up the painful scrubbing of my arm as of yet. "That means I have to get up and walk over there. I don't think I'm in the mood to do that just now."

"Then why did you call me?" She sounded close to giving up and tossing the phone out her window.

Her sweet frustration made me laugh. "I told you, because you gave me your number."

"Not that again," she whined.

"Fine..." Lowering my tone, I reverted to a seductive voice. "Then maybe to ask you to go out with me?"

"What?" she screeched into the phone. Then, in an exasperated huff, she added, "You must be kidding me!"

Of course, I was. What would I do with a nerd on a date? But taunting her was fun. "Nope. Why would I?"

"Because I want to talk to your brother and not you, to begin with. And aren't you supposed to be dating Lara?"

"Hmmm, who's Lara?" Did she think I had a girlfriend? Because I didn't.

"Asian supermodel?" Sue snorted. "Long black hair?"

"Oh, you mean Lauren?" I concluded. "Well, I did date her yesterday. And I might again sometime." Although the word "dating" probably had a different meaning in my books than in hers. "But there's always a free spot in my calendar to squeeze you in, sweetness," I kept teasing.

"Are you actually mental?" she blurted, putting real

emphasis on the words: *are, you, actually,* and *mental.*

"I hope not." Biting back a snicker, I said in the most serious tone I could manage, "Why? Are you not a safe girl to date?"

"I'm the *perfect* girl to date, just not for you, dumbass!" she barked into the phone.

Dumbass? Really? Now I couldn't hold back the chuckle any longer. "Aw, don't say that, little Sue. You don't know me yet."

"And God willing, I never will. Please, go get Ethan now and stop wasting my time."

Oh, so curt and professional. She could be a great lawyer in a few years. "All right, you win." I laughed and added just for good measure, "But tell you what. If it doesn't work out between you and Ethan, which I know it won't"—*because he just doesn't seem interested in girls the way you're hoping for, Little Miss Sunshine*—"you let me take you on a date. Deal?"

Sue's voice was stone-cold as she told me, "When hell freezes over."

As far as that went, last summer Theresa Alber had asserted that she'd only let me do her when hell froze over, too. Since I slept with her on Halloween, I supposed hell was a chilly place by now. "That happens more often than you think, sweetness," I drawled. Rising from my chair, I walked out of my room and knocked on Ethan's door.

Without waiting for an invitation, I entered and tossed him the phone. "Call for you."

Ethan, who seemed to have started his homework after the

shower, leaned back in his swivel chair and held the cell to his ear, giving me an odd look. "Hello?" he said somewhat curiously into the phone.

"By the way, she said thanks for the latte," I shouted over my shoulder before I left the two sweethearts to themselves. Pulling the door closed behind me, I couldn't bring my legs to move. Normally not big on eavesdropping, this time I just couldn't resist. My possibly gay brother had a girl on the phone. I needed to know what was happening. Unfortunately, I didn't hear much because Ethan spoke so low. Did he suspect I was listening in? Nah, doubtful.

When the door suddenly opened, my heart gave a start. I stood guiltily frozen in the hallway and met Ethan's gaze as he came out of his room. He studied me for a moment. Then he cracked up laughing and held out my cell. "Are you spying on me?"

"Umm..." At least he took it in good humor. "I was—"

"Snooping?" Ethan finished as I tucked my phone into my pocket. "I can see that. So to make it easier for you, Susan is coming over now."

My eyes grew wide with surprise. "You invited her?"

"Yes."

"Over *here*?"

"Yes."

"To do what?"

Ethan shrugged. "Hang out. Watch some TV maybe. Why? What do *you* do with the girls you have over?"

Oh, brother... I pursed my lips, arched a brow, and let

Ethan figure out the answer for himself.

"Ah, right. Well, I'm not going to mack on her all evening, if that's what you want to hear."

"Not even a little?" I heard myself say, even though that was not what I wanted to ask. Or it was, but it was also the wrong thing to *say*.

Once again, Ethan surprised me by laughing, totally untouched by my probing. "No, I don't think even a little. Susan's a girl I met just this week. You do know that boys and girls can hang out and have fun without dropping their pants, right?"

"I'll believe it when I see it." I was serious. When I wanted to play foosball or watch a movie without making out in the dark, I invited one of the guys over, not a girl. How could Ethan—the person I'd shared a womb with for nine months—be so much different from me? But I didn't quite yet believe he had absolutely no intentions with this girl, so I gave it one last try. "You really aren't interested in her in any way?"

"She's a friend."

Right, let's put that theory to the test. "And if, let's say, someone else asked her out?" Tucking my hands into the pockets of my sweats, I shrugged. "Would that bother you?"

He gave it serious thought for exactly two seconds. Then he shook his head. "Nope. She's free to pick whoever she wants."

That was fairly disappointing news. I spun around and walked back to my room, but he called out my name, making me glance back. "Can I have Susan's CD now?" he asked, still

ANNA KATMORE

amused from our very disillusioning conversation.

Like he had, I gave it two seconds of serious deliberation, then said, "Nope," and grinned. "But I'll turn up the volume again, so you and Sue can listen, too."

Ethan rolled his eyes, slightly less amused.

With the music blasting from the speakers, I popped a mint, which I had a box of sitting on my desk, in my mouth, sprawled out in my comfy chair again, and opened my Spanish book to prepare for next week's test and the informal lesson with Lauren tomorrow. Gee, learning Spanish was so not what I wanted to do right now. *Estoy aburrido. Estas aburrido. Es aburrido.* Snorting, I continued to conjugate in my mind how bored everybody was. When I had that down pretty well, I tried to conjugate how lame my brother was next.

A loud bang jerked me out of my studies a little later. I looked up and was completely stunned. The textbook nearly slipped from my fingers. It took me a moment to catch myself, then an intrigued smile pulled at the corners of my mouth.

What the deuce did Susan Miller want in my room?

I couldn't even ask her because the music was so loud, but since she'd shut the door, I was sure she'd sought me out for a reason. My eyes fastened on Sue's shy face, I rose from the chair, dropped the textbook, and went to turn down the volume. Her gaze followed like it was glued on me—and it was focused on my bare chest for a good deal of that time.

"Um, hi," she croaked when we could hear our own words again.

The first thing I noticed was the absence of her glasses. Her eyes really were a vibrant green. They were beautiful. Big, warm and, right now, a little insecure.

"Sorry for breaking into your room." Her shoulders twitched with a reluctant shrug as she grimaced. "Sort of."

I prowled toward her. Where was Ethan? Did he send her for the CD?

Since she stood there, all lost and lonely in my room, I took a moment to let my gaze roam over her body. She wore the same lemongrass-green tee from school. Not exactly revealing, that rag. The girls I usually spent time with made an effort to show as much of their curves as possible. Sue presented nothing. At all. Her collar was cut wide and loose, but she wore it so that it showed more of her bare shoulders than the upper curves of her breasts. It left a lot of room for imagination. Weird how that imagination kicked in right now.

After taking a deep, encouraging breath, she told me, "Your mom let me in."

And there I knew. She hadn't even seen Ethan yet. Once again, she'd found the wrong twin, and she was totally clueless. I suppressed a chuckle as she explained, "She called you, but with that noise fending off the cats and dogs of the neighborhood, I get it that you didn't hear—"

This time, with a little mercy, I placed a hand over her mouth before she could shoot herself in the foot again. Science club or not, this girl had lips as soft as cotton candy. Putting my index finger in front of my lips, I made it plain to her that she'd said enough.

Deep breaths through her nose feathered against the back

of my hand. The shock in her eyes was priceless. Having her in my room like this, I just couldn't resist teasing her. I took my hand away from her mouth and said in a low, seductive voice, "I didn't expect you to jump at my offer so fast." My lips stretched into a smile. "Especially after you turned me down so mercilessly on the phone."

First she just stared at me, incredulous. Then she moaned. "Nooo. Chris?"

"The very same."

Sue took a step back to distance herself from me and demanded with fierce reproach, "Why are you listening to my CD?"

Oh, that was a good question. "I could tell you, but you might not like the answer."

Completely ignoring my good intentions, she arched her eyebrows, demanding I tell her anyway. So I closed the distance between us again and leaned down to speak softly in her ear. "Because you gave it to me."

When she sighed with exasperation, her breath tickled my bare chest. "That, as well as my number," she snarled, emphasizing every word, "you should have passed on to Ethan. Why didn't you?"

Well, her annoyance, if nothing else, spurned me on to taunt her a little more. I rubbed a strand of her hair between my fingers, feeling the silky softness. It made me think really strange things. Things that I'd never done with a nerd before. "I wanted to learn what taste you have in music, so I know what to put on when we make out on my bed."

Sue swatted my hand away. "In case you haven't figured it out all by yourself, let me make it clear now: You have a screw loose."

To put it mildly, I thought as I pictured how I was going to silence that girl with a hot kiss she certainly wasn't used to from her former geek boyfriends.

"More importantly, it's considered rude to hit on someone who actually came to see your brother."

No worries about that, sweetness. Ten minutes ago, he was totally fine with you hooking up with someone else.

"Why? You think he'll be mad?" I teased, grinning at her obvious and unrequited interest in my twin brother. My possibly *gay* twin brother, to be clear. "You think he'll date you?"

For the first time, worry crept into her eyes. "Why, don't you?"

At this point it was really hard to say, but I doubted it very much. I couldn't say that straight to her face, of course. That was Ethan's job. I wasn't going to *out* him to anyone. What kind of brother would that make me?

Deliberating a respectful retreat, I stroked my chin with my thumb and forefinger. "In fact, I think I'll just watch for a while and let myself be entertained by how things go from here." Should be quite an interesting show. I winked at her, then took her by her shoulders, and turned her around to face the closed door. Gentleman that I was, I even leaned forward and opened it for her.

Sue let me steer her out of my room and five steps down

the hall to Ethan's door. I opened that for her as well, because by now I deemed her too shocked to manage by herself.

Ethan lounged on his bed, playing Wii. He looked up when I gently pushed our guest into his room, but his smile was noncommittal. They really were only friends—at least as far as he was concerned.

"You've got a visitor," I told him and left Susan to her fate. Oh, this was going to be a priceless show. Fits of laughter rocked me as I retreated, and Susan slammed the door shut behind me.

Back in my room, I turned up the music so the two of them could listen with me as I picked up my Spanish textbook once more. It was hard to say how long I'd been engrossed in studying, but at some point my stomach started to rebel with hunger.

In the kitchen, along with the emergency numbers, was also the menu of Lou's Pizza Oven and a twenty-dollar bill from Mom. Before I made the call to order, I went to ask Ethan what he wanted. Outside his room, I halted. It was quiet in there; Sue had probably gone home by now. I gave a quick knock on the door before I walked inside. "Hey, E.T., I'm going to order pizza—" My heart skipped a beat, and I stopped dead in the middle of the room.

Sue was trapped underneath Ethan, on his bed, her leg angled, their faces inches apart. He was about to kiss her. Fricking *kiss* Susan Miller!

"You're shitting me!" Damn, it was too late to censor my words. The scene had obviously knocked all sense out of me.

My throat went bone-dry, and all I could do was stare at them, open-mouthed.

Both pale from shock, they scrambled up. Whatever had been going on in this room, I'd effectively ruined it.

When my gaze met Susan's and I saw the fiery reproach in her eyes, I felt a slight sting in my chest. "I'm sorry, I didn't know you were still here," I apologized in a voice that sounded strangely raspy to me. To save them and myself a last bit of dignity, I spun on the spot and strode back to the kitchen without another word.

"Pizza sounds good," Ethan's voice followed me. Probably his attempt to rescue an irremediable situation.

Gah! I rubbed my hands over my face, shaking away the vision of them lying on his bed. Now I had a pretty good idea of how embarrassing it must have been for Mom to walk in on Lauren and me a couple of months ago.

While I dialed Lou's number, leaning against the island, somebody stormed past the kitchen and made me look up. It was Susan dashing to the front door, Ethan close on her heels, whining, "Look, if it's because of what—"

"No, it's not," she cut him off.

Had they started fighting in the ten seconds since I'd left them alone? I refused to walk into the hall to witness it, but I could do nothing about the fact that their conversation carried clearly back into the kitchen.

"Mom needs the car," Sue explained, "and I've got about three minutes to make it back home."

Ah, considering that new bit of information, she should

actually be happy that I'd interrupted them. Otherwise, she might have gotten in trouble with her mother.

When Ethan's hesitant "oh" drifted to me, however, I felt really sorry for him.

"Hey, it was nice. We should totally do that again," Susan suggested, but next she got caught in a light stutter. "I mean—I—"

Okay, that was it. Now I just had to poke my head into the hall and watch what was happening. Her back to the front door, Susan spotted me over Ethan's shoulder, but other than a disapproving frown marring her forehead, she decided to ignore me and said to him, "Ah, heck, I guess I'll see you." She turned around and opened the door, but Ethan didn't let her slip out just yet. He held her back by her wrist. Good boy. I would have done the same. Was he going to kiss her goodbye?

No, he didn't. Instead, he told her with a hopeful edge to his voice, "It was nice, Susan. Come over again tomorrow? Or let's go have that soda we talked about."

It was a shame I couldn't see Sue's reaction, because she stood hidden behind the open front door as she told Ethan, "Okay. Call me after school." Then she leaned around the door and fixed me with a scowl. "Give him my number, dickhead!"

Swallowing, I nodded, and she was gone.

As Ethan trudged back through the hallway, I stepped out of the kitchen and blocked his way. "Hey, man, I'm sorry."

"Yeah, right." He rolled his eyes. A moment later, he shrugged it off, though. "Maybe next time wait until I invite you in."

"I thought she'd left already," I rushed to explain. "It was so quiet in your room."

Now he laughed. "Guess why!"

Shit, I was such an idiot. With a grimace, I groaned, "Not gonna happen again, I promise."

Ethan slapped me on the shoulder and grinned as he passed me. "No worries. I suppose there will be other chances."

To kiss her? Two hours ago, he'd assured me he wasn't interested in that girl. *Just friends*—those had been his words. What in the world had changed his mind in there? Then again, there had been a lot of popcorn on his bed when I'd stormed in on them, and his mouth hadn't yet been on hers. What if I'd read it all wrong?

I spun around and blurted, "Did you kiss her?"

My brother's answer was deadpan. "Now wouldn't you like to know?"

Chapter 4

I DIDN'T GET any more information out of Ethan while we ate pizza in the living room that evening, and as much as it disappointed me, I felt even worse for Mom. The moment she got home from seeing her client, she burst into my room, about to explode with curiosity.

She closed the door, pressed her back against it, let out a long, girly breath that she was much too old for, and demanded, "Tell me everything!"

Playing dumb, I left her drowning in her personal torture a second longer. "Umm...about what? How my Spanish is going...or how the pizza we had while you were gone was?"

"I'm warning you, buddy," she threatened with a finger pointed in my direction as she suppressed a laugh. "Don't make me ground you for the rest of the month. You know I'm talking about Ethan's female visitor."

"Why don't you go ask him yourself?"

"Because *you* always tell me not to push him. Now spill,

buddy, or I'm going to wash your favorite shirt with my pink socks next time. What do you know?"

This woman knew no limits. I cracked a smile. "Don't run off to buy a dress for a wedding just yet. Ethan said they're only friends. But if you ask me, they were close to making out in his room."

Mom crossed to my bed and sat down on the edge. I turned in my swivel chair to face her. "Close to?" she asked, pulling my pillow into her lap and hugging it.

"Yeah." I scratched my head with a pen. "I kinda walked in on them and stopped whatever was going on, though."

Instantly, Mom stiffened, and her brows shot upward. "You did what?"

"I didn't know it was the wrong moment," I defended myself as the pillow barreled straight for my face. Catching it, I threw it back at her. "Believe me, I really wish I hadn't."

With a deep sigh, Mom put my pillow back in place, stood up, and walked to the door. With a mocking glance back at me, she snarled, "I really *should* ground you for that, you know. For an entire year. With no basketball ever again."

"It was a flipping mistake, Mom." Biting back a chuckle, I swiveled back to my computer and finished my email to Dad. I hadn't written him in a while, and since I was the only one in this family who still kept in touch with him, I thought it was okay to give him an update on Ethan's dating life. He would like to hear about Sue.

*

"So…" I began, as Ethan drove us to school the next morning. "Are you going to tell me what happened yesterday?"

An annoying smirk tugged at his mouth. And like I expected, he didn't respond.

My dear brother enjoyed tormenting me by holding back the information I tried to squeeze out of him a little too much. Did I deserve that for being such a nice *older* brother? Because, yes, twenty minutes of a head start in life made all the difference.

"Know what?" Ethan finally said as he parked in front of school. "I'll tell you whether I kissed Susan if you give me your autographed Lakers ball."

My basketball signed by Kobe Bryant? "Dream on, E.T." Laughing, I climbed out of his car, slammed the door shut, and headed into the building. It was my holy treasure. I wouldn't give that ball away for anything in the world.

However, Ethan's stubbornness left me no choice but to come up with another strategy. Two mornings in a row, I'd met Susan Miller in the same section of the school this week. Odds were she had first period close to my history class. With watchful eyes, I walked down the corridor, hoping to glimpse a girl with a honey-blond ponytail and glasses. But damn, she didn't show up.

Tyler and Rebecca caught up with me before I reached history, giving me an excuse to hover outside class a little longer. "So, are you and Lauren going out again today?" Rebecca asked as I kept sweeping the hallway with my gaze.

"She's coming to my place later," I told her absently. I didn't know if this counted as going out in Becky's book, but from the grin on her face, it made her happy enough. A moment later, I mirrored that grin, yet for a totally different reason. "I need to talk to someone. See you guys later." I darted away, following the red backpack that zigzagged through the crowd.

Within a few seconds, I caught up with Susan Miller, matched her stride, and casually put my arm around her shoulders. "Hey, Sue."

She looked at me, and the first thing I noticed, apart from her surprised smile, was how perfectly she fit under my arm. She was a little smaller than Lauren, which made walking with her like this just...comfortable.

Unfortunately, her delighted face crunched as fast as it had come, and her back went stiff. "And you are...?" she demanded with a wary edge to her voice.

I rolled my eyes. "Chris." When would she finally be able to tell us apart? It wasn't that hard, really. I was the charismatic ladykiller, and Ethan was the...ah, whatever.

"What do you want, Chris?" Sue snarled. She made every effort not to touch my hand more than necessary as she lifted it off her shoulder with only two fingers and dropped it behind her back.

Seriously, this girl had the charm of an enemy tank.

Suppressing an irritated groan, I slid in front of her, making her stop, and leaned against the row of lockers to my left. Little Miss Sunshine wouldn't get away from me so fast.

ANNA KATMORE

"I'm curious," I said with a smirk and cocked my head. "Did you and Ethan kiss yesterday?"

Obviously shocked by my bluntness, Sue opened and closed her mouth twice before any sound came out. "Keep your drool in, Spike," she snapped eventually. "What happens between your brother and me isn't any of your business."

That meant: *No fricking kiss*! "I knew it," I blurted, laughing out loud now. If they'd really been making out, she'd be eager to brag about it, especially in front of me, if only to make me leave her alone. Ethan had been serious when he'd told me he didn't intend to mack on her all evening. "He didn't have the guts."

That elated comment must have stabbed Little Miss Sunshine's feelings, because she just stared at me with frank annoyance. Then she strode off, smacking her shoulder against mine, which certainly hurt her more than me.

I turned around and shouted after her in my sweetest voice, "Have a nice day, little Sue." Her retort was her middle finger high up in the air, which I deemed as enough attention to assume she was starting to take a shine to me.

With a broad smile on my face, I went to history, and the grin didn't vanish until the end of third period. Only when Lauren sank more gracefully than anyone into the chair next to mine before Spanish and scrutinized me with curious eyes did I realize I wasn't behaving quite like myself this morning.

"Why are you grinning? Can't wait for your extra lesson later?" she asked with a knowing look.

I cleared my throat. "Always looking forward to seeing you,

Parker."

Lauren gave me her *You want in my pants?* smirk and slowly traced the bold letters on the textbook in front of her with her pen. "I hope you've been a good boy and studied your grammar."

Oh, I'd been a good boy, and studied really hard. "My brain is so full of Spanish crap, I was dreaming of it last night."

"Full of crap? Yeah. Spanish? I doubt it." She giggled, then we both fell silent with the rest of the class as Mrs. Sanchez entered the room and greeted us with her ever so cheerful, "*¡Buenos días!*"

After class, I headed off to the cafeteria for lunch while Lauren went to gym for one more period before her lunch break. At the buffet, I met Cody Giles and Tyler, and immediately we started hollering and plotting how we were going to kick some Clearwater High ass when they came for the game on Saturday.

Sitting down in my usual spot at the basketball table, my glance swept the room for another try at catching Susan Miller with the geek squad. Again, there was no ponytail among those kids. Well, actually there were several, but not the one I kept an eye out for. Eating the apple first, the only item on my food tray that wasn't dripping with fat and mayo, I leaned back, stacking my feet on the empty seat beside me. It was reserved for Rebecca, but she hadn't shown up yet.

"Where's your much prettier half?" I mocked Tyler, tossing one of the French fries next to the burger on my plate, hitting him right on the forehead. He was lucky the thing wasn't dipped in ketchup. His answer didn't register, however, because my gaze caught on a girl standing near the seated crowd around my brother. Nervously, Susan Miller twirled a strand of her ponytail around her finger and gave him a small smile.

As she wiggled her fingers at him and headed off, I expected her to walk to the food counter and get something to eat, but she sauntered empty-handed across the cafeteria to the table farthest away from ours. The one also known as the soccer table. What in the world was she doing there?

"Ow!" I winced when something stung my left eye and tore my attention away from Susan taking a seat. The grape that rebounded from my face hopped away on the floor. I rubbed my sore eye, considering fishing the pickle out from my burger and starting a food fight with Tyler for catching me off guard. But one of the lunchroom monitors had just walked past our table, saving T-Rex from a pickle attack. My clean record of no detention in my senior year couldn't be ruined with something as stupid as gooey food hitting the wrong person.

Taking a bite of my burger instead and stuffing a handful of fries into my mouth, I listened to my friends with only half an ear. Ninety percent of my attention was nailed on the soccer table. The Bay Sharks had never interested me much, so it was probably normal that I'd never noticed the bunch of girls sitting with Ryan and his team. Of course, I assumed they were team members' girlfriends, but how did Little Miss Sunshine fit in with the gang?

A brief conversation she was having with Alex Winter made everyone at that table burst out laughing. The sound drifted to us from the other side of the room. Sue turned a horrible shade of pink. Okay, it wasn't really horrible but quite sweet for a girl. She busied herself peeling a kiwi and chopped it into bite-sized pieces.

I wondered what they found so funny.

And then I wondered why I actually *wondered...*

That girl was on my mind way too much these days, and no one but Ethan was to blame for it. I couldn't even enjoy my burger without sneaking peeks at her every so often. This wasn't just weird, it was annoying, especially when another grape hit me in the face.

"Dude, are you listening?" Tyler asked, the next grape at the ready.

Opening the top of my burger and fishing out the pickle slice, I answered his tilted eyebrows with a smirk and countered, "Try it, and you'll have this splattered on your forehead."

Tyler's hands lifted in surrender. "White flag, man!" He popped the grape into his mouth with a big grin. A truce was fine with me, as long as no more fruit nailed me in the eye.

After lunch, as everyone started off in different directions, I caught up with Ryan and walked with him to biology. Curiosity was a curse that I couldn't seem to shake off today. "What's the deal with Miss Snappy and Rude sitting at your table? Thought she'd be friendly with the volcano-builders."

"Miller? She's cool." Ryan glanced at me sideways. "Why? Are you interested in her?"

"No. She's hanging out with my brother, and that's just a

little strange, considering we're talking about"—I shrugged and frowned at him—"*Ethan.*" Ryan was the most discreet person I knew and one of the few people who also knew about my brother's supposed preferences. When the rumors had almost made it outside the basketball team and Ethan quit playing, I talked to Ryan quite often. One of his cousins was gay, too, so he could talk a lot about it with me.

"Give Ethan a chance. I think they'd make a fine match." Hunter chuckled and slapped me on the shoulder. "While you, my friend, don't seem to be healthy company for the book lover."

I lifted both eyebrows. "Sorry, what?"

"For the first time in—I believe her entire life—she's been put in detention."

Thinking that news over, I walked through the door into biology, but then stopped when Hunter didn't follow. "Where're you going?"

With a grin, he explained, "Done with school for the day. Got some class president stuff to do."

A meeting? Oh, the lucky dude. Now that he mentioned it, I remembered that this was also the reason for Rebecca not joining us at lunch. She was his VP, and Tyler had said something about that before he nearly blinded me with a grape. Before Ryan could head off, I shouted after him, "What got Miss Snappy in detention?"

He laughed, cutting me a quick glance over his shoulder as he walked away. "As if you don't know."

Heck, should I? Dumbfounded, I stood on the threshold to

biology until the bell rang half a minute later and Mr. Murphy shoved me into the room as he came around the corner. The stout man, who always wore a white lab coat with big white buttons on it, pushed his glasses up his nose and coughed.

"Have something better in mind than listening to my lesson, Mr. Donovan?" he asked in a voice that broke on every other word, sounding like he was stuck in a pubescent voice change for the rest of his life. Everybody liked the teacher, who had the face of a koala, mostly because we couldn't do bad enough at any of his tests for him to give us a grade worse than a C, ever.

"You're lucky, Mr. Murphy, I think I'm going to stay today," I bantered back and walked to my seat by the window. Shrugging out of my leather jacket, I made myself comfortable for watching yet another film on the dissection of a human brain, which laid free all the slimy stuff. It was one of the most disgusting things they showed in high schools but most of my classmates enjoyed the view. For me, it was easy to zone out and let the hour pass without registering much.

Carefully, so as not to be seen by koala Murphy, I threaded the cable of my headphones under my Dunkin' Sharks jersey from bottom to top. At the collar, I fished them out and plugged them in my ears from behind my neck. The volume on a minimum, just loud enough so it tuned out the sound of the nasty documentary, I leaned back, scooted lower in my chair, and focused on the clock above the blackboard instead of the TV.

My music always on shuffle, I counted the minutes ticking

away to my favorite song, "Take Me to Church." When that song was over, a random band came on next. It took me a couple of seconds after the first few beats to recognize the group. The album was new on my iPod, only downloaded yesterday from a CD. Susan Miller's CD, to be exact.

A smile crept to my lips at the memory of Sue standing in front of me in my room, checking me out from head to toe. I would bet my soul that she liked what she'd seen.

She was an awkward case. A geek sitting with the Bay Sharks. And then a girl like her in detention? I just couldn't picture that. But Ryan wouldn't lie about it, so what the heck was that last comment of his supposed to mean? Should I have any clue as to why Miss Snappy got in trouble? I didn't think so, but suddenly it was all I could think about. She didn't look like the typical troublemaker to me, and Ryan said she'd never had detention.

Kneading my bottom lip with my thumb and forefinger, I wondered which of the guys I could ask about it as I watched the minute hand on the clock move way too slowly. Ryan was busy for the rest of the day, and none of the soccer team had English with me next period. I could ask Ethan after school. He might know.

Suddenly a much better idea took hold, and my leg started bouncing impatiently under the table. Maybe it was time to break my clean record of detention-free days and find out for myself.

With the ringing of the bell, I shot up from my seat and out of Mr. Murphy's class. I had a plan and only five minutes to put it into action.

Trevor North, Jake Olsen, Tyler, and Brady Baker, all guys from my basketball team, stood gathered by Jake's locker. Coming here was a detour through half the building on the way to my next class, but I knew I'd find some of them here and needed them all for Operation Detention.

"Gentlemen, I need your help," I told them, a little out of breath, shoving Jake aside and reaching into his open locker. Usually, he kept a basketball in there, and today was no different.

Jake raked a hand through his black hair before he put his ball cap back on. "What's up?"

"I need detention, and you have to help me get there." All four questioned my sanity with incredulous expressions, so I explained, "I want to meet a girl there."

Tyler narrowed his eyes at me. "Lauren was put in detention?"

"No, it's not about Lauren." I started bouncing the ball on the floor. "Remember the girl from the other morning? The one who thought she had a date with me?"

He took the ball away from me and spun it on his finger, chuckling. "Right. The cute nerd. So now you actually *are* dating her?"

"Nah." I rolled my eyes. "Turned out she's friends with my brother. Confusion. Long story." I waved a dismissive hand. "The thing is, Ryan said she's in detention this afternoon, and I want to find out why."

"Thought about asking her?" Trevor suggested, leaning his

burly shoulder against the locker next to Jake's.

"I will." A smirk pulled at the edges of my mouth. "Why do you think I want detention?"

"But you could just ask her now or after school."

"Sure, I could. But you haven't seen that kitty in lion-mode yet. I don't want to give her a chance to escape. An hour in the same classroom as her seems like just the time I need."

T-Rex slapped my shoulder, barking with laughter. "That, I have to see, dude. Count me in."

"What about Becks?" I reminded him. His girlfriend would wait for him after school just like every other day.

"I'll text her later. Bros before hoes, you know it."

When Jake slammed his locker shut and faced me with a wicked grin, it was settled—they all had my back. "Well then, let's play some ball!" He stole the basketball from T-Rex, bounced it against the wall above his head, and then jogged down the corridor.

As I raced after him, a familiar excitement crept up my spine. I intercepted the ball, bounced it twice, and passed it back to T-Rex as we hollered above the crowd around us. Everything went exactly to plan, and we didn't even last a minute.

A woman I didn't know by name, but who looked much more like a nursery teacher with her petite figure than somebody dealing with teens, stopped us at the corner, slamming her small fists on her hips.

I grinned down at her reprimanding face. Detention was settled.

*

"Hey, Mr. E.," I greeted my English teacher once again at the beginning of eighth period—after actual English—with the basketball still clasped under my arm. The classroom started filling with random students, all finding seats in corners, fishing out Game Boys or their phones to while away the next fifty minutes.

"Mr. Donovan? I was wondering when I'd finally be seeing you in detention again." He snickered, putting his newspaper down. "Mr. Moss, Olson, North, and Baker, no surprise to find you here either."

The guys saluted Mr. Ellenburgh as we sauntered to the window side of the room and huddled in a group of chairs that we moved together. There were only three girls here so far, and none of them was Susan Miller.

"So which of these chicks you want to talk to?" Jake asked in a low voice, sweeping the classroom with a glance. I shook my head at Jake, keeping a close watch on the door. Randy McDowell from my history class entered next and, after him, one particular girl with glasses.

"Here we go," I drawled with a grin. In response, my friends all turned to look at who had arrived.

"Geek squad," Brady and Jake deadpanned at once.

"Funnily enough, soccer table," I informed them, even though I had yet to find out why. That, however, among other questions, was the reason I'd come here, right? "Apparently, she has a crush on Ethan."

"And that pisses you off why?" Tyler chuckled and poked his elbow into my ribs.

I glanced at him sideways. "Not pissed at all."

"Yeah, right. Our friendship is older than dirt, dude, and I know that frown. What did she do to stomp on your ego?"

I did frown now, deliberately. "What are you talking about?"

"I'm talking about you having always been a sore loser. If she prefers your identical twin over you, you must have done something to fall right through her cracks. What was it?"

Yeah, what was it indeed? Sue was still talking to Mr. Ellenburgh in a hushed voice, and she seemed to be really friendly with my English teacher. She was also nice to a lot of other guys I knew. So why did I, of all people, bring out this kitten's claws? "Actually, I have no idea." She could hardly hold our first encounter against me. That was just an unfortunate moment.

Susan scurried to an empty seat in the back of the room as if it was her personal walk of shame. Her chin was dipped so low, she wouldn't notice a street lamp in front of her, let alone any of the students in this classroom, me included.

Quietly enough to not draw anybody's attention, she took a couple of books from her schoolbag and started doing homework. Her ponytail fell over her right shoulder, and she kept tossing it backward every so often. Sometimes she chewed on the end of her pen, but not once in all that time did she look up or around the classroom.

The guys had to feel the unsociable vibe radiating off her, because no one goaded me to walk over and talk to her. Yet, if I waited any longer, detention would be over without me being any wiser. With the basketball under my arm, I finally rose from the chair and sauntered over. She didn't notice me coming. What a *huge* surprise.

If I said something now, I'd probably make her jump in her seat. Instead, I put the ball down on her desk and gave it a gentle push so it rolled over her math book. Mystified, Sue watched the ball roll until it dropped over the edge and bounced on the floor. That was the moment she got a real start. Her tiny squeak was so out of place...but kind of sweet.

While she bent down to pick up the ball, I stepped in front of her, greeting her with a smile as she straightened again. "Hey, Sue. Never seen a basketball?" I reached for Jake's ball in her hands and let it spin on my finger. A quick glance at the back confirmed, yep, the guys were avidly observing each of my movements. Nosy suckers.

Sue followed my gaze and was rewarded with a bright grin from T-Rex and the rest. "My name is *Susan*," she snarled at me when she turned back.

Ah, Miss Finicky today, was she? I chuckled. "I'm wondering...does my brother know that his girlfriend is in detention?"

"If you tell him, I'm going to shoot you," she fired back at me, as if I'd hit a nerve—which, on second thought, I probably had. In a slightly lower voice that was no less annoyed, she added, "And I'm not his girlfriend."

"Yeah. I know that." The non-kiss yesterday was evidence enough. Sue gaped at me for a tense moment and then turned her attention to the math stuff in front of her, deliberately ignoring me. Maybe that was what Tyler had meant about her stomping on my ego because, frankly, it annoyed me like hell. Girls didn't normally brush me off, and I didn't have to do much to get their attention either.

But with Sue, it was like crashing into a brick wall. Over and over...

From the corner of my eye, I saw the guys snickering, so I glared at them before lowering myself into the chair next to Sue. I'd come here for some answers, and she wasn't going to get rid of me until she provided them. Stacking my feet on the table, I balanced the chair on two legs and spun the ball on my finger. "So, what got you in here?"

After a long moment, in which she said nothing at all, she put down her pen and crossed her arms in front of her chest. "You, in fact."

"Me?" I caught the spinning ball, staring at her in surprise. "Wow." So Hunter wasn't kidding. If I got her in here, I should know why. Only problem was, I had no clue. "How?"

"My history teacher saw me flipping you off this morning."

I cracked up. So it really was *not* me who landed her in detention. She just had to be careful about her indecent gestures in public. But I feigned a hurt look anyway. "Yeah, that was actually rude." I wiggled my finger in her face. "We really need to work on your manners if you're going to keep going out with my brother. Speaking of which..." I resumed spinning the ball and looked innocently at her from under my lashes. "Are you two going to meet up again today?"

"Why are you so interested in your brother's privacy?" Sue whined. "You should stop poking your nose where it doesn't belong. Especially when it's also concerning *my* privacy." She arched her eyebrows. "Because I'm not going to tell you shit."

"Ah, such a cute mouth and such bad words," I teased her. "Now I get why you've been put in detention, Miss Miller. Must be a soccer thing with the language, eh?"

Sue frowned at me as if she had no freaking clue what I was talking about. I shrugged and went on, "It was a surprise to see you sitting with the Bay Sharks at lunch today. I assumed you'd be with the geek squad."

She cut me a sharp glare. "Why would you think that?" Quickly enough, her face lit with understanding. "Oh, no, let me guess. The glasses, right? You really think because I'm wearing them I'm a nerd?"

"Hmmm. That was the idea, yes." And the ponytail, and the Harry Potter shirt, and the modest clothes, and... Hey, hadn't Ryan even called her *book lover* today?

"And Ethan didn't tell you that I was"—she interrupted herself with a sweet eye-roll—"*am* on the soccer team?"

Whoa. She was? *Sexy, Miss Miller.* I was impressed. Just envisioning her in a soccer jersey... Hmm, that thought had a lot more potential than imagining her with the volcano-builders. Now why hadn't Ethan told me this?

Remembering how he was maintaining a low profile lately and how much it annoyed me to be left guessing, I murmured,

"Ethan doesn't say much these days."

Sue leaned back in her chair, frustration etched on her face. "For good reason. It's none of your business."

"Maybe." *Probably.* "But now I'm curious. Why does he suddenly go to soccer practice?" Was it because of her?

"If you must know, he's taking my place for a while because I hurt my knee."

"Is that so?" Chewing on my bottom lip, I contemplated this new bit of information. Eyes still focused on hers, my mind strayed, and I wondered which knee it was.

"Yes, that is so," Sue imitated my drawl. "And for your information, just because someone's wearing glasses doesn't mean he or she is a geek. I only need them for reading, not for playing. And now, if you don't mind"—she waved me off with a dismissive hand—"go and grate on someone else's nerves. I've got homework to do."

No one could say I didn't get a hint when it was slammed in my face. With the ball tucked under my arm, I tipped the chair forward until all four legs were back on the floor and rose to my feet. It was an awkward new feeling to be brushed off by a girl. Any girl. It stabbed me right in the gut.

Just as a form of protest, I contemplated actually weaving my charm around her now. See how long little Sue was capable of keeping me at a distance when I decided to really woo her instead of just teasing.

But then there was my brother. Even though he'd claimed not to have a romantic interest in her, I couldn't be sure after walking in on them yesterday. This was a tricky situation. I wasn't going to steal Ethan's girl simply to prove that no chick could resist me.

About to head off, I cast Sue a pensive look. "Just tell me if he kisses you. I'd really like to know."

"The hell I will. Now go away."

Like I said, the charm of a tank. Unfortunately, something about her abrasive attitude worked like a damn lasso on me. It must've had to do with her "when hell freezes over" statement on the phone yesterday. Every cell in my body rebelled at the thought of retreat. Like I was a slave to my own damn ego.

Since the guys were observing our conversation like it was the most entertaining daily soap, I tossed T-Rex the ball with a hard look at them all so they'd mind their own business. Then I let my ego get the better of me and did something rash and really stupid.

Deliberately slow, I leaned across the table toward Sue. When she glanced up at me, I pulled her spectacles off her nose and stared into her gummy-bear eyes. "My offer for a date in a week is still on." Until then, I wouldn't know for sure if Ethan was into her or not. Once he was out of the way, I could teach this little kitten a lesson.

"Give them back, dickhead!" she hissed, reaching for her glasses, but I moved my hand out of her reach before she could grab them. Susan put on a glare so hard it could've cut holes in concrete. "And I'll never go out with you. Not today, not next weekend, and not in ten thousand years."

Oh, wanna bet? A slow smile tugged at the edges of my lips. "You *will* go out with me, sweetness. And I'll show you how fast hell can freeze over when I want something."

Sue gulped. I could see it, I could hear it, and I knew I already had one foot in the door. "You see?" Capturing her gaze, I carefully laid her glasses back on the desk. "The fire's already reducing to a soft glow." Since her mouth hung open so sweetly, I couldn't resist closing it gently with my finger. The satisfaction of having the last word made me grin as I walked back to my friends.

"Dude, what are you? Five?" Tyler snickered as I straddled my chair, folding my arms on the backrest in front of me. "For a minute there I thought you were going to *push* her to get her attention. Is that how you talk girls into dates now?"

"Shut up. I told you she's difficult."

"But you didn't say you wanted in her pants," he teased.

A humorless laugh left me. "Because I don't."

"Sure." Brady rolled his eyes and made air quotes with his fingers. "You *will* go out with me?"

"It's just to teach her a lesson," I defended myself.

"In what? Charming the pants off a girl, kindergarten-style?" Tyler mocked me. Would it also be kindergarten-style if I smacked that stupid grin right off his face? "Anyway, I thought she was into your brother. Do you really want to steal her from him?"

"Ethan said they're just friends." He'd practically given me permission to hit on her yesterday. If that changed, he'd have to tell me straight.

"Hey, Chris!" Susan's saccharine voice made us all immediately turn our heads in her direction. A gloating grin took form on her lips. "It takes a little more than a cute smile to get on my good side. And luckily your brother comes equipped with the whole package."

Whoa. That was a shot below the belt.

Abandoning some of the sugar in her voice, she added, "You want to freeze hell? Go ahead and try. It'll get you nowhere with me."

I could do nothing but stare at her for an endless moment. The thoughts running wild in my mind during that time ranged from wanting to walk over and prove her wrong with a kiss, to laughing out loud, to telling her she was messing with the wrong guy.

When I'd finally stomached the surprise of her boldness and came around, I licked my lips, never taking my eyes off hers. The left side of my mouth tilted up in a challenging smirk. Everybody's eyes were on me, even Mr. Ellenburgh's. The entire room waited for my next move, and I wasn't going to disappoint.

"Game on, little Sue," I told her in a wicked drawl that rendered her silent.

Her shocked stare amused me. Chuckling, I turned back to my friends, who studied me with open mouths. Until Brady shook his head and burst out laughing. "No freaking way, dude! You don't stand a chance with *that* girl."

Oh, was that so? I cocked my head, pursing my lips, then cast them all a brilliant smile. "Watch me."

Chapter 5

I HEARD ETHAN trudge into the kitchen while I was raiding the fridge for some ice cream to cool down after detention. Casting a glance around the open door at my brother, I presented an unmistakable ask-me-what grin.

"What?" Ethan demanded, pulling off his jersey, which was soaked after today's soccer practice, and tossing it over a chair. He got us both spoons from the drawer in the island, then waited at the table for me and the raspberry-almond dream to join him.

"I got detention today," I declared, licking a scoop of ice cream off my spoon. A moment later I was fighting brain freeze.

"And that's big news why?" Ethan rolled his eyes. "You've spent more time in detention in the last year than in any class." Obviously, he had no clue as to what I was about to spring on him next.

"It was my first time in detention *senior* year. But that's not the point." Another load of ice cream made it into my mouth. Around the spoon, I said, "Gueth who wath there wib me."

"Susan."

What the hell? I choked on the spoon, spit it out, and coughed like a dying grizzly. "How did you know?"

Unimpressed by my near-death experience, Ethan kept scooping raspberry ice cream from the box and shrugged one shoulder. "The guys talked about her being in detention at soccer practice. They didn't tell me the reason, though." He lifted his chin, scrutinizing me with a thoughtful look. "You wouldn't, by any chance, know why she ended up there?"

By chance, I would...

With a little more excitement from his end, I'd have been willing to spill all the good parts, too. Since Ethan once again seemed far too uninterested in Susan Miller, though, the girl who'd challenged me in public to make her fall for me, the necessity to tell him everything rapidly lost its urgency. I shook my head.

"Ah, never mind," Ethan said. "I'm going out with her in a bit anyway. Guess she'll tell me what happened."

"Going out with her? As in—"

"Going to have a soda with her," Ethan cut me off with unmistakable annoyance. "We are *friends*. So stop the hell jumping to conclusions, Chris. You and Mom are the worst suckers for romance in town. What's wrong with you lately?"

A sneer almost made it to my lips. "Nothing. Just..." Seducing my brother's new girlfriend would be a shit move and

ANNA KATMORE

I'd have to back out of that challenge. But since he seemed to be happy being single, and Susan was just a *friend*, there was nothing to worry about, right? Nevertheless, I was really starting to feel for him. From the look on his face, Mom had probably cornered him last night to squeeze out all the information about his latest female guest.

When Ethan prompted me, with a quizzical stare, to finish my sentence, I ended it with an amazingly creative, "Nothing."

We ate in silence for a couple of minutes. Curiosity nagged at me to find out more about his afternoon...hangout? Because it certainly wasn't a *date* with Sue. I cast him the same quizzical look he'd given me moments ago, which he probably misread as me fighting another brain freeze, because he didn't say anything. When the silence got annoyingly long, words burst out of me. "So, where are you taking her?"

Ethan hesitated a moment before he revealed, "Charlie's." It was barely more than a mumble, and he didn't look up either. Just his cheeks turned a heated pink in spite of the cold ice cream we were shoveling into our mouths.

As far as I knew, Ethan wasn't a big fan of Charlie's Café in town. Apparently the menu bored him, and he didn't want to waste money on drinks when he was saving for a car—that's what he'd said last spring. Yet today he was a lucky car owner and still didn't want to go there with me on the occasional Saturday night. My conclusion was that he just lacked the guts to bring a date, and being the fifth wheel has never been Donovan style. His choice was always staying home on the weekends and playing Wii. Pathetic.

Sticking his spoon in the ice cream, Ethan rose and left the kitchen to go hit the shower. He was done in ten minutes—shaved, dressed, and styled—and by that time I'd annihilated the entire raspberry-almond dream by myself. Hands tucked into my pockets as I leaned against the wall in the hallway, I watched him tie his shoes. "When are you meeting Sue?"

"Five."

I glanced at my watch and narrowed my eyes. "It's quarter past four. You'll be at Charlie's in five minutes. Three if the traffic lights favor you."

Ethan smoothed out his black jeans and adjusted his collar. "Yeah, but I'm not going to drive. I'm taking a walk." If the tremor in his voice hadn't betrayed him, the way he fumbled with the strands of his hair to make them stand perfectly in place as he looked in the mirror certainly would have.

"Antsy?" I teased.

Drawing a deep enough breath to inhale every dust particle in the room that Mom hadn't caught on her last cleaning day, he turned to me. His larynx bobbed with a hard swallow. "See you later," he said and walked out the door.

Holy cow! I'd never seen my brother this nervous before. If Sue really wasn't the reason, then what was?

Scratching my head, I stared at the closed door for another moment before I walked into my room and did some quick cleaning. Afterward, I booted up my computer. It was five thirty, and Lauren would be here in half an hour. She liked *tutoring* me to the background singing of Enrique Iglesias. I couldn't say I enjoyed that wailing, but as long as it made her

ANNA KATMORE

happy and, more importantly, got her in the right mood, no one was going to hear me complain.

When I heard the front door slamming shut a little later, I peeked out into the corridor. It couldn't be Ethan coming back already. That would be like the shortest date ever, even if we were only talking soda here.

But no, it wasn't Ethan. Mom trudged into the kitchen, her arms loaded with groceries. I helped with the paper bags. "Are you cooking tonight?"

"Yes. Salmon fillet and potatoes." She set her purse down and started putting all kinds of food into the fridge. "Unless you and Ethan want to cook?"

When Mom hopefully waggled her eyebrows at me, I almost felt bad for telling her, "Ethan's gone. He won't be back for dinner. And Lauren's coming over in a minute. We're going to study. No time for cooking, sorry."

"Oh." She scrutinized the vacuum-sealed fish in her hands, her brain certainly rattling through the options. Ethan was the biggest eater in our house. If we lacked one mouth, the fish would probably be wasted. Eventually, Mom lifted her head with a contemplative look. "Maybe Lauren wants to—"

"Nope, she doesn't," I cut her off and went back to my room. Even if Lauren did want to eat with us, I wouldn't let her. Having a girl over for dinner, lunch, or even breakfast came too close to commitment. No way!

My phone went off in my pocket as I settled on my bed with a car magazine. It was a message from said girl who would never eat in this house.

You there?

Lauren always texted me when she was outside. It was her way of ringing the doorbell.

Last room down the corridor, I answered. *Be naked when you enter. ;-)*

Very funny. Come to the door. Unless you don't want to see me naked at all tonight?

Ah, I couldn't risk that. Getting off my bed, I jogged to the front door to let my sexy tutor in. She turned around and let me help her out of her purple leather jacket. Lauren knew her way around my house and was in my room before me, shouting out a hello to my mother on her way.

I made a detour to the fridge and brought her a Dr. Pepper, her favorite. I popped the can open for her and put it on the desk before sitting down on the edge of my bed with a sly grin, totally ready to be tutored for an hour or two.

Lauren sank into the chair across from me and started thumbing through the pages in my textbook. "Now, where did we stop last time?"

Right at her black lacy underwear, but that was probably not what she wanted to hear. So instead of pushing her, which I knew she hated more than anything when I was with her, I was a good boy and conjugated the verbs she randomly tossed at me. I translated some of the text she told me—and I got all of it right—but when she wanted me to explain how to build the past perfect subjunctive of some crap, I just stared at her with a cocked head.

At my silence, Lauren's gaze lifted to me. "What?"

ANNA KATMORE

What? Seriously? "If that was a test, I'd have gotten an A plus plus plus! So do you intend to take off your top any time soon, Parker, or are we going to study without any rewards at all today?"

A very light blush highlighted her cheekbones as she lowered her chin for a moment and then batted her lashes at me. "Why don't you come and do it yourself?"

Yep, that was an invitation to my liking. A smirk of anticipation tugged on my lips as I got off my bed, ambled toward her, and pulled her to her feet by taking her slender hands in mine. This was the part of the evening when Enrique Iglesias actually came in handy. I started to sway Lauren gently to the low music and began unbuttoning the front of her shirt, all the time humming softly against the side of her neck.

Her hair tickled my nose. Suppressing a sneeze, which was the epitome of unromantic, as I'd found out with my ex-girlfriend quite a while ago, I gathered her long strands with both hands and slid them to her back, out of the way.

Lauren brought her hands up and started to unbutton my shirt, slowly sliding it down my shoulders and arms until it landed on the floor. Oh yes, we were definitely getting to the good part.

When she hooked her fingers in my belt, working it open with the same slowness as she did the buttons, it was a foolproof sign that the actual Spanish lesson was over. A very physical part of me was quite happy about that fact.

Hands on her hips, I leaned my forehead against hers and, with a grin, looked into her eyes. Until some strange sort of disappointment struck. Lauren's eyes weren't pretty. They were dark and striking. But they fit nowhere into the delicious candy spectrum.

For Christ's sake, this wasn't supposed to bother me right now! Not when I had her half undressed in front of me. But once I started to wonder, my thoughts went totally astray. Was it normal for girls to have such thin eyebrows? Lauren's were no thicker than a line drawn with a charcoal pencil. She must pluck them. Jeez, did that hurt? And did all girls do it? What the hell for?

My gaze ran lower over her flawless face. No spots, no birth marks, and, just for me I was sure, no lipstick today. I swallowed, looking at those lush lips I should've been kissing.

"Chris, is something wrong?" she asked in a soft voice, obviously unsure if she should smile or frown at me. She went for both.

"Nope, everything's fine." I gave her the smirk she needed to relax again and leaned in to kiss her. Only, our lips never touched.

"Mom, we've got a guest for dinner! Is that okay?" a voice boomed through the house, through my door, and through my brain—making me jerk back.

Drawing in a quick breath, Lauren jumped, too. "Was that your brother?"

Most definitively. And he hadn't come home alone. Ethan and Sue...on a date in our house? Dammit, I just had to see that.

Lauren and I could make out any other day. This, however,

ANNA KATMORE

was extraordinary entertainment and got top priority. I let my hands slip away from her hips and raked them through my hair. "Uh, yeah..." Now what to say to end this tutoring session without kicking her to the curb? After all, it wasn't her fault that I wouldn't ask her to eat with us. "I thought Ethan would come home later, but since he's here now, I have to help him with...uh....his school project," I said, pulling the excuse from thin air. "It's a biology assignment, and I promised to work on it with him. He needs it done by tomorrow."

Lauren's frown deepened as I buckled my belt and then picked our clothes up from the floor. "Really?"

No, not really. "Yep. Sorry." I handed her the black top I'd peeled her out of not two minutes ago and began buttoning my shirt in haste. "Do you mind if we continue the lesson some other time? Maybe tomorrow or this weekend?"

Lauren knew my *no dinner, no lunch, no sleepover* rule, so she didn't complain when I rushed her to the door, chin low, still struggling with these goddamned shirt buttons. Something was going terribly wrong down there, but there was no time to right it. I all but shoved Lauren out of my room.

Okay, that was a bit harsh, so I corrected my bad behavior by sliding my fingers through hers and pulling her along with me. She shouldn't get the feeling that she was being kicked out of my house—which, let's face it, she actually was.

Ethan walked straight for his room, only raising his eyebrows at us in a feeble greeting. Susan appeared right behind him and—

Jesus Christ. Had she been on the catwalk tonight?

She'd abandoned her jeans and usually decent shirts for a dress that put even Lauren's Saturday-night outfits to shame. Tight on top, flaring at her thighs, it was a striking red that called up the bull in any guy. *Hot damn, Miss Miller!*

Letting my x-ray gaze run up her body to her face, which was completely spectacle-free this evening, I didn't miss her checking me out in return. From her clandestine look, *she & I* was starting to become a serious possibility in her book. Was it because she hadn't gotten what she was after from Ethan? Or had the little flirtation in detention already had an impact?

As we passed in the hallway, I smirked and winked at her. Her cheeks turned red with alarm. Like being ripped out of a daydream, her eyes grew wide, and she rushed after Ethan. The door banged shut behind her, apparently her own subtle way of saying hi to me. It made me chuckle. In addition to the fact, I realized Ethan wasn't behaving like a gentleman with her, which was another surefire clue that he wasn't into her.

Susan Miller was free to take and seduce. Goodbye, bad conscience—hello, freezing-hell challenge.

Someone squeezed my hand. Oh, right. Lauren. She led the way to the front door and turned on the threshold with a quizzical look. "That's the girl who talked to you in school the other day, right? Is she your brother's new girlfriend?"

I wasn't sure how much she knew about my brother, but I definitely wasn't going to discuss him with her. "Guess I'll find out later," I answered, shrugging one shoulder. Then I kissed her on the corner of her mouth. "See you tomorrow." It certainly wasn't the kind of goodbye kiss she'd expected, nor was this abrupt ending to our Spanish hookup lesson. Yeah, whatever.

When she was gone, I closed the door and made a beeline for the kitchen. "Mom?"

"Hm?" She turned with the smile of a bunny in carrot heaven. That alone answered the question I hadn't yet asked her.

"Is Sue staying for dinner?"

"Hhhyesss," she hissed, frantically nodding her head. "And isn't she a nice girl? So polite and *so* pretty."

"Yeah." I laughed. "Pretty." It was hard not to pick up on her happiness and feel a slight bit of joy about it myself. Not quite because Ethan finally seemed interested in a girl, but because it gave me a chance to get to know my target a little better.

After re-buttoning my shirt in the correct order, I started peeling the boiled potatoes Mom had put in a bowl. "Ethan said he was taking her out to Charlie's. I wonder why they came home so early."

"They want to play video games," Mom informed me, leaning her back against the counter next to me and wiping her hands on her apron. "I hope that's just a new teenage code word for being alone." Her crumpled look turned a shade of soulful. "Is it a code word?"

I rolled my eyes, suppressing a snort. "Yeah, Mom. It's a code word." And it stands for: *Ethan is a douche.* Video games, gee! I could think of a hundred things to do with Sue in my room, and none of them involved a console or controller.

But when my mother returned to preparing the salmon fillets and began humming joyfully under her breath, I didn't have the heart to burst her bubble. I could actually *feel* her excitement, and it made me shake my head, amused.

After I'd tossed the potatoes in hot butter with French parsley, she asked me, "Would you please get the two of them, Christian? Dinner's ready in three minutes."

Did she for real just call me by my full name? Gross. Laughter rocked my chest. Beverly Donovan hadn't been this nervous since the day she applied for her dream job as a real estate agent. And here I'd thought nothing in this house could surprise me anymore. Total error.

Leaving the spicy-smelling kitchen, I walked to Ethan's room, knocked, and opened the door—by God, almost. Fingers gripping the doorknob, a terrible memory made me shudder and jerk my hand away as though the metal was shriveling my flesh. Video games, my ass. I'd learned my lesson last time and would never again walk into Ethan's room uninvited. Instead, I shouted, "Feeding time!" and trudged back to the kitchen.

Less than a minute later, the supposed sweethearts showed up, not holding hands or anything a couple would do. I deemed it a good sign. The challenge of seducing Sue was on until Ethan told me to lay off—directly.

Having a girl I wanted to seduce in the same room with my family was a little out of my comfort zone, though. Also, it would break my mom's heart if I stole Sue from under Ethan's nose right in front of hers. I wasn't that kind of an asshole.

Needing a distraction, I fetched a jar from the island and

made a tour around the dinner table to fill our glasses with water. New plan: Catch Sue alone sometime.

But, screw me sideways, not staring as she followed me around the table to lay out the plates required more self-control than expected. Her already short dress rode up her thighs a little higher each time she leaned forward.

She sidled up to Ethan after she was done and asked him in a low voice, "Isn't your father coming home for dinner?"

"My father lives in L.A. with his former secretary," Ethan huffed, scowling at the chair that once was Dad's. "He hasn't been home for dinner in almost six years now."

The color of embarrassment zoomed across Susan's face. "Oh."

She could be a kitten with claws, all right, but tonight she was a guest in our house. Ethan shouldn't make her uncomfortable. He deserved a slap upside his head for that retort. Since I could hardly slap my brother in front of her, I covertly poked him in the ribs with my elbow as I passed him and coughed.

Ethan jerked his head to me. I narrowed my eyes, which he also did in return. At least he got the hint and told her quickly, "No worries." Then he offered her a seat. *Any* seat. Dammit, that guy could drive me up a tree sometimes.

Unknowingly, of course, Sue lowered into my chair. Call me finicky, but in this dining room, we'd had a certain seating order for years, and not even Ethan's first female guest since elementary school would change that.

I could just ask her to move over, but there was another

possibility, which allowed me to touch her and might get us a lot farther. Holding my tongue, I took Susan's hand and made her sit in the chair to the left of mine. She seemed all right with that and didn't even flinch at the contact. Yep, we were definitely making headway.

After dishing out salmon and potatoes for everyone, Mom lowered into the chair across from me, and Ethan sat down to my right. "I think my car needs to go to the shop," he said around a mouthful of fish. "It's been pulling slightly to the right since last week."

"Might be low air pressure in one of the front tires." I didn't know much about cars, but that's something my dad had detected on Mom's car during my last visit with him in L.A. "We can take a look tomorrow, if you want."

"Mm-hmm." He sipped from his glass, and Sue did the same. Did she even know that she'd been mirroring his every movement for the past three minutes? The girl sat shy and hunched at the table, obviously trying not to draw attention to herself. Well, major fail with that red dress, sweetness.

But where the heck was the tank with the bad manners tonight? If I hadn't known better, I'd have said this was a total stranger and not snappy geek Sue Miller. Then again, she might've only been playing the nice girl for my mother...like I was playing the gentleman. We both knew better, and yet it could turn out to be fun.

I decided it was time to include her in our conversation as Ethan had obviously shipwrecked in that department. But Mom beat me there. "So, Ethan said you know each other from school. Are you in the same classes?"

"Umm, no." Susan picked at her fish. "I'm a junior."

"Ah. Ethan wants to go to UCLA next year, did he tell you? How did you two meet, anyway?"

Throwing a wary glance at Ethan, Sue looked like she was fighting a blush. But after a quick cough, she straightened and informed the Spanish Inquisition, "We met at soccer practice this week. He made me late getting home." Obviously a memory that made her smile. "It was my granddad's birthday, so I almost got in trouble that evening."

"Sorry for that," Ethan mouthed at her across the table and grimaced. Although, for once, it looked more flirtatious than anything he'd done since we sat down.

It didn't surprise me that soon enough my mother steered the conversation toward houses. She loved talking shop when she got a chance, and grilling Sue about her living situation was obviously a must on her list. Ten minutes later, I knew that Susan Miller lived in a yellow two-story on Rasmussen Avenue—two bedrooms upstairs, a small but cozy kitchen downstairs, an open fireplace in the living room, and too much junk in the garage to fit a car in. Nice.

When my mother next demanded to know the year of construction, Sue's face went blank.

"Don't mind her," Ethan came to her rescue, ending the interrogation and offering her the bread basket, from which Sue sneaked a slice. "She's like that with everyone. Mom's a real estate agent, always on the hunt for houses to sell."

"Wow, that's a cool job." Sue's eyes gleamed with a whole

new interest. "Must be awesome to see so many houses from the inside."

"It's the best job in the world. I love houses." Mom, who'd finished her meal by then, wiped her hands and mouth on a napkin and then leaned back in her chair with a friendly smile. "Do you already have plans for after high school? College? Traveling? Any job you'd like to do?"

"College," Susan shot back without a millisecond of thinking. I didn't expect anything less from the girl that actually did homework in detention. "I want to study languages and later on find a job that gives me the chance to work with books. That's what I love. Great stories. So I was thinking maybe a librarian, or a literary agent, even."

"Sounds like you have a plan," I chipped in for the first time, though the term *literary agent* was something I'd have to Google later in my room. Sue nodded with real pride as she looked at me.

The clock struck eight a couple seconds later. All of us seemed equally surprised about how long we'd been sitting in front of our finished plates, just talking—or in Ethan's and my cases, mostly listening. "All right, guys," Mom said then and clapped her hands once. "Dishes to do. Go play it out."

"Oh, come on, Mom," Ethan whined. "I've got a guest."

Heck, it was so clear that he was going to try to worm himself out of the dishes contest. He wouldn't stand a chance against me at hoops in the yard, which usually decided which of us had to clean the kitchen when Mom did the cooking.

But I wasn't in the mood to wash plates, pans, or pots

either. Just for fun, I picked on Ethan's tactics and cast a smirk toward Sue. "Yeah, right. *She* can do the dishes."

Mom pointed a criticizing finger at my face. "Your brother's girlfriend won't be doing your chores."

In that very instant, I could hear Susan's surprised intake of a breath from where I sat. In a shy way, she lowered her eyes.

"Mom, she's not my girlfriend," Ethan contradicted—fast. Despite Susan's disappointment, this clearly wasn't him being embarrassed by Mom calling him out on dating a girl. It was him telling Mom to lay off, because he really *wasn't*.

"See?" I said to my mother. "She's not his girlfriend." With a grin, I rose from the table. "She *can* do the dishes."

But of course Mom wouldn't let me get away with that. "No way, buddy. You do your job first." She grabbed me by the back of my collar, stopping me from leaving the room, and I laughed out loud.

"Ah, all right, I'll do it!" Anything to stop the *mom*ster from strangling me. With a quiet chuckle, I stacked the dishes and winked at Sue as I took her plate. Her shyness seemed to have eased out of her during dinner, and she even smiled at me this time. Hell was starting to cool off already... Mmm, I liked how this evening had developed.

Since I'd evidently cracked open the door to Sue's good side, I decided to sweeten my chances a little more. "Dessert in twenty!" I called to her and Ethan before they left the room for yet another game of Wii.

Everything a nice cream and fruit dessert needed was there

in the fridge. I lined the ingredients up on the island counter: different fruits, coconut juice, a lemon, powdered sugar, vanilla beans, yogurt, and some mascarpone. Sweets were my specialty, and Sue was going to get wooed in an unforgettable way.

Mixing everything except the fruit in a bowl, I got ambushed by the *mom*ster again. She slung her arms around my waist from behind and squealed in my left ear. "Oh, isn't she lovely?"

"Mom..." I moaned as some of the cream splashed on my front during her attack. Unbuttoning this damned shirt for the third time today, I escaped my mother's clasp of excitement and draped it over the backrest of a chair.

Of course, she couldn't keep her fingers out of my dessert in the meantime. Licking cream off her forefinger, she smiled brilliantly. "They make such a sweet couple."

"You heard Ethan. They *aren't* a couple."

"Yet."

I rolled my eyes. She was a hopeless case. "Why don't you take a timeout, relax in the living room, and sip a glass of wine?" I suggested with a less-than-subtle nod toward the door.

Mom pinched my cheek. She stuck her finger into the cream a second time and walked out in a happy skip. Half a minute later, she popped her head in once more and tossed me a fresh t-shirt to make amends for the stained shirt.

When she was gone, I finally finished the cream and poured it into four dessert bowls from the cupboard. Ethan had bought them for us a couple of years ago. While his name was painted on the green one, he'd found it funny to give me a blue

ANNA KATMORE

bowl with the name *Christopher* on it. That was his way of rubbing it in that so many people got on my nerves by assuming my full name was Christopher. I'd liked the colors of the bowls, though, and had just used a sharpie on mine to replace the *opher* with *ian*.

The yellow bowl was Mom's, and it said so on the side with *Best mom in the world* in cursive. But which one to give Susan? There were two left. A red one with the word *Milk* on it, and an orange one that would have marked her as *Cereal*. I picked *Milk* because the color fit her dress.

A small radio with a CD deck stood next to the microwave, and cooking was more fun with music—that was one of the few things my family agreed on. Mom's latest discovery was Sam Smith. His voice blared through the house most of the time she was home, therefore it didn't surprise me that his album was in the CD player. I turned it on and, knowing all his songs by heart by now, I sang out loud to "Stay With Me" while peeling and chopping the oranges, kiwi, bananas, and peaches.

From the corner of my eye, I saw a shadow move past the kitchen door. Or maybe not quite *past*, because when I looked up, I found Sue standing close to the doorjamb and casting an intrigued glance into the room.

Our conversation from detention was certainly as apparent in her mind as it still was in mine. So had she come to spy on the foe? Intrigued by what I had to offer?

Because she didn't walk away when I caught her watching me, it was worth a try to beckon her closer. Still singing this stupid song, I crooked my finger at her. And, heck, she moved. Slowly. In the right direction.

Come here, kitty, kitty, kitty...

When she stood directly across from me with the island between us, her gaze roamed over the bowls filled with cream. Although her mouth obviously watered, she didn't dip her finger into it like Mom had.

From the plate holding the chopped fruits, I picked a peach wedge and dunked one side into the cream. All this time, I sang the lines to "Stay With Me" like I was giving an exclusive concert for Susan Miller. It was the weirdest thing to do, but I also knew, if I stopped singing, I would say something imprudent, probably about her hot dress—and she would stomp away.

As I held the peach wedge out to her, to either take it or simply bite off the tip, Sue shook her head. Fine. Perhaps not her favorite. With a casual shrug, I bit the cream end off myself and put the rest of the slice back on the plate. There, my gaze got stuck on the heap of kiwi slices. She'd eaten one of them at lunch today. Were they more to her liking than peaches?

Putting that theory to the test, I reached for the kiwi and watched her reaction. Her mouth tugged up at the corners. Ah, there we go. Smiling, and still singing along to this nagging song, I dipped a round kiwi slice into the cream then held it out to Sue. Only problem was she couldn't take it like she could have taken the peach. Cream was all over the kiwi and my fingers, too. If she wanted this bite of dessert, she had to let me feed it to her. I was fine with that. Was she?

ANNA KATMORE

Sue looked at me intently, yet she didn't move an inch.

Aw, c'mon, don't leave me hanging, sweetness. We've come so far. There was, after all, a challenge to win and, as everybody knew, the love of a girl was won with dessert.

I could almost hear the silent argument she was having with herself. Her eyes switched back and forth between mine and the fruit between my fingers with a hunger that made even *my* mouth water. Just not for kiwi.

Anticipation tickled the inside of my stomach. I stopped singing. A gambler must feel this way when he puts all in and waits for his opponent to show his cards.

Seconds ticked by.

What's in your hand, Sue?

Lips pressed together, Susan started to lean forward. Her flaming gaze captured mine. Or maybe it was the other way round, I couldn't tell by that time. When she warily parted her mouth, I could barely keep my glorious smile in check, so I ground my teeth behind closed lips and tilted my chin a little lower.

Her teeth caught the kiwi, and her lips caught my fingers. That was the plan. Yet when it happened, adrenaline shot through my body in all directions. Had to be the anticipation of getting a head start in the challenge.

Sue pulled the fruit away, and it vanished in her mouth completely. A tiny spot of cream remained on her bottom lip. She wiped it off with her thumb. Too bad for me. If I'd been a little faster, I could have wiped it away for her and would certainly have dazzled her with that move. All I could do now was lick the rest of the cream off my own fingers. Delicious. The cream *and* Sue's blush as she watched me.

Once again shocked out of a world where the possibility of *she & I* existed, she sucked in a sharp breath. Then she spun on her heel and stalked away without looking back.

Still trying to fight me? Laughing, I dragged my gaze away from her swaying backside and the swinging ponytail. But I'd read her face. She had let me in once, she would let me in again. Susan Miller was in for a ride to hell. And by the time we got there, the North Pole would seem like a warm place in comparison.

Chapter 6

I HELD A handful of chopped fruit over Susan's dessert bowl. About to drop them into her cream, a wedge of peach sticking out caught my eye. She hadn't bitten into that one, probably hated it. To be on the safe side, I made sure no peach landed in her bowl.

Once done, I headed for Ethan's. A quick knock on his door and a shout to Mom in the living room was enough for the entire pack to file into the kitchen two minutes later. Sue's wary glance didn't escape me. She seemed guarded, kept a wide distance, and wore a stern face. If she was worried I was going to out her to my brother for enjoying being fed from my hand...well, it was kind of tempting.

But Mom would never forgive me.

As Sue sat down, I reached over her shoulder and placed the dessert bowl in front of her, casually brushing her shoulder with my arm while I whistled the melody of "Stay With Me." A personal reminder of how much fun we'd had in this room five minutes ago—just the two of us.

She threw me a furtive look from the corner of her eye, probably getting a mental cramp from willing me to stop whistling already. I responded with a tight smile and slid into my chair. Under the table, my knee knock against hers. Couldn't waste a chance to make her aware of me.

Sue obviously tried very hard not to look at me after that, but I sneaked a peek at her every now and then. One spoonful of cream and fruit after the other disappeared into her mouth. After the fourth or fifth, I started fantasizing. Me holding out a juicy green grape as she stole it with her teeth, her lips closing around my fingers like before. A warm tickle spread in my stomach. The next grape I would put between my teeth and—

Jeez! My spine stiffened with shock from that image. Or rather because of the anticipation that gripped me by the neck. Daydreaming of fooling around with a geek. At which point in this evening had the challenge actually become so appealing to me?

I shook off the thought and concentrated on my own dessert—which was cream and not *Susan*.

When Sue left the house with my brother that night, my head was still filled with visuals of a hot red dress and stupid things I wanted to do to charm it off her. Much, *much* too appealing.

To clear my head with some distraction, I logged on to Facebook. Lauren had posted from the shopping center. *Change of plans* it said beneath the picture of her and Rebecca, each toasting the camera with a fancy cocktail and smiling big.

ANNA KATMORE

Looks like more fun than a Spanish book, I typed in a comment under the picture.

Lauren was fast with a reply. *Come join us. ;)*

Heck, maybe I should. I grabbed my phone from the desk, navigating to the recent calls list to dial her number. At the very top of that list appeared *Weird Geek.* My thumb hovered.

No. *No!* I wouldn't call *her.* Not now and definitely not when she was with my brother. I gritted my teeth and pressed *Lauren 10* right beneath Sue's entry. That was the moment I heard Ethan's voice outside my room.

What the hell was he doing home already?

Before Lauren's phone started ringing, I ended the call and walked into the hallway. Ethan said "good night" to my mother and "hey" to me as we passed each other in front of his room.

"Hi," I replied before he disappeared inside and shut his door. Confused, I sauntered into the kitchen to see if he'd brought Susan with him again. For all I knew, she might be chatting with my mother.

Well, Mom was watching a movie in the living room all by herself, and the kitchen was empty. A quick peek around the corner to check the front door. No girl there. No shoes or jacket either. Ethan had returned alone. And *much* too soon. Made me wonder if he'd even stopped in front of her house for her to get out, or if he'd just slowed down a little and made her take a reckless jump.

Shaking my head, I returned to my room, my phone still clasped in my hand. Hmm, Ethan was home. Sue was back at her house. Odds were he once again hadn't kissed her. And no one would blame me if I dialed her number now. After all, my brother just wasn't interested, right? Considering she'd worn that hot little dress that had sorely tempted me throughout dinner, yet *he* was obviously immune.

Or maybe a text would do for starters. Settling on my bed with the pillow squeezed between my back and the wall, I typed a message. *Not like a geek.* Tonight's outfit kicked her right out of that department.

Some minutes ticked by, and nothing happened. Annoyed by her lack of response, I tossed my phone to the side just as it beeped with a message. Ah, somebody changed her mind.

Weird Geek wrote: *What?*

Since she seemed ready to talk to me, I took the chance and dialed her number instead of sending another text. Sue picked up quickly, although her voice sounded anything but delighted. "Chris, why are you calling me?"

"To wish you a pleasant night and to answer your question," I told her, suppressing a laugh.

An audible sigh traveled through the line followed by her grumbling, "Does your brother know that you're talking to me?"

"No. He just came in...too soon after he drove you home, if you ask me." Contrary to her growl, I strived for a light, playful tone. "Does that mean he, once again, didn't kiss you?"

"None of your business!" Whoa, her saliva had probably just turned a radioactive green from the venom in her voice. But after having her almost plant a kiss on my creamy fingers tonight, I begged to differ.

"Come on, it's a simple yes or no question," I teased her. "I'll sleep a lot better if I know the answer."

"Why don't you ask him yourself, if you want to know so badly?" hissed the kitten.

Did she hate me because she'd liked when I'd coaxed her to eat the fruit from my hand? Or because I looked like the guy she had a crush on and she just couldn't deny it? Her attitude about this was quite immature, considering she wouldn't stand a chance in this challenge anyway. I rolled my eyes but gave her that. "Okay... Since you told me to..." I rose from my bed, walked out the door to my brother's room, and stuck my head inside. He was doing a workout on the floor. "Hey, Ethan," I interrupted, hiding the phone behind my back. "Did you kiss Susan tonight?"

He turned only his head toward me. "No." A grunt as he did a pushup. "Why?" Followed by another grunt.

I waved at him to continue his evening workout and shook my head, mouthing, "Never mind." On the way back to my room, I pressed the cell to my ear. "Ethan said no." Then, as I slumped into my desk chair and started to swivel, I innocently added, "I wonder why he didn't. Could it be that he's just not interested?"

"FYI, he asked me on another date." It wasn't a snappy remark as much as a self-assured jibe. Or maybe it was simply her wishful thinking. Someone should rattle her awake.

"Aw, playing video games again? Is that really your idea of a successful date?"

"We're going to the movies. *Your* idea of a successful date is probably coming out of your room with bed hair and a messy shirt."

I stopped spinning in the chair. Dammit, she *had* been checking me out when we met in the hallway! And my incorrectly buttoned shirt had certainly given her some wild ideas. A sly grin escaped me at the memory of her almost eating me up with her eyes. "I knew you noticed that." Now the far more important question was, "Did it bother you?"

Sue gasped. "Why the hell would it?"

Obvious, girl. "Because, for one, I look exactly like my brother and, from what I can tell, you're totally into him. Means you're totally into me, too." Some rules of the universe just couldn't be broken, no matter how hard she fought it. "And two, only one out of us seems to be dying to snatch a kiss from you these days." Even if it was only to come out of this game the winner.

The absolute silence on the other end of the line shocked me. No snappy retort for once? I must have hit a nerve. "You stopped breathing, Sue," I told her warily, unsure if she was still there. Her quick intake of air then made me chuckle. "I guess that means you agree with me on both points."

She was breathing again, good, yet she took a long moment before she asked me something in a very low and, for her, unusually soft voice—when she spoke with *me*, anyway. "Chris, tell me one thing." Another pause. Gee, I was really itching to hear where this was going. "You had the most beautiful girl in your room this afternoon. Why do you want to kiss *me*?"

Oh, I would tell her why. "Because Lauren, like most other girls, is an easy catch." Spanish lessons or not, I only had to snap my fingers, and she would make room in her calendar for me. "You, on the other hand," I drawled into the phone, hoping to stroke Susan's senses awake with it in spite of the late hour, "challenged me today—and in front of my friends, too."

"So you want me because you can't have me?" Her voice traveled up an octave at the end of the line.

"Who says I can't have you?" I teased.

"I do."

Think again, sweetness. You have no idea who you're dealing with. But her naivety made me smile. "Oh, okay. So yes, then I definitely want you."

Now, Sue actually laughed out loud, but I wasn't so sure whether she sounded amused or frustrated. "You need to understand that I could never kiss a guy without having true feelings for him," she informed me as if making an official statement, "which I don't have for you, Chris."

"Really?" Could somebody enlighten me now as to what one had to do with the other, please? "I've kissed more than twenty girls the past few months, and it was lots of fun. But not one of them made me *feel* anything." No, that wasn't quite the truth. In fact, it depended on how the word *feel* was interpreted here, so I added, "Well, other than—"

"Stop it!" Sue cut me short. "I don't want to hear it."

No? I laughed. "Okay, okay." I wouldn't like to hear about her ex-lovers either. If she'd had one yet. A geek and sex in junior year? Mmm, I wouldn't bet my life on it. Then again, tonight she'd totally busted the geek image of herself. Which got me back on track. "Anyway, there's another reason why I want you."

"What's that?" She sounded truly curious. A good sign.

Eyes closing, I recalled the sexy sway of her hips, then cleared my throat, and said in a low rumble, "You looked *way* hot in that dress today. Definitely not like a geek, which should answer your question to begin with." After a short pause in which I stared into the distance and suddenly saw myself in Ethan's place, taking Sue home earlier, I added in an even lower drawl, "If I'd been the one driving you home tonight, I would have kissed you. And you would have liked it."

Sue stopped breathing again. Mission accomplished.

Blinking a couple times helped free myself from the beguiling vision of kissing her. "Sleep tight, sweetness." It came out as a whisper. Smiling, I hung up, so she could revel in that fantasy herself.

Phone dropped to my lap, I expelled a long breath. When was the last time a girl had gotten me edgy like this? The feeling of not knowing if I could really land her in the end began to screw with my mind. It came with a load of excitement and weird anticipation. I had to go back in my memory as far as Amanda to recognize a similar feeling. Amanda hadn't been a challenge. She'd been my first love...and my last, for that matter.

Love. What a strange word to bring up now. I wasn't feeling anything remotely close to it for Sue. Nevertheless, the

ANNA KATMORE

girl had something about her that made me think of funny ways to crack through her walls. It wasn't only about showing her that she was no different than any other chick and I could have her if I wanted. Tonight, the course of this challenge had taken a turn. Now I needed to have her to actually prove to *myself* that I could.

*

Two hours later, lying in my bed, bored and wide awake, I wondered if it had been a mistake not to meet with the girls in the shopping center. If Becks was there, Tyler couldn't be too far, and some foosball would have provided the distraction I needed. Lauren could have been that kind of distraction too, but somehow I wasn't in the mood.

Eyes shut, I planned my next move with Sue. I kept replaying our encounter in detention, followed by the delicious moment of me feeding her a piece of kiwi tonight. Now if that wasn't some serious progress, I didn't know what was. And then we had that phone call to boot.

Although I didn't know if making her aware that—with the twin thing—she was actually sort of crushing on me too made things about this challenge easier or more complicated. The trouble was, even if she was aware of her attraction to me, she would only try harder now to keep me at a distance.

Counterproductive.

Exhaling a sigh paired with a smile, I rolled onto my back and put an arm beneath my head, the other hand flat on my stomach. Sue really was a piece of work. Considering her resistance, winning her in the end would be an even bigger glory.

Another wave of anticipation swamped me. I hoped it would finally put me to sleep with some happy dreams, but no such luck. At some point, and it felt like hours later, I started making faces at the ceiling, only because the silence in the darkened room was killing me. Gah! Foosball would have been so much better than this.

*

Sleep-deprived, I trudged through the house with a foggy head and glassy eyes on Friday morning, struggling to get into my routine. A hot shower and coffee so strong it could burn a hole in my stomach helped matters a little, but not much.

"Want a ride?" Ethan asked as he walked past the kitchen, where I lounged, half lying on the table.

I gave him a thumbs-up for a yes.

"Then shake a leg. It's late."

A tired grunt left me. After chugging down the rest of my coffee, I put the cup in the sink and rushed to get my stuff for school. Ethan was already waiting in the car, engine humming, by the time I walked out the door.

Head lolling against the window, I caught three minutes of sleep on the ride, but if anything, the short nap put me in a worse condition than before. With my current tunnel vision, I felt like Grover Beach High's in-house zombie as I shuffled

ANNA KATMORE

through the hall to first period.

Luckily, the caffeine kicked in over the morning, and the yawns I had to smother during history and trig stopped when we played a hard game of basketball in gym. Done with the second shower of the day, I jogged to Spanish afterward and sank into the seat next to the one already claimed by Lauren. "Hi," I greeted her with a bright smile.

She said "hey" a little curtly and didn't even look at me for a full three seconds.

Uh-oh.

My brows knitted together. "Everything okay?"

"Yep. Everything's fine."

Shit. *Nothing* was fine. But what had I done? Gaze uncomfortably darting around the room, I cleared my throat. "Are you pissed because I didn't come down to the shopping center last night?" If she was, I really didn't see why, but with girls one could never know.

Now Lauren turned her head in my direction as slowly as the velociraptor in Jurassic Park when it scented its prey. It gave me the chills. She inhaled deeply, slanted her head like she was pondering how to answer that, then obviously decided not to answer at all, and just rolled her eyes.

Mrs. Sanchez walking into class as the bell rang cut our not-so-funny conversation short and forced me to retreat. I could only speculate for the entire next hour. Sometimes I sneaked a glance to Lauren's side, but each time she noticed she expelled an angry snort. She might've breathed smoke the next time I looked at her, so halfway through Spanish, I stopped and kept my gaze to my notes in front of me.

When the bell heralded my lunch break and Lauren slipped out of her seat faster than a viper, I dumped my books in my schoolbag and hurried after her. Just outside class, I caught her arm, stopping her in her tracks. She would talk to me now whether she liked it or not. It was Friday, and I had an important basketball game tomorrow that I wanted her to come watch. And on top of that, I didn't handle parting in anger very well, because I'd had enough of that shit when my parents were still together.

"What is it?" I snarled at her face, clasping her arm harder as she tried to jerk it free. "Tell me what your problem is, *please*, because I really don't know."

For an extended moment, she tried to kill me with her stare.

"Please," I repeated more insistently.

Lauren knew about my issues with arguments, and that was probably the only reason she relented now. Her voice, however, was like a lethal injection. "How did the school project with your brother go?"

I swallowed, hard. "Uh—"

When my grip on her loosened, she finally pulled away and folded her arms over her chest, a muscle jumping in her jaw as she waited for my reply.

"It...umm...went good?"

Her mouth fell open, and her eyes grew wide. Dammit, wrong answer.

Next, she shook her head and rolled her eyes. "Oh, get lost,

ANNA KATMORE

Chris!" She stormed away, but I was on her heels and stopped her again before she rounded the corner.

Snatching her wrist, I made her face me and blew out a breath when she stopped growling at me. "Okay, so there was no project," I admitted.

"No shit."

Hell, what could I say? I had felt bad when I made her leave yesterday. My mouth opened and closed, but words...? Not one came.

At my incompetence, Lauren took over the talking, and there was a lot she had to say. "I heard from Becky what happened in detention yesterday. Tyler told her everything about your intentions to seduce that girl. The one your brother took home yesterday, isn't she?"

Should I say yes? Should I nod? Heaven help me, I was scared of this girl.

"Chris, you're not my boyfriend," she continued then, with the intensity of a harvester riding over me. "You can go out and hookup and do *what*ever with *who*ever you want."

Okay, good to know. It wouldn't work any other way with us, anyway. But what exactly did we have to talk about then?

The answer to that came with a reproachful quirk of her eyebrows. "The point is, I don't like to be lied to. So next time you have something better to do than hang out or study Spanish, for Chrissake, just say so."

My heart pounded a nervous beat. Lauren was a close friend, but at times like this, I wished I could duck my head and just run. She was unpredictable when she got mad. I sucked my bottom lip between my teeth and nodded slowly.

"Fine. See you on Monday," she snarled, eyes still slits. When she turned away from me for the third time, I didn't follow her but called her name loud enough for her to catch over the mumbling of kids in the hallway. She stopped and glanced over her shoulder. "The basketball game tomorrow?" I asked. I did want her to come.

After an endless moment of deliberating, she finally grunted, "Maybe." Then she headed off to her next class, and I went to meet my friends in the cafeteria. My conscience was a bitch that kicked me in the ass the whole way.

Chapter 7

THE MOMENT I entered the overcrowded cafeteria and sat down with T-Rex and the others, I glanced at the soccer table, and it made me forget all about Lauren and our conversation three minutes ago.

Dammit. Watching Sue eat another kiwi gave me all kinds of funny quivers in my stomach. For fun, I considered walking over there, snatching a cup of cream on the way, then dipping her kiwi slice in it, and feeding it to her like yesterday. Would she eat it? In front of all her friends?

In front of Ethan, who was actually sitting with them today?

I doubted it, so the walk would be a waste of time. I ate my pizza and kept my attention close to the neighborhood instead of letting it run astray to the soccer gang. If the saying was true and third time was really a charm, my brother would bring Susan home again that evening. Another visit should offer enough opportunities to get a few minutes alone with her then.

But when I came home from basketball practice that afternoon, Ethan was hiding in his room all by his lonesome. It seemed he had other plans for today. Whatever they were, they didn't involve Susan Miller.

While I was playing with the thought of giving Sue a call myself and inviting her here, my mother slashed that idea when she knocked on my door and called my name.

"'S open," I answered.

"Peggy Ann delivered the rosebushes this morning," she informed me, slipping only her head through the door. "Would you mind helping me plant them?"

Rosebushes? For real? I made a face and whined, "Can't we do it this weekend?"

"They'll dry out before then. Come on, please? I can't do it alone."

"Ask Ethan then…"

"He's studying for his math test."

Rolling my eyes, I suppressed a grunt and dragged myself out of the chair, tossing my phone on the bed. Mom backed away when I pointed a finger at her nose. "You know what that means, lady."

As I squeezed between her and the doorframe, she lifted her brows at me. "Hmm?"

"Allowance raise," I told her with a smirk.

"Yeah, right." Mom knocked her elbow playfully into my side. "Dream on, buddy."

Plans busted *and* no payment? Seriously, the house rules needed an amendment, and fast. Then again, how long could it take to dig a hole and put a stupid bush in? Ten minutes?

Together, we walked into the yard and—*jeez!* There was a trailer loaded with an entire rose jungle in the driveway.

"What the heck are you going to do with *those*?" I wailed.

Her innocent grin came a little too late. She pointed at the twenty-foot line of bleak soil along the wooden fence. Great. If we started now, we could be done by midnight...if we hurried. "Terrific," I muttered, going to retrieve the shovel.

Saturday morning, I slept in. During the night, an annoying pain had started in my lower back, which was probably a result of all that manual labor in the garden, bending and planting those prickly bushes. Trying to ignore the twinge as the morning sun tickled my face, I turned over, but the ache didn't go away. Grandpa must've felt like that when he woke up every morning—stiff and hurting all over. At least that's what he looked like when Ethan and I used to spend our holidays at our grandparents' house up until ninth grade. Getting old? Not something one should look forward to.

It was well past eleven when I finally rolled out of bed and did a serious series of pushups and crunches to get the kink out of my back. A long, warm shower soothed the pain some more. Hungry as hell after the workout, I threw on a white polo shirt and my favorite washed-out jeans, then made myself an awesome breakfast. An omelet with pretty much everything the fridge had to offer and coffee so thick and black it could've been the devil's spit-out soul.

A breakfast like that demanded some relaxing in front of the TV afterward. Zapping through the channels, there was nothing to hold my interest, so I didn't fight the pull when my eyes started closing.

It might've been minutes or hours later when the doorbell yanked me out of my light sleep. "Chris, can you get it?" my mother's voice drifted into the living room from outside the house. Her face popped up behind the door leading to the backyard. Obviously, she was busy with her rosebushes. Running a hand over my face, I rubbed the sleep from my eyes and sauntered to the door.

A delighted smile tugged on the edges of my mouth when I saw the girl with a ponytail standing in the sunlight on our doorstep. "Hi, Susan."

She gave me a once-over, her eyes narrowing the slightest as they returned to my face. Ah, she had no idea. Cocky, I crossed my arms over my chest and tilted my head slightly. "You're trying to figure out who I am, aren't you?"

All of a sudden, her gaze lightened. "Nope, I just got the answer. Is Ethan in his room?"

"Yes," I drawled, wondering what the hell gave me away. Sue didn't even wait for my answer but pushed me out of the way and headed down the hall, leaving me to close the door like her damn servant.

I rushed after her and grabbed her arm before she reached my brother's room. "How did you figure it out?"

"Simple."

Simple? It shouldn't be simple, dammit. But then she let me in on her secret by grabbing my massive silver chains and winding them around her finger until they almost cut into my

ANNA KATMORE

flesh. "Your *I rule* chains gave you away."

"I rule" chains? Excuse me? They were the only things my dad had left behind when he moved out. Mom had asked Ethan and me if we wanted them, since she didn't intend on spending a single dime to mail anything to our father. Ethan had deadpanned, "Are you kidding me?" So I'd worn both ever since.

A mischievous grin on her face now, Sue dropped the necklaces and then flicked me on the forehead.

"Hey, that's rude," I blurted with narrowed eyes.

"What? The flick or calling your chains what they are?" The girl had the nerve to flick me again. Oh, God help her, but she shouldn't have done that twice. Obviously, she needed to be taught another lesson.

"Both," I said, snatching her hand and twisting her around fast, so her back was pressing against my front. My arms around her in a tight embrace, I growled in her ear, "And if you do that one more time, I'll give you a hickey the size of Ohio." Lowering my head, I let my lips brush over the satiny skin of her neck with my next words. "Right here."

Shit, but this girl smelled good. Like she'd taken a bath in coconut milk.

Sue froze in my arms. As her skin quivered under my mouth, I wanted to make good on my promise this instant.

Gasping, she tried to wrestle free from my hold. "Go away, Chris! You're disgusting!" Either she was a really weak girl, or she just didn't want to get away as much as she wanted to make us both believe, because she didn't seem to be trying very hard.

Her girly resistance coaxed a chuckle from me, but I gave her that and let her go. One arm braced on the wall then, she caught her breath. "Never," she warned me, "do that again!"

"Why?" Playfully, I waggled my eyebrows at her. "Afraid you might get addicted to it?"

"Yeah, either that"—she all but stuck her finger down her throat to make herself gag and rolled her eyes—"or throw up."

Seriously? I laughed out loud now. "Every addiction starts with denial, so I'll let you believe that." Suddenly it struck me what day it was, and my laugh died abruptly. "Why did you come here, anyway? Are you coming to my basketball game tonight?" I didn't quite dare to believe that, but why else would Ethan have invited her over?

Sue mirrored my narrowed gaze. "What? No!"

"Then why are you here?"

"Movies? Ethan and I?" She lifted her eyebrows in a way that called me dimwitted. "I told you on the phone, remember?" She started to walk away, but Little Miss Sunshine was mistaken. She couldn't drop a bomb on my head like that and just run.

Slamming my hand on the wall in front of her face, I cut off her escape. "Wait. That's today?" I wanted her to suddenly remember that she got the time of their date wrong. But, alas, my luck with this girl was non-existent.

"Yes."

That one word left a bitter taste in my mouth.

"But you can't," I muttered. All right, maybe *she* could, but

Ethan couldn't. Like shit would I let him skip the game. My argument with Sue was over that instant. Instead, I decided to talk to the culprit, the one who'd betrayed me. Stomping down the hallway, I entered Ethan's room without bothering to knock. "Hey, what's this crap about you going to the movies tonight?"

My brother, who sat at his desk doing whatever, looked up. "I'm going with Susan." Confused, he shook his head slightly. "What's your problem?"

His casual brush-off stung. "My problem is that it's my last game this year. The big rematch against Clearwater High. You were supposed to come. You promised!" His face was still as blank as a piece of paper. My shoulders dropped as my hope drained. "Mom's coming, too."

Something soft touched my arm. My head jerking around, I found Sue's compassionate eyes on me. "If it means so much to you, we won't go to the movies tonight. Ethan can go to your game."

"I can?" I heard Ethan's stunned voice at the same time I blurted, "He *can*?"

"Yes," Sue answered with a soft, amused chuckle—something that was definitely rare when I was around. "The movie won't run away. And if it's the last game before winter break, you really should go," she prompted Ethan. "It would kill me if my family didn't come to my big games."

Of course. She was a soccer player, she could relate to my feelings. Right then I wanted to hug and kiss her more than anything.

"Okay, but you have to come, too," Ethan told her.

For a moment, she deliberated the idea. In the end, she shrugged and gave us both a small smile. "Basketball, it is."

I ignored the urge to grab her and spin her around, but seriously, the smile tearing at my lips right now was nothing I could hold back. Turning a little more in Sue's direction and less in Ethan's, I mouthed a genuine, "I owe you."

The wicked gleam in her eyes spelled trouble; yes, she would collect that favor sometime soon. But I was good with that. Whatever she wanted, she would get it for making my brother come to my game.

Sue walked past me and shut the door in my face, shutting me out of Ethan's realm once again. For a bit, it nagged at me not knowing what the two of them did inside this well-sealed fort. But soon enough T-Rex called, and we built each other up bragging about how we were going to kick some Clearwater High ass tonight.

My mind chock-full of basketball, I packed my jersey and shoes in a duffle bag. From a drawer, I grabbed my lucky socks, the white ones with the two green loops, and tossed them on top. Spraying some Axe under my shirt, I stuffed the bottle into the bag too, then zipped it closed.

Mom had changed into one of her elegant dresses by the time I came into the kitchen. It might seem awkward to dress so formally for a game where people usually left with hot dog stains on their shirts and maybe some Coke splashes, too. But not in this house. The dark red dress was my mother's way of showing me what a proud basketball mom she was. One who didn't doubt for a second that her son's team would win the game tonight.

"I'm ready to eat steak today," she stated with a big smile and kissed me on the cheek. That was the whole point of the dress anyway. If my team won, she would be treating Ethan and me to a fantastic meal in a nice restaurant afterward. The alternative was Burger King and my treat, but that wasn't in the stars tonight. I could feel it in my excitedly bouncing ankles.

I rubbed the spot on my cheek where she'd left a damp, mama-kiss spot. "Are we taking one car tonight, or does Ethan want to drive with Sue?"

"I don't know. Can you ask them?"

The duffle bag dropped with a thud on the floor. Heading for Ethan's room, I knocked gently, but with the fun they must've been having inside, they didn't hear. I could even tell through the door that they were playing Wii bowling, what with Sue cheering, "Ssttt....*rike*!"

Certain not to interrupt anything unpredictable this time, I cracked the door open. Sue slammed another virtual ball down the lane and asked my brother, "When does the game start?"

"In forty-five minutes," I answered, which made them both turn around. "Mom's ready, and we're leaving in five. If you two want a ride, you better finish this fast."

The sound of pins being shot to hell and a ringing chimed from the TV, drawing everyone's attention for a moment. Obviously, Sue was a pro at Wii bowling. With a happy grin, she spun back to Ethan and me, bouncing on the heels of her feet. "I'm done. We can go," she declared, hands clasped behind her as she proudly stuck out her chest.

Ethan didn't share her joy about winning the game. He folded his arms over his chest, and from his grumpy voice, I guessed his face, turned away from me, was none too happy either. "I don't care how much you complain. Next time it's *Mario Kart* again."

"Fine with me." Susan beamed, shining like a new nickel, no doubt taking this as another invitation to a Wii hookup in her crush's house. The two of them definitely took the term *virtual dating* to a whole new level.

I knew my brother was that kind of innocent but, seriously, Sue too? The tight blue top and hip-hugging jeans made me think otherwise. After the red dress from dinner yesterday and now this white blouse that hung loosely, unbuttoned over her top... It did a damn good job of spiking my imagination once again. How in the world did she do this, making me think of things by actually hiding them? That shouldn't even be possible. Heck, she'd slain the image of a frumpy geek in my mind forever.

With a smirk on my lips, I headed for the door, the two of them following. As I tossed my duffle bag into the trunk of the SUV, Mom offered the car keys to us with an outstretched arm. "Does anyone want to drive?"

I snatched the keys without even waiting for Ethan's answer. This was as close as I could get to having my own car. He could drive his, but I would drive Mom's. Period.

The volume low, we listened to some music. With my

ANNA KATMORE

mother on board, I drove at a leisurely speed. She'd never let me drive again if she knew how fast this car could go without her inside keeping hawk eyes on the speedometer. Halfway to the high school, she shifted in the passenger seat and addressed Sue with a friendly voice. "Susan, darling, how long can you stay out tonight?"

In the rearview mirror, I saw how Sue's surprised gaze snapped to the front. She leaned forward, her face between my mom's and mine. "Um...my curfew on weekends is usually midnight."

"Great!" Mom said and turned fully in her seat to explain, "You know, we have a little tradition on game nights. If the Sharks win, I take my boys out to the St. James Steakhouse in Oceano. If they lose, my boys have to take me out to Burger King in Arroyo Grande. Whichever it is, you're in for a treat tonight."

Laughing, Susan accepted the invitation to another dinner with my family before looking at me. "I better cheer for your team tonight, so you and Ethan get a proper meal, huh?" Her tone was light and happy. Friendly, even though she was talking to me.

I cut her a teasing glance. "He and I...and *you.*" There should be tons of opportunities to catch her alone for a minute tonight and make a move. The girl was in for a treat, all right. A Donovan-style treat.

I expected her to lean back then and revel in my brother's silent company some more, but she totally disconcerted me when she continued staring at my face. After another couple of seconds, I started to grin and demanded, "What?"

"You smell nice." She sounded like nothing could surprise her more than this. To be fair, it was indeed the last thing I expected to hear from her. Sweet, regardless. It made me chuckle.

"Well, thanks," I said. When, with another quick sideways glance, I saw her face redden with shock, it was clear that it had been a crazy slip of her tongue more than an actual thought-through compliment.

Mom and Ethan laughed, too, while Sue dropped back into her seat, and our gazes locked in the rearview mirror for a second. What? Were we finally warming up to each other?

"Hey, if I'd known you like Axe, I'd have put some on as well," Ethan taunted her.

Ah, you can try, dear brother, but the first score with Sue is mine.

Susan was obviously too embarrassed to answer and kept her gaze away from my brother—and away from the rearview mirror, too. Smiling to myself, I took a right turn, then circled the high school in search of a parking spot.

Addison Hayes sat behind the ticket table at the gym's entrance. She let my family and my guest pass without charging the usual five dollars and fifty cents on a game night. "Thanks," I told her, sneaking a handful of shelled peanuts from the bowl next to her roll of tickets. Shoving them all in my mouth at once, I led the way down the hall to the locker rooms.

Mom wished me good luck while she squeezed me in a

tight embrace. From Ethan, I got a smack on the shoulder. "I want a steak, bro."

"Done deal," I assured him, then turned to Sue. It was her turn to wish me luck—maybe with a kiss, if she liked.

But this little piggy just shrugged and grinned at me. "You made us all come and watch you tonight, so you better try not to slip out there on the court."

So much for encouragement. It coaxed a hearty laugh from me. Picking up my bag from the floor, I swung it over one shoulder and headed into the changing room. We had time for hugs and kisses later—after my team had won.

And I planned to collect.

Chapter 8

"READY?" COACH SWANSON barked, adjusting his Dunkin' Sharks ball cap.

"Ready!" we confirmed as one.

Prowling like caged tigers, we listened to the song blasting from the speakers in the gym and the murmur of people finding their seats in the bleachers. The clock above the door said seven minutes to eight. Seven minutes until we got to prove that we were the best high school team on the West coast. When Tyler met my gaze, he smirked with barely controlled excitement. I waggled my brows in return.

The music outside stopped, and a trumpet and drum fanfare set it. The announcement of our entrance.

"Get 'em, Sharks!" Coach shouted as he opened the doors for us.

Like stampeding horses, we conquered the court, cheering and whistling with the fans, sinking some balls and high-fiving each other. This was our place. Our home. Nothing would stop

ANNA KATMORE

us today.

Each time one of us made a basket, the Grover Beach High announcer, with a very nasal and irritating voice, yelled our names and numbers so the audience would know who they were cheering for. Tyler did a pirouette when it was his turn, and I poked him in the ribs for it, chuckling along with him as I nicked the ball from him.

My turn. Some dribbling toward the hoop and a perfect throw. The announcer, full of enthusiasm, shouted, "And here, number twenty-one, we have Chris Donovaaaan! With a field goal percentage of an unsurpassable sixty-three percent!"

The audience's cheers resonated in the arena, putting a wide smile on my face. Ah, what the heck! I bowed to them before jogging back to my friends.

A couple minutes later, a different fanfare played out and we retreated to the sidelines, letting the opposing team roll in and have their moment. Clearwater High had brought their mascot, a lion wearing their colors—blue and white. The crowd followed his cheerleading and gave the team a nice welcome.

Somebody bumped a shoulder against mine. Turning, I saw William Davis with a mischievous smirk on his face. "Who's the girl with your brother?" he taunted.

It was clear which way this conversation would go. I took a deep breath, cutting a quick glance to the middle section of the bleachers, where my family always sat. Ethan, between the women, stuck his fingers in his mouth and whistled when our gazes met. They had come to watch me win. It was all that mattered tonight.

"That's my mom," I answered Will with a tight grin. He rolled his eyes, but I didn't care. I'd come here to play some ball and not discuss who may or may not be gay.

As Coach clapped his hands, we gathered around him. "Tyler, you'll do the opening jump," he said. Of course the team captain would get to do that. It wasn't like he hadn't done it the past twenty times, too. I almost grunted with disappointment but held back.

"Jake, no fouls tonight." The coach gave him a pointed look, but then he added in a very low voice, "Unless it's absolutely unavoidable." He cleared his throat and adjusted his cap as he glanced at Will next. "Team play, Davis. I know you're one hell of a dunker but, in God's name, pass the ball."

William nodded.

"Baker—" Coach looked around. His brows knitted together. "Where the hell is Baker?"

We all glanced around and found Brady leaning casually against the barrier in front of the bleachers, talking to a smiling redhead, whose cheeks blushed to almost the same color as her hair.

"Dude!" I yelled. "Save the flirting for later and come play now."

He loped over, a wide smirk on his face as he ran a hand through his shaggy hair and shoved the bottom of his white jersey into the top of his green shorts.

"Baker," Coach snarled again with a pointed look, but then all he did was shake his head and sigh. "Ah, what the heck, just give your best and make me proud, guys!"

As we stormed onto the court, Coach ran a few steps with me. "Don't show off, Chris! Just play a good game and win this," he warned before striding off to the side of the court.

Grinning over my shoulder, I called, "I would never!"

T-Rex ran to center court to meet with a blue shirt. The referee tossed the ball in the air and in a spectacular jump, Tyler caught it. My team had possession.

And we put it to good use.

Trevor scored first. Then Brady. Then Trevor again, and I sunk two in a row. In all that time, the blue shirts only scored two points. We were in excellent form tonight.

When Brady passed me the ball next, a lion attacked me from the side. I shot the ball on to Will before tripping and slithering along the floor. Skin chafed against polished wood. *Ouch!* I clamped my jaw in pain. Was that the stench of burnt hair and flesh? I quickly rubbed over my bruised knee, then scrambled to my feet, and headed back into the game.

The first two quarters were over soon enough. Between halves, we all gathered around the water cooler to take a sip. Trevor had sprained his ankle, which I didn't realize until Coach replaced him with Peter Allister at the beginning of the third quarter. The opposing team changed some players, too.

Will tried to pass me the ball, but a guy the size of Mount Everest suddenly blocked me and easily grabbed the ball out of the air. He wasn't as speedy as the guy who had been marking me before, but his height evened out that disadvantage perfectly. Brady and Will found themselves blocked by similar giants. The suckers were everywhere. Within minutes, our advance was smashed.

Dammit, I didn't get to touch the ball once the entire quarter.

Grinding my teeth, I chased even harder after the basketball in the final quarter, quickly taking a new strategy. I jumped, feinted a throw, but kept the ball and passed it sideways in a low toss to another teammate. This way, Brady and I each managed to sink two more baskets.

After checking the countdown on the scoreboard, my nerves were strung taught. Thirteen seconds left, and we were two points ahead. Exhausted, I willed the damn digits to count down faster. We could win if only—

Tyler lost the ball to Clearwater High at that exact moment.

A player on their team maneuvered across the court, evading any white shirt like an incurable disease. He threw the ball. And he scored...just as the final whistle blew.

"Nahhh!" I groaned, glaring up at the ceiling, rubbing my hands over my sweaty face. "This can't be happening!" But if the cheers of the opposing fans weren't enough, then certainly a peek between my fingers at the scoreboard proved the ball had gone through the hoop. Two more points.

With a tied score, the referee announced five minutes of overtime. I was dying for some water.

Summoning all my strength, I attacked like a real shark, along with the rest of my team, once more. We scored. They scored. Twice. The five minutes were almost over. "Chris!" Brady called out to me as he passed me, bouncing the ball in front of him. "High—low!"

I nodded. He would feint another toss at Tyler under the basket but actually pass it to me. I was so ready to hit this shot and earn us another five minutes to win the game.

Brady jumped, feinted, tossed, and I caught the ball as it bounced toward me from between Mount Everest's feet. There was no chance to glance at the time, but I'd learned to read the tension of the crowd. It was downright tangible. There had to be less than ten seconds to play.

Like a derailed engine, I rolled across the court, dribbling the ball at my side. The bright orange hoop practically begged me to sink the ball in its mouth. With a jump shot that put me at eye level with the giants of the other team, I threw the ball.

My aim was good, I knew that. But I never saw if the ball slid through the hoop or not. A striking pain exploded between my shoulder blades. I was tossed forward and landed on my knees. A groan left me, the pain excruciating.

Disoriented, I flexed my neck and back, looking around. Where was the hoop? The ball? Did it go through? *Come on, announcer with the irritating voice. Tell me if I saved the game!*

"What an amazing throw, ladies and gentlemen!" the voice I was dying to hear finally cried out. "Twenty-two to twenty-two! Chris Donovan saved his team with a spectacular shot."

Phew. That was close. The score of tonight was absurdly low, but at least for now it was even. All right then. Where was the damn ball? Foul shot for me. My aching back said so.

I jogged to the free throw line, and the referee tossed me

the ball. A silver whistle between his lips, he nodded at me and then stepped back. Holding the ball tight in my hands, I zeroed in on the basket, sweat dripping from my brow. I let it bounce on the floor twice, and the sound echoed in the silent gym. Exhaling a long breath, I wiped my eyes with the back of my forearm, then gripped the ball again. *I can do this!* I took a small jump and tossed the ball in an elegant arc. The ball dipped into the hoop, triggering a bombastic roar of the crowd.

Done.

It was over. 23-22. The Grover Beach Dunkin' Sharks were masters of the season.

Hands fisted in the air, I let out a long breath, grinning broadly. The next instant, I was rushed by my teammates. Some clapped me on the shoulders, T-Rex caught me in a bear hug, and then the rest of the guys tackled us. Coach announced his congrats, beaming proudly. We all slammed our hands together in the air, jumping around like little puppies. This was our night. Our victory! And I was ready for a steak.

At the sidelines, Mom waited with Ethan and Sue, their eyes filled with at least eighty-five percent of the joy I was feeling. High on adrenaline, I loped over to them, throwing my arms around my mother without mercy for her outfit or perfect hair.

She laughed, hugging me back. "Oh, sweetie, I'm so, *so* proud of you!" she squealed in my ear. "You played wonderfully!"

"Thanks, Mom." Smiling, I let her go and draped an arm over Ethan's shoulders. When I reached out to catch Sue with the other, she swiftly ducked and took a wary step back, fending me off with outstretched arms.

"Nuh-uh!" she chided. But then she started grinning and, with a nod toward the court behind me, said, "That was pretty cool."

I chanced my luck and leaned in closer, suggesting in a low voice, "How about a kiss for the winning team?"

"Yeah..." She laughed. "I actually think I'd rather kiss that stuffed loser lion over there, thanks."

"So you have a thing for wild cats? What the hell are you doing with Ethan then?" I teased quietly and smirked.

Playfully, Sue pushed my shoulder, totally getting the hint. I winked at her and hurried away to celebrate with my friends some more before we hit the showers. "Fifteen minutes!" I called back to Mom as I ran.

*

I rubbed my hair dry, tossed the towel on the bench, and pulled on my jeans. The shower had been reviving, but now my stomach was growling in rebellion, and all I could think of was tearing into a steak as thick as the yellow pages in another half hour.

"Good game, guys! See you on Monday," Trevor called out before he left the changing room, which was still thick with male euphoria twenty minutes after our glorious victory.

"St. James for you tonight?" Tyler asked as he sat next to me on the bench while I tied my shoelaces.

"Yep. Mom's treat. It's tradition." I grinned at him sideways and tied my other tennis shoe. "You celebrating with Becks?"

"Becky and Lauren. The girls want to go to Charlie's." He zipped his backpack closed and shut the locker above the bench. "I think Lauren was hoping you'd come, too. She huffed when I mentioned your name earlier, but then she asked if I knew what you were doing after the game."

"Did she now?" I scratched the back of my neck. "Dammit, I didn't even see her in the crowd." Not that I had actually been looking for her. What the hell—I should have. It did mean a lot to me that she came after all.

Or it should have...

"What's going on between you two anyway?" T-Rex asked.

"Nothing. She's just a friend. You know that."

"Yeah. But I was ready to bet a grand on you caving in eventually and us being a quartet soon. Doesn't look like that's going to happen."

Heaving a sigh, I stood and slipped my black hoodie on. Then I shrugged. "Don't see it happening, no."

As Tyler shouldered his backpack, pursing his lips, he said, "Someone will be very disappointed about that."

"Lauren? She knows I'm not interested in a relationship." It was never up for discussion, from the beginning. "She's cool with that."

"Rrrrright." He cut a glance to the ceiling.

I stuffed all my things into my duffel bag and sent him an annoyed look. "*What?*"

Before he answered, he expelled a long breath. "Dude, either you're blind or just plain stupid."

I lifted my brows, prodding him to go on.

"The chick's *hawt* with a capital H. And she certainly *is* interested. Ever thought that just maybe she was waiting for you to come around and take the next step?" he asked. "I mean, you two are hanging out—what? Three, four days a week? You might as well make it official, man."

"Even if I wanted to"—which I absolutely didn't—"I can't. I've got a challenge going, remember?" Eyes narrowed, I took my watch from the locker and fastened it around my left wrist. "You don't do that with a clingy girlfriend."

"Ah, this is still about your brother's girl then? Sue. That's her name, right?"

"So it's true? Ethan has a girlfriend now?" Will laughed scornfully, suddenly standing near us, arms crossed over his chest, head slanted. "What did you do to make that happen? Brainwash him over the summer?"

"Shove it, Will," I grunted and turned away, zipping up my bag.

"Why?" His laughter died. "If you ask me, he's only using the girl for cover."

"I'm not asking you, though," I gritted out. Argh, why tonight, of all nights? I was fed up with his shit.

As expected, he ignored me and just kept spilling bull. "Somebody should tell her that she's not the type of *person* he's looking for. Maybe if she grew some balls—"

"You know what?" I snapped, slamming the locker door

shut, cutting him off abruptly. "I'm wondering why..." It came out slowly, all right, and it would probably have been wise to think again before saying what was on the tip of my tongue. But when I turned around and locked gazes with my teammate, there was no going back. Eyes in slits, I scrutinized his face, gritting my teeth, and drawled, "There was just a gym full of hot girls, ready to be picked up by a player after the game. And the only person *you* checked out was my brother." I lifted both eyebrows in an unmistakable way. "How come?"

First, Will Davis's face turned white, and then red with fury. A vein pulsated hard at his right temple, but words eluded him completely.

Silence from the idiot. At long last. But my mood was successfully ruined. Ignoring T-Rex and the other bystanders, I grabbed my duffel bag and headed for the door.

"I'm not checking out a *fag*," Will spat behind me.

And that was that. The bag slipped from my hand, landing on the floor with a dull thud in what was suddenly a way too quiet changing room. I whirled around, bristling with anger, and planted a fist right on his chin.

Will staggered back into the metal lockers behind him. Everyone stood frozen, watching in stunned silence as he spit out a mouthful of blood. His face marred by a furious grimace, he lunged at me.

Fists were flying, his and mine. The pain hardly registered. Before I knew it, he'd tackled me, and we both fell over the low bench in the middle of the room. Someone was pulling hard at my collar. It couldn't be Will, because the asshole was lying

ANNA KATMORE

under me, slowly turning blue in the face with my forearm pressing on his throat.

"Chris, man—get off him!" Tyler's voice exploded in my ear among other shouts. "You're gonna kill him!"

I would, indeed, for insulting my brother one too many times.

More hands grabbed me, pulling me away from Will and twisting my arms behind my back as they hauled me to my feet.

"Stop it, dude," Brady pleaded with me. "I think he got it."

Jack shit he got. But with three guys holding me back and two more taking up protective positions in front of a coughing Will on the floor, the fight was over. Muscles still taut with anger, I yanked myself free from my friends.

Blood was dripping down my nose and over my lips. I wiped it away with the back of my hand, striding to the sinks in the shower room. One look in the mirror and I knew I was in trouble. My right eye already turning all shades of *punch-me*, there was no way I could hide this from my mother when I walked out of here. She'd have a fit.

I washed my face with cold water to at least get rid of the red trails, then sniffed back the blood, and shoved a piece of crumbled paper towel into my left nostril, the one still bleeding.

"Feeling better?" T-Rex asked from behind me.

Jaw tight, I met his gaze in the mirror. "Hell, yes."

He folded his arms over his chest, leaning against the doorjamb. "You know you have to talk this out with Will before next practice."

"And you know you can bite me." I turned around, meeting his gaze for real, grinned cynically at his face, and walked past him without another word.

"Before next practice, Chris..." his annoying, sing-songy voice followed me.

Screw the team captain.

"Whatever," I grunted. The next basketball practice was Monday. That gave me forty-eight hours during which I would *not* think about that jackass Will Davis, who was still hunched over on a bench, struggling to recover from a little shortness of breath.

I grabbed my duffle bag, pulled up my hood, and walked out the door. Time to face the *mom*ster.

Chapter 9

AS I PULLED the door open and stepped out into the hallway, I froze. My brother stopped dead, too. One look at my face, and he stiffened. His sharp breath echoed in the corridor. *That bad, huh?* Obviously, he was just about to walk into the looker room, maybe to find me. Mom and Sue sat on the vinyl chairs along the wall. Luckily, Ethan blocked me from their view.

He opened his mouth, but I didn't give him a chance to say anything. "Let's go," I mumbled. Head dipped low, hiding my face inside my hood so my mother wouldn't see my swelling lip and the shiner just yet, I strode off toward the exit.

The clacking of Mom's high heels followed me fast. "Chris, wait!" Grabbing a fistful of my sleeve, she spun me around. "What's up with—" Her face paled with shock, her mouth dropping open.

An endless moment passed in silence. I was prepared for her to explode on the spot, bringing down the entire gym with her when she did. What staggered me, though, was the brief pain in my brow as someone suddenly dabbed at the cut there with a tissue. Wincing, a hiss left me. Then I narrowed my eyes at Sue. What the hell was she doing?

Startled by my reaction, she gasped. Her hand hovered in midair. "Sorry," she mumbled.

I closed my fingers around her wrist and slowly brought her hand down, searching her face, trying to understand the worry in her eyes. Heck, I didn't need a nurse right now. But after her unexpected compliment in the car earlier and the way she tended to me now, she made me believe she was feeling a twinge of concern for me. In spite of all the jibes, she actually cared. A funny warm feeling started in my gut.

"I don't like seeing anyone hurt," she explained in a low voice, apologizing for her mindless action.

"I'm fine," I replied, somewhat stoic, not wanting to give away how much her concern touched me just now.

Her hand with the blood-stained tissue slipped away from mine as she dropped her arm. As if she needed to be protected from me, Ethan sidled up to her, locking a hard gaze with mine.

"What in the world happened?" my mother squeaked then, reaching for my chin and forcing me to face her once more.

I heaved a deep sigh, turning my face away. "Leave it, Mom. It's nothing." I was a boy. Fights happened between boys sometimes. "Can we go now? I'm hungry."

"No, we certainly can*not* go," she hissed. "Look at you! Who did this?"

Thank God, we were alone in the hallway. But I didn't intend to stand around and wait for my teammates to file out of the changing room and get a front-row seat for the Donovan family drama. Without responding, I strode through the double glass doors out into the parking lot wrapped in darkness. Street lamps flickered here and there and gave away the position of Mom's lonely SUV.

Fetching the keys from my pocket, I unlocked the doors and tossed my duffle in the trunk. I didn't get a chance to open the driver's door, though, let alone climb in. Mom yanked the keys out of my hand and snapped, "Where do you think you're going?"

What the heck? We had deal. I won the game, now she was going to take us out for dinner. "To Oceano," I muttered. "As was the plan."

"But not with that black eye." Furious, she folded her arms over her chest, pulling her cardigan closed over her dress. "And we're not leaving until you tell me what happened."

Will called Ethan a goddamn fag. I tried to kill him. "Someone had to shut up Will Davis, that's what happened."

That bit of information didn't sit well with her. "What?" she whispered, more than just angry now. Oh no, I had *disappointed* her. "You started it?"

"I didn't start it, no," I defended myself. "He got on my nerves, and I broke his face." Since Ethan was near again, I leveled the briefest scowl at him. If anyone was responsible for this fight, it was my brother. He kept playing hide-and-seek with us. Left us guessing. And now he brought a girl home. What for? To fool our mom? Our friends? The entire *town*? Perhaps Will was right. Sue wasn't his girlfriend, no matter how much Ethan tried to act like it. And in the end, *she* would be the one getting hurt.

Mom should leave me alone and have a go at Ethan instead.

But then, how would that change anything? If my brother felt how I believed he did, there'd always be morons like Will who'd make his life hell. He shouldn't have to endure that for something that just *was*.

Anger swamping me once more, I grabbed the keys from my mother, pulled the soaked piece of paper towel out of my nose, and tossed it away. "He deserved it, so can we drop it and go eat?" For me, the argument was over.

For Mom, it obviously wasn't. "What restaurant do you think will let you in with a bloody face like that? Certainly not St. James Steakhouse!" she barked. "And what will Susan think of you now? We promised to take her out to celebrate your team's and *your* victory tonight."

Ugh. As if the throbbing pain in my head and getting a lecture weren't enough, she also had to give me a bad conscience. Mom stabbed a finger at my chest and then pointed at Sue. "You will apologize to your brother's friend this minute for ruining our evening. And she even tended to you."

Slowly, I moved my gaze to Susan. More than sorry for a ruined celebration, I felt sorry for her being pulled into an argument with my mother. If I could have, I would've kept her out of this. Ethan should have taken her for a walk the moment the argument started. Instead, the bastard simply stood there and watched the tragedy unfold.

To avoid making her feel any more uncomfortable than she already did, judging by the obvious horror in her eyes, I caved. There was time to discuss things with my family later, when we were alone. For now, I inhaled a deep breath and told Sue, "I'm sorry."

Definitely not expecting that from me, she nervously chewed on her bottom lip. A second later, she moved closer to Ethan, again, like she needed protection from me. What the hell was wrong with the two of them? Jaw set, I narrowed my eyes, not at her, but at my brother. He and I were going to talk about a few things tonight, whether he wanted to or not.

As if being ripped out of a trance, Sue suddenly stepped forward and placed a hand on my mother's arm. She didn't look at me as she told her, "Really, there's absolutely no need to apologize to me. I don't care much for fancy restaurants anyway. We can just leave and...and...you can drop me off at my house. I'll be fine with that."

Her unease made my heart twinge with sympathy. She was apparently wishing for this night to be over already as much as I was.

It was Ethan who changed tack then and startled us all out of the awkwardness. "Bullcrap," he said in a light tone as he rolled his eyes. "Of course you're coming with us. We'll go get a winner's meal." He clapped me on the shoulder next, like he'd done so many times before in real brotherly moments. "No one cares about your ugly face at Burger King."

A smirk pulled hard at the edges of my lips. "Right back at ya, bro."

Next, Mom's hand shaped to my cheek. Carefully, she turned my head back to her and sighed. "I'm sorry. I shouldn't have yelled at you." There was a tremble in her fingers that made me think she was in more shock with all this than I'd assumed.

I nodded at her, not ready to rehash this conversion, then turned away, and climbed into the car. Silently, the others got in, too. Before I could drive off, though, my mother dropped a bomb as she buckled herself in. "By the way, you're grounded for the next two weeks, buddy."

I fixed her with an open-mouthed stare. Did she still not understand that none of this was my fault?

On the other hand...I'd picked a fight tonight. One that left my nose bruised and swollen and my right eye shining probably violet by now. The punishment could have been a lot worse.

*

Nobody spoke on the drive to Arroyo Grande. The air in the car was so thick with embarrassment, worry, and regret that one almost had to shovel it aside just to see through the windshield again. As for me, I only felt a throbbing ache in the right half of my face and the stinging pain of my tongue as I

ANNA KATMORE

bit it to keep myself from asking Sue what the hell she thought she was doing tonight.

Coming to my game instead of going out with my brother. Telling me I smelled good. Tending to my injury. *And* defending me in front of my mother.

She hated my guts. At least that's what I'd read in her continuous jibes the past few days. Was I wrong? Did she actually have a softer side, too? Like that moment when she let me feed her a piece of kiwi? What did I do in those moments to bring out this far more likable side of her? A side that fit her gummy-bear eyes and sassy ponytail a lot better than a snappy tongue. A side that intrigued me.

Stopping at a red light, I sneaked a glance in the rearview mirror. Sue's eyes were on me. She didn't look away when our gazes locked. We couldn't do this forever, I needed to concentrate on the road, but now I knew she was watching me. Why was she, when Ethan sat beside her? She should talk to him. Call him out for not caring for a girlfriend. But she didn't. Every damn time I checked the mirror after that, I found her mesmerized eyes pinned to my face.

I'd known this girl for five days now, and she confused me more than anyone else I knew. Challenge be damned, I was starting to want to understand her. Like really get to know her and find out what was behind that snappish façade of hers. I wanted to find out what it would be like to share a laugh with her like Ethan so often did.

A new song started to play on the radio. A duet from Charlie Puth and Meghan Trainor. For some reason I was sure this song would forever remind me of the copper taste on my tongue...and Sue shyly looking into my eyes through the mirror.

There were a number of empty parking spots in front of Burger King, so we had free rein. Except for a few stray patrons, the restaurant was mostly empty, too. Obviously, we'd picked a good time for dinner.

While I followed Mom to the counter, Ethan secured one of the tables in the back. Halfway through, he obviously noticed that Sue wasn't following him. She stood, indecisive, between him and us, probably too shy to let us place her order, too. "Come on," Ethan prompted her, nodding his head toward his chosen table.

Sue cut us a brief glance and then started to walk away, but I reached for her hand and spun her around. Surprised, she stared into my face while I took my time studying hers. "What do you want?" I asked in a low voice, but with more persistence than I should have, considering she was Ethan's...girl...friend?

Did she notice how I still held her hand and brushed the tip of my index finger back and forth over her skin? Because I had trouble not noticing how velvety soft her hand felt. Soft...and *cold*.

She swallowed. Two or three seconds passed, but to me it seemed like minutes, and she still owed me an answer.

Ethan and Mom must have assumed she was struggling to decide between a chicken sandwich or cheeseburger. Maybe that's what I'd asked her anyway. Or not.

Casting a brief glance in Ethan's general direction, she

cleared her throat, then looked at me again with a small smile on her lips. "I have a soft spot for sweet and sour."

Oh-kay. Make sense of that, Donovan.

A chuckle rocking my chest, I let her hand slip away. And only when she was gone did I realize I'd been the one to let go first.

Shaking my head at how this affected me, I sidled up to Mom with a smile and ordered a stack of cheeseburgers, one of them for Sue, and fries for everyone.

Sue and Ethan were having a hushed chat across the table as we walked toward them, but when they saw us coming, all conversation died. I parked myself next to Susan and handed the food out. Three burgers remained on my tray. I annihilated them while discussing the game with my brother. Mom didn't like me talking with a full mouth, I could read that by her continuous narrow-eyed look. But she'd never played a hard game of basketball in her life. She didn't know how exhausting it was. I was hungry. There was no time to waste on manners. My body felt like someone had stuck an IV into my arm and made me bleed out all my energy over the past hour. I had to refill. When my fries were eaten up before I'd finished my last burger, I sneaked one from Sue's tray. And another. And one more.

She didn't seem to mind, didn't even give me a funny look, so I assumed it was okay to help myself to another handful. Her pile of fries was vanishing fast. Soon, only one lonely stick of fried potato lay there helplessly. I reached for it, but Sue was faster. She stuffed it into her mouth before I could.

"Meany," I whispered, amused as she provocatively munched the last fry with extra pleasure, grinning at my face.

"Hey, you can't promise to treat me for dinner, then eat half my meal," she complained. Then she leaned in a little closer and added in a low voice, "Anyway, it's not my fault you gave away your chance at an unhealthy, half-pound steak that might have filled you up a little better."

Was that a jibe again? Funnily enough, it didn't feel like one. It felt more like she was drawing me into a bubble of conspiracy. A place where only she and I could be right now. "Ah, I don't care." I shrugged it off and let her in on a secret of my own. "Ethan's steaks are much better, anyway."

"True," Ethan confirmed. Immediately, I regretted mentioning his name. I didn't want anyone inside this bubble with us right now. But it was too late. "You have to let me cook for you one day," he told Sue.

"What? Was that an invitation for dinner next Saturday?" And of course, all of her attention was nailed back on my brother. Great. How would I ever win this challenge if she was distracted so easily?

"It certainly was. But I can't do it alone. Chris has to help me." Ethan shot me a look that surprised me. It wasn't a simple request for support. On the contrary, I got the feeling he was trying to help me here. Almost as if he'd read my thoughts and wanted to make up for it.

But cooking for Sue? I grimaced. "No. I don't like cooking for guests, Ethan. You know that." I rummaged through the empty wrappings on my tray. There was nothing left. Still hungry, I sneaked a few fries from my mother's plate, the only person at the table who still had some. Without a word, she held out the rest of her burger to me. Dammit, have I already said I love her? Regardless of the forthcoming house arrest, my mom was the best in the world.

"Oh, come on," Ethan said then. "Why are you always playing down your talent?" I hated that he wouldn't give it a rest when I'd already said no. But that didn't stop him. "She'll love it. You're an excellent chef."

And then he got backup. Sue turned her head to me and drawled the word "pleeease" with a cheesy smile.

God, but she was sweet. Still, my answer was no. Seducing a girl was one thing; breaking my rules for her was another. Not gonna happen. Chuckling and shaking my head, I shoved the last bit of burger in my mouth.

"Come on," Sue whined, "don't be a spoilsport. I promise I'll eat up, even if it tastes terrible."

What the heck? How could she assume my food would be anything but awesome? I cast her a slow, provocative glance. *Remember the kiwi and cream, sweetness?* And if she was tired of kiwi, we could try something else. She'd love it—anything I served her, not just the food. "It won't be terrible."

Spellbound by my stare for a second, she took two deep breaths. Then she answered with a dry throat, "So you're going to cook for me with your brother?"

With Ethan in the kitchen, too? What fun would that be? "Mmm..." I faked thinking about it real hard, pressing my lips together. "Nope."

At her disappointed sigh, I thought the discussion was finally over. How stupid of me. Susan leveraged a sizzling hot look at me that begged me to throw her over my shoulder and carry her outside for some alone time in the car. Shit, was that look intentional?

Heck yeah, it was, because just when she had me catching my breath and struggling to control my testosterone, she dragged out, "You owe me."

Oh, that vixen! If she hadn't messed with my feelings so badly just then, it might have made me laugh. "I do, indeed." I owed her for bringing Ethan to my game tonight. Only, was that enough to break my rules? On the other hand, having her in my house again would put me at an advantage. Funny things did happen sometimes. Kisses, for instance...

Wiping my fingers on a napkin, I leveled a smug look at her. "You're lucky I'm grounded and don't have anything better to do next Saturday."

Susan's mouth curved up. I was starting to fancy that smile of hers. It was infectious, and for the second time today, it managed to warm my gut. The only problem right now was that her happiness had more to do with being with Ethan than looking forward to spending time with me. It sucked ass.

"Ah, that's lovely," my mother joined in the conversation. "But you have to make sure to come early. Be there when they actually cook." She reached out to touch Sue's hand for emphasis. "Their meals are always delicious, but it's even more of a delight to watch them in the kitchen together."

What? She wanted us to give Sue an exclusive show, too?

ANNA KATMORE

Had we already adopted the girl? From the look in Mom's eyes, she was certainly considering the option.

Hearing that, Susan leaned her head against the window on her left and gave my brother a dreamy look. "Is that so?"

With a flirtatious tilt of his eyebrows, he said, "Well, if my mom says so, it must be."

Hey! Could he stop doing that? He never showed any real interest in Sue, but the instant she seemed to warm up to me, he had to go stealing her back. Not fair! And with what intention, anyway? I doubted he was going to be passionately kissing her good night later like she was obviously dying for him to do. The most he would grant her was probably another invitation to play stupid Wii bowling tomorrow.

Shit, why did it bother me so much?

A daring theory began forming in my head. The theory was that our challenge was beginning to lose importance. If Susan let me kiss her now, I would probably enjoy it for a totally different reason. I would like it because I loved how her eyes gleamed whenever we bantered. It was actually starting to annoy me that she preferred Ethan over me.

"Are you finished, guys?" Mom interrupted my hazardous train of thought, and I shook it away.

I helped her clean up the wrappings and stuffed some into the empty French fries packs. Anything to keep me from watching Susan swoon over my possibly gay twin brother.

As my mother slid out of the booth and swung her handbag over her shoulder, I didn't see it coming. But I bloody well felt it. Like someone head-butting me on the nose. Hard.

Abysmal pain forced my eyes shut, but they teared anyway. I pressed my hands over my face, groaning. "Darn it, Mom!"

So that's what it felt like to have your face broken twice over. I didn't want to cry, I really didn't. Not in front of Sue. But the pain almost had me on my knees.

"Oh, sweetie, I'm so sorry!" Mom came to my side, fussing like I was five and she'd accidentally trampled my Lego house.

Please, no touching. You've damaged enough.

But she ignored my silent prayers and kept caressing my head in an overload of motherly guilt. When I lowered my hands to tell her she should stop it and give me a minute to recover, I found my palms bloody. "Fuck!"

In the blink of an eye, I was up and on my way to the restrooms. There was already enough blood on my sweatshirt. No need to add more stains.

Shoving through the door as another man exited, I rushed to the sink, leaned over the basin, and turned on the water. Let's do this one more time.

With cupped hands, I rinsed my face and splashed some cold water onto my neck. If one could believe Coach Swanson, then it was supposed to help. I did this for a couple of minutes and also rubbed my glassy eyes. Sometime during that, the door behind me opened. Not hard to guess who'd come in when no one walked toward the stalls in the back. A deep sigh also gave my brother away.

"Why did you really pick a fight with Will?" he asked me.

I was in no mood to talk. "Go away, Ethan. I'm bleeding."

"You did this because of me, didn't you?"

Why didn't I just try talking a stone into jumping rope? I would have been about as successful with that as with trying to make my brother leave. A part of me wanted to growl at him: *Yes. Hell yes, I did it because of you!* But he didn't need to feel bad about it. He didn't need to feel bad about *anything*. My God, the only thing I wanted from him was a little trust and the truth.

Hands braced on the edge of the sink, I straightened and gazed into the mirror, letting the blood drip from my nose. Ethan was leaning against the wall next to the door, hands in his pockets. His gaze was sober, searching my eyes in the mirror. After a long moment, he said in a sad voice, "You know, you didn't have to do this."

I had no idea what it was, but something caused me to snap. I spun around and, tasting blood on my lips, hissed, "You're wrong! I did have to. And I don't regret it either. Will has been asking for an ass-kicking for a long time." Only, it should have been Ethan standing up for himself. He couldn't keep acting like there wasn't something *different* and expect that I would have his back forever. He was hurting people, didn't he see it? And not only Mom and me, but now Sue too. However hard it was, he needed to understand that. So, gripping the sink behind me for support, I added, "But you, on the other hand, shouldn't have brought Susan home."

Ethan lowered his chin and studied the tips of his shoes. "I don't know what you mean."

"Don't play stupid, Ethan!" I wiped my nose and mouth with my sleeve. "You know what I mean." Folding my arms over my chest, I cocked my head as he looked up at me. "What do you want to prove with her?"

Ethan pushed himself off the wall, walked two steps, and then slumped back against the door. His eyes moving up to study the ceiling now instead of his toes, he heaved a sigh. "I'm not trying to prove anything. I like her."

Rrrrright. Only there was a tiny difference between like and *like.* "The same way she likes you?"

His gaze found mine. Seconds ticked by before he answered, "Maybe?"

"And maybe not." I gritted my teeth, because I hated where I was going next, but there was no return from here. "Sue seems like a nice girl. You're going to hurt her if you don't tell her the truth soon."

Immediately, his eyes narrowed to slits, and his entire body stiffened in shock. The air in the room almost bristled. "You know what?" he spat then. "I don't care about this shit. Come outside when you've stopped the nosebleed."

Yeah, that was the reaction I had foreseen.

"Ethan," I begged as he pulled the door open. Relief filled me when he did stop and look at me over his shoulder. "I'm your brother. I don't *care.*" I tried to infuse all the truth and power possible into an honest look. "And neither does Mom."

A muscle ticked in his jaw, and his throat twitched as he swallowed. I was hoping he was going to relent. Come back and talk this out with me. But he didn't. Instead, he turned around and walked away.

At this point, I was pretty sure I had ruined our

ANNA KATMORE

relationship for good.

Slamming my fist against the wall in anger, pain seared through my already hurting knuckles. Fights sucked, physical ones as much as verbal ones.

When the bleeding eventually stopped, I washed my face one last time, wiped it dry on my sleeve, and headed out to the car. Everyone sat inside already, no one talking. The moment I opened the driver's door, Mom shot me a worried look. "Is everything all right, sweetie?"

"Yep," I answered curtly, starting the engine.

She reached out and placed her hand on my forearm. "I'm really sorry. What can I do to make up for it?"

Chancing my luck, I gave her a sideways glance with a wry grin. "You could undo the house arrest."

She gaped at me for a long moment, eyes shiny and bright. Then the corners of her mouth moved up. "You wish."

Yeah, it was worth a try.

I drove off, ignoring her snicker, but soon I dared a glance in the rearview mirror to check on the other passengers. As far as I could tell, Ethan's entire interest was in the sidewalks and streetlamps we passed. Sue stared out her window, too, though every now and then she sneaked a peek at Ethan—and never one at me through the mirror.

I didn't like the feeling accompanying me. I'd messed up things with my brother and the girl who was obviously into him. But what almost troubled me more was the fact that this girl had started to claim a permanent place in my thoughts.

Susan had said her curfew was twelve. Even though it was

still far from midnight, asking her if she wanted to come back to our place would certainly be the worst idea of the evening. So I cleared my throat as we drove into Grover Beach again and said, "Sue?"

Her eyes jerked to the mirror to meet mine. "Hm?"

"Would you tell me how to get to your house?" At the last dinner she'd told my mom she lived on Rasmussen Avenue, but where the heck that was, I had no idea.

"Yeah, sure. Just drive toward school and take a left before the parking lot. It's not far from there."

I did as she told me, but whenever I glanced back in the mirror, her eyes were either glued to the dark outside or on Ethan. I didn't like it. In truth, it had begun to annoy the hell out of me. How could one night—the one of my greatest victory—go so terribly wrong in such a short time? Sighing deeply, I took the left turn at school, then asked her, "Where next?"

"Follow this road for half a mile. I'll tell you when to turn left again." It turned out that the next was also the final turn. We'd reached Rasmussen, and a little ways up, there was her house. Yellow and neat, just like she'd described it. There were still lights on in two downstairs rooms, but no movement behind the curtains.

Coming to a halt right in front of her drive, I pressed my lips together and gave Sue a sheepish smile in the mirror.

"Thanks," she mumbled, not holding my gaze for longer than necessary. As my mother turned to her, Sue said, "It was a very nice evening. Thank you for taking me."

ANNA KATMORE

"You're very welcome, dear."

Then Sue stared at Ethan with a hopeful expression that he totally ignored. "Call me if you want to do something next week."

Ethan nodded once. "Mm-hm." From what I could see, he didn't even look at her when she got out. What a douche.

I shook my head and waited until Sue had disappeared inside her house before driving off. Once home, Mom got out wearing a soft smile, not in the least aware of how terribly wrong this evening had gone for my brother and me. Ethan followed her silently. After I'd grabbed my duffle bag from the trunk and slammed the door closed, I locked the car. Then I walked into the house and dropped the keys in my mother's handbag.

"Thanks for coming to my game tonight," I told her, kissing her on the cheek. As she tried to caress my face—the swollen side—I winced. "Please, don't. You already broke my face once."

She jerked her hand back, concern on her face. "Sorry, sweetie." Then she carefully raked her fingers through my hair instead and sent me off with an air-kiss. "Good night."

Ethan was already in his room. Passing his door, I knocked once and shouted, "Hey, E.T., can I come in?"

"No," was his curt answer.

Like a damn tree, I stood there for a couple seconds longer. But when it was obvious he wouldn't change his mind, I rolled my eyes in frustration and went to my room.

Chapter 10

IT WAS AROUND eleven, and I was beat. Not only from the game, but that useless argument with Ethan had exhausted me quite a bit, too. Stripping down to my boxers, I slipped into bed and turned off the lamp on my nightstand.

All too soon, though, my mind wandered to Susan's house. Her room was supposed to be on the second story of that yellow house. What would it look like in there? *May the force be with you* bed sheets and a Harry Potter cape hanging on her door? After starting to get to know her a little better, I actually doubted it. And the *Weird Geek* as a name for her in my contacts list didn't do her justice any longer, either. I should have changed it a while ago.

Feeling for my phone in the dark, I squinted as the bright blue light of the screen came on. Scrolling down to the very bottom, I found Sue, the last entry before *Wendy 3*. Who the hell was *Wendy 3*? Obviously I hadn't talked to that girl for a long time, or the name would ring a bell. The 3 wasn't such a good sign, either. Maybe that was the reason I hadn't talked to her in such a long time in the first place.

Retyping *Weird Geek*'s entry, I wondered what number I should give her. It was a rating of "doable," or how much I enjoyed kissing that particular girl. I hadn't done either with Sue yet, so the system wouldn't really work.

But I did want to kiss her. And heck, I wanted to really badly. So much so that my mouth suddenly watered at just the thought of it.

Right now, she was probably sitting on her bed, moaning over another missed good-night kiss and waiting in vain for a call from my brother. Since she had no idea about the conversation that had taken place between Ethan and me in the restroom, she must have felt totally alienated by his behavior on the drive home.

If only she knew...

If only she had the slightest idea which sex truly interested my brother. Maybe then she would stop chasing after him and see what she could have with me instead. I would be the right kind of boyfriend for her.

Crap, did I really just think that? *The word with a capital B?* No way—this couldn't be happening...

Or could it?

Dammit, I didn't know what to think anymore. It certainly wasn't the way I should've been thinking of Sue. Or any girl. *At all.* I never did. At least, I hadn't in a long time. So why now?

I wanted to put my phone away and ignore these odd

feelings that had taken me over tonight. Except I couldn't. Instead, my heart started pounding harder as I typed a message for Sue. *Good night, sweetness.*

Maybe it was the absolute wrong thing to do to send it, but my quick thumb beat common sense. If Ethan didn't come around fast and sort things out, he couldn't hold it against me that I was acting my age and running with my hormones. Sue was a girl too sweet to miss out on.

Unfortunately, she was also a girl not interested in me. That much I figured when no good-night text came back. Disappointed, I rolled to my side, dragged the covers up to my chin, and closed my eyes. I'd never had this much trouble cracking through a girl's barriers before. Regardless of the challenge, maybe that was a sign that I should stop wasting my time with her. For some reason, I got the feeling I was going to break my teeth trying to crack this special nut. On the other hand, I wasn't quite sure that, even if I tried, I could make myself stop going after this girl...

Shifting to my stomach, I managed to fall asleep eventually. Then a beep paired with something vibrating against wood pulled me out of unconsciousness.

With no idea how much time had passed, I lifted my head, drowsy, wondering what was going on. The blue light of my phone illuminated my dark room. No ringing meant no call. A text? Rubbing the eye that was not swollen from getting punched in the face, I reached for my cell. Right, text. From *Ponytail Sue*. The name didn't ring a bell, couldn't be important. With a moan, I closed my eyes again, wanting

ANNA KATMORE

nothing more than to fall right back into sleep.

Until the name jerked me wide awake an instant later. *Ponytail Sue?* That's what I had replaced *Weird Geek* with! I lifted my head and read what she'd written: *Are you still awake?*

Rolling onto my back, I sat up and typed a reply. *I am now.* With my eyes still sticky from sleep, I had to correct three typos in that short message. Only after sending it off did I check the clock. Quarter past midnight. That was awkward, to say the least.

Another text arrived. *Can I talk to you about something?*

In fact, if she wouldn't, I doubted I could go back to sleep now. I answered: *You can call me anytime. ;-)*

Twenty seconds later, the phone went off in my hand. Dammit, and I'd almost believed she wouldn't really do it. "Hey, sweetness," I answered. "What's troubling you?"

After a moment of hesitation, she confessed, "Something that you did earlier." Even though her voice was low and wary, it felt nice to hear it again. But what exactly had I done wrong?

"Starting with offering to give you a hickey, that could be many things." I chuckled. "Could you be a little more specific?"

Sue let out a long breath into the phone that I could almost feel on my ear rather than hear. "I did something terrible tonight," she whined. "When you went to the restroom after your nosebleed, I did, too."

That was the drama? *OMG! The horror!* I shook my head, smirking into the darkness. "Okay, that's really not a big issue, Susan. Everybody needs to pee sometimes."

"I was outside when you and Ethan were talking in the bathroom." Her voice dropped even lower. "I heard you."

My breath froze in my lungs. Shit. I raced through the conversation earlier at Burger King. Did I say the word *gay* tonight? Or something about "into guys"? Or whatever the hell else could have revealed Ethan's secret to her?

"Chris...?" Sue's cautious voice flowed through the phone.

Little hysteric shivers zoomed over my skin, making it hard to concentrate. I cleared my throat. "What did you hear *exactly*?"

"There's something going on, and you know it. Since it's concerning me, I think you should tell me."

Was she kidding? "No, I don't think I should."

"Then at least tell me why you got in a fight with that guy—Will."

Goodness, she was onto something. And she had a right to know. But what could I do? Nothing, goddammit. With the same curtness as before, I answered, "Sorry, can't."

"Fine," she muttered. "Then there's no need for me to talk to you anyway." And she frickin' hung up.

No way, sweetness! We weren't done yet! I'd dialed her number before she could finish that frustrated huff of hers, and when she picked up, I immediately told her, "That was rude."

"Keeping secrets from me when you know that I like your brother is rude," she snapped back.

God help me out of this! I didn't want to make her angry. And she didn't deserve to be lied to, either. But who was I to spill Ethan's secrets? I just couldn't. Why didn't she understand that?

"Fair enough, but I can't help it," I told her honestly. She was starting to mean *something* to me. But my brother meant more. And because Sue was relying on *me*, of all people, to help her with him, I knew that he really meant a lot to her, too. In a way, it stung. A hint of cynicism sneaked into my voice. "It's not my business, as you told me so nicely the other day."

Sue heaved a deep sigh. "How about I take a guess, and you just say yes or no?"

To her credit, it was a good try. In spite of the twinge of jealousy stabbing me, it made me chuckle. "Nope. It doesn't work that way."

And then Sue totally stumped me when she moaned into the phone.

My jaw dropped, because the sound of it, so incredibly sexy, ignited a series of X-rated visions in my mind. "Do that again, and I might ask you what you're wearing right now," I told her, no longer master of my own tongue and mind.

Sue sucked in a sharp breath, but the next second, her tone was heavy with frustration as she said, "Chris, you're such a blockhead."

There was no use in denying that when the visuals kept coming with unstoppable force. Some of them involved kiwi and cream and reminded me that I just might get another chance to feed her soon. "Yeah, maybe," I purred, sinking a little deeper into my pillow. "But you have a date with this blockhead in a week."

"No I don't," she huffed.

"Oh yes, you do." After practically begging me on her knees today to cook for her, she couldn't have forgotten so fast. "You're coming to my house, I'm going to cook for you, and we're eating together. Sounds very much like a date to me," I explained, carefully leaving out the part about my brother being with us as well. "And like it's customary for a *real* date," I drawled, "I will kiss you before the evening is over."

For all I knew, Ethan wouldn't even mind.

A shocked laugh escaped Sue. "You're insane if you really think that."

"So? I've been called worse." I chuckled. "You should consider the possibility that Ethan, nice as he may be, just isn't the right guy for you." Honest enough, but still safe. Mentally, I patted myself on the back.

"But you are?" Sue challenged next.

"At least I don't have dark secrets."

After a moment, she grumbled evasively, "I think it's late and time to end this conversation."

Aw, did that mean she actually agreed with me and was taking the easy way out? It could only be that, since we hadn't solved the original problem yet. "Really? Shame." I held back a smug laugh, enjoying teasing her just a little more. "Before you go, could you moan for me again?" It would totally make my night.

"In your dreams," she snarled, but I saw right through her defiance. Who was she trying to fool? She liked my teasing as much as she'd enjoyed the kiwi, me breathing a kiss on her neck, and us holding hands at Burger King tonight.

Maybe it was too soon to throw in the towel just yet. The fight for Sue wasn't over, and as I saw it, I stood a fair chance. "I guess I'll be seeing you around." A smile pulled at my lips. "Night, Sue."

The disconnecting signal was her reply, but I would swear I'd heard the softest chuckle before she hung up.

With a surge of joy, my hand fell to my lap, clutching the phone. My gaze wandered to the window, and I stared out into darkness. Hopefully Ethan would invite her over tomorrow.

I couldn't wait to see her again.

*

Sunday morning, a call from Hunter caused me to open my eyes while I was still lying in bed, daydreaming. He wanted to know if the Sharks won the game last night.

"Yep. I took a blow to my back and sunk the winning point with a free throw. It was awesome!"

"Congrats, dude!"

"Thanks." I got out of bed and booted up my computer to have a little music fill the room. "By the way, your friend Susan came with us. She and Ethan wanted to go to the movies at first. Jeez, I still can't believe he would do that to me." There was a slight sting of betrayal stabbing me again. "But she made him go to the game."

"Whoa, how did that happen?" Ryan demanded.

I scratched my head. "No idea, actually. But it was an altogether crazy evening."

"Crazy how?"

With the cell squeezed between my ear and right shoulder, I put on my jeans and buttoned them up. "Well, for one, your nerd friend gave me a freaking compliment. And later, I got in a fight with Will Davis from my team."

Hunter's laugh echoed through the line. "Aha. Want to explain any of it a little better?"

I detailed most of last night, leaving out only how Susan Miller stared at me in the rearview mirror and how we sort of held hands at Burger King. Those things were just too personal to spill. But since Hunter knew about my speculations about Ethan being gay, I also told him about the conversation we'd had in the bathroom and how my brother had run from it.

"Mmm, that's bad," he admitted. "Are you going to try again?"

"Talking to him?"

"Yes."

I heaved a sigh. "Maybe."

"Good luck with that, man." As Hunter said goodbye, I heard a doorbell ring somewhere on his end. Apparently, he'd arrived at his girlfriend's house. "See you tomorrow."

I hung up and slumped in my chair, my head lolling backward. We couldn't act like nothing had happened last night, so a visit to Ethan's room seemed inevitable.

After I'd finally donned the rest of my clothes, I walked over to Ethan's door and knocked. "E.T., can I talk to you for a minute?"

He grumbled something that sounded a lot like *fuck off.*

ANNA KATMORE

Ah, okay, so the current status of our relationship was still *complicated*. It didn't change for the better during any of the next three times I gave it a try. Sunday dragged on, and I got bored as hell.

My brother's reluctance to talk to me about Susan also stopped me from giving her a call just for distraction. Before continuing with this challenge, which in fact got more and more appealing to me, a few things had to be sorted out. Number one on that list: Ethan's sexual orientation. He could no longer claim Sue if he wasn't interested in girls. And I needed to know. As the afternoon carried on, the urgency of it became almost unbearable.

"Come on, E.! Let me in." Another knock on his door. "We need to talk!"

"Go away. I'm busy."

Yeah, I totally got that as the music of *CoD* played in his room. "Dammit, Ethan. Stop being an ass." Turning the door knob, I found it locked, so I rattled it angrily. "Come out now and talk to me. I'm sorry about yesterday, okay? But really... We. Need. To. Talk!"

The music of the game he was playing became five times louder. Great.

Frustrated to the bone, I spun around and sank against the door, banging my head on the wood. Surprisingly, Mom stood in the hallway, scrutinizing me with worried eyes. "What's wrong with him?"

A sigh zoomed out of my lungs. "Nothing. Fight. He's an idiot," I grumbled, then walked back to my room.

My mood thoroughly ruined, I turned on the TV and watched some stupid shows. *The Big Bang Theory.* Could anybody even understand the crap these guys were talking about? Certainly not me.

Sometime after nine in the evening, I finally muted the TV and grabbed my phone instead. Without getting too deep in thought and wondering whether it would hurt my brother or not, I typed a message for Sue. *Fancy another chat after dark?* ^^

Not tonight came back pretty fast.

To say I was disappointed was quite the understatement. But I wouldn't give up just yet. *Why not? I thought yesternight was nice with you. ;-)*

Only a few seconds went by before my phone vibrated in my hand with another reply. *Because you're trouble of the kind I just don't want to deal with right now.*

Trouble? Well, if she thought talking to me was trouble already, then she better not hear what I actually had in mind for Saturday here in my house. Smiling, I touched the keys on the screen. *Aw, every girl loves a little trouble. And you shouldn't hate what you haven't sampled yet. You have no idea what you're missing out on, sweetness.*

Anxious to read her comeback, I stared at my phone until the screen lit up again. *Seriously, you're like a sample bottle of perfume in a drugstore.*

My jaw dropped to my chest. What the hell? Was she for real? And what did that even mean? Mouth still open, I didn't bother to reply with another text but swiped my thumb over

ANNA KATMORE

the call button.

As the sound of her picking up drifted down the line, I burst out, "I'm *what*?"

"You know those cheap perfume bottles they put in stores for promotion?" No greeting, but that was okay. After all, I hadn't given one either. "Every woman walking by sprays a little of that bland scent on her skin and in the end, they all smell alike."

Okay. Sense please?

"But not me. I'm very selective, Chris," she continued. "I don't have to sample everything that's offered to me for free. And most of all, I don't like *bland*." Stunned silent, I could only listen to her rambling, even as she said, "Good night," and hung up.

She *hung up* on me. Again. What was wrong with this little nerd-cake? Catching my breath, I hit the call button a second time but then disconnected before the first ring. I didn't want to sit speechless through another lecture of hers. Better to get back to writing.

You think I'm boring? Ouch. That hurt, Miss Miller.

Would she reply? My heart beat against my rib cage...hard. And there came the beep. *I said bland, not boring. There's a difference. One means you make me fall asleep. The other means each time you open your mouth I want to go on an exploration and delve deeper to find out if there's more inside that hollow shell.*

The only words standing out to me in that message were *open mouth* and *explore*. Ah, sweetness. I chuckled. She ran right into this one... *You want to explore my mouth? Go ahead.*

Messages were then exchanged so fast, it almost felt like we were chatting with each other, both sitting on my bed.

Chris, do you ever hear what I actually say?

Of course. Your last text said you wanted to kiss me. And thinking of kissing her gave me a tingly feeling in my stomach again.

Excuse me, I need to go bang my head on a wall now and get that image out of my mind. That she wrote to me rather than actually doing what she suggested proved I was right at the beginning. I had her quite where I wanted her.

That's what they all say...before they beg me to date them... :) I was laughing quietly as I sent it off. She was so easy to tease.

I'm not going to beg you to take me on a date.

Oh, she wouldn't have to. Even though she already had... **cough* I remember a certain someone begging me to cook for her on Saturday *cough**

Her reply took a bit longer this time, and it was short. Must have taken her a great deal of thinking. *You're delusional.*

There, she was mistaken. Thoroughly. Nothing had been this clear in my mind in a long time. Could she say the same about herself? Who was chasing after clouds here—she or I?

Yes, one of us is, definitely. Sleep tight, little Sue, I typed and sent it off.

A sigh swished out of my lungs when she didn't answer with good night. In fact, my phone remained silent for the rest of the night. Jeez, it would've been so much easier if she already knew the truth about Ethan. If we *all* knew. We could move on and concentrate on more important things then...like how to make Susan Miller kiss me.

For hours on end, I wracked my brain over this, as sleep was once again a stranger in my room that night. In the morning, one sleepy and one swollen eye stared back at me from the mirror. Seriously, lack of sleep didn't become me.

On the way to the kitchen, Ethan knocked into me, his head dipped as low as mine. From his crumpled look and his shuffling, he hadn't gotten much sleep last night either. "Hey," I mumbled. "Can we—"

Shaking his head, he cut me off. "Just leave me alone, would you?"

It didn't surprise me that I couldn't catch a ride to school with him either. Mom lent me her car, and once again the wish for my own came up. It was fights like this that made being car-less a pain in the ass.

First thing at school that morning, I ran into Will Davis as he came out of the guys' restroom. I froze. Hell, his face looked like someone had wiped the floor with it. And that someone would have been *me*. But the marks on his throat—they really looked scary. I swallowed hard. No matter what he'd said to provoke me, stepping out of line like that shouldn't have happened.

"Dude, you look like shit," I blurted out, running a hand through my hair.

"Sporting a nice shiner yourself," he replied curtly. Then

his gaze dropped, and his voice followed. "T-Rex said I have to sort this out with you before he lets me come to practice again." Hands in his pockets, he seemed to be trying to dig a hole in the linoleum floor with his right toe.

"He told me the same," I confessed.

Will looked up and stared me hard in the eye. "I'm not going to say sorry, Donovan."

I smirked. "Neither am I, *assbucket*." When Will held out his fist after a moment, I bumped it with mine. "See you at practice."

He nodded, half grinning, and headed in the opposite direction. I didn't get to move one foot, because a familiar-looking redhead stepped in my way the next second.

I couldn't recall where I'd seen her before, but the tight black top she was wearing, pushing up a chest that actually screamed *stare at me*, clashed a little with my memory of her. "Uh, hi," I said, rubbing the back of my neck and forcing my gaze back to her face. Was this maybe *Wendy 3*? She looked like a freshman, and I usually didn't rate those in my list.

"Hey," she replied with a decent smile that vanished soon enough as she took in my multicolored face. "You're Chris Donovan, right?"

"Uh-huh."

"My name's Cassidy. I'm looking for your friend Brady." She gazed at me with hopeful eyes. "You wouldn't know where I can find him right now?"

Bang! The hint I needed. She was the girl Brady was flirting with before the game on Saturday. Chuckling, I slung my arm around her shoulders and pulled her along with me. "He's got English first period. Let's see if we can find him for you." My friend would be delighted to find this cute chick roaming the hallways searching for him. "You'll make his day."

Cassidy giggled. "You think?"

"Absolutely."

A couple of steps down the hallway, I spotted Sue walking with the oncoming traffic. Her hard stare bored into me. Jealous of the girl at my side. Yep, she was definitely developing an interest. And I couldn't say I didn't like it. Keeping my grin in place, I cooed, "Good morning, sweetness."

A funny sound drifted from her closed mouth, like teeth gnashing. She refused to greet me, or Cassidy for that matter, and stomped off. Her reaction was quite entertaining. Definitely something we could work with.

Of course, I was going to set the record straight later. Admittedly not *just* for the sake of our challenge, Sue shouldn't be thinking I was unavailable. Bad enough that she'd once thought Lauren and I were a couple and I'd had to convince her otherwise.

Ugh, that thought brought me right to my next problem. Lauren. She hadn't texted or called me all weekend. Nor had I contacted her. After being mad at me and still coming to my game Saturday, she had to be furious now. I hadn't even talked to her afterward.

How had I managed to get into so much girl trouble lately?

Speak of the devil, in front of Brady's English class, Lauren stood with him and Becks, who had intertwined her fingers with Tyler's. I stopped dead, my arm finally sliding off Cassidy's shoulders. "Look, Brady's over there," I told her, pointing at the group of my friends, who hadn't noticed us yet. "Go talk to him."

At the sight of them all, she gave me a shy look, probably hoping I would change my mind and walk her the rest of the way.

"He'll be happy to see you," I assured her with a smile. Then I started off in the direction we'd come, but after a single step, I glanced back at her once more. "Oh, and don't mind the black-haired one. She's not his girlfriend." At my wink, Cassidy relaxed and started toward her obvious crush.

I, on the other hand, beat it to history, stalling for time before I had to confront Lauren in fourth period.

Chapter 11

I WAS LATE to Spanish. "*¡Lo siento, Señora Sanchez!*" I mumbled an apology as I slid into my seat, silently taking my books out of my backpack. My teacher didn't mind, but Lauren obviously did. From her narrowed eyes, she didn't buy that coach Swanson had held me up after gym. Or maybe that was just a shock reaction to my black eye. Who could tell with that girl? Whatever. My being late bought me another hour before she'd confront me about Saturday and the game...and not finding her after it.

The lesson sped by much too fast, and Lauren still caught me unprepared when she blocked my exit to lunch.

"Nice," she said, arms folded over her chest as she leaned in the doorway, nodding at my eye.

"Uh, yeah... I got in a fight over the weekend." Kids shoved past me, and I stepped aside, but Lauren didn't. In her books, they obviously didn't need more than one foot space to squeeze through.

"I heard about that. Becky told me. The only thing she didn't know was why. Tyler didn't tell her." She cocked her head, nailing me with a reproachful stare. "And none of the other guys would spill either."

Lips pressed together, I briefly arched my brows, not answering her unspoken question. She wouldn't get shit out of me.

After a thirty-second staring battle, she slid away from the door, moving back into the classroom. Her backside against the wall, she waited until the room was empty and told Mrs. Sanchez goodbye as the teacher left for her next class.

"Chris, what's wrong with you lately?" Lauren demanded then, her voice a notch lower than before. "What's changed?"

"What do you mean? Everything's still the same." Because her eyes were not a good place to look when pulling off this total lie, I stared at her slim legs plastered with tight white jeans.

"No, it's not." She wrapped her fingers around the strap of my backpack where it hung over my right shoulder. Suddenly I found her nearness extremely suffocating, like all the air had vanished from the room. "Something's off. You getting into detention when you haven't been at all this year. Then last week, you canceled tutoring for the first time. Picking fights—"

"*One* fight," I corrected her sharply, making the mistake of looking at her face again. Huge dark eyes searched mine. Immediately, my voice turned a note softer, though still sullen. "I already sorted it out with Will this morning, so you don't have to worry about *that*."

"I'm not worrying." Her hand slipped away from the strap, and she crossed her arms over her chest, appearing suspicious once more. "I'm wondering..."

My gaze sweeping over the room, I shrugged it off. "Maybe it's just the stress before Winter finals."

A silent moment passed. "Yes, maybe." Clearly, she didn't believe me. But she sighed and appeared to let it go. "We have a Spanish test Friday. If you want to study, let me know."

Deep down, I knew she was hoping I'd suggest meeting after school today, before basketball practice, like we'd done so many times over the past weeks. But I couldn't. After all, I was grounded and pretty sure Mom wouldn't let me go out, even to study with a friend. Not that I was going to ask her.

Clearing my throat, I adjusted my backpack on my shoulder and produced a tight-lipped smile. "I'll call you about that, promise." When she gave a reluctant nod, I ducked out of the classroom and hurried to the cafeteria.

Lowering my butt into the chair next to Rebecca with my food tray in front of me, I shoved a handful of fries in my mouth.

T-Rex leaned around his girlfriend. "Why so late, man? Got held up?"

"Yep. Lauren," I answered, searching my tray for the packet of ketchup I'd grabbed at the counter. It was hiding under the burger plate. I ripped it open and squeezed the sauce over my fries. Then I cast Becks a quick look. "She felt the need to talk about things *changing*."

Rebecca held my gaze, lips tight, eyebrows arched. She

suppressed a grin and shrugged innocently. "Well, you know, maybe it's time?" Stealing a French fry from my tray, she bit off the top.

I answered her amused grin with a cynical smirk. "And maybe it's not."

Or maybe it was, just not in the way she was hoping for. My gaze wandered between the rows of tables right to the soccer corner. Sue was nibbling on a sandwich. She didn't see me, only having eyes for Ethan. Of course.

Grunting in irritation, I finished my meal. Since I'd come late, break was over much too fast, and I hadn't even gotten to my damn dessert yet. It was time to head to my next class. Grabbing the dark red apple from my plate, I rose with the others and walked toward the cafeteria exit, rubbing the fruit on my sleeve. Casting one last glance at the soccer table as I bit into the apple and—damn! The piece lodged in my throat.

Susan was still sitting there with my brother...alone. The rest of the soccer thugs were gone, and the two of them were staring at each other like they had a crapload to say. Things like, *Be my girlfriend? I love you?* Or maybe, hopefully, *I'm gay?*

On the other hand, what if Ethan had realized over the weekend that he was totally into her after all? In spite of Sue warming up to me, she was clearly still waiting for *him* to come around. Had she finally gotten what she wanted? What the hell was Ethan saying to her? I didn't want to continue chasing Sue if she was my brother's girl now. Heck, I *couldn't!* But at the same time, I simply couldn't stop staring at her.

ANNA KATMORE

The uncertainty was killing me. Shivers rolled down my spine. Only when Becks crashed into me from behind did I realize I'd stopped dead in the doorway.

"Chris?" she asked, her gaze switching back and forth between me and Susan. When she had my attention, she lifted her eyebrows. "Coming?"

Teeth clenched, I nodded and tossed the apple in the trash on the way out, having lost my appetite.

The final two periods of the day were hell. Constantly, my thoughts returned to Ethan and Sue in the cafeteria. The devil only knew how long they'd been sitting there—*alone*. What was so important that they needed to discuss it without the others? This annoying restlessness wore a hole in my chest.

Twice during biology, I fished my phone out under the desk and typed a message for Sue. But instead of sending it, I deleted it each time and finally put my cell away. She wasn't the one I needed to talk to about this. Ethan was the one I wanted. We'd started something on Saturday, and this afternoon we would finish it. No escape. I was going talk to him, and he was going to listen. And in the end, he would give me a damn answer.

Now I just needed to figure out how to start this conversation and stop him from running. Or keeping his door locked once again.

"Hey, man, guess what?" Brady tore me out of my musing with a bump against my shoulder on the way to English. He didn't give me time to answer. "I've got a date tonight."

"Cool. Who is she?"

He grinned. "Cass."

"Hm?"

At my lost look, Brady made a face, as if that name should ring a bell. "The chick you sent to me this morning. Red hair, hot body. How could you forget her? She's one cute thing."

"Ah, Cassidy." I rolled my eyes at myself and chuckled. "Yeah, she seems kinda sweet."

He shook his head, clearly deeming me a lost cause. "What's happening on the dating-the-nerd front? Did the girl from detention give in to you yet?"

I sucked on my teeth and then let out a long breath. "Not yet, no. I'm still working on it."

Brady laughed. "What's the problem, dude?"

"My brother. She likes him, and I have yet to figure out if he's into her too. I'm not going to interfere if he is."

"Right." Thoughtfully, Brady stroked his chin with his thumb and forefinger. "That would actually suck." Then his expression changed to a grim smirk. "Figure it out fast, because I bet twenty on you kissing her before next week."

I laughed out loud. "You bet money on me?"

"Yeah. Tyler said you'd have her smitten by the middle of this week. North and Olsen think you're never gonna get that girl."

I dropped my schoolbag on my seat in English class, turned around, and folded my arms over my chest, leaning against the corner of the desk. "You guys have a few screws loose, you know that, right?"

"Yep, I told North and Olsen they did." Brady chuckled,

totally twisting my words. Then he smacked me on the shoulder. "This weekend, dude. Don't let me down."

Heck, I wouldn't—if it was in my hands. I wouldn't even disappoint T-Rex. But from where I stood at the moment, things didn't look so bright. One more reason to make my brother cough up the truth.

After school, I sat on my bed, staring at the wall. Ethan had come home at the same time, but he'd disappeared into his room. Balling my hands into fists in frustration, I got up and started pacing the room. Was he gay or not? It was the only thing that decided whether I was going to continue chasing Susan Miller. And after that crazy Saturday, I really wanted to do that.

From the shelf on the wall, I grabbed my original NBA-regulation basketball. It held the autograph of Kobe Bryant, and it was my most sacred treasure. He'd signed the ball for me after a game when I was fifteen. No one in this family, and not even my best friends, were allowed to touch it—ever.

Grinding my teeth, I slammed the ball against the wall and caught it again.

An angry grunt pushed out of my lungs. Ethan had given me the runaround long enough. Time to sort this out once and for all. And I had just the idea to make him talk.

I stomped out of my room and right into Ethan's without a flipping knock. He could hide and tell his excuses to someone else; I was done with that shit.

"What the f—"

"Shut up," I cut him off and tossed him the ball, hard.

From his place on the bed, he dropped the Wii controller on his lap and caught the basketball with both hands. "Do you want it?"

"Want what?" he asked, eyes slitting with suspicion.

"The ball," I snapped. "Do you want it or not?"

Ethan studied the black signature on the orange surface for a long moment. His brows smoothed out, but he didn't look at me. "I'm guessing it doesn't come free?"

Of course not, silly brother. Face hard, I gritted out, "We play for it. If you win, it's yours. If I win, I keep it and you have to answer a question."

His head jerked up. "*Which* questions?"

"It doesn't matter. Just one. No excuses, no back doors, no running. You answer plain and simple."

Ethan swallowed. He was practically salivating. It was clear how much he wanted this ball. Kobe Bryant was his greatest idol. He'd envied me ever since the day I got it. I couldn't remember when he'd last made a bid for it, but it had been as high as two hundred and fifty dollars. But no price would do this ball justice as far as I was concerned.

With some reluctance, he rose from his bed, not letting go of the grand prize. "What game do you have in mind?"

"Not Wii," was all I said, because that was something I could never win.

"And not basketball." Right, he didn't want to take a risk, either.

We both glared at each other, until Ethan's gaze slowly wandered to the side. I tracked it and spotted the chessboard

ANNA KATMORE

on the shelf he was focusing on.

After considering the idea for a couple of seconds, I walked to the corner, picked the game off the shelf, and strode out of his room. "Chess it is," I snarled on the way out.

Ethan followed me to the living room, where we silently set up the game on the coffee table. When all the glass figures were lined up and ready to ride into battle, my brother moved one frosty pawn. I mirrored the move with my clear one. Ethan couldn't have picked a better game—this was the only thing in the world that we both sucked at equally. A fair chance for both of us.

Let fate decide.

One by one, Ethan robbed my pieces, and I took some of his in return. Soon, there were only a handful of pawns, both our kings, my queen and a rook, and two of his knights left on the board. How was one supposed to win with so few pieces?

My chances waned even more when he took my last pawn with his king. Dammit. I had to do something, and fast, or my plan was going to be shot to hell. After an endless time of thinking, I moved my queen closer to his king, then leaned my chin in my hand, and stared at the board, waiting for his next move.

The doorbell rang at that moment. With a new spark in his eyes, Ethan shouted, "It's open!"

"Are you expecting someone?" I demanded.

The next instant, a familiar voice called out, "Ethan?" That cleared up the situation.

I lifted one brow. "You invited Sue over?"

Ethan nodded and yelled, "In the living room!"

Normally, I would have greeted the girl with a smile, but at the moment I was too tense to even glance at her. Looking away from the board would have given Ethan a chance to cheat, and that couldn't happen. I needed that free question.

"Hi, um...guys?" Sue stuttered by the door.

Since Ethan and I not only looked alike but were also wearing almost the same clothes today—he in a white polo shirt and I in a black one—I immediately felt bad for Susan and her dilemma of not being able to tell us apart. Having mercy, I reached for the chains that had given me away to her in the past and pulled them out from under my collar. It should be enough to make her understand.

Ethan then pushed his king into a corner at his side, away from my queen. Apparently happy with that move, he tore his gaze away from the board and said, "Hi, Susan."

Her reluctant footsteps drew nearer. The smell of her coconut perfume, body lotion, or shampoo drifted to me. Whatever it was sneaked up my nostrils and drove me crazy. Dammit, if only I had won this game already and could concentrate on her instead of how to slay a frosty king with my queen.

To my surprise, Susan's hand appeared in my vision. She took my rook and slid it along the line to the very end. "Checkmate."

Checkmate? What the freak? How? Where? When? I scrutinized the game one more second, then my eyes widened. "Hah!" I held out my hands, presenting Ethan with the awesome end of this terrible game and beamed at him. *I fricking won!*

Without thinking, I snatched Susan's wrist and yanked her down onto my lap. "That's my girl!" I laughed and hugged her to my chest.

Sue draped one arm around my neck and joined in my euphoria. Was she serious? Holding on to me like that? The fact that she didn't wiggle out of my embrace filled me with an extra shot of delight. But of course, Ethan had developed a talent for ruining any moments I had with her, so why not now? "Why did you do that?" he snapped at her, incredulous.

That was Sue's cue to calm down and get off me. I was reluctant to let her go. She felt good in my arms. I wanted to keep her.

Her voice sobered as she stood, facing Ethan. "Because I need to talk to you. And it has to be now and not in twenty minutes." Damn, I hadn't heard her sound this earnest since I met her. Trouble?

My brother pressed his lips together for a moment. The shock in his eyes vanished fast, overridden by concern. "Okay, talk in my room?"

Sue gave a quick nod and walked ahead. Ethan followed her, but before he left the living room, he shot me a warning glance over his shoulder. "You did *not* win. We're going to repeat this when you're on your own. No cheating!"

Great. I knew he'd worm out of this if he could. Leaving the Kobe Bryant ball and the board on the coffee table, I strode to my room and started packing my duffle bag. I had basketball practice in thirty minutes. Better to get out of the house, anyway, instead of shuffling about, wracking my brain over the things he and Sue might be doing in his room right now. Like fooling around and making out and laughing together and...

Gah! The idea became more irritating by the minute!

I'd never been jealous of my brother before. He could have taken any girl he wanted. But with Sue... Dammit, something was going on here that was totally screwing with my mind. I couldn't deny the edgy feeling I'd had when she sat on my lap and I'd held her. And not only then. It had begun a few days ago. Maybe not as intense at the start, but the wish to touch her—to kiss her—had been there ever since the weekend. It was new. And so awkward.

The mystery to solve was why I couldn't just shake this longing for her away. I could do it with Lauren, and Tiffany, and Theresa, and the devil knew who else. Only, this particular girl with the plain ponytail wouldn't get out of my head these days. She made me think and do stupid things.

I was starting to worry...

Had I lost my head in this challenge?

Playing ball worked wonders in clearing my mind of all images of my brother kissing the girl who haunted me. The only thing I concentrated on was making baskets. Unfortunately, practice was over within minutes—okay, maybe not, but it certainly seemed that way to me—and I had to return home. Mom hadn't lifted the restrictions on my house arrest. Too bad.

Susan's car was gone by the time I got there. *Done kissing*

ANNA KATMORE

my brother? I thought, annoyed that I'd missed her but glad at the same time because I wouldn't have to endure watching them being sweet to each other.

Shrugging off my jacket, I kicked off my shoes and then dumped my sweat-soaked jersey and shorts in the laundry. On the way to my room, Ethan emerged from his. My throat tightened in annoyance, because the bastard looked flipping happy. Unable to bear his grin, I avoided his gaze altogether and slammed my door closed behind me.

It didn't take long—I had hardly glared at the wall over my desk long enough—before the door opened without a warning knock and my brother strode in. My Kobe Bryant ball clutched under his arm, he towered over me, standing at the foot of my bed. My scowl did nothing to send him away.

"What?" I snarled after a while.

Ethan shot the basketball at me. Even though I caught it, the toss was so hard it knocked the air out of my lungs. His face in hard lines, Ethan snapped at me, "One. Freakin'. Question."

"I don't un—"

"You have one," he cut me off sharply. "Ask now or never."

Slanting my head, I studied him for so long, I got a kink in my neck. Was he for real? Sue had won the chess game for me, but he was still going to let me ask? What in God's name had changed his mind?

My mouth fell open as the truth sank in fast and hard. Ethan had known from the beginning what I wanted to ask him. And the one thing that had changed in the past couple of hours must have been his answer.

Sue had been here, and he was happy when he came out of his room. They'd sorted things out, no doubt. They'd talked about relationships and shit and now they were together. Ethan had finally figured out that he wanted Sue. Great.

"Go away, Ethan," I mumbled, letting the ball roll out of my hands. It bounced on the floor and rolled toward the open door. "I don't know what I could ask you that matters now anyway."

Hesitantly, my brother walked to the ball, picked it up, and studied it for a moment while spinning it slowly in his hands. "That's it? You pull off this bullshit, offering your holy basketball in a wager, and then you back out?"

What would it change to hear that he wasn't gay? Nothing. The challenge was lost, and Sue was no longer free.

Why did this simple truth hurt so bad? I'd had no intention of getting too close to her from the start, so a fair retreat for my brother's sake should be all right now. It should be easy, goddammit.

A sigh escaped me. I dropped my gaze to my hands in my lap, sadly picking at my fingernails. "It is what it is."

"Yep. So go ahead and ask your stupid question now. Because if you don't, I'm going to keep the ball anyway."

Lifting my head, I locked my stunned gaze with his.

Ethan prompted me with an arched brow. But I didn't need to ask him whether he was gay anymore. The answer was self-explanatory—he was dating Sue. I should get over it and be happy for him. For her, too. After all, she'd gotten what she wanted—the nicer twin. Hopefully Ethan appreciated her. She was someone special and deserved a great boyfriend. Someone who saw more in her than a challenge. Someone who loved her.

And there it was all of a sudden, the one thing I really needed to know. Swallowing hard, I licked my lips and angled my legs to sit Indian-style. After a final, dry cough, I asked my brother, "Are you in love with Sue?"

Ethan sucked in a breath to answer, but then he held it and tilted his head. Yep, he wasn't prepared for that one.

Almost apologetically, I pressed my lips together and lifted my brows, sighing. It wasn't cool to admit you'd been chasing after your brother's girl behind his back, but since this was a moment of pure honesty, it would be unfair to hold back, right?

Narrowed eyes scrutinizing me, Ethan expelled a breath. "No," he said then, grimacing even more. He made that one word sound like a goddamn question, like it was the last thing on earth he'd expected to have to answer today.

My head started spinning. What in God's name was going on here?

Shaking his head, Ethan tossed me the ball again and walked out of my room. In the doorway, he hesitated. We stared at each other, both obviously mystified. Then he asked quietly, "Are you?"

Seconds ticked away, and I had no answer. Only the sound of my heart beating loudly in my chest filled my ears.

An odd smile appeared on my brother's lips before he nodded slightly and disappeared from the threshold, leaving the door open.

"Ethan," I called out after him. He poked his head in once again, brows lifted in question. A worried sigh escaped me. "If I were...would you mind?"

He laughed and stepped forward, leaning one shoulder against the doorjamb. "Don't be stupid. If you were, it would hardly be something you could turn off by will, right?"

It felt like he was trying to tell me more with this simple answer than was obvious. That he couldn't turn off whatever he felt... Was that it? "Probably not," I agreed in a low voice. "See, it all started with this silly challenge. She was always so snappy, and I just wanted to tease her a little. But now..."

"Now what?"

I inhaled a deep breath and hugged the ball to my chest. "Now, I hate to think about her kissing someone else."

"Well, you don't have to worry about me then. I'm certainly not going to kiss her."

"Seriously? Because I... I'd really like to go out with her."

Ethan smiled. "I think you should."

Ah, if only it was that simple. Courting Sue had seemed like the ultimate challenge to begin with. And then there was still their friendship. "It wouldn't be a problem for you? I mean, if I tried to steal your girl? You know, I wouldn't do it if you told me not to," I added.

Kind of playing the big brother here, Ethan crossed his arms over his chest. "I told you, I'm not in love with her. She understands that we'll never be a couple. That's all you need to know, right?"

Jeez, he made it all sound so easy. Could it really be? Warily, I answered, "Rrright." It wouldn't be stealing anymore if he gave me permission. But that didn't mean Susan would let me take her out on a real date in the first place. I hung my head. "I don't see how I can even start to convince her I'm worth a shot."

A throaty bark erupted from Ethan's chest as he laughed at me. "You'll find a way, bro." He closed the door, and I was alone in my room, totally derailed.

Spinning the Kobe Bryant ball—which, thankfully, was still my possession—on my finger, I tried to sort my thoughts in a way that made sense. Ethan was no longer mad at me, and his playing around with Sue had come to an end today. What the hell had he told her if not that he wanted to be her boyfriend? He'd looked far too happy for having just had a serious chat like that.

Whatever it was shouldn't trouble me, as long as Susan Miller was still single and I had the green light to officially court her. Now I needed a plan. Talking to her at school often backfired. She obviously didn't want to be seen with me, not least of all because of the challenge, I assumed. Even if she started to like me, it would probably be her main plan to hide it and stick with her stubbornness.

Fine. I could be stubborn, too.

The nicest reactions I'd gotten from her were when I talked to her alone, like on the phone or when she was in my house.

Best would be if Ethan invited her over again. But I didn't plan on missing any chance I had to sneak under little Sue's skin, so I decided to text her tonight as well.

After eating dinner, cleaning the kitchen for Mom since she cooked, and doing my homework, I turned off the ceiling lights in my room and switched on my bedside lamp. It was close to ten. I'd been waiting for hours for this moment.

Settling on my bed, I navigated to texts on my phone and typed a message.

Have fun with my brother today? He came out of his room a happier man. About time too, his cranky mood all Sunday was a pain to cope with.

Staring at the screen after sending it off, I counted the seconds until her reply. The display light went out a couple of times. Each time I swiped my thumb across the glass and waited.

Beep. There! A message from *Ponytail Sue*. My heart beat faster.

We had the best date ever. Guess what, we played video games. :P

Ethan had rejected her, and she called it the best date ever? How was that possible?

I began my next text with an emoticon that scratched its head in confusion, because that's what I was actually doing, too. *I'm starting to believe that playing* Mario Kart *is the only way to seduce you. Never done that before with a girl.* Hmm, maybe that was the crux of the matter.

Sue answered faster this time. *Oh, you should try it. You*

ANNA KATMORE

might be surprised. And then the corners of my lips tilted up involuntarily as I read her last words. *Sleep tight, sweetness.*

Ah, she had me on my knees with that. Shaking my head, I chuckled and wrote: *You stole my line.* ☺ *See you tomorrow.*

After that, I turned off the light and went to sleep. Whatever dream was going to haunt me tonight, I hoped Sue would be in it.

Chapter 12

ETHAN WAS LEANING against the hood of his car, ankles crossed and arms folded, as I walked out the door on Tuesday morning. "Need a ride?" he asked, lifting his brows.

Smirking, I pulled the keys out of my pocket and dangled them in the air. "Taking Mom's. Basketball after school." I walked up to him anyway and held out my fist for him to bump it. "Thanks for the offer, though."

As my brother gave me a fist bump, we both knew we were back to square one and the things that had happened over the weekend were forgiven and buried. A huge rock broke away from my chest.

I ambled to Mom's car and opened the door while Ethan walked around his. One leg inside and a hand on the wheel, I halted and called, "Hey, E.T.!"

He turned. "Hm?"

"Would you do me a favor and ask Sue what her favorite kind of cake is when you see her?"

ANNA KATMORE

"Sure." He scrunched his forehead. "Why?"

"She's coming to dinner on Saturday, right?" I asked in a casual tone, trying not to give away too much of my excitement. "I thought I could make some dessert, too."

Studying me for a couple of seconds, Ethan smirked. "Best way to a girl's heart, huh?"

I shrugged nonchalantly before sinking into the driver's seat of the SUV, but I knew he totally saw through me. Ah, whatever. He seemed cool with it, so why bother hiding anything from him? Pressing the horn twice in goodbye, I drove past him and headed for school.

Roaming the halls with Brady that morning, I realized little Sue was obviously playing hide-and-seek with me, because the kitten was nowhere to be seen. Brady spotted Cassidy and smacked me on the shoulder. "See you at practice."

He sneaked up on the girl from behind, and I headed on to first period.

The morning went by fast. Lauren was exceptionally quiet in Spanish—she glanced at me for the briefest moment as Mrs. Sanchez entered the room, and then ignored me the entire lesson. I found this highly unnerving. Lauren had grown on me, much more than I'd expected her to, considering I didn't usually run buddy-buddy relationships with girls. Her cold shoulder now showed the reason for that particular rule in the first place.

To ease the situation, I confronted her after Spanish by snatching a fistful of her knitted sweater and dragging her back to me. "Hey, Parker, not so fast."

Her straight black hair fanned out as she swung around to me. Giving me a polite but distant smile that trampled on the friendship we'd built in the past few months, she lifted her thin eyebrows. "What's up?"

Uh... "I thought we could do another Spanish lesson today." One that concentrated on Spanish—with no sex involved for once. After all, I wanted an A on the test Friday.

Obviously, it was the right suggestion, because her gaze lit up a notch and her smile turned a hint warmer. "Sure." She paused a moment. "Want to meet up later?"

Why not? Other than being a great language tutor, Lauren was also a girl. Maybe she could give me some good advice on how to win Sue's heart, too. "I have basketball practice after school, but I'll call you when I'm home."

"'Kay, do that." Then she looked down, where I still clasped her sweater. "You want this, or what?" Giggling, she pried my fingers loose.

"Sorry." Letting go of her top, I ran a hand through my hair. "See you then."

*

After showering off the sweat from playing basketball for ninety minutes, I grabbed my duffle bag and went to the parking lot where I'd parked Mom's car that morning. I'd just dumped my bag on the backseat, and was about to get in, when a girl in the distance caught my attention. Heck, not just any girl...

The handle of the car door clasped tightly in my hand, I watched Susan standing there by the entrance to the soccer field for several minutes. Was she waiting for someone? Maybe for me?

Nah... Discarding that thought, I clamped down on my teeth. But then...she was here. Why waste a nice opportunity? I reached for my leather jacket on the passenger seat, then slammed the door of the SUV shut, and punched a button on the key fob to lock the car. Shrugging on my jacket, I ambled toward Sue and popped a stick of gum I found in the jacket pocket into my mouth.

Susan was so preoccupied with staring at a forgotten ball in the grass in front of her, she didn't even notice me coming. Hands tucked in the front pockets of her light pink sweatshirt, she heaved a sigh.

I leaned against the pole of the open gate. When she still didn't notice me after a minute, I asked in a quiet voice, "Having a chat with the ball?"

Like a shocked bunny, Sue whirled around. Taking in my face, especially my healing black eye, probably for proof that I was *the other twin*, she cleared her throat and demanded, "What are you doing here?"

"Tuesdays I have basketball practice. I was about to head home but then I saw you. Which brings on my counter question: What are *you* doing here?" I slanted my head. "Other than trying to move the ball with a telekinetic stare, that is."

Sue looked me in the eyes for a long moment. Whatever she found there made her talk in a soft voice, not bark at me like usual. "I don't actually know why I came here." One of her shoulders lifted and dropped in a helpless gesture. "Probably because I miss playing soccer."

"Which you can't do because of your hurt knee." I'd sprained an ankle really bad some time ago and couldn't play basketball for two weeks. That was a hell of a long time, so I understood how terrible she must be feeling.

Sue stared at me open-mouthed like I'd just built a house in front of her with my bare hands in three minutes. Surprised I remembered about her knee, was she? "Yeah, I do listen sometimes, you know," I told her and chuckled. Then I walked to the ball and picked it up, an idea forming in my mind. "Hey, want to play some soccer now?"

I bounced the ball on the ground like a basketball, only in the grass it didn't rebound. "Rubbish." I picked it up and spun it on my finger. Yep, that worked well with any ball. "Which is your bad leg? You can shoot with the other," I suggested with a shrug, when she still stared at me as if struck by lightning. "And I'll stand in the goal."

"I'm a righty, which is my bad knee, so that would hardly be fair on me." Susan made a long face, but I didn't intend on giving up that easily.

"Ah, don't be shy." I squeezed the ball under my arm and wrapped the other around Sue's delectable waist, pulling her along with me. "I've never played soccer in my life, so that should pretty much even out your chances." And that was nothing but the truth.

She did walk with me but arched her brows and gave me a

ANNA KATMORE

sideways glance. "As far as I know, you're grounded. Doesn't that imply you should go home right after practice?"

"This *is* practice." Sort of. Just not mine, and not the sport of my choice. Mom would understand. Then again, she wouldn't know. "If I get in trouble for it later, I'll totally blame it on your sad puppy eyes when I found you at the gate."

With my arm still around her, I could feel her giggle. A sweet sound. And finally she gave in. From her pocket she fished a rubber band and raked her hair to the back of her head. "Fine. Let's play."

Sad Sue turned into playful and cute Sue, and my chest welled with the wish to yank her closer.

As we reached the end of the soccer field, I threw her the ball, took my leather jacket off, and dropped it on the ground. The goal was huge. Much taller than it looked from a distance. "Whoa, who defends this? A baby elephant and its mama?"

Sue snorted. "Nick Frederickson is our goalie, and he does a darn good job."

Nick Frederickson was a giant—half a head taller than me, and I wasn't on the short side. No surprise they put him in this position. I rubbed my hands, blowing out a breath, and then I placed them on my thighs, slightly bending my knees. "Okay, bring it on, girl."

Sue dropped the ball on a white line, then shoved it a couple feet closer with her toe.

I straightened and gave her an uncertain look. "Is that the right spot to put it?"

"Absolutely!"

Sure. Her snicker said something else. I rolled my eyes but, in no mood to start an argument in a moment like this, I got back in defending-the-house-size-goal position.

Sue squinted against the sun as she focused on me. A second later, she gave a whopper of a kick. The ball came barreling toward me, but much too high. Even as a complete soccer outsider, I knew it would never land in the net. Tilting my head up, I watched as it smashed into the crossbar above me and bounced back to Susan. Once more, she set it on the invisible mark she'd chosen for her free shot.

Her next kick scored—my headlong dive to the right was a jump into nothingness and I smacked into the ground. Dammit. I'd need three of me to block this goal. "Beginner's luck!" I muttered as I got to my feet and saw how Susan danced on the spot like she'd just won a world championship.

"Why? You're the beginner." She laughed and only stopped dancing when I threw the ball at her again.

I waited for her next shot. Sue pretended to move right, but when I started to move there too, she went the other way and kicked. The brat! She'd tricked me. I stood there gaping at the upper left corner as the ball smoothly sailed into the goal.

Admittedly, she was good. But I didn't need to inflate her ego even more. "I totally let that slip through for you," I teased.

"Yeah, yeah, keep on dreaming." The gleam in her eyes said she was enjoying our little one-on-one. Her fourth shot was another goal, right over my head. My jump was a tad too low to stop it.

Gnashing my teeth, I picked it up. "No one can possibly

keep this goal safe, unless they're an elephant. On a trampoline."

"Give up?" Sue asked delightedly as I walked to her.

"You wish." I let the ball bounce a couple times on my right knee. "We play against each other now."

"Not a good idea." Susan lifted her leg to remind me of her injury—like I'd forgotten. "Knee, remember? I can't run."

"But you can jog," I countered, "slowly. Right?" To sweeten the prospect some more, I added, "And I'll clasp my hands behind my back."

Her ponytail swayed as she tilted her head and gave me a wry look. "You play soccer without your hands, smart ass."

This girl was hard to please. In more than one way. "Fine. I'll do that *and* run backward. Is that better?"

Not waiting for her approval, I shoved my hands in my back jeans pockets and went for the ball backwards, practically blind. Okay, not blind—I looked over my shoulder—but running like this was definitely out of my comfort zone.

Sue got to the ball first. She didn't seem convinced of my suggested game and just shoved the ball out of my reach, seemingly ready to discuss new rules. That didn't stop me. Using my heel to kick, I tried to steal the ball from her. Finally, she accepted that I wouldn't give up, and engaged in the game with more enthusiasm. With short kicks and at a lazy jog, she headed for the goal.

Not a chance, Little Miss Sunshine! I cut in front of her and snatched the ball, but even right in front of the goal, there was no chance to shoot. Knee injury and all, Sue was just too fast. Obviously, she found pleasure in playing with me, even if she tried to hide her wide grin every so often.

Suddenly that grin was wiped right off her face, and her eyes shot wide open. "Watch out!" she shouted. Next thing I knew, something hit me on the back, and the breath exploded out of my lungs. I swallowed my gum.

The damn goal post had gotten in the way.

Unhurt but feeling a slight ringing in my head after the collision, I dropped to the ground, feigning a faint. Susan's hysterical laughter quaked around me. I decided to give her a moment to compose herself before opening my eyes again. Only, she didn't calm down. *Yeah, glad you find it so hilarious when I hurt myself, sweetness.* Behind closed lips, I clamped my jaw shut, fighting to bite back a grin. Oh, she was going to regret this.

"What's up? Did the goal knock the air out of you?" She sounded much closer now, probably right above me. Her voice still shook from her laughing fit. "Come on, I'm sure that little bump didn't hurt as much as Will's punch to your face probably did."

I didn't answer, not even when she poked her toe into my ribs.

Her chuckle died. "Are you okay?"

Oh yes, I was. And she was in for a surprise the moment she squatted down beside me.

After another beat of silence, I felt the shift in the air as she lowered and leaned over me. Worry crept into her voice. "Chris?"

Perfect! With her head blocking the sun from my face, I knew exactly where she was and reached up so fast, she had no chance to back away as I grabbed her neck. Gently enough not to hurt her, but still firm and determined, I yanked her down to me until she was so close I could see my reflection in her shocked eyes. Hands braced on my arms, she sucked in a sharp breath.

My expression as sober as can be, I said, "You laughed at me." Then I gave in to the smirk I'd been fighting back so hard for the past sixty seconds. "That will cost you."

Her gaze still locked with mine, she licked her lips and then swallowed. Her eyebrows went up in a suggestive way. "Let me guess. You want a date?"

A kiss would be better, but a date was fine. "Sounds like a good idea to me."

"Seriously, when are you going to lay off me?" The annoyance edging her voice was hard to understand. It said she wanted to punch me while her eyes told a different story. A much more romantic one...

"When I get what I want, sweetness. Or to put it in your words," I teased, "when hell freezes over."

Sue snorted, and her expression went flat. "That's not gonna happen, dude."

Really? Without wasting another second, I shifted under her, rolling us both around so that she was trapped underneath me. A gasp escaped her but at the same time she started another giggling fit that rocked her body. Using only part of my weight to keep her trapped on the ground, I fixed her with an unflinching stare.

"Get off, Chris! You're squishing me!" she squeaked, the words ripped apart with laughter. Working her arms free, she reached out and flicked me on the brow.

What the hell? I narrowed my eyes at her. Hadn't she learned her lesson last time? "Oh, you shouldn't have done that, sweetness," I drawled. The surprise in her eyes was pure joy for me as I gripped her wrists and pinned them on the grass above her head. It was time to make good on my promise. *A hickey the size of Ohio.* "Remember what I told you last time, if you did that again?"

Her jaw dropped as realization struck. "No, you wouldn't—"

I arched one eyebrow. "You bet."

At that moment, Susan began wrestling and squirming beneath me like mad, but the prospect of getting necked by me coaxed another fit of laughter from her nevertheless. High on anticipation, I leaned my head down and nuzzled the side of her throat.

"Don't you—no—don't—don't you dare suck on me!" Sue cried out, chuckling uncontrollably.

Grinning, I pressed my lips to her tender skin. Dear God, she smelled delicious. All coconut and summer love. Kissing her neck felt so much better than I'd dared to dream. A moan escaped me, one of pure pleasure. Mouth slightly open, I let Sue feel my tongue on her skin. Nothing more than a gentle brush, and she shivered beneath me. I loved it when a girl was responsive, but with Sue it was more than that. Her excitement

ANNA KATMORE

crawled under my skin and made me want to tease her tongue rather than her skin.

"Agh! Take your slobbery mouth off of me!" she ordered— only it lacked conviction. Not my fault that she was still squealing and giggling. At this point, I was pretty sure she'd hate for me to stop but was just too stubborn to admit it.

Trailing a line up her neck with my tongue, I finished with the slightest of kisses and whispered, "Why, that was just foreplay, Sue." Then I sucked on her neck, delivering the promised hickey.

"Ugh! You branded me," she whined. I wondered if she noticed how she pulled me closer instead of pushing me away.

Her indecisiveness made me laugh. "And you should show it proudly," I told her as I finally rose and helped her to her feet, clasping her wrists.

As soon as she stood, she took a step back and rubbed wildly at the spot on her neck that was already starting to turn a deep red. "That was so—"

Nice? Sexy? Enticing? Yeah, I'd agree to all of that.

But back to her not-so-convincing resistance, Sue grimaced. "Ew!"

Ew? Seriously? "Yeah, that was probably the reason you were laughing so hard, right?"

She flushed a deep scarlet. *Gotcha!*

Smiling, I went to find my jacket and slipped it on. A glance at my watch, and all fun was blown away. This little game had lasted longer than expected. Mom was home. She'd be waiting...and she was going to kill me.

"Sorry," I said to Sue. "I'd really love to fool around with you some more, but I'm still grounded, so I have to go home now." I started walking toward the parking lot, but when Susan didn't follow, I stopped and glanced over my shoulder, waiting for her. Hesitantly, she caught up with me, the red vanishing from her cheeks. "Where are you going, anyway?" I demanded then. "Can I give you a ride?" I was in trouble already. A few more minutes couldn't make my death any worse.

She coughed quietly and lowered her gaze. "Actually, you can take me home with you."

Now, if that wasn't interesting news. "Oh, sweetness, you don't know how I've been dying for you to suggest that."

Groaning, Susan pinched the bridge of her nose as if she couldn't get any more annoyed with me at the moment. This time, I had the feeling it wasn't faked. "Let me rephrase: You can take me home with you, where our ways will part at the front door, and I'll spend a nice afternoon with your brother. How does that sound? Better?"

"Lame." I rolled my eyes. We'd had such a good time on the field just now. Why stop there? I took her hand and pulled her along with me. Hers was so cold, a shiver raced up my arm—and after getting heated in a sexy soccer game, too. "Whoa, what are you? Frosty the Snowman?" I squeezed her hand a little tighter to warm it with mine.

Her phone dinged in her pocket, and Sue pulled her hand away. She tugged it out and stared at the display. Curious about her smile, I glance at her phone over her shoulder.

A text from *Charlie Brown*. My forehead creased with a

frown. "Who's Charlie Brown?"

"Your brother," she told me and laughed when I gave her a clueless expression.

I shook my head. "You two are strange." Charlie Brown? How in the world did that fit? But wait, if she called him a *Peanuts* name, what the hell did she call me? "Do you have a name for me, too?" I asked. Her face went blank, and my eyes grew wide. "You do? What is it?" Couldn't be something as silly as Snoopy, right?

"Nothing," she said quickly and turned away to read the message from my brother.

Nothing my ass! She did have a special name for me, and I wanted to know what it was. After she'd typed a reply, I snatched her phone before she could put it back in her pocket.

"Hey! Give it back!" She jumped around me like a frisky puppy, but I hadn't found what I was looking for yet, so she couldn't have it back.

"Let's see," I said, fending her off with my free arm. Twisting out of her reach a couple times, I thumbed my way to the text folder, holding the phone higher than she could reach, and searched through the texts there. It should be easy enough to find mine, because there were a lot from last night.

I stopped dead. Staring at the name, my smile slipped. My throat hurt as I swallowed, and I lowered my hand. Slowly, I turned around and studied Sue's guilt-ridden face.

"*Arrogant Dick*? You can't be serious." Okay, since it was right there, white against a black background, she had to be, but jeez! Couldn't she have come up with something a little nicer? I called her *Ponytail Sue*, for goodness sake!

She gave an apologetic shrug. "What can I say? That's what I got to know you by."

Okay, but that didn't mean she was allowed to go on like this. Leveling her a stern look, I held her cell out to her. "You are so going to change that. Now."

A grin sneaked over her face. "Nuh-uh. It is what it is."

"Fine, then I'll do it for you." Turning away, I began to change *Arrogant Dick* to something more appropriate. Like...oh, I knew! *Dream Guy Material.* There. Much better.

Sue was still jumping around me like she was being bitten by spiders, trying to stop me from messing with her phone. I successfully warded her off until I was done and handed her the cell. She ignored my grin and slid the phone back in her pocket, not even checking the new entry. *Fine then, don't.* She would see it soon enough, anyway.

From a couple feet away, I unlocked the SUV, and Sue climbed in without a word. I started the engine while she fumbled with the seatbelt, and drove off. It seemed like she was taking extra time with that, paying a lot more attention to the process than was necessary. When the belt was secured and provided no distraction any longer, she began picking things from her jeans that weren't really there. For a moment, I watched her from the corner of my eye, but after some time I just had to ask, "Do I make you nervous?"

Susan's head jerked up. A cynical grin was her answer. "You never give up, do you?"

"Not as long as there's a hint of a chance," I said, showing

ANNA KATMORE

the tiniest amount between my thumb and forefinger. But since I had her alone in this car with me, I soon forgot all about mocking her and wondered if now was a good time to discuss something else with her. "Can I ask you a serious question?"

Biting her lip in a cute way, she blinked at me twice and stated, "I'm almost certain you can*not*, but please, go ahead and give your best."

"Very funny." I rolled my eyes, but a smile escaped me. "Anyway, tell me... Why would you go out with my brother, who's my absolutely identical twin and who told you yesterday that a romance was not in the cards for the two of you, but not with me?"

Susan was silent for so long, I threw her a quick sideways glance to make sure she was still with me and hadn't spaced out for some reason. Eventually, she cleared her throat and said in a low voice, "You think it's only about looks, don't you?"

Of course! But that didn't seem like the answer she wanted to hear. So I narrowed my eyes at the windshield and murmured, "No." Then I added with a smile, "I think I can also be quite charming."

"Yes, you can be," she agreed. "If you want to." Folding her arms over her chest, she nailed me with an intense stare that distracted me like hell from driving. "But it's not enough to make me want to go out with you. You may look like your brother, but other than that, you're two totally different people. Like day and night, really."

"So you'd rather kiss a guy who's shy and insecure," I probed.

Head still turned to me, she started to smirk before she answered. "I thought we were talking about going out, not kissing?"

I waggled my brows at her. "That goes hand in hand."

"Okay then..." She inhaled a deep breath. "I'd rather go out *and* kiss a guy who doesn't date a different girl every day."

Couldn't begrudge her that. If I had a girlfriend, I wouldn't want her to sleep around either. Heck, I'd prefer someone who hadn't done so in the first place. It was probably natural that this player side of me turned someone like Sue off a little. But neglecting all the good sides of being single for a possibility with Sue that she hadn't even considered yet?

I parked the car in front of our house and cut the engine but didn't get out. Instead, I hung my arms on the steering wheel and rested my chin on the backs of my hands, studying Susan for another intense moment. A wary smile sneaked to her lips. Her hair was still in that sweet ponytail, with strands sticking out now from fooling around in the grass with me. Her eyes held a million questions.

I *could* give up dating other girls for her. It would be easy, too. All I needed was an incentive. "Give me a reason not to," I demanded, not breaking eye contact.

Sue's chest lifted and fell with a long breath. "It doesn't work that way, Chris."

It didn't work which way? Her agreeing to be more than a challenge so that I'd stop hooking up with other girls? Then what did she want from me? For me to behave like a boyfriend before actually *becoming* her boyfriend?

Shit—did I *want* to be her boyfriend?

Well, it was something to consider. Of course, it was too late to undo my record of hookups, but maybe if I kept it clean from now on, she'd give me a fair chance after all.

Yeah, excellent plan. She'd have no reason to back out then. Intrigued by this idea, the corners of my mouth curved up. "All right. Let's do it your way." An immediate surge of excitement sparked through me as the words left my mouth. Pulling the key out of the ignition, I got out of the car. This day was getting better and better.

As I skirted the hood, Sue was still fumbling with the seatbelt and cast me a shocked look through the windshield. She got out and slammed the door shut. Fast, light footsteps followed me on the pavement as I held the key over my shoulder and locked the car.

"Wait!" she called after me. "That's not... Just..."

Just what?

"*No!*"

After unlocking the front door, I turned around to face her. One look at her neck, and my blood ran hot in my veins. My mark on her throat was turning a beautiful shade of purple. With a mischievous smirk, I clarified, "Your rules. You laid them down, so you better stick to them."

Silently, Sue shook her head.

Oh no, she wouldn't back out! Determined, I nodded, then I took her hand and dragged her inside the house with me.

"Chris? Is that you?"

Ah, that was Mom in the living room. I really would have

loved for the world to know Susan Miller was going to be mine soon, but since the girl was still a little reluctant, I decided it was better not to push it. The hickey would stay our secret for now.

Meeting Sue's uncertain gaze, I placed one finger over my lips to keep her quiet. Then I said out loud, "Yes, Mom!" My mother didn't need to know we had a guest just yet.

And neither did Ethan.

My mind set, I pulled Susan along with me into my room, pushing the door almost closed but not all the way. We wouldn't be in here for long—unless she insisted on it. I let go of her hand, which made her stop abruptly in the middle of my room.

In one of the drawers was my dark red bandana, but in which one, I couldn't recall. The drawer with my socks was a no-go, but in the drawer with all the random stuff like biking gloves and sweatbands—there was the bandana I was looking for.

Silent as a mouse, Sue watched me shake the thing out and fold it into a triangle. Only when I walked toward her did she take a hurried step back. Her wariness made me chuckle. "Hold still," I said as I followed her and carefully tied the bandana around her neck to cover the hickey. Breathing hard, she let me do it, her eyes on mine the whole time.

When the knot was tight enough, I withdrew my hand, skimming my fingers along her soft skin. One last glimpse at my mark on her as I hooked one finger into the bandana and pulled it down a little, then I told her truthfully, "You know, I wouldn't have done that if—for only one second—I'd had the feeling you weren't enjoying it."

Like a stranded fish, Sue gaped at me, no sound coming out of her open mouth. It took her several seconds to close it, and then she swallowed hard. Then she whirled about on the spot, her honey-colored ponytail flying. As if what I'd said had hurt her feelings, she stormed out of my room. Except, I got the impression she wasn't hurt at all—just realizing that I'd told her the truth.

Chapter 13

BEING A NICE brother to Ethan and a decent hopefully-soon-to-be-boyfriend for Sue, I stayed in my room the entire time she was in my house. She shouldn't feel as if I was stalking her or anything. Accidentally running into her was cool. Sneaking after her and disturbing her time with "Charlie Brown," her obviously new best friend, was not. It didn't matter. I intended to talk to her again that night, when she was home and her mind unfettered by Ethan.

To kill that unbearably long time with more than studying for Winter finals, I got Hunter on the phone before dinner and sounded him out about Sue.

"So her best friends are your girlfriend, and Alex's and Mitchell's, correct?"

"Include your brother on the list, and you got it, I'd say," Ryan replied.

"Okay." I made a mental note of that, then scratched my head. "What's the name of Mitchell's girl again?"

"Sam."

"Right. She's the tiny one with choppy black hair?" I knew Alex Winter's hot blond girlfriend, and I'd met Lisa the other day. But Tony hadn't yet come around to introduce me to the quirky little thing that had been flanking him recently.

"Exactly." There was a light chuckle through the line. "Why do you need all this information? I thought her 'charming personality' wasn't your type?"

"Could be I changed my mind."

"Is it about the challenge?"

Fuck, he knew? "Who told you about that?"

"Dude, half of the school is talking about it."

"Yeah..." Of course they would be, after what Sue and I pulled off in detention. T-Rex and the guys probably weren't the only ones betting their money these days. "See..." A sigh escaped me. "Things have changed...somehow. I kinda like her." If only I had never challenged Sue in public. Dammit, I wished I hadn't challenged her at all. "I'd love to take her out and see where things go."

Something whizzed on Hunter's end of the line, and next I heard him gulping, probably from a can of soda. "What's stopping you?" he wanted to know. "Just ask her on a date."

"Nah, we're not really there yet."

"Rough start, huh?"

"Hit the nail on the head."

"Okay, anything else you need to know to make the hunt easier for you?"

"Hmm." I scratched my left eye. "Who was her last

boyfriend?" One from the geek squad? Or even someone from the soccer team? It would be helpful to know how he looked and what Sue had liked about him to begin with.

"I don't think she's had one yet."

Stopping before I scratched my eye out, my mouth fell open. "You're kidding me, right?"

"Nope. As far as I can tell, she's very selective."

The fact that she'd had no random hookups made something inside me happy. But no boyfriends? She was too sweet for me to believe that. Then again, maybe all the guys she'd dated in the past were total jerks and not worth anything lasting longer? The thought appealed to me.

After thanking Ryan for the information, I hung up and went to the kitchen for a drink. Ethan's door was open and his room empty. Too bad. I would have liked to catch another moment with Sue before my brother drove her home.

Ethan came back minutes later. He was silent through dinner, didn't even respond to one of Mom's happy beams when she asked him about Sue. But he threw me a glance once or twice, lifting his brows in an odd manner. Like he was trying to communicate the silent word *sorry*. For what? Because Mom still wanted to see him in a relationship with the girl I now wanted? It wasn't his fault—not entirely, anyway.

Still a little irritated, I started tidying my room after dinner. So many things stood between me and Sue, and now my Mom did, too. As if winning Susan Miller's heart wasn't hard enough already.

Funnily enough, it only took my brother sticking his head

through my door and delivering a short message later that evening for my mood to brighten. "Greetings from Susan. She wants me to tell you she likes cake with cream and fruit."

Cracking a major grin, I stopped sorting through my CDs and faced him. "She called you and told you to tell me that?"

"Nah. Text."

Same difference. And that sneaky little brat. There had to be a reason she'd sent the message to Ethan and not me. Was she avoiding a confrontation after the hickey incident? My smile widened at the thought.

I walked to Ethan and handed him Sue's Volbeat CD, which had lain on my desk all this time. Nobody had asked for it, so the thing had fallen into oblivion under a pile of school books.

Ethan looked at the cover and laughed. "Finally." Then he left and slammed the door shut. Seconds later, the rock music drifted through the walls.

In the glorious mess that was my desk, I hunted for my cell and wrote a message for Sue. *LOL. Why didn't you tell me that yourself?*

In the middle of stacking the rest of my CDs and DVDs, her reply arrived. *I didn't know if I'd reach you at an inappropriate moment. What if you were with another girl right now? For all it's worth, you're dream guy material.*

All thoughts of cleaning abandoned, I parked my backside against the edge of my desk and punched in another text. *I'm glad you finally realized that ;-) But I'm grounded, sweetness. And you're the only girl coming to our house these days. No need to worry.*

I was hoping for another fast response, but minutes passed and Sue let me down. That hindered my plan to keep her talking for a while longer, so I quickly came up with a change of topic and typed: *What's your favorite?*

My favorite what? she wanted to know.

Fruit. For the cake. If I was going to make one for her, it had to be perfect.

My cell dinged, and I bit my lip, smiling, while I read: *I like kiwi.* She'd also added a smiley face sticking its tongue out. Aiming to taunt me? She'd succeeded. Ah, what a delicious memory...

Flopping on my bed, I went to YouTube and searched for a special song. If she remembered the kiwi moment, she probably wouldn't have forgotten about Sam Smith, either. To sweeten her night, I pasted the link to the song in the message and wrote *Sleep tight, sweetness* underneath.

*

Wednesday morning, after first period, the need to relieve myself had me rushing to the boys' restroom. As I exited, I heard Hunter's voice. Pivoting, I realized he wasn't alone.

Tony Mitchell's quirky little girlfriend was with him, and so was Susan Miller.

Ryan had his arm around Sue's shoulders, as if he was steering her right in my direction. A smirk stretched my lips. He let go of her as soon as they'd caught up with me. Leaning

ANNA KATMORE

closer to Sue so that only she could hear my taunting voice, I said, "Sleep well last night?"

Her cheeks flushed a soft pink, and she lowered her gaze briefly as she smiled. "With a catchy song in my ears, actually."

"Oh, I bet it was," I wanted to answer—but didn't get a chance to. An all-too-familiar voice interrupted me from behind.

"Good morning, Chris."

A quick shiver zoomed down my spine. *Not the best moment, Parker.* Clearing my throat, I took a step away from Sue and put on a nonchalant expression. "Hey, Lauren, what's up?"

Her eyes fixed on me, she did that thing with her hair—brushing it over her shoulder with the back of her hand. It was a clear sign of her hunting for attention, and it usually wreaked havoc with me, because it tilted her head in a way that presented her kissable neck. Only today, I wished she'd left her raven mane where it was. With Sue next to me, it made me quite uncomfortable.

"You said you'd call me about tutoring you in Spanish again," she reminded me, her eyes warm and alluring.

Spanish! I scrunched my face. "Ah, right. I totally forgot about that."

Lauren laughed. "Yeah, I noticed."

Dammit, couldn't this conversation have waited until fourth period? I was in the middle of something here. And dealing with Lauren's seductive gaze wouldn't help me with Sue. Was she doing that on purpose? I rubbed my neck. "You see, it's a little difficult right now…because…" *Dammit, find an excuse, idiot! Fast!* "I'm grounded," I blurted out.

"I don't mind if we study at your place," she replied with that typical I'm-up-for-some-afternoon-fun smile of hers.

Man, had I really thought we could study without sex involved? Strike that. "Ah, no. That's not a good idea right now," I told her, cutting an uneasy glance at Sue, who seemed to hang on every word we said. Did she realize what Lauren really wanted from me right now? God, I hoped not. But then again, she couldn't be that blind.

Swallowing, I shifted my weight from one foot to the other and adjusted my backpack on my shoulder, focusing on Lauren again. "In fact, I don't think I'll need extra Spanish lessons for a while."

Lauren blinked her dark eyes a couple of times in disbelief. "Are you sure?"

Of course, or I wouldn't have said so. Restraining myself from tossing that in her face, I averted my eyes and nodded. An instant later, Sue dragged my attention back to her as she coughed loudly. Her shy gaze darted around when everyone looked at her. Eventually, it came to rest on me, and she mumbled, "Excuse me," like she'd disturbed an extremely important meeting.

I raised a curious eyebrow at her, but Lauren dragged my gaze away again when she brushed my forearm with her fingers and whispered, "So, nothing has changed, huh?"

A sigh expanded my chest. How could I possibly answer that?

Back in a normal voice, she said, "See you in Spanish." Then she gave the rest of the group a quick smile and headed on to her next lesson.

Ryan left us, too, so only the two girls and I were still standing by the lockers in the hallway. Sue scrutinized me with sharp eyes. All kinds of thoughts must have been running through her head then, but the one most apparent was total confusion. Knowing her well enough by now, I guessed she was probably surprised I'd sent Lauren away.

I lifted my hands, palms up in surrender, and said, "Your rules."

With that reminder, I left the girls before Sue could come up with another argument as to why we wouldn't work. I swear she had one ready at the tip of her tongue.

*

Since I was bored as hell all day, not allowed to leave the house per my mom's restrictions, I was almost happy when it started to get dark outside. The past few evenings, it had sort of become a habit to tell Susan good night through a message. A little fun right now was just what I needed, so I typed a line for her. *What are you doing?*

Susan answered without delay. *Just moved in with my grandfather.*

What in the world did *that* mean? Stripping off my clothes, I settled on my bed and wrote: *Want to explain?*

Long story.

She didn't know this about me yet, but I liked long stories. *You have three and a half hours. If I get less than six hours of sleep, I'm grumpy in the morning.*

By the time her next text arrived, I was pretty sure I had her undivided attention, because mere seconds passed between each of my messages and hers. *Ha ha, so we better make sure you go to bed early.*

I'm in bed now. I always am when I text you. Why aren't you?

My parents are having a rather noisy argument. My grandpa lives next door, and I came here to sleep on the couch.

Jeez, that didn't sound like fun. *Wow. You do that often?* After I sent the text off, I leaned over the edge of my bed and fetched a pack of Skittles from my nightstand. Picking out all the green ones from the pack, I slipped a handful in my mouth while waiting for her answer.

My phone dinged again. *Sometimes. I'm used to it. So you go to bed this early every day, so you can text me?*

Ah, I would text her all day, if that were possible. *Yeah. I don't like being disturbed when I talk to you. ;-) How's the hickey doing?* Just as I was about to hit send, my phone suddenly went black. WTF? Eyes narrowed, I turned it around, examining it, but of course, there was nothing to be seen. And for good reason. The battery had died was all. Had to be that, considering I hadn't charged it since last weekend.

The cable was on my desk. Fortunately, it was long enough to plug in and reach my bed. Sitting on my mattress once more, legs under the covers, I retyped the message, then finally sent it off.

Sue replied fast once again. *Turning violet. How's your black eye doing?* I could so visualize her taunting grin with that answer.

Actually, I had no idea how my black eye looked, so I sat up and stared at my image reflected off the dark window from the light in my room. Aha. Ugly-as-hell yellow. Settling back, I wrote: *Turning yellow-ish. Makes me a whole lot more attractive, doesn't it?* ^^

I like flawless. :P

Of course she would, that witch. Never missing a chance to make a jibe at me. I laughed and replied: *I like ponytails.*

Almost immediately, my phone chimed with a new message. *I like charming Chris.*

Whoa! Was she serious? I wouldn't have thought she'd tell me something this nice *intentionally*. The "you smell good" thing last Saturday was amazing, but certainly a mere slip of the tongue. While this— Dammit, my heart started knocking a little harder against my rib cage.

I like kissing your neck. You taste like coconut cream. And hell, I still had that awesome smell etched in my memory after our friendly wrestling match in the grass.

Body butter. I'll get you some if you like it so much. :P It's late. Have to go to sleep now, or I'll be grumpy in the morning.

Yeah, yeah... Lame excuse. The chat was getting hot, and she felt it. That was the reason for her backing out, and nothing else. No matter. She could have her way tonight, because with the past few texts she'd given me enough to make me go to sleep with a broad smile on my lips. There was only one thing left to say: *Sleep tight, sweetness.*

As if she was scared too much would change, she didn't reply to that text. I didn't mind, hadn't reckoned on it anyway. Turning off the light after ten minutes, and with the silly grin still pasted on my face like someone had duct-taped it there, I closed my eyes.

Chapter 14

FOR THE REST of the week, Sue seemed to avoid me like I had some deadly disease. How else could it be that I didn't meet her once in the hallway even though I hung out much longer than usual in places I knew she would be? It was only at lunch that I got a glimpse of her. Once or twice, she sneaked a peek across the cafeteria in my direction, but that was about it.

At least things seemed to be back to normal at her house. That's what she told me in a text on Thursday night when I asked whether she was still sleeping on her grandpa's couch. I knew firsthand how bad it was when parents kept up an endless fight.

Fourth period on Friday, we had the dreaded Spanish test. Having received the cold shoulder from Lauren over the past couple of days, it was no surprise she didn't wish me luck.

The test was easy enough. An essay about a vacation in Spain. Ask for directions, order some food, call an ambulance at some point, and go souvenir shopping. I could say all of these things in Spanish. The only problem was that at every translation, I involuntarily remembered which part of Lauren's body I'd gotten to explore when I'd gotten the answer right. At the ambulance part of the essay, I banged my forehead on the desk, biting the inside of my cheek, because I really didn't want to go there right now.

Lauren cut me a sideways glance. No doubt she thought I was failing the test. Narrowing my eyes at her, I cursed her silently for being such a *practical* tutor.

By the end of the test, I was feeling a little too warm inside my clothes.

In no mood to explain myself to Lauren about the head-banging, I rushed out of class when the bell rang and headed for the cafeteria. My lunch today consisted of a bottle of ice water, which I chugged down in big gulps.

Seeing Susan across the room ruined the soothing effect of the cold water. Instantly, my mind took a beeline back to *practical studying*, and I wondered what little Sue could teach me—or what I could teach her. Deciding not to gawk at her all through lunch, I made a serious effort to distract myself by joking around with my friends at the table. The rest of the school day went by quiet and fast.

Sue hadn't come to see my brother the past two days. Stuck in detention in a boring house, my hopes rose when Ethan slipped on a fresh shirt later in the afternoon and styled his hair.

"Is Susan coming over?" I asked, leaning in the doorway to the bathroom, watching him in the mirror.

ANNA KATMORE

"Nope. Meeting her at Charlie's," he told me as if this wasn't a big issue. Hell, he should've known how desperately I wanted to see her again. They both should've. Did they actually find this funny? Torturing Chris Donovan for entertainment on a Friday afternoon?

Clamping my jaw shut, I turned on the spot and retreated to my room. Might as well do my homework early and not save it until the last minute before school on Monday.

Ethan came home from his date with my girl before dinner. It didn't appear that anything exciting had happened between the two of them, and it better not have. But the way my brother remained seated at the dinner table after Mom left the room and bit his lips made me a little uncomfortable. Something was on his mind that he didn't want to tell me—but he would.

"What's up?" I grumbled, taking our glasses and carrying them over to the sink.

Ethan's sigh drifted to me. *Uh-oh.* I turned around and leaned against the kitchen counter, gripping the edge hard. "Spit it out already."

Ethan cleared his throat, his eyes on the unlit candle in the middle of the table. Slowly, his gaze slid to me. "Susan canceled."

"Today?" I asked, confused.

"No, for tomorrow."

My jaw dropped, my eyes growing wide. "She did what?"

"She doesn't want to come for dinner tomorrow."

A surge of disappointment rushed through me so fast, it

felt like the ground beneath my feet had slipped away. "But why?"

Blowing out a long breath, Ethan leaned back in his chair and tipped his head on the backrest to stare at the ceiling for a long moment. "I'm not exactly sure what's going on between the two of you right now"—his eyes rolled in my direction—"but I would guess she's feeling a little apprehensive about what you want from her."

I frowned at him. "And will not seeing me help with that?"

"Hey, don't blame me." He straightened. "She's the one who took a rain check. I would have loved to cook for her tomorrow."

And so would I.

Growling, I pushed myself away from the counter and strode to my room. Under a pile of freshly laundered clothes that Mom must have brought in after dinner, I finally found my phone and sent little Sue a text. It was only one word, and it said it all.

Please.

She didn't reply. By quarter to eight, I wanted to throw myself on the bed and sulk like a five-year-old. In fact, I did throw myself on the bed, but I switched on the TV, too, and watched more reruns of the *Big Bang* nerds. What else was there to do on a Friday night when you're grounded?

After twenty minutes of trying to follow the conversation of the four oddballs, I'd reached the point where I aggressively wanted to smack the Jewish guy with the turtleneck, slap the Indian upside his head every time he went mute on a woman,

ANNA KATMORE

and knock *myself* out when the one with the glasses slept with his girl with a flipping t-shirt on. At least the mantis-like guy named Sheldon was funny. He was the only reason I watched the episode until the end.

On the nightstand, my phone dinged. A text. *Finally!*

Please what? Sue replied. Oh my God, I waited twenty minutes for that? What the hell?

I punched in more information. *Please come tomorrow.*

Five unbearably long minutes went by, and my cell remained silent. That was enough. My blood still boiled from the bomb Ethan had dropped on me earlier, but Sue giving me the silent treatment now? No freaking way! I found her name in my contacts and called her.

She didn't answer. "Ah, dammit!" I growled, almost crushing the cell in my hand. I hung up and typed another message for her. *Pick up the phone!* Then I called again.

At long last, she answered with a raspy, "Hey."

Feeling at the end of my patience, I came straight to the point. "What's up?"

"Nothing," she replied, innocent as a delicate butterfly.

"Yeah, sure." I rolled my eyes. "And my brother moved into the Playboy Mansion."

That coaxed a chuckle from her. It felt good to actually hear the tension drop out of her. "Come on, Sue," I prompted. "What's the problem?" We were getting closer to each other, was that such a bad thing in her book? "Why don't you want to come over tomorrow? And don't think I didn't notice that you haven't been at my house most of this week."

"Things have been a little stressful with my family these past few days," she explained.

"Oh…" I knew that was true to some extent from texting with her, but I also knew it was just another lame excuse for not wanting to see me. She wouldn't get away with it. "I'm sorry about that, but it's even more reason for you to come tomorrow."

"Is it? How so?" Her tone was a challenge.

"Because it'll take your mind off the trouble at home for a while." There! She couldn't worm out of it now. Obviously, she realized that, because nothing but silence pressed against my ear. "Come on, Sue. Let me cook for you," I pleaded. "It'll be fun and it'll taste good."

A moment passed in which Sue kept me waiting. Eventually, her deep sigh traveled through the line. "All right. Tell Ethan he can pick me up at two." Right after surrendering, however, she warned me in a snappy tone, "But you better not put any peaches in that meal."

Goodness, I wouldn't. Staring at the ceiling, I laughed at her stubborn determination to keep a distance between us.

"Goodbye," she said quickly.

"Bye, little Sue," I replied, but she didn't hear it because she'd already hung up on me.

*

I woke up late on Saturday morning. Too late. There were a lot of things on my to-do list, and if I wanted them done, I'd better get out of bed this instant. Well, a moment's delay was all right. Yawning widely, I sat up and shot Sue a text. *Please don't change your mind!*

This was all that had been on my mind the entire night. She couldn't cancel again.

When no reply rolled in, I put the cell away, got out of bed, and slipped into my sweats and a tee. Ethan was up already and sat at the kitchen table, hunched over a shopping list. "What do you need for your cake?" he asked while I poured a cup of coffee and slumped down in the chair next to him.

"Let me think..." Another yawn, and I stretched my spine to loosen up. "Flour, eggs, sugar, and some butter for the cake, but I think we have enough of that stuff here. For the topping, I'll need some fruit. Whatever you like on yours, and then strawberries and grapes for Mom and me. Sue said kiwi, so I need three of those as well."

Ethan wrote everything down in his neat handwriting, which I couldn't pull off for the life of me. "And for the cream you need what?" he mumbled, still scribbling things on his list. "Yogurt and..."

"Mascarpone, some whipped cream, vanilla sugar, and an organic lemon." I'd made this cake before. Several times, actually, because it was Mom's favorite. It only remained to be seen how Sue liked it. "Oh, and bring me some bitter chocolate, too."

"Got it." Ethan looked up. "You know it's impressive how you persuaded her to come after all."

Yeah, the charming side of me must have taken over again last night. Grinning, I shrugged. "No big deal."

"Rrright." Ethan cast me a smirk, then tapped the end of his pencil on the shopping list. "Anything else?"

"Nope, that's all." I glanced at the paper in front of him. Two pages were filled with ingredients for today's special dinner. "Can you run to the store *now*? I'd like to start on the cake early."

"I'd been planning on it, anyway. The meat needs to soak in the herb marinade a few hours."

Yep, Ethan was the steak expert, while I was all about desserts. We did make a great team in the kitchen. At one point, we'd even thought about opening our own restaurant when we were older. But with a basketball scholarship practically under the belt, I dreamed of going pro. There wouldn't be much time for cooking if that happened.

After Ethan left, I glanced at my phone. No reply from Sue yet. She hadn't called Ethan to take a rain check, but with her silence this morning, one could never know. I decided to send her the same message again, just to be sure. *Please don't change your mind!* I would send it so many times it was bound to coax an answer from her.

It turned out my lucky number was seven, because she replied then, *Calm down, tiger. I'm coming, I'm coming...* The cake was already baking in the oven by then.

When we were done in the kitchen, Ethan changed to go pick up Sue, and I went to take a shower. I hadn't yet stripped down when a knock sounded on the bathroom door and Mom called out, "Chris! I got a call from a client. Have to go."

"What about dinner?" I asked, peeling off my socks.

"I won't make it, sorry. But you guys have fun."

"Okay. Bye."

I showered quickly, toweled off, and slipped on a white tee with my favorite dark gray shirt on top. Leaving the buttons open, I worked some gel into my hair and made it stand in all directions like a forgotten stack of straw.

Through the closed door, I heard my brother return with Sue and Mom telling Ethan that she was off now. One last spray of Axe on my chest, and I was out of the bathroom, dying to see Little Miss Sunshine. And not only did I see her, she knocked right into me when I walked through the door.

Quickly, I cupped her elbow, steadying her. A smile pulled up the edges of my mouth. The light green t-shirt she was wearing highlighted her beautiful eyes. And dammit, her hair was in a ponytail. "Hey now, look who found the way to our house again," I teased her in welcome.

Sue looked up at my face, her gaze warm and happy. She didn't pull her arm out of my grip but smiled back at me. "Look who's dressed up for cooking."

"It's how I dress up for a date, actually."

Her smile grew even wider. "Well, then you dress up nicely."

A compliment again. And an intentional one this time? It must have been, because she didn't look away. My gaze, on the other hand, dropped to her tight t-shirt, which enhanced her petite figure perfectly. "Right back at you." Sadly, all evidence of my hickey on her neck was gone already. "I see there's no need for a turtleneck any longer."

At that innuendo, Sue's focus zeroed in on my black eye, which wasn't black or blue any longer, but only a shadow of yellow with a bit of violet. It would be gone completely in another couple of days, but for now it held Susan's interest. Her hand twitched, as if she wanted to reach up and touch it, but she held back. Would she like it if I took her hand and placed it on the spot for her? I was still holding her arm, and she didn't complain. Our gazes locked for an infinite moment, thoughts of leaning in and brushing a kiss on her mouth invaded me. I swallowed.

"Bowling or baseball, what do you want to play, Susan?" a very annoying voice disrupted our moment.

Sue sucked in a barely audible gasp. She quickly found her composure again and carefully pulled her arm out of my hold. After a soft cough, she slipped past me and called to Ethan, "How about golf for a change?"

I loved my brother. But sometimes I wanted to strangle him. Gnashing my teeth, I spun on my heel and followed Sue into Ethan's room. He might have ruined a perfect kiss moment, but he wouldn't hide Sue from me for the next two hours, oh no.

Susan had already made herself comfortable on his bed while he set up a game. I flopped on the mattress beside her and suggested, "Three players?"

Ethan turned around and shot Sue a questioning look. She rolled her eyes, sneaking a glance at me, but at the same time

ANNA KATMORE

she smiled. I guessed she was fine with me staying.

Ladies first. Ethan handed Sue the controller. She climbed off the bed, not caring that my legs were in the way, simply making her way over them. Ready, she took up position in front of the TV and took a swing with the controller. That shot was a major miss. At least one hundred and fifty virtual yards past the hole.

Ethan was next, and he wasn't any better. My turn. I'd played this game a lot with T-Rex when we were younger, so I had enough practice to get a hole in one. In the following forty-five minutes, I squashed them at Wii golf.

When it was Sue's turn again, I cringed at how she took up a lax position. "You're holding it wrong. It'll never work with that shot." Sliding behind her, I reached to her front and placed my hands over hers on the controller.

Sue stiffened in my casual but not entirely innocent embrace. The soft strands of her ponytail tickled my chin, and I blew them away...maybe very, very, absolutely unintentionally also blowing on her neck.

"Please, this is so cliché, Chris," she scolded me, wiggling her shoulders to shake me off. But her voice trembled, and her breathing was much too fast for merely being irritated. She was turned on by my sensual hug. Maybe she would have let me hold her longer, if my brother hadn't been in the room with us.

Um...Ethan? Could you get lost for a moment?

But of course that wasn't happening, so I let go of Sue and sat down on the edge of Ethan's bed, chuckling. Sue stared at me hard, then she teed off and missed, again, by miles.

"Told you so," I teased, arching my brow. The blush that had cooled off a second ago after my sneaky embrace flared up again. She was one scrumptious little thing. Trying not to get dragged too deep into the thought of nibbling on her, I cleared my throat. "Anyway, it's time to stop playing and get to work, or we'll be eating at ten tonight."

We all moved to the kitchen, where Ethan and I had already laid out everything we were going to need for preparing the meal and dessert. Susan sat down at the table and watched us with open curiosity as my brother and I got busy. While Ethan chopped vegetables and checked on the marinated steaks, I began pouring all the ingredients I needed for the cream into a bowl.

But cooking without music was no fun, so I switched on the radio. It was what Mom liked so much about my brother and me cooking anyway.

An Italian song played, with a rhythm you could shake to. I twisted across the room—passing Ethan, who danced to the other side—and got three eggs from the fridge. On the way back to the island, which I'd completely covered with my bowls, chopping board, and hand-held blender, I juggled the eggs. Yep, it was totally to show off to Sue, and I prayed to heaven none would drop to the floor. Cutting a glance at her every now and then to make sure she appreciated my skills, I found that she was sitting much too far away from me.

At Ethan's request to pass him the vinegar, I put the eggs down, gripped the bottle by its neck, tossed it in the air, and caught it again behind my back. Seven months, I'd practiced this move—and I'd shattered close to fifty bottles in that time, much to my mother's chagrin. But it paid off, even if just for this very moment.

Susan caught her breath and slowly let it out again, seemingly horrified, yet equally impressed when I didn't break the bottle. I chuckled as I patted the empty spot on the counter for her to come sit with me. Eyes narrowed, she shook her head.

Why so shy? I crooked my finger, beckoning her.

At that, she mouthed the word "no."

Now, come on... I expelled a deep sigh and rolled my eyes at her. Always needed an extra, *extra* invitation, didn't she? Fine, she could have it. I walked toward her and, ignoring her shocked gaze, took her hand to pull her up from the chair. Not giving her a chance to protest, I twisted her around me and caught her to my chest. Another hug—the second of today— and my heart rejoiced. She smelled so damn good.

Startled, Sue laughed as she placed her hands on my shoulders for balance. I took one of them in mine again and danced her in a sexy Latin style to the corner of the kitchen island. Once there, I grabbed her hips and lifted her onto the counter.

Like a shy little girl, she clasped her hands in her lap, crossing her legs at the ankles. It was fine with me, as long as she was close.

I mixed the yogurt and mascarpone, added the other ingredients, and tasted it once the mass was smooth. Yummy. Sue should taste it, too. Without a whole lot of thinking, I dipped my finger into the cream and held it out for her.

Sue scrunched her face in disgust. "Seriously?" Her gaze moved to my finger. "Gross."

All right, it seemed we weren't exactly where I wanted us to be yet. No problem, the afternoon was long. I laughed and sucked the cream off my finger myself.

Time to chop some fruit. Sue was blocking the drawer with the knives, and I had to move her a bit to get in there. One hand on her hip, I slid her over a foot, which made her squeak with surprise. After I'd retrieved the knife, I slid her right back in place, and this time—apparently prepared for the move— she just giggled.

Whatever Ethan had prepared in the meantime, he was finished, because he told me he was going to need the oven in a minute. The cake I'd made this morning was still in there—no longer baking, of course, but so that it wouldn't dry out.

Pulling out the tray holding the cake, I placed it next to Sue on the counter. Ethan turned on the oven and put a ceramic bowl of meat and sauce inside. "Half an hour," he announced while I put the cream on my cake.

I juggled some oranges to the next song that came on, until one dropped to the floor. Thank God it wasn't an egg.

Ethan picked the orange up with a reprimanding look. Yep, he knew I could do better than this. Anyway, enough juggling for one day. Ethan was done, and I still had to chop the fruit for the cake, lay it out, and prepare some liquid chocolate for decoration.

Picking the bananas and grapes from the fruit bowl, my

heart sank when I didn't find the most essential topping for my cake. "Where are the kiwis?"

The breath that Ethan sucked in through his clamped teeth just then caused the hair on the back of my neck to stand up. "Crap," he said, looking like a boy who'd accidentally burned his little sister's Barbie Dreamhouse. "I completely forgot about them."

An irritated growl rolled out of my throat. "Go get me some, now."

Ethan folded his arms over his chest. "How about you go get them yourself?"

Why not? Uh, I knew why. Leaning forward, I braced my hands on the counter and leveled the same taunting look at my brother. "I'm grounded." Smart ass.

Ethan grimaced, grasping my dilemma. "Right."

"Hey," Susan spoke up, making us both turn toward her. "I can go get them." She gripped the edge of the counter and slid forward, moving to hop down. But I didn't let her.

Placing one gentle but firm hand on her knee, I kept her where she was. "Ethan can go. *You* stay right where you are." No way would she leave this room now. I made that clear with a fiery look into her eyes. She swallowed, totally understanding my intentions.

"Be right back," Ethan's voice drifted to us as he left the kitchen. Good. The corners of my mouth tilted up as the slamming front door announced he was gone.

I was alone with Sue. Finally.

Chapter 15

SUSAN MILLER'S NERVOUSNESS was charging my kitchen to a point where touching metal might be dangerous.

To give her a chance to adjust to the new unchaperoned situation, I turned off the radio and tried to be very *un*intimidating. But heck, was that even possible when I was practically sweating excitement? Yeah, better shut up too, or something stupid might pass my lips to make her go all defensive again.

Half expecting to get zapped as I passed her to fetch a bowl from the cupboard, I gave Sue a quick glance. With wary eyes, she watched my every step as I went to melt the dark chocolate with some butter.

As the chocolate heated, I stirred it with a whisk and tested the slowly melting mass with my finger. It couldn't get too hot or it would taste bitter later. From the corner of my eye, I could see how Sue sat rigid where I'd put her on the counter, thighs pressed together, hands still nervously clasped in her lap. Not relaxed yet. Oh dear.

What in the world could I do to make her feel comfortable with me? If we kissed now, chances were that she'd bite off my tongue by accident. A shudder raked through me. Not the best way to get intimate.

I didn't want her all keyed up and sweating because of me. It stressed me out, too. Maybe that was the reason I burnt my finger when I dipped it into the bowl again. The chocolate sauce had gotten too hot too fast. I jerked my hand back, swallowing a pained yowl, and a dark drop of chocolate landed on my white t-shirt.

"Damn." Pulling my tee away from my chest, I tried to wipe the stain off with my thumb, but that only made the smear worse. *Terrific.* I turned off the burner and put the sauce aside, then I shrugged out of my gray shirt and pulled the stained tee over my head. Sue watched me like she actually wanted to lick her lips—badly. Yep, she totally loved what she saw. As I tossed the tee across the room, where it landed with perfect aim on the backrest of a chair, I couldn't stop myself from smirking at her. Her throat twitched hard as she swallowed.

To give her a moment to cool down again—and myself too—I turned away, buttoned up my dark gray shirt, leaving the top buttons open, and went on to season the chocolate sauce with rum and grated orange peels. A nice smell of citrusy, warm chocolate enveloped us, making my alone time with little Sue all the sweeter.

While chopping some orange wedges, an idea took shape.

It was risky, oh yeah, but that wouldn't stop me. I tested the temperature of the molten chocolate. It had to be warm, but not too hot for what I had in mind. Sue shouldn't burn her mouth on it.

All this time, she hadn't spoken a single word. The only sound in the room was the knife hitting the board as I sliced through a banana and the whisk brushing the stainless steel side of the bowl when I stirred.

Eventually, the chocolate had cooled down enough for my plan. From the fridge, I got a plate of strawberries and set it on the counter beside Sue, playing my part with nonchalance. "Close your eyes and open your mouth."

Surprisingly, Sue followed my order. I wouldn't have thought it would be that easy. But of course, it *wasn't* that easy. The next moment, one of her eyes shot open again and she looked at me sharply. "You're not going to stick your finger in my mouth, are you?"

A laugh escaped me. To use her own word, "Now that would be a little *gross*, right?"

Expelling a relieved breath, she closed that eye again, only to open both half a second later. "And you're not going to kiss me, either?"

Cutting her a quick sideways look, I kept stirring the chocolate sauce next to her. "I wasn't thinking about it." Okay, total lie, but what the hell. I teased her with a smirk. "But now I'm wondering why you were."

"You better play nice, if you want me to stay through dinner," she warned me with an almost-growl.

ANNA KATMORE

"I always play nice, little Sue." Not *fair*, maybe, but nice for sure. "Now close your eyes."

This time, she obeyed.

I put the eggbeater away, tilted my head, and just looked at the girl in my kitchen for an endless moment. Did she even know how beautiful she was? How much her bare neck tempted me to stroke my fingertips gently down her skin each time she had her hair in that sassy ponytail? The lashes of her closed eyes rested calmly on her cheekbones, but her almost erratic breathing gave away how nervous she still was.

Pulling myself together, I resisted the urge to brush my knuckles down her cheek and instead moved a little closer, so our legs touched through our jeans. "Open your mouth," I said again, softly.

She did, but only so much that a tiny blackberry would fit through her parted lips. We were dealing with oranges and strawberries here, so she would have to open up a little more. With an amused smile, I asked her, "You don't trust me?"

Her lips parted a bit wider. Good girl. I picked up an orange wedge, bit off one half, and dunked the other into the warm chocolate. When it had stopped dripping, I carefully placed it in Susan's mouth.

With her teeth, she pulled the half wedge out of my fingers and ate it. A pleasurable moan escaped her.

Captivated by that sound, I swallowed with a dry throat. "Good?"

Eyes still closed, she frowned and gripped the edge of the counter, finally loosening up. "Jeez! This is *awesome!*"

Happy about our small progress, I chuckled. "Next one."

When she opened her mouth for me again, I put a chocolate-coated strawberry right on her tongue. Slowly...

Sue closed her lips around my fingers. At that instant, I could see and also feel how she stiffened next to me. It didn't stop me from dragging my thumb across her bottom lip to wipe a small drop of chocolate away. I licked it off my finger.

She'd practically been panting since the moment my brother had left us alone, but now her breaths almost came to a standstill. Yet she was a good girl and kept her eyes closed.

"Susan?" I whispered.

Sucking her bottom lip between her teeth, she croaked, "Hm?"

I leaned closer and drew in the mellow scent of the coconut lotion coating her skin. She smelled illegally good. Intoxicated, I gently nuzzled the spot behind her ear with the tip of my nose. "What's the temperature in hell right now?"

Sue's eyes shot wide open. Staring at me in total astonishment, she couldn't find the breath to give me an answer. I didn't care. Her silence was answer enough, and it was the perfect moment. I stroked my fingers over her cheek, tilting her face a little more toward me.

For an instant, her eyes screamed, "Oh my God!" but a second later, they lazily closed.

I brushed my lips over the corner of her mouth and then breathed, "Are we getting close to freezing point?"

Again, she didn't answer, but turned her head even more to me. That was all I needed to know. Pleasant waves of excitement rolled through me. Shaping my palm to her cheek, I placed the first real kiss on her mouth.

Ah, God, finally. I'd never waited this long for a kiss. And Susan was ready for it, too. She let me in and, from the way she met the play of my tongue with her own, she enjoyed every moment of the kiss as much as I wanted her to.

With my hands softly splayed on her cheeks, I tilted her face a little farther up as I stepped in front of her. Sue opened her knees for me to stand between her thighs. Her hands moved to my chest, shyly flattening against it. They were trembling ever so slightly. She dug her fingers into my shirt to stop them from shaking.

Enjoying every warm breath of hers on my face, I explored her mouth with a lazy slowness that allowed me to stroke her tongue into total surrender. She tasted of chocolate and strawberries—my favorite.

Dying of hunger for her, I lowered my hands to her waist and pulled her closer to the edge of the counter so her front was flush to mine. Her fingers crawled up my chest, over my shoulders, and to the back of my neck. Heck, they felt cold there. A chill ran down my spine.

Nibbling a trail along her jaw to her ear, I teased her, "Hey there, Frosty."

She immediately pulled her hands away. That was not what I wanted, so I caught them and put her arms back where they felt best—around my neck. Her cool fingers weren't uncomfortable on my skin. They were thrilling.

My hands braced on the counter on either side of her hips,

I began kissing down the side of her tender neck. Small, gentle kisses that would remind her of the hickey after our soccer match a few days ago. Susan breathed a dreamy sigh.

In response, a heated moan escaped me, and I returned my attention to her sensual mouth and nibbled on her bottom lip with gentle demand. Her forehead dipped against mine. Sue was totally relaxed now. I kissed her harder, deeper, pulled her tighter against me, and then—

A fucking car stopped in front of the house, and someone slammed the door shut.

Ethan. *Hell, no!*

Go away, I silently prayed, letting out a growl as I inched back from Sue. I wanted to keep making out with her. But with her reluctance to surrender to me the past couple of weeks, it was probably best not to nail the fact that we'd finally kissed on a billboard for all to see. I wanted to leave it up to her to decide when it was time to come out with the truth. Even to my brother.

I skimmed a few stray wisps of hair out of her forehead and then nudged the tip of her nose with my finger. Looking into her flushed face and warm eyes made me smile. "Now...that wasn't so bad, was it?"

A slow grin tugged at the corners of her mouth as she shook her head.

Happy with the new direction this afternoon had taken, I stepped away from her and stirred the molten chocolate. Ethan entered the kitchen seconds later.

"Hey, guys," he called out. "Here are the kiwis." He threw

me the fruits one by one, and while he went to check on the steaks in the oven, I sneaked a final glance at Sue. Her intense gaze was on me, so I winked at her and gave her a crooked smile. Shy again, she looked quickly away.

I was still busy laying the fruit out on the cake as Ethan prepared three plates with his meal. Susan hopped off the counter and helped him.

"God, Ethan, this is delicious," she complimented him later as we all sat around the table, eating steaks with veggies and pepper cream sauce. She was right; my brother had outdone himself today. That meal would be hard to top, but hopefully Sue would still like my cake.

I checked on it after I'd carried our plates to the sink, but the cream wasn't yet cold enough. "It could do with another twenty minutes," I told them from behind the refrigerator door.

"Maybe we should clean up the kitchen before dessert," Sue suggested.

"Good idea." I closed the fridge and smirked at the two of them. "Ethan can do it."

Obviously irritated, my brother leaned back in his chair and crossed his arms defensively over his chest. "Why me?"

"Because you forgot the kiwis today."

His brows dipped into a frown. "Well, I actually drove to the store again and got them. You clean up here."

Damn. I wanted more alone time with Sue, and having Ethan clean the kitchen would have given me that time. I stared Ethan down, but he wouldn't cave. When had he become such an annoying brother? There was nothing he would get out of the situation if I had to do the dishes—apart from more time to play Wii. *Screw him!*

Since all this hard staring was an obvious impasse, there was only one possible solution. He must have come to the same conclusion, because we said at once, "Let's play it out."

With Susan in tow, we stalked to the back door and out into the yard. Ethan fetched the basketball from the shed and brought it to the small paved square that was our court. There was only one hoop fixed on an iron bar that my father had cemented into place for us when we were little. Ethan gave Sue the ball and asked her to throw it in the air.

When she did, we both jumped for it. I grabbed it first and started running for the basket, bouncing the ball along with me. Ethan tried to cut in, but he had no chance. Smoothly, the ball slid through the hoop. "Two—zero," I hollered and tossed the ball to Ethan. Round two...

Though I'd have much rather spent the time kissing Susan in my room, I did enjoy the game with Ethan. Basketball was the only thing in the world that could turn off my mind completely. When I played, there was only the ball, the opponent, and me. I loved it. But the incentive of winning some more alone time with Sue made me give my all to the game.

From the corner of my eye, I noticed her returning to the house. Tired of watching us? No one could blame her for finding one-on-one basketball boring.

"Twenty-two to twenty," Ethan finally grumbled almost half an hour later. It was a tight victory, but it didn't matter. I won, and while my brother could do the dishes now, I'd get pretty little Sue all to myself again.

Wiping the sweat off my forehead with the hem of my shirt, I walked back inside and left the ball for Ethan to put away.

As I came back to the kitchen, I stopped dead in the doorway, my heart thumping in my throat all of a sudden. Sue stood by the table, holding my stained t-shirt to her face. She didn't notice me but, holy damn, she was sniffing my tee! Like she really loved my scent or something. She heaved a dreamy sigh, as if she might be auditioning for a romantic chick flick.

For a tiny moment, I wondered if I should sneak out again and give her another private moment with my shirt. But heck, the scene in front of me held me captive. I couldn't bring myself to leave.

Touched by such secret devotion, I leaned against the doorjamb and finally coughed to get her attention.

Sue jerked around to me. Her hands dropped immediately, and her eyes shot open wide. I teased her with a half-smile. "Would it make you feel better if I pretend I didn't see that?"

She stared at me in utter horror.

"Hey now, don't look so bashful," I told her in a soft voice as I slowly walked toward her. "It was just a matter of time until you fell for my irresistible charm." Pointing at my t-shirt in her hands, I added jokingly, "And scent."

Warily, she backed away until she knocked into the island behind her and came to a dead stop. That particular place in my kitchen evoked nice memories. I followed her at a slow prowl and told her, "I won. Ethan has to do the dishes." As I stood in front of her, I took my t-shirt out of her trembling hands and tossed it aside. One look over her shoulder, and I knew Ethan wouldn't find much to busy himself with in here. "I see you already did his job. Nice." I shrugged and locked gazes with her once more. "So we can go straight to dessert..."

My hands on her hips, I laced my fingers through the belt loops of her jeans and carefully pulled her against me. For balance, she gripped my upper arms, sending another shiver from her cold fingers through my body. I cracked a smile. "We have about twenty seconds for us."

As our brows touched, me leaning my head down, she lowered her gaze. Oh, her sigh was the sweetest surrender. I breathed a kiss against her lips...and heard the back door slamming shut. Ethan.

"Make that five," I corrected myself with a frustrated growl. But I wouldn't just sit back and watch my dear brother ruin one good moment after another for me. Five seconds were better than nothing. Trying to tame my hunger for this girl, I pressed a quick, hard kiss on her mouth. Then I let her go and went to check on the cake in the fridge.

At Sue's high-pitched "hi!" my attention snapped back to her.

"Hi," Ethan replied, looking as surprised by her nervousness as I was. "Everything okay?"

Susan fumbled with her fingers. "Yeah! Sure! Why?" Still too loud and much too squeaky. A moment later, she dashed from the room. What was the matter with her?

ANNA KATMORE

Ethan cast me a worried look. I returned it with a puzzled shrug and decided not to tell him that Sue's awkward behavior might have to do with us kissing just moments ago. I couldn't be sure anyway.

"On the plus side," I said to Ethan, picking up our wordless conversation, "she did the dishes for you."

He shot a glance at the sink. "Ah. Awesome." Next he came around the island unit and switched on the coffee machine. Putting the first of three cups under it, he shot me a sideways glance. "Maybe she broke a glass or something and feels uncomfortable now."

"Mmmmaybe..." Or maybe not. I rubbed my neck and turned away from him. The room was thick with secrets, and I refused to be the one to clear them. As I cut the cake into square pieces and Ethan prepared cappuccino for the three of us, Susan returned from wherever she'd left to in a hurry before. The bathroom was a good guess.

As if, for some reason, she was no longer invited to sit with us, she froze on the threshold and just watched with wary eyes as my brother and I set the table. *What the hell, girl? Don't be silly!* I put the two plates I was carrying down on the table and went to her.

Wordlessly dragging her along with me, I made her sit in the chair that had been hers since the first time she ate with us and assured her with a small smile that everything was okay. No need to freak out now that we'd reached the next level of whatever was between us.

Earlier, I'd prepared a special piece of cake for her. One

that sported a heart-shaped, chocolate-dipped strawberry surrounded by kiwi slices. I got it from the counter and put it in front of her, then sat down too. Sue cast me a scrutinizing look from under her lashes. Yep, cake art was my way of telling her how I felt about us. If I couldn't kiss her in front of Ethan yet, I could at least make her eat my declaration of love.

"Thanks for doing the dishes, by the way," Ethan told her sometime through dessert. He put a forkful of cake in his mouth and added while chewing, "You know you didn't have to do that."

"Of course." Sue swallowed the bite she'd just taken. "But between watching two hunky guys playing basketball or doing dishes..." A laugh escaped her. "Well, I guess I'm just weird."

My brother joined in her laugh. "Only a little. I'll drive you home for it later."

"No," I protested, shoving the last bite of my cake into my mouth. "I can drive her home." No way would he trample on another perfect occasion for me to be alone with Sue.

Ethan licked his fork clean, grinning stupidly at me. "No, you can't."

Bet your ass on it, bro. "Sure can."

"Nope."

I threw him an annoyed look. "Why not?"

"You're grounded."

Dammit. I hated the grin on my brother's face. And Mom would be home soon. Ethan was right, I couldn't go. "Ah, fu— sh—" Hell, I shouldn't cuss in front of Sue. "*Craaap.*"

My fishing for a decent word coaxed another laugh from

ANNA KATMORE

Sue as she got up and carried her plate and empty cup to the sink. "Well, thanks," she told me over her shoulder. Her sexy look fired me all up. "That was a very...*interesting* and delicious dessert."

I agreed with a nod and got to my feet, not caring about the rest of the dishes on the table. When she came back and passed me as she headed for the door, I covertly stroked her hand with the back of mine. "Good night, sweetness," I whispered so low that only she would hear it.

Chapter 16

MOM SAT IN the kitchen and ate the warmed-up food we'd saved her from our dinner. While waiting for Ethan to come home so I could finally start an undisturbed chat with Sue on the phone, I joined her at the table to kill time with another piece of cake and a cup of coffee.

"Hey, sweetie," Mom said, scooping up veggies with her fork. "How was the afternoon with Susan?"

She didn't say *my* afternoon with Sue, she said *the* afternoon. Keeping it general meant she still hoped it was *Ethan's* afternoon with her. Terrific. I sipped the cappuccino and licked the foam off my lip. "It was nice."

"Just nice?" She smiled in a very demanding, very conspiratorial way. "Did Susan like Ethan's meal?"

"Umm...I guess." I lowered my gaze together with my voice. "And she liked my cake, too."

Mom cut another piece from her steak and chewed it with way too much enthusiasm. "Are they out together now?"

"Yeahhh...no. Or *maybe.*" Heck, where were they? Ethan had said he'd drive her home, not stay with her for two and a half hours. "He was just going to give her a ride. I don't know what's keeping him so long."

"Good." She grinned at her plate, dragging the word out unnecessarily.

Dammit, had she even heard what I said? I spun my cup on the saucer. Ethan was supposed to be home already. Mom should be worrying where he was, not happy that he was out with my girl. To cut off her delight, I muttered, "I don't think the two of them would make such a great couple."

"Oh," she said around a mouthful of green beans. "Why would you say that?"

As the weight of dejection grew heavier in my chest, I looked up and stared into her hopeful eyes for a few seconds, then sniffed defiantly, "Because I kissed Sue today. And she kissed me back. I intend to do it again. Is that okay with you?"

My mother's jaw dropped, giving me an exclusive view of chewed-up green stuff.

Since I was well on the way to destroying her wonderful evening anyway, I added, "Oh, and Mom—I think Ethan's gay. You know you can do nothing to change that, not even if you push the girl *I* like upon him at every given moment." Eyes narrowed, I let go of the coffee cup and rose from the chair. On the way out of the kitchen, I told her without looking back, "There's a piece of cake for you in the fridge."

Now didn't that go well...

Crabbier than I'd already been the past hour, I trudged to

the living room, belly-flopped on the couch, and turned on the TV. Whatever was on didn't hold my interest, so I started zapping through the channels. It was nine thirty—my special time with little Sue. Where the hell was Ethan?

It took Mom about fifteen minutes to stomach the shock, but when she finally came into the living room, her look was one of pure guilt. She stopped in the doorway, and we locked gazes for several long seconds.

As she started walking toward me, I bent my legs to make room for her on the couch. She sat down and gently rubbed my shin, ignoring the ending of *Up* on TV. "I'm sorry, darling," she told me in a low, pleading voice. "I had no idea."

She must have meant she'd been clueless about Sue and me, because the thing about Ethan wasn't a big secret between us. It was something she didn't like to talk about, all right, but definitely not something she hadn't thought about a lot this past year.

"It's okay, Mom," I replied flatly.

"No, it's not." She pulled both my legs onto her lap and held my ankles in a warm grip—something she used to do when I was younger, upset, and didn't want to talk about things. Somehow, that has always been her way of connecting with me and making me talk. "I'm really sorry, Chris. Of course it's okay if you and Susan have feelings for each other. I never meant to... I didn't know... Ah, it's just..." She sighed.

Taking a deep breath myself, I shifted to my back, leaving my legs where they were, and searched her face. "Mom, I like her. Really. And Ethan doesn't. At least not in that kind of way. I checked with him."

"I know." Another sigh pushed out of her chest as she tipped her head back to stare at the ceiling. "Well, I *guessed* he wasn't in love with her from the way he..."

"Treated her like a friend?" I supplied when she couldn't find the right words.

Head tilted toward me, she nodded and blinked slowly. "Yeah, that."

"So...since you already sort of adopted Susan anyway," I said with a small pout, "can I keep her?"

Mom laughed. "Of course you can."

I held her gaze with a stern look of mine. "And could you try to be happy for me, too?"

Her laugh died, and a stricken expression washed over her face. Gently, she put my feet away, rose from the couch, and stepped toward me. Closing my eyes as she leaned down and her hair fell on my face, I turned my head to the side so her loving mother-kiss would hit me on the cheekbone and not the nose. "I *am* happy for you, baby. Very much, in fact." She ruffled my hair and then stroked my cheek. "Susan is a nice girl, and you deserve someone like her."

I agreed with that. But it meant a lot to me that she was finally on my side. "Thanks, Mom."

She straightened, giving a tiny nod, and wrapped her black cardigan tighter around herself. "I'm tired. I think I'll go to bed now."

"Okay. I'll stay here and wait for Ethan." It could only be minutes until he came home. Right?

"Good night, sweetie."

"Night, Mom."

She walked out and turned off the lights as she passed the switch by the door.

Heaving a sigh, I rolled to my side again and stared at the TV. The flickering light from the screen was my only company for the next hour. But between my mulling over Sue and why Ethan hadn't returned yet, not much of the movie registered.

At some point, I must have snoozed, because when I heard the sound of a door clicking closed and blearily lifted my head, the room was dark and drool dripped from the corner of my mouth. I wiped it away with the back of my hand, groaning. The sleep timer had turned off the TV. Fine with me.

Barely able to fully open my eyes, I glanced at my watch, which had glow-in-the-dark numbers. It was two in the morning. *What the heck?* Had Ethan been out until now?

I couldn't be bothered to get up and walk to my room, much less follow Ethan into his and make him talk. Not in the dead of night. My cheek sinking back onto the cushion, I closed my eyes and saved grilling him—and texting Sue—for the morning.

*

Next time I woke, it was because my neck hurt like hell and my arm had gone cold and stiff when it dropped off the couch. I rubbed my eyes and groaned when I saw what time it was. Not even six o'clock. If I hurried to my bed now, I might catch a few Zs before the day really started.

Swinging my legs off the couch, I scrambled to my feet. As I shuffled to the door, a sound made me freeze on the spot. It wasn't so much a sound as a voice, actually. *Sue's* voice. And from what I could tell, she'd just come out of my *brother's* bedroom. *What in the hell—*

"Not my family," Ethan whispered to her as they tiptoed past the living room, completely unaware of me. "You just don't want Chris to find out."

"I don't want him to ask stupid questions," she shot back in a whiny hiss. "This is really something I'd like to keep between you and me."

Stupid questions? My heart gave out, my mind did, too, my breathing stopped, and I wanted to die right then. Ethan had banged my girl. The girl I worked so hard to win and who he claimed to have no interest in. The girl that had made me fall in love with her in just two weeks.

My brother had slept with that very girl, and he didn't even waste a thought on how he would break my heart in doing so. And neither did Sue.

Raking my hands through my hair, I turned on the spot, feeling so helpless it hurt. What was I supposed to do now? Be quiet? Walk out there and talk to them? Bang my head against the wall until all thoughts of wanting Susan Miller were crushed? The truth was, I didn't know.

Ethan's sigh drifted around the corner. "Fine. I won't say a word about it."

Even lower than before, Susan thanked him for that. When

a traitorous silence followed, I had to step up to the door and sneak a glance into the hallway. My brother was holding my girl in a really tight embrace. Her face was buried in his shoulder, and his face was pressing against her hair. Neither of them noticed that I was standing merely a few feet away.

When Ethan let her go, I slid back into the living room, out of sight. With my throat tightening like I was stuck in a noose, it wasn't a good idea to confront them now. Chances were I'd break my brother's face.

The front door opened and closed moments later. With my back against the wall, I sank to the floor and hugged my legs to my chest. I dipped my forehead toward my knees. Furious and trying not to cry out at the sense of betrayal flooding me, I bit my tongue so hard I tasted blood in my mouth.

*

Spending Sunday in bed was the only thing that kept me from running amok. Ethan's treachery stung so hard, I didn't want to leave my room and risk seeing him. Mom called me to breakfast, she called me to lunch, and she sent Ethan to call me to dinner. I refused to open my door for either of them.

"Sweetie," my mother said outside my room, gently knocking after seven o'clock in the evening. "Won't you come out and eat something? You must be hungry."

"I'm not. Leave me alone."

"Chris, please. If it's because of how I—"

"It's not you, Mom."

She sighed so loudly, the sound penetrated the door. "Okay," she said then, defeated, and walked away.

I, on the other hand, kept doing what I'd done the entire day. Lying in bed, still wearing yesterday's clothes, I stared at a message from Sue. *Good morning. Are you still asleep?* She'd sent it two hours after I saw her coming out of Ethan's room.

Each time the display light of my phone diminished and the screen turned to black, I swiped my thumb across it and scowled at the words for another ninety seconds. I hadn't replied. And I wasn't going to. Her betrayal had been ingrained too deep for me to want to talk to her. I really didn't need to hear all the ugly details.

When Ethan passed me in the hallway the next morning and offered me a ride to school, I cut him a scornful look and walked away without a single word. I showered, brushed my teeth, drank my coffee black and thick, and asked Mom for her car.

On my way to history, I ran into Justin Andrews. He was limping, which was usually a sure sign that something about his suicidal hobby—extreme BMX—had gone wrong over the weekend.

"You have an accident?" I asked, nodding at his left leg.

"Yeah, sort of. A stray cat ignored a yield sign and I took a flight."

"Ouch..." I grimaced. "Did you have a doctor look at it?"

"Nope. It's not that bad. Just bruised. I'm going biking again later today." His gaze wandered away from my face to somewhere behind me. He smiled and lifted a hand to greet somebody there.

Turning around was a reflex. But when I met Sue's eyes across the hall, all air was sucked out of my lungs. She stood rooted to the spot, her smile waning as I frowned at her. Was she going to come over? Was she going to say something? Did she expect *me* to start a conversation?

Right. She could wait for that until the cows came home. I turned back to Justin, ignoring what was happening behind me.

"Wow. What a warm greeting," he said, narrowing his eyes in confusion. "Something up with you and her?"

I cleared my throat. "No. Why?"

"Well, wasn't she the girl you wanted to seduce?"

My backpack slipped from my shoulder. "You know about that, too?"

"'Course. Thought I wouldn't?"

At this point, I actually doubted that anybody *didn't* know about the stupid challenge between Sue and me. With a sinking heart, I adjusted my backpack and told him, "It doesn't matter. In fact, the challenge is over."

"Seriously?" As I headed down the hallway to my class, he walked with me. From what I knew, he had math two doors down. "What happened?"

"Nothing. She's just not interested."

Justin threw me a sideways glance. "And you couldn't convince her to be?"

That cost me a chuckle. "Obviously."

"So that's it? You gave up?"

"Yep." In front of my history classroom, we stopped and I pivoted to him. "Got a problem with that?"

Slowly, he shook his head, but his eyes gleamed with humor. "Not at all. But you'll make some people lose a lot of money."

"Of course..." I grinned. "You bet on me, too?"

"Nope. Against you. Twenty that you wouldn't land her this year."

I burst out laughing. "You suck, Andrews!"

"Maybe." He shrugged and chuckled. "But I got to know Susan quite a bit from hanging out with Hunter and the guys. She's pretty decent. From what I can tell, she wouldn't stoop to throw away her principles for a meaningless winter fling."

"Meaningless, huh?" Lips pressed together, I expelled a sigh through my nose. Maybe he was right. After all, the kiss couldn't have meant much to Sue if she couldn't wait even a day to jump my brother.

My silence obviously made Justin suspicious. "You okay, man?"

Dragging my gaze away from the floor, I looked him straight in the eye and swallowed the lump in my throat. "Sure. See you in gym." Heading into class, I felt his gaze follow me for a couple of seconds before he disappeared from the doorway.

Great. If this was the kind of conversations that awaited me today, it was going to be a long morning. The only light at the end of tunnel was the fat B plus scribbled with a red pen on my Spanish test, which Mrs. Sanchez returned in fourth period. I would have proudly shown it to Lauren. Only, she wasn't there. Her seat was empty, and I hadn't seen her this morning, either. For some strange reason, she was the only person I really wanted to talk to today. Perhaps because she was a girl...or because she would be one of the very few people who hadn't bet money *on* or *against* me in this goddamned challenge.

Rebecca informed me at lunch that Lauren had the flu and would probably be out of school all week. "But I'll tell her you asked about her. She'd like to hear that."

"Yeah, sure...go ahead," I agreed absently, my gaze fixed on the soccer table, where Susan joked around with my brother.

"And when she's feeling better, you can tell her how much you missed her and how deeply in love with her you are."

"Mm-hm," I answered, not really paying attention. Ethan was having pizza for lunch today, and he held the piece out for Susan to take a fricking bite. When she did, he pulled it away quickly, so she bit into the air. Laughing, she smacked him on the shoulder.

"Can I borrow your phone for a moment?" Becky asked next to me, and someone snickered along with her. "I'd like to send Lauren a text asking her if she wants to be your girlfriend."

"It's in my backpack, side pocket." The giggles got louder around me, but I had no time to see what was amusing them so much. Instead, I narrowed my eyes, focusing on Susan's mouth. Maybe I could figure out what she was saying to Ethan

ANNA KATMORE

by lip-reading.

A smirking Becky popped up right in front of me, startling me out of my observations. "Jesus Christ!" I blurted out.

Hands braced on the table, Becks leaned forward until her face was in mine. "Chris, are you listening?"

I frowned at her. "Yes." Man, what was her problem? "You said she's ill. Fine. I'll call her later and ask her how she's feeling. Now sit down, for Chrissake."

T-Rex burst out laughing behind his girlfriend at that moment, and Brady smacked his hand on the table, shedding tears. Trevor was just rolling on the floor.

"What the hell—"

"Dude," Tyler shouted between eruptions of glee, holding his stomach. "You're hopeless."

I got it, the joke was on me. Only, I had no flipping idea what was going on. Nor did I care. "*God...*" I rolled my eyes at them all. "Grow up, guys." Abandoning my soccer-table observations for today, I started to eat my burger. Whatever Susan and Ethan did during lunch, watching them wasn't worth becoming a running gag to my friends.

Later that afternoon, as I drove to school again for basketball practice, I remembered what Becky had said. Lauren was sick. A good friend would call her and ask how she felt. I retrieved my cell from the console. But a better friend would drive by and check on her personally. Tossing the phone on the passenger seat, I took a right turn at Grover Beach High, zooming past the parking lot, taking the highway out of town.

In front of her house, after parking at the curb, I finally

dialed her number.

"Chris?" Surprise rang in her watery voice, and she snuffled as she answered.

"Yep. Becks told me you're ill. Are you home?"

She hesitated a couple of seconds, then huffed, "I have a fever and, in case you didn't hear it, the sniffles. Where do *you* think I am?"

I rolled my eyes at her cynicism. "Okay, Miss Grumpypants, then come and get the door."

"*What?*" she screeched.

Climbing out of the car, I slammed the door shut and walked up the front steps to her house. "Come to the door and let me in," I repeated slowly.

"What—*now*?"

"Yes."

"No!"

"Why not?"

"Because...because..." Some rustling was going on in the room she was in. What the hell was she doing?

"Because why, Lauren?"

"Well, because I'm in bed." A clicking sound like someone drawing the curtains drifted through the line. "Oh my God, you're really here!"

Had she checked for my car in front of the house? Because she wouldn't be able to see me standing outside the door from the window in her room. But she would hear the doorbell ring. "Come on, Parker. Open the door. I've seen you in bed before. No big deal."

"I wasn't sick when you saw me in bed. Now go away. Please."

What? I laughed and rang the doorbell again. "No way. I'll keep ringing until you open up. I can do this for hours, so get your sick ass out of bed and—"

The door cracked open. Almost like in a haunted house, nobody invited me in. There was only the dark gap waiting for me. I tucked the phone into my pocket and pushed the door open. Leaning around it, I glimpsed Lauren flitting back to her room at the end of the hallway. Were those flannel pajamas she was wearing?

I shut the front door and followed her, knocking on her door before I entered, even though she'd left it open for me. Sitting on her bed, wrapped in her comforter, Lauren eyed me warily. Her messy hair was raked to the top of her head and fastened with a clip. And yep, those PJs were flannel. Dark green, with tiny dinosaurs all over them. I bit down a smirk. "Sexy, Parker."

"I said I'm ill, idiot."

Ah, charming, that little virus vessel.

"Why did you come?" she growled. "Didn't you say you were grounded?"

A thick smell of cough syrup hung in the air, and all kinds of meds were piled up on her nightstand. Ugh, better take caution while in this room. I pulled the collar of my sweatshirt up to cover my mouth and nose, so as not to breathe in the airborne germs, and took a seat on her desk chair, wheeling as far away from her bed as possible. "Officially, I'm playing basketball right now."

Her glassy eyes grew wide. "You ditched practice?" I nodded. "To come here?"

"Mm-hm."

"For God's sake, *why*?"

Folding my arms over my chest, I held her hard gaze. "Because you're my friend, and friends do that when someone's ill."

"I get that." Lauren tilted her head. "And now tell me why you really came."

Lowering my gaze to the parquet floor, I expelled a long breath. "Well, first, I wanted to apologize for..." For blowing her off the other day? No, too direct. I cleared my throat. "For being a little distant lately."

"Distant?"

Carefully, I looked up at her face. "Well, unavailable."

"Unavailable..."

"Would you stop repeating everything I say, for heaven's sake?"

Lips sealed, Lauren gaped at me.

"So, what I'm trying to say is, I really liked our arrangement, but something has come up."

"Some*one*," she corrected with a reproachful edge to her voice.

"Yes...some*one*." I inhaled deeply, but then I remembered the viruses in the room and decided it would be best to just adopt a shallow breathing technique, even through my improvised sweatshirt-surgical mask. "Her name's Sue."

ANNA KATMORE

Lauren sniffed. Her gaze escaped to somewhere outside the window. "I know."

Of course she did. And she knew all about the challenge, too. Now I just couldn't stop myself from asking the question that had been bugging me all day. "Did you bet money on me?"

Startled, she glanced back at me. "What? No."

I hesitated a beat and then asked, "Did you bet money *against* me?"

"*No!*" Her eyebrows furrowed to a line. "Stop being stupid."

"It's just, a lot of people—"

"I know that, from Becky and the others," she cut me short, her voice turning more nasally than before, like her nose was filling up pretty quickly. "But you should know me well enough, Chris. I wouldn't do that."

I gave a small, appreciative nod.

From the box on her nightstand, she pulled a tissue and blew her nose. Wow, quite the trumpet.

After she tossed the used tissue in the trash can next to the bed, she wrapped the blanket tighter around her again. "So, how's the challenge going for you?" she asked, but she didn't look like she was really interested in the answer. In fact, with her lips pressed tight and her gaze focused on my crossed ankles instead of my face, she looked like she'd rather avoid the entire topic.

"It's over."

That made her look up. "You got what you wanted?"

Staring at her for a long time, I wondered what the right answer to this question was. In the end, there was only one thing to say honestly. "No." Sue wasn't my girlfriend; I hadn't gotten what I wanted. But that wouldn't come past my lips. Instead, I shrugged it off. "She's just not interested."

Scrutinizing me with her glazed dark eyes, Lauren cocked her head. "But our tutoring arrangement is still off." It was a statement, not a question.

"Well, there are no Spanish tests for a while," I mumbled, swaying back and forth in the swivel chair.

Lauren's gaze sharpened. "That's not what I meant."

Avoiding her stare, I confirmed, "Yes, the arrangement's off." I couldn't see myself with another girl at the moment, no matter if Sue was with my brother now or not. For me, it was either her or no one. Dammit, what had this girl done to me in the past couple of weeks?

Rubbing the back of my neck, I threw Lauren a wary look. "Are you angry?"

She hesitated a long moment. Then she gave me a small smile and slowly shook her head. "No. But I'm glad you finally had the guts to end it." Her smile grew a fraction wider. "It means I can accept Wesley's hundredth invitation to a date now."

Scandalized, I grabbed the collar of my sweatshirt and pulled it down, straightening in the chair. "The guy with the elephant ears?"

Her cheeks flushed a little as she nodded. "He's cute, and he's been asking me for a date since the beginning of the semester."

"Really? Then why didn't you go out with him?"

A soft, bashful laugh escaped her. "You're an idiot, you wouldn't understand."

I couldn't deny the idiot part, but I had a feeling her reasons had a lot to do with me. That was bullshit, though. "We never said we wouldn't see other people."

"No, we didn't," she confirmed.

My voice lowered. "But you weren't seeing anyone else, were you?"

"No...I wasn't."

And I was a dipshit. Dragging my hands down my face, I sucked in a deep breath and let it out slowly. "I'm sorry."

"Apology accepted." She smiled again, but then her face scrunched up and she sneezed. Three times in a row. During the last sneeze, half of her hair got loose and spilled down one side of her face, the black strands matted and stringy.

Lauren must have noticed my quiet inspection, because she looked away from me, embarrassed, while she wiped her nose again. "It's not washed. I told you I didn't want to see you."

What a stupid reason. "Parker, I've seen you at your best. It doesn't change anything to see you at your worst." Then a smirk escaped me, and I cast her a teasing frown. "But maybe you should keep Wes away from this place until you feel better."

She bit down a grin. The next instant, though, she tipped to the side and leaned against the wall, grimacing like a headache or something was coming on. That was my cue. "I've been keeping you up long enough. Get some rest."

Lauren nodded, looking wan, and said in a nasally voice, "See you at school next week."

Rising from the chair, I pushed it back into its place and headed for the door. Before I left, I turned around once more. "Did Wesley ever hear you blow your nose?"

She made a puzzled face. "No...?"

"Good. Don't let him," I teased her with a wink.

She stuck her tongue out at me, and when she grabbed the tissue box from her nightstand and aimed, I quickly closed the door.

After the visit and good conversation with Lauren, I felt a little happier than I had all day. Since basketball practice was over by now, I had no excuse to stay out any longer, and drove straight home. I parked in front of the house, tossed Mom the keys as I walked inside, and headed for my room. In the hallway, I ran into Ethan. He smiled at me and said, "Hey."

And all the happiness evaporated.

Chapter 17

I AVOIDED MY brother as much as possible the entire week. Every time I saw him anywhere in the house, the urge to physically hurt him—like really, *really* hurt him—was hard to resist. It was far too soon to talk to him.

Every morning, he asked me if I wanted a ride to school, and each time I told him, "Fuck off." One would think he was clever enough to get the hint at some point, but he was as persistent as a bee buzzing around a honey pot.

Wednesday evening, I was watching some crap on TV in the living room. And by crap, I mean the nerd show that I had somehow gotten addicted to. It was close to nine when Ethan showed up in the doorway, hands tucked in his pockets and lips puckered like he was contemplating what to say.

God, no! What was coming now?

Ethan cleared his throat. "Hey, look. I don't know what happened last weekend, or whether it's something that *I* did, or if it's *Sue* that pissed you off, but..."

Deliberately, I moved my gaze away from him, back to the screen.

"Shit, Chris, what's your damn problem?"

Teeth clamped together, I scowled at him again in the flickering light of the TV.

A sigh left him, and he rolled his eyes, throwing his hands in the air. "Yeah, yeah, I know. *Fuck off, Ethan.*" He spun on his heel and left the room, leaving me to my much-desired solitude.

As the week progressed, my mood didn't exactly improve. One reason for that could've been because I reread every single text Susan and I exchanged each night before bed. Yep, all of them were still saved on my phone. Of course, that was pathetic, but thoughts of Sue just wouldn't go away. Who could have foreseen that a shy nerd girl with a Harry Potter shirt would be my downfall one day? Definitely not me.

With my hunger on hiatus, coffee as thick as tar was all I had for breakfast on Friday morning. As I rose from the table and carried my mug to the sink, my pants slid lower on my hips. I reached to my back and tugged up the waist. Whoa, being depressed was starting to show. My favorite jeans, which usually fit perfectly, now hung loosely on me. Without a belt, the damn things wouldn't stay in place. Had I really lost that much weight since last weekend? Then again, I couldn't remember the last time I'd finished a full meal.

Because Ethan had soccer practice right after school, he didn't offer me a ride for a change. Mom needed her car all day, so my only alternative was my bike. I secured it near the parking lot behind the school building and went inside with my head hanging low. By now, I knew exactly where to find Susan in the morning, and I really didn't want to see her. Having to sit through lunch in the same room and not being able to walk over to her was hard enough. I didn't need to bump into her at every corner of the hallway, too.

The sound of heels clacking alongside made me aware that a girl had fallen into step with me. I lifted my head and mumbled, "Hey, Becks," then looked around her in search of my friend. "Where's Tyler?" It was rare to find either of them roaming the halls alone between classes.

"Spilled juice on his shirt. He's changing into his jersey." She pointed her thumb over her shoulder to the restrooms behind us. I stopped, and she did, too. Her gaze rested on my face, her eyes wide and inquisitive. Her curiosity couldn't be about Lauren; she already knew that I'd paid her friend a visit after school on Monday, and she certainly knew what we'd talked about, too. But when Becky started biting her lip, there was no doubt she was about to grill me about something else.

"What?" I tried to ease her into the conversation, but it came out as a grumble.

"I was wondering..." Rebecca began wryly. "You look quite miserable. Is everything okay with you?"

I studied her for a second. Had she noticed my weight loss, or were there actually worry lines on my face now? "I'm good," I said a bit too harshly.

Immediately, she lowered her gaze and shoved her long, blond hair back over her shoulder. "Right. It's none of my business." Her voice loaded with regret, she flushed an embarrassed pink and tipped backward against the wall next to the restroom. I waited with her.

"Listen," I said, bumping my shoulder against hers. "I didn't mean to grunt at you. I just had a really tough week is all."

Her eyes switched to mine. "We noticed." Lifting my brows in response, I curled my lips, and Becky shrugged. "Tyler said I'm not supposed to talk to you about it, but Tyler's not here, so... It's about that girl from the soccer table, right?"

Tucking my hands into my pockets, I turned toward her and leaned one shoulder against the wall. "T-Rex told you not to talk to me?"

"Not about that, yeah. He thinks I've been pushing you enough with Lauren and should keep my nose out of your love life." She grinned and rolled her eyes. "Like that would ever work."

A laugh escaped me. After enduring her nonstop requests to go on a double date, I could see that was true. "Have any advice for me?" I asked, more to make conversation than for my benefit.

"Umm..." She pressed her lips together for a moment. "Actually, I'm not quite sure what to tell you, because I don't know the whole situation. Tyler said you gave up chasing her before anything happened between you and...what's her name?"

"Susan."

"Right. He said that Susan wasn't interested in you. But I

don't buy it."

"You don't believe she isn't interested?"

"I don't believe that nothing happened between the two of you."

A hard lump clogged my throat. "What makes you think that?"

Becky shrugged one shoulder again and let her gaze skate from one student to the other as they passed us in a hurry to get to their first classes. Then she tilted her head to me. "The way she stares at you when you're not looking."

A sizzling shiver zoomed through me. "She does that?"

"Yep. A lot. At lunch." A knowing smile on her lips verified her words. "But it's not like she's admiring you from a distance. There's something in her eyes...more like wonder." She paused to lick her lip and gave me a shrewd look. "I think you kissed her."

I almost choked on the spit in my mouth. When the hell did she figure that out? And why hadn't she told anyone? She could have saved a few people some good money. Then again, she had no proof. "You can't know that."

"You're right. I didn't..." Her grin spread wider. "Until now."

Shocked, my jaw dropped. "What?"

"Chris!" Fisting her hands in frustration, she cut an exasperated glance to the ceiling. "I don't have to work for the FBI to know a little about body language."

I let out a breath but didn't exactly know what to say to that.

"What I don't get," she added, "is why you gave up so easily when you're so obviously in love with her."

Folding my arms over my chest, I stared at Becks for a long moment. Finally, a sigh escaped me, and I told her why. "She's with Ethan now."

Her eyes grew wide. "Your brother?"

"Yes."

"No."

"No, what?"

"No, she's not."

"With my brother?"

"Yes."

"Yes...what, *no*? Becky, I lost you."

While I scrunched my face, Becks erupted in a fit of giggles. She brushed her hand down my upper arm and explained, "Susan is single. She's not with Ethan. They're just friends."

"And you know that how?"

"She's not acting like they're together," she informed me, as if that was the most obvious thing in the world. "They have fun. But they never touch like couples do. Believe me, she's not interested in your brother."

"But she slept with him. How does that fit into your brilliant body language analytics, Miss Evers?"

"She did?"

"Yes," I growled.

"Wow, that's tough." Her voice lowered dramatically, her next words merely a stunned breath as her eyes narrowed in

ANNA KATMORE

sympathy. "I'm sorry, Chris."

Tyler came out of the restroom at that moment, wearing his white, sleeveless Dunkin' Sharks jersey. He slung an arm around his girlfriend and greeted me with a cheerful, "Morning, dude."

I said "hi" but, at the same time, cut Becks a warning look to make sure our confidential conversation was now over. She pressed her lips together, breathing deeply through her nose.

During first period, all I could think of was Becky's statement that Ethan and Sue weren't a couple. She was right—they didn't touch. At least not when I peered over at them during lunch breaks. So how did they land in bed together after she kissed me? Was she trying to prove something to me? That our kiss meant nothing at all?

On the other hand, Becks had said something else this morning that badgered me all through history, trig, and gym. Sue apparently stared at me when I wasn't looking her way; the same thing I did with her. She wouldn't do that if she was completely uninterested, would she? So what weird game was she playing? What did she want?

Because I knew exactly what I wanted. *Her.*

And yet, her betrayal still stung. It was as if I'd only just watched them come out of Ethan's room this morning instead of a week ago. She had no idea what kind of hell she'd put me through.

It was that exact thought that was racing through me when I saw her rounding the corner between third and fourth periods. Her honey-colored ponytail hung drearily over her right shoulder, like she'd forgotten to pump it up with her magical spray of cheerfulness. Wearing tight white jeans and a soft pink sweatshirt—the same one she wore when I'd found her at the entrance to the soccer field last week—she looked like a lost unicorn, completely in the wrong place. Her gaze pasted to the floor in front of her, she didn't notice much of what was going on around her. My entire body started to quiver with longing at the mere sight of her. But also with anger.

She needed to know—feel exactly what I felt. If Becky was right and Sue still had feelings for me—which I could hardly believe after she slept with my brother—then I knew a surefire way of finding out.

In a rush of determination, I reached for Becky's hand and shot Tyler a stern glance. "Can I borrow your girl for a moment?" Startled, he nodded, and I pulled Rebecca away from our group by the wall before he could change his mind.

Becky stumbled along with me. "Chris! What—"

"Shush! I'll explain everything later. Now, just come with me and don't freak out, okay? Please." As I laced my fingers through hers, she gaped at me with huge eyes but caved at my pleading look and walked with me.

The next moment, we blocked Susan Miller's way in the hall. She knocked straight into my chest. A loud "oof" burst from her lungs as she bounced back.

"Whoops," I said in a sickly innocent voice and waited for her to look up at me. When she did, I could almost feel the shiver of shock racing through her as her eyes widened. Didn't

ANNA KATMORE

expect to run into me, did she?

Quickly regaining her composure, she cleared her throat. "Hi." I didn't return the greeting but gave her a hard glare. "Sorry," she added then and dropped her eyes, breaking free from our locked gazes.

Her chest quivered with a sharp intake of air. I knew exactly what she was staring at now. My fingers intertwined with Rebecca's. I squeezed her hand a little harder to give Sue the right signals. *Yep, baby, I found another girl. You're not the only one who can play this game.*

I sneered inwardly, but the next instant, Susan lifted her gaze back to my face, and my chest tightened at the hurt in her eyes. Her throat moved. That she was shocked beyond words said a lot. Her face had paled. Dammit, was that too much?

Suddenly, I was aching for the two of us. But I couldn't show her that. Not here. Not now. Not after she'd turned her back on me and run to my brother.

"Anything wrong?" I snapped with more hostility in my tone than I actually meant. Rebecca's burning gaze bored a hole into the side of my head, but she played her part well and kept silent.

Reluctantly, Susan shook her head. Her beautiful green eyes misted under the thatch of too-long bangs, and her mouth dropped slightly open in horror. More than anything, I wanted to let go of Becks, clear up the situation, and pull Sue into my arms. But I didn't. Instead, I waited for her to step aside, then walked past her, dragging a baffled Becky along with me.

My plan had worked. I could be proud of myself.

"Are you completely insane?" Becky hissed under her breath as we rounded the corner and the show officially ended. She jerked her hand out of mine, cut in front of me, and smacked me hard on the chest. "What the hell, Chris?"

"I...er..." Rubbing the sore spot on my sternum, I stumbled for an explanation. Words completely evaded me while trapped in her mad glare.

"You used me to hurt this girl! You're such a dipshit!" Her eyes were sharp and narrow as a viper's. It wouldn't surprise me if her saliva turned poisonous this minute. I took a wary step back. Didn't she see the brilliance of my plan?

Pointing her manicured nail at my face, she hissed, "You're going to apologize to this poor girl right now, or I'll never speak to you again!"

"She's already gone," I argued in a small voice.

"Go find her!"

Thank God the bell rang, saving me from a very uncomfortable situation. I did feel like an ass for the look I'd put on Susan's face, but going after her and apologizing was the last thing I could imagine myself doing right now. On the other hand, I knew how persistent Becks could be. She would never let me live it down if I was stubborn about this. Having my best friend's girlfriend breathing down my neck was not something I wanted. And Becky could do this forever, if she thought she was in the right.

We were at an impasse. *Terrific.*

I rubbed my neck, bouncing on my feet, eager to leave. "I have Spanish now, and she's probably already in her class, too."

Becky stabbed her finger against my chest. "Fine. At lunch then," she warned. My cheeks actually turned warm at that growl of hers.

A moment later, Tyler and Brady rounded the corner and found us. A big smirk rode Tyler's lips. "Dude, did you just use Becky to make that girl jealous? Clever move!" He slapped me on the shoulder, while Brady nodded in awe.

Ten seconds ago, I might have welcomed their approval, but not anymore. Sadly, there was no way to warn T-Rex before Rebecca snarled in his face, lips compressed and eyes still in evil slits. Surprised, he leaned back and whined, "What?"

"You guys are such idiots!" she hissed, then stalked away to her next class.

At Tyler's baffled look, I shrugged and mouthed the word "sorry." He only shook his head, still confused, and followed his girlfriend. Brady and I moved through the swarm of students to get to our classes in time, too.

It was a good thing we'd already had our big Winter final in Spanish and the holidays were nearing, because nothing Mrs. Sanchez said that day registered. My mind was constantly in the clouds—dark clouds, actually, hovering above my head for purposefully misleading Sue and making Becks angry. She was right; I was a dipshit.

But Susan had hurt me. Part of me still believed I had a right to get back at her that way. Another part of me was sorry about it. And a third part, a very small one, dreaded the moment when I had to face her at lunch and straighten things out, per Becky's demand. To hell with this day! Why couldn't it already be over?

Eyes lowered, I walked into the cafeteria after fourth period and headed for the basketball table. Most of my friends were already there; unfortunately, so was Rebecca. T-Rex sat silently beside her and ate his burger, obviously trying hard to avoid her still pissed-off glare.

"Hi, guys," I said, dropping my backpack on my chair and quickly dashing off to get my lunch. While I waited in line, I chanced a peek over at the soccer table. My conscience still looming above my head with a baseball bat in hand, I wanted to see if my show with Becky had left any obvious marks on little Sue. Probably not. Considering how things were going with her these days, she would probably be jesting with my brother, as she'd done all week.

But when my gaze skated over to the tables by the windows, her usual seat was empty. I scanned the other faces and then looked around the cafeteria. Sue hadn't moved down a chair or two, or even switched tables. She just wasn't there. Had she decided to eat her lunch outside today? Maybe she was simply avoiding being in the same room with me. But that was stupid. Also, if she really was, surely my brother or some of her other friends would have joined her. The strange thing was, they were all there. The only one missing from the soccer bunch was Sue.

Staring openly now, I started when the lady behind the counter tapped me on the shoulder. She prompted me to take my meal and make room for the kids behind me. Hastily, I grabbed the tray and returned to my place, sinking into my chair, lost in thought.

"So, what are you going to do about Susan?" Becky grumbled as I stared blankly at my food.

"She isn't here," I replied in a low tone, not looking up. And even if she were, I doubted I'd be capable of walking up to her and offering an apology. The small part of me claiming that Sue deserved what I'd done today had quite a loud voice.

After a short pause in which Rebecca probably checked out the soccer table for proof, she said, "Strange. But I'm assuming you have her number. Talk to her. Or *I* will." At her sinister warning, I lifted my head. She was frowning at me. "What you did was awful, Chris. *Mean*. I'm not going to be a part of that."

Looking around our table, I tried to find support from my friends, but they just ducked their heads and pretended not to be listening. "Fine," I grunted, clenching my teeth. Dammit, this girl had an attitude that would open doors to the military for her one day. Picking a slice of cucumber from my salad and chewing on it, I lied, "Over the weekend." At least it would get Rebecca off my back. She didn't need to know that I didn't intend to call Susan ever again.

Obviously pleased, Becky nodded and then asked Tyler to pass her the salt for her fries. When he looked warily at her, she offered him a conciliatory smile. Tension visibly eased out of his muscles. I wouldn't be able to say that about me as long as she was sitting at the same table. Man, the end of the day couldn't come fast enough.

The November afternoon was warm and the ride home

from school on my bike a nice change. The sun shining on my face dispersed some of the depression that had followed me around all week. If only I could hold on to that warm feeling when I was indoors. Yeah...no such luck. Walking past Ethan's room stirred the familiar glumness inside me. The painful spikes of treachery were back in full force. In a rush, I discarded my dark gray shirt, fetched some fresh clothes from my wardrobe, and headed to the bathroom to shower off the events of the day, and all the anger with it. It was Friday, after all. My detention was over, and I should've been be finding a hookup for tonight. A real date, not a fake one.

Only problem with that—I couldn't make myself even think about being with another girl. Not yet. It was insane, but I only wanted to be with one. The girl I wasn't going to talk to ever again.

After the shower, I'd barely toweled myself dry when somebody rang the doorbell. Mom was at work, Ethan at practice, and I sure wasn't expecting anyone. Slightly annoyed at the prospect of having to deal with a door-to-door salesman, I slipped into my jeans, foregoing boxers and socks, and donned my black hoodie over my wet skin. It was nasty but, unless I wanted to answer the door half-naked, I had no other choice. Buttoning up my pants on the way, I hurried to the door and pulled it open, prepared to face a sweating man with a mustache trying to sell me a vacuum cleaner or some special car polish. When my gaze landed on a soft pink sweatshirt instead, my jaw smacked against my chest.

Chapter 18

BEFORE SUSAN COULD say a word, I pulled my crap together and closed my mouth. She shouldn't see me in utter shock. I was over her. *Or not.*

She cleared her throat and pushed out a croaky, "Hi, um..."

Right, we were back to square one—she didn't even know whether she was talking to me or my brother. Irritated by her lack of attention, I crossed my arms over my chest and clarified, "Chris."

"Right." Her voice wavered with awkwardness as she lowered her eyes quickly. "Is Ethan home?"

Wow, wasn't that a surprise? Resisting the urge to roll my eyes, I fixed her with a cold gaze and gritted out, "Soccer practice."

"Okay, um..." She shook her head slightly. "Never mind."

Sue turned away, but I couldn't let her go, because at that very moment, I noticed a sparkling tear rolling down her cheek. *What the fuck?*

Before she could slip away from me, I reached out and, with my knuckle under her chin, gently tilted her face up. "Susan, why are you crying?" Did Ethan have something to do with it? What had the bastard said to make her cry?

Whatever it was, I was going to kill him!

For an unfathomable moment, Sue gazed at me, wounded and shattered. Her face turned pale, she swayed, and she was breathing much too fast. Dammit—she was going to break down on my doorstep any second.

In a rush of worry, I grabbed her arms, ignoring the anger that stood between us, and pulled her against my chest, catching her before she fell. A second, then two, passed before her arms slid around me. She dug her fingers into the back of my hoodie, probably appreciating the support.

"I broke up my parents!" The hoarse cry burst out of her, the words muffled by the fabric of my sweatshirt.

That was definitely not what I'd expected to hear. "You did what?" I demanded, holding her against me with my hand in her hair.

While that first, lonely tear on her cheek had surprised me, her full-on breakdown in my arms knocked me for a loop. Her body shook, and her voice broke as she sobbed against my chest, "My parents are getting divorced. It's my fault!"

I'd never had to deal with a crying girl before, and heck if I knew what to do with Sue. Say things like *shhh*, or *there, there* maybe? God, it all sounded so stupid. I couldn't really say that aloud. For now, it seemed like a good idea to just keep focused and calm her down. "Tell me what happened." Well, that came out more anxious than soothing, actually, but she had me in a knot of concern, even if I was the one who was supposed to be calm and strong for her.

Her arms tightened around me. They pulled at the back of my sweatshirt, choking me a little as the collar bit into my throat, but I remained silent. Only she mattered right then. I stroked up and down her back, trying to give her the comfort she needed. With a huge gulp, she sucked in air and hiccupped a little before explaining, "I went home after third period today. My parents were both there." She wiped her face against my shoulder, wetting it with her tears. That was okay. I wasn't fussy. "They told me they want to get divorced."

Uh-oh, that was bad.

"They've been fighting for so long, and last weekend—" She broke off, the pain in her throat apparent. After a quick moment, she tried again, "Last weekend, Ethan wanted to see my room. I showed him. But my parents started fighting again—they didn't know we were home. It was so embarrassing. I said some horrible things to them. Then I ran away."

Giving her all the comfort she needed, I continued caressing her back as she coughed out more and more details. I listened to her, gazing over her head into the street.

"They didn't fight after that. I thought things would finally work out. But it just got worse. They must have been plotting this all week. Today, they told me they didn't want to be together anymore. Because of me. Because of what I *said* to them."

She sounded like she was carrying the misery of the entire world on her shoulders. Silly girl. How could she ever think she'd made a mistake to split up her parents? It wasn't her fault.

"They said they don't want to hurt me with their fighting," she sniveled. "But I don't want them to break up because of me."

When she was finally done and only quiet sobs escaped instead of more of her deluge of words, I continued to hold her. My bare feet grew cold on the doorstep, but I didn't care. The only thing that mattered now was to be the rock she needed to ground her. I loved how she held on to me, and I loved how she allowed me to be the one to soothe her. Whatever the reason she'd come here today, I never wanted to let her slip away from me again.

After a while of quiet embracing on my doorstep, it seemed to be time to get one thing straight. Easing back, I didn't let her go completely, only held her slightly away from me and wiped a few strands of hair out of her face. Tear-soaked, they were sticky like spider legs, so that proved to be a bit of a challenge. "Sweetness, you certainly did *not* break up your parents." A brush of my thumb caught the last tear on her cheek and brushed it away. "They have some shit to deal with, but it's not your fault."

Sue looked at me like she wanted to dive into my arms again, and I wouldn't have stopped her. Yet she held back, her green eyes glassy like a pond in moonlight.

A car drove by. It was Miss Bloomington, her Dalmatian,

Cecil, sitting in the passenger seat, sticking its head out the window, its ugly pink tongue lolling in the wind. We'd been standing out here for the neighbors to spy on for long enough. Sue wasn't done grieving, and I knew of just the thing to make her feel better. Carefully, I took her hand, dreading the moment she would pull back and push me away. She didn't, thank God, and let me tug her inside with me.

The best place to take her was probably my room. If Mom decided to come home early, she wouldn't disturb us there. Susan certainly wouldn't want just anyone to find her in this condition.

With a gentle push on her shoulders, I steered her toward my bed. As she lowered down on the edge, she looked so wretched, it was like Bambi sat in my room, after a collision with a truck. The cuffs of her sleeves pulled over her palms, she dried her eyes with them.

To spare her nice sweatshirt, I got her a pack of tissues from my desk. As she pulled one out and was about to blow her nose, a thought struck. The girl on my bed was perfect, even when her face was swollen from crying. What if she blew her nose like an elephant now, like Lauren did the other day? Would that ruin some of the fascination she held for me?

Sue wiped her eyes with the tissue and cleaned her nose— gently. A relieved smile almost escaped me, but that would have been *so* out of place. Remembering why I'd brought her inside at all, I quickly braced myself. "Don't go away. I'll be right back." After she gave me a nod, I loped to the kitchen.

In a hurry, I put the kettle on and searched for a good

brand in the box of tea bags. Strawberry-vanilla. That was the right flavor to soothe Susan's agony. When the water was hot, I poured it into my breakfast coffee mug and dipped the tea bag into it until the water turned a pretty, dark pink. The sweet smell unfurled fast. Hopefully she was as much a fan of strawberry tea as she was the real fruit.

That thought made me pause a moment, turn around, and stare at the spot on the island where she'd sat the last time she was in my house. Where I'd kissed her. What a sweet treasure of memories in my chest. Except the familiar feeling of betrayal, which had haunted me all week after she'd sneaked out of my brother's bedroom, returned just as quickly and I had to tamp it down—hard. It wasn't about me and my hurt feelings right now, it was only about Sue and the trouble with her family. She needed someone to lean on, and right now I was that somebody.

When I returned to my room, I found her standing by the window, gazing out onto the yard. At my soft cough, she pivoted. I held out the steaming cup. A little confused, she looked first at the cup, then at me.

"Tea is good for the soul," I told her, offering a small smile instead of a sugar packet, which I'd totally forgotten to add to the tea.

Carefully, she took a sip. Her face didn't scrunch up in disgust, so she probably liked the taste, even without the extra sweetener. Holding the cup between her hands, she turned back to the window, staring outside.

Worried, because I had no idea what to do or say next in a

ANNA KATMORE

situation like this, I stood beside her, looking through the same window. Our arms touched, and she quivered. Was that too close? Did she want more distance? She didn't move away, so maybe it was all right to just stand here with her.

Should I offer her more comfort? Heck, I wasn't good at things like this. Ethan would know what to do. He would know exactly what to say to make her feel better. Me? I hardly knew her, much less her parents. What could I actually offer?

The weight of silence quickly became too heavy. "You're lucky your parents still have that base where they talk to each other and to you about things like a divorce. When my parents broke up, they'd long gone past that point." That was the best conversation starter to come to my mind, and I was intensely hoping it brought Sue out of the turtle shell she'd retreated into while I was in the kitchen.

It seemed to work. She tilted her head, her curious look resting on my face. "How was it for you?"

"Well, it was pretty hard at first," I admitted with a quick glance at her. I grimaced. She didn't need to know all the details, only enough that she understood she had someone who could empathize. "I came home one day, and my dad was no longer here. No goodbye, no letter, no phone call. He was just gone."

Her mouth opened slightly in shock, her eyes even wider. She didn't interrupt me, though, so I continued, "The first sign of life Ethan and I got from him was after two freaking months, and I know he only called because Mom begged him to talk to us. She was the one who saw how we suffered every day, not him." My gaze got stuck on the tiny basketball court he'd paved for us in the yard. Part of me was still angry at my dad for leaving, but I'd mostly forgiven him by now, and refused to let old wounds reopen. I tore my eyes away from the paved square and cut a glance at Susan, who sipped her tea, her eyes still fastened on me.

"What did he say to you that day?" she asked.

"Something about how he needed time to sort out his life and shit." I paused and laughed. "Well, he did sort it out pretty quickly. He moved in with his secretary two days after he moved out of here." *The fool.*

Okay, maybe I wasn't completely over it. So what?

"Two years ago," I went on, "I started seeing my dad again. Not often, just for birthdays and Christmases, and maybe one or two other times a year. That's all right now. We have a comfortable relationship."

"And Ethan?" Sue asked, her head angled in curiosity.

Of course she would want to hear more about his life than mine. Typical. I suppressed a sigh and told her, "It was harder for him. Ethan never forgave him. They haven't seen each other once since the day my dad moved out." It was a shame, really. "I believe Ethan just needs a little more time. Maybe when we're at college, or just one day…" I shrugged. "Whenever."

Sue had stopped crying, which elated me. My tactic had been right and my soothing successful. Heck, I was a genius!

Suddenly, the longing to touch her again overwhelmed me. Not thinking at all, I reached out and brushed some stray wisps

ANNA KATMORE

of hair behind her ear, skimming over her soft skin with my fingertips. "The fact that your parents talk to you about it and even try to do what they think is best for you means they care a lot for you. You're not breaking them up," I assured her. "If anything, you were the one holding them together. But you can't do that forever."

Giving in to another impulse, I took the cup out of her hands and placed it on the desk behind her. Next, I carefully pulled her toward me, looping my arms around her waist. "And know what the best thing about it all is?"

Again, Susan didn't squirm out of my embrace, even though she was supposed to be Ethan's girl. Whatever was I supposed to make of this? A sigh escaped me.

She tilted her face up and stabbed me in the chest with her chin, waiting for my answer.

"The fights will stop," I told her in a confident voice. I wanted to give her hope.

She inhaled deeply while our gazes stayed locked for several long, silent seconds. What were we doing here? I should be mad at her. Hurt. And I still was in some ways. But for the life of me, I couldn't let her go. It was like last weekend in the kitchen was happening all over again. Just the two of us in here—so damn close. I only needed one tiny sign from her, and I wouldn't have given two fucks about my brother. I would have kissed her.

That sign never came.

Instead, Sue broke eye contact a moment later and detached from our hug with great care. I stiffened but let her slip away. She picked up the cup of tea, staring into the slight swirl of liquid. Right. Her mind was probably set on Ethan. No matter what Becky had said, Sue and my brother must've had something going. Being with me now certainly counted as cheating in her mind, even if what she and Ethan had done to me was much worse than what I'd intended to do now.

Anger swelled in my chest, hardening the muscles in my jaw. Sue must have noticed it, too, because she became fidgety all of a sudden and handed me the half-empty mug in a rush. "I should go," she murmured around to head out.

Panic struck me. Without thinking, I reached for her hand, pleading, "Wait." I didn't know exactly why I held her back, but she turned to me anyway. "I..." The word slipped over my lips, then nothing followed.

Sue searched my face, almost as if she was burning for me to say something. But *what*? She'd come here feeling miserable about a family fight. How could I add to that reproaches about ditching me and replacing me oh-so-quickly with my brother? "What is it?" she prompted.

When I let go of her hand, it dropped sadly to her side. Feeling helpless, I pivoted to the window and put the cup down on the ledge, hoping the lump in my throat would dislodge. But that took time, and Susan seemed to lose her patience. "*What*, Chris?"

I drew in a deep breath. She was still here, God knew for how much longer. This was my only chance to get the answer I needed. So, squaring my shoulders, I snapped, "Fine!" Before I could backtrack, I spun to her. "Tell me one thing. Why did you let me kiss you last weekend and then sleep with my brother the same night?"

There. It was out. Too bold? Probably.

Susan gaped at me. Then she scrunched her face and blurted, "What bullshit are you talking about?"

"*You* tell me."

"There isn't anything to tell!" she shot back, and much louder, too. Her eyes narrowed to angry slits. "I didn't sleep with Ethan. What in the world made you come up with something so stupid?"

Stupid? Or true? "You came back that night with him"—I crossed my arms over my chest, digging in my heels—"or should I say, *in the morning*? And you sneaked out before sunrise." Duh! How was she going to explain that?

Actually, she didn't. Instead, her jaw dropped with the realization of being caught—and the pain of betrayal stung me again like it was the first time. "How did you get that out of Ethan?" she whispered, defeated.

"I didn't have to. I *heard* you!"

She contemplated that for a second and suddenly took on an offensive stance. "And your point is?"

"Wha—" Staggered, I threw my arms in the air. How could she turn the tables on me so easily? *I* wasn't the one who'd screwed up here, dammit. *She* was! "That you spent the night with him!" That was my point ,for shit's sake. "And *after* you kissed me the same day!"

The volume of my voice might have gone a little over the top, because Susan flinched back. Barely managing to calm myself, I added in a hurt tone, "I thought you liked it."

Sue didn't back away any further, but she studied my face long and hard. Her eyes gleamed with understanding, along with a surge of anger. She raked her hands through her bangs, shifting her weight from one foot to the other, and the lines around her mouth hardened. "I spent the night here for the reasons I told you fifteen minutes ago. I had a fight with my parents and ran off. But I didn't have sex with your brother." Looking helpless now, she sniffed and took an exhausted step backward so she could sit on my bed again. "I can't believe that you'd really think that. And if you were so sure, why didn't you ask Ethan?" Reproach hung heavy in her voice. "For Christ's sake, why didn't you ask *me*?"

Because I was so hurt, I thought I'd never talk to you again.

Now, as the core of her statement sank in, I suddenly felt like a complete idiot. She'd sent me a text last Sunday morning. What might have happened if I'd answered it? "Are you saying I hit rock bottom over nothing?"

Her face turned red with frustration. "I'm saying, please, for once in your life, think before you act. Do you know what a horrible week I've had because of you?"

Because of *me*? Thrown for a loop, I leaned back until I felt the window sill behind me and gripped the cold ledge for support. "What do you mean? I thought you were feeling miserable because of your parents."

Horror suddenly zoomed through her eyes, and she pressed her lips together. If I hadn't known better, I would have thought she wanted to take back whatever she'd just said. After a moment of silently staring at me, she dropped her forehead in her cupped hands, avoiding my gaze. "Yeah, that too," she murmured into the cuffs of her pink sweatshirt.

"So what did *I* have to do with it?" I had to know, and right this moment, too.

She didn't look up. "Nothing. Forget it."

Yeah, as if!

She couldn't come here, break down in my arms, let me hold and comfort her, and then backpedal when things got sticky. Her parents' fight was one thing troubling her, but another one was *me*. So what the hell—

And then, slowly, one piece after the other clicked into place, completing the puzzle of Susan Miller.

She hadn't known I'd heard her with my brother on Sunday morning, so she must have thought I was ignoring her for a different reason. The challenge. Was that it? She thought I was done with her after our first—and let me add *amazing*—kiss. She sent me a text the next morning, and I ignored it. We met in the hallway on Monday, and all she got from me was the cold shoulder. And dammit, today I'd purposefully mislead her with Rebecca Evers. What kind of an asshole would do that?

The answer was simple: me. Because I'd fallen for little Sue and foolishly thought she'd abandoned me for my brother. I rubbed my hands over my face, sighing deeply. Jeez, what a mess I'd maneuvered myself into.

I needed to get this straight, and fast. So, first on the list of amends was clarifying what happened at school today, when we ran into each other—or rather, when I'd made her knock into me and Becky. Suddenly a small detail of our earlier conversation resurfaced in my mind. Had she actually said she'd left school after that incident? That's why I hadn't seen her at lunch. So what if the Becky thing had struck her harder than I'd guessed?

"Susan?" I asked in a softer voice than I actually thought I was capable of.

She lowered her hands, but she didn't lift her gaze to me yet. "Hm?"

"Why did you go home after third period today?"

Head low, she remained silent.

"Susan," I pushed again, with a little more insistence, and walked over to where she sat on my bed. "Tell me."

All she did was shake her head.

"Why not?" I squatted down in front of her and tipped her chin up with my knuckle. Damn, she was close to tears again, and this time I couldn't deny that it was my fault. I wanted those tears to go away, more than anything. But for that to happen, we needed to talk about things. So, once again, I prompted her, "Tell me why you left school after we ran into each other in the hallway today."

With her chin in my hand, only her gaze broke free from mine. The damage was done; she wouldn't talk to me. I felt so helpless, I wanted to tear my hair out. In the end, it was clear I couldn't make her talk if she didn't want to. There was, in fact, nothing I could do, so I dropped my hand from her face and sank onto my knees, defeated.

She didn't stand up, didn't go away, and didn't say a word. She just sat there, silent and hurt.

Carefully, I took her hands in mine. They were cold as ice. The slight tremble didn't escape me either. I liked her fingers— long and fragile—and remembered how they'd felt at the back of my neck when we kissed. I stroked the inside of her hands for a moment, then gently laced my fingers through hers, wishing for a miracle so that the Becky thing could disappear— never happen in the first place.

"I'm sorry I hurt you." My voice was thin and drained of all strength. A weak whisper. "But she means nothing."

"Now that's a hell of a relief, isn't it?" Sue snarled, looking directly at me at last. "As if any of them ever mean something to you."

What she said hit me straight in the center of my ego, but of course she had a point. Ultimately, I was happy she was talking to me at all. Drawing slow circles around her knuckles with my thumb, I told her with deeply felt honesty, "You do."

"Oh, do I?" A cynical laugh escaped her. "Obviously so much so that you couldn't wait to replace me with your next challenge right after you kissed me."

"I swear there's nothing going on between Rebecca and me," I protested, holding her reproachful gaze. "She's only a friend."

"Rebecca..." Susan repeated the name as if it held all the gravity in this room, then she paused for a deep sigh. When she spoke next, her voice was edged with resignation. "Maybe we come from two different places, Chris, but from where I stand, it does mean something when a guy laces his fingers with a girl's."

She tried to pull her hands out of mine, but I didn't let her. Instead, I squeezed them even tighter and confirmed, "Yes, it does." Her slight gasp reassured me that she'd understood my meaning. "But not this morning." I rolled my eyes, hating myself for making that stupid mistake. "Heck, I was a complete douche, okay? I used my friend's girlfriend to make you jealous."

Lowering her chin a little, her gaze settled on me with trepidation. "You did what?"

I swallowed. There was no getting out of this without coming clean with her, but the thought of confessing my stupid idea scared me. "This entire week, you seemed so happy when you were with the guys...with Ethan. Oblivious to how I felt about you. It was a stupid thing to do this morning, but I wanted a reaction."

"And that was your plan?" She grew what felt like ten feet in front of me, even though she remained seated. "To shove a random girl in my face?"

Feeling small and intimidated, I shrugged. "Well, it did work."

"If you only wanted my reaction, a phone call would have done, Chris!" she yelled.

I hung my head, not knowing how else to escape her anger. "Yeah, I get that... Next time, I know."

"Next time?" Sue squeezed my hands, yet it wasn't for

ANNA KATMORE

affection. Rather, she balled her hands into fists, but because I refused to let go of her, her fingers wrapped tighter around mine. "There won't be a next time," she clarified. "Not with you and me, anyway."

"Why not?" Fair enough, she had a right to be angry at me. But to throw everything we had away because of a fricking mistake? That was stupid. "Last Saturday was an amazing date, and we didn't even leave the house. Don't you think we should do it again?"

Her eyes widened with a horror I didn't even begin to understand. What had I said that was so terrible?

After a moment, she seemed to gather herself and said in a low, contained voice, "No, I really don't. I'm not that type of girl."

"What type?"

"The type that's available whenever you fancy a brief roll in the hay, or that you can send away when you're bored of her."

What—

Understanding dawned on me. She didn't want to say the name out loud, but she didn't have to. The name *Lauren* hung rich on every syllable.

Slowly, I shook my head. Silly, silly Sue. "You wouldn't be that kind of girl for me."

"No? I'm not sure you even know a different kind, actually."

Whoa. That was harsh—and undeserved, too. "I do know how exclusive works," I bit back.

"Really?" Sue angled her head. "When was the last time

you had a girlfriend?"

At a time I refused to talk about now. "It doesn't matter."

"It matters to me."

Of course it would. Her eyes and low voice revealed as much. But now was not the time to talk about my ex-girlfriend. In fact, there would never be a right moment to unfurl that part of my past. Staring into her eyes, I silently begged her to let it go.

A mix of anger and hurt crossed her face as she interpreted my silence totally wrong. "See, I knew you didn't know how it works."

My molars ground together in frustration. She wanted the truth? Fine! If it meant so much to her... "Tenth grade. Amanda Roseman. We lasted seven and a half months. She broke my heart when she left me for my once-best friend. So I decided to take a little time off from being *exclusive*." *Happy now?*

Susan's chin dropped with surprise. For once, she was short of a reply.

I drew in a deep breath and took advantage of her silence to further my point. "That doesn't mean I'm not willing to try it again with the right girl."

"You think I am the right girl? Why?" She sounded sullen, the snappiness in her tone disappearing. "Because you had to wait two weeks before I let you kiss me?"

"That, and because I did stuff with you that I've never done with anyone else." Except with Amanda, so I added, "Not in a long time anyway. Apart from you, my mom is the only girl who ever gets texts from me. And when I took random chicks to my room, I never cooked for them." I rolled my eyes at the memory of last Saturday. "Or freaking played Wii golf."

Her green irises started to gleam with a new spark of reproach. "Oh, that justifies everything, does it?"

Hell, why was she still on the offensive side? Had I not opened up enough to her yet? What did she want to hear?

"The way I see it, yes, it does," I proclaimed. But dammit, judging by her look, it would take a miracle to soften her up. And it seemed, just today, I'd run out of miracles. I squeezed her hands a little tighter, pleading with her sense of reason. "Let's give this a shot. We could be awesome together."

A small, doubtful V grew between her eyebrows. "We didn't even last a day. How is that awesome?" She shook her head and pulled her hands out of mine. "Seriously, I just don't think we'd work together."

No, no, no, no, no! She couldn't say that.

But Sue rose from my bed, and on what seemed to be shaky legs, she walked away from me. Panic made me race after her. "Where are you going?"

"I don't know," she breathed as she headed to the front door, not turning around.

This couldn't be happening. We weren't finished. Screw it, but I refused to accept her retreat. "Wait, please!" Before I knew it, my fingers had wrapped around her wrist, and I pulled her back into me in the hallway. "I was an arrogant dick when we met, you were right about that." The words flew out of me as the fear of really losing her manifested. "But I thought I showed you a different side lately. Someone you could actually like." What about the deal we'd made after playing soccer together? Had she forgotten about that? "I even played by your rules."

A hopeless shrug rolled off her shoulders. "You did." She paused. "I meant what I said the other day—that I probably couldn't kiss a guy without having true feelings for him. You made me believe you could be that guy."

Great! So what's the damn problem?

Sue held my pleading gaze. "But it wasn't for real, Chris. *You* weren't for real. You said yourself, you played by my rules—you tried to be different for me." Reluctantly, she shook her head. "That's not what I want."

Dragging her a little closer by the hand I still held, I lowered my head slightly to gaze into her eyes. "What *do* you want?"

As if she had no idea how to answer, she cut a glance to the ceiling, then pulled away from me, and tipped against the wall. She looked lost and sorry. "I want someone who is all that you showed me, but naturally so. Someone who doesn't have to force himself to be the kind of guy I want."

Force? Was she crazy? Being around her was the best thing that had happened to me in a long time. There was nobody forcing me into giving her that hickey on the soccer field, or writing the messages we sent back and forth, and there was certainly nobody forcing me into that kiss last Saturday.

"Most of all, I want someone who doesn't come with the tag 'trouble.' Do you understand?"

Oh. So that was the whole problem. Being with me scared her. Of course, it would. I wasn't a nice hero cut out from one of her books. I actually had a life *before* she scribbled her number on my arm. And there was still the challenge. She'd never get over that.

Her ideal boyfriend was a low-key guy. A dude who'd ask her three times if the orange juice he'd served her was the right temperature instead of blindfolding her and dripping the juice into her open mouth.

"I do understand." My words came out cold and toxic. "You want someone safe and boring. Someone who doesn't give you that exciting tingle in there." Angling my head, I brushed my fingers over her stomach, giving her a suggestive look. "In short, you still want Ethan."

She was quiet for too long. The silence pressing in on us threatened to make me ignore her wishes and just pull her into my arms. A kiss, that's what she needed in order to see clearly again. She could deceive herself all she wanted, but I knew what her heart really desired. Not the nice guy next door. She wanted adventure. It had been there so clearly—in our first kiss. Why didn't she see it?

Just when I was about to reach for her and make her understand in *my* way, she murmured, "I do like the exciting tingle. I just don't want the heartache that comes with it."

Oh, sweetness! "Give me a chance to show you that you and I can work without heartache. I'm not Ethan—" The dorky thought of it gave me shudders and made me roll my eyes. "God, I'll never be like him. But I can do *safe*. Give us a shot and let's start again."

For a split second, the lines around her eyes softened. She almost smiled as she looked at me and doubtlessly deliberated simply saying yes. In that fathomless moment, she wanted to reach out and put herself in my arms, I could feel it. The air tensed with sheer excitement, and I was ready to catch her if she made this one small step toward me.

The spellbound moment between us ended when Susan slowly shook her head. All my hopes tumbled down like a sandcastle in a strong wind. My chest tightened in despair. God only knew why she'd changed her mind.

Without explanation, she sniffed and turned around, then walked out through the front door, and closed it behind her.My throat clogged. I squeezed my eyes shut and sunk against the wall. Running after her wouldn't change anything now. But letting her go was harder than anything I'd ever done before.

Chapter 19

I WAS STILL sitting on the floor in the hallway when Ethan came home from soccer. He paused in the doorway in surprise for a couple of seconds, then closed the door, and quietly kicked off his shoes, his back to me. Maybe he wanted to give me a chance to pick myself up and retreat to my room to avoid him. Any other day this week, I'd have done exactly that. But things had changed, and today was different.

His clothes sweat-drenched from training and glowing red in the face, he slowly shuffled down the hallway. When he reached me, he stopped, biting his lip as he deliberated with a wary look. "Fuck off, Ethan...?" he asked.

I inhaled deeply. "Sit down."

Still cautious, he took his time to lower to the floor opposite me, legs crossed Indian-style. "I'm seriously worried now, you know."

Damn, I'd given my brother shit this whole week for nothing. What was the right thing to say to make this okay? A simple "I'm sorry" didn't seem to be enough. Yet it was the only thing I could offer at the moment. "I feel like a complete and utter ass. Please forgive me."

Obviously uncertain as to how to take the change in my mood, Ethan glanced down the hall to his open room and then back at me. "Apology accepted..." he said, his expression guarded as he scrutinized me sideways. "Subject to modifications."

I smiled.

"Now tell me what the freak happened, so I can sleep better at night."

Ah, where to begin? I pulled my heels to my butt, mirroring Ethan's Indian-style, braced my elbows on my knees, and fumbled with my fingers. My gaze pasted on my hands, my explanation took some time to come. "I thought you slept with Susan."

Preparing for a rant, I waited for his answer, but Ethan didn't say anything. I dared a glance at his face. His mouth wide open, he sat there frozen. His appalled eyes were fixed on me.

"Ethan?" I probed carefully.

He shook his head as if to free himself of a momentary blackout. "When... I mean, what..." He expelled a breath. "Fuck, *why?*"

"Last weekend, when we cooked for Sue, I kissed her. Specifically, when you were gone for the kiwis." Expecting another round of shock from him, I grimaced.

His reaction, however, was a stern look and a *duh*

expression. "I know that, dickhead."

"You do?"

"What did you think?" He rolled his eyes at me. "We're friends. She tells me stuff."

Right. How could I have doubted that? "So, after our kiss that night, you took her to your room."

Ethan shifted his mouth to one side, contemplating. "I know *you* two aren't that good of friends, so now I'm wondering how you know about *that*?"

"I was waiting in the living room for you to come home and fell asleep on the couch. In the morning, I heard both of you coming out of your room, and she asked you not to tell me. Because she didn't want me 'to ask stupid questions,'" I quoted Susan's concern, my voice sharp with irritation. "Seriously, what would you have thought in my place?"

"Well, first of all, you should have talked to us about it, if it really worried you so much."

"Of course it worried me! Heck, I told you I kissed Sue that afternoon."

"So? You kiss a lot of girls and never care what they do afterward."

"It's different with her."

"How?"

"I don't know."

"I do."

"Yeah?"

"Yes."

"What's your theory?"

"You're in love with Sue."

I wrapped my arms around my bent legs and planted my forehead on my knees, squeezing my eyes shut. "Hmm. Could be true."

"Could be, all right." Ethan laughed. "So how did you find out we did *not* sleep with each other?"

I lifted my head and planted my chin on my knees instead. "Sue showed up today. She said she ran off because of a family fight that night."

"She actually came here to tell you that?"

"No, she came here because her parents are getting divorced."

"*WHAT*?" His outraged shout startled me stiff, and my head snapped up. "And you're only telling me this now?" He slid his phone from his pocket and hastily dialed a number.

"What are you doing?" Alarm rang in my words.

"Calling Susan, of course!" He pressed the cell phone to his ear, his sharp gaze on me while he waited. "Her parents are breaking up—she'll be devastated."

That about summed it up.

Ethan listened for a few seconds, then he put the phone down and grumbled, "Voice mail."

I sucked in a breath through my teeth. "She's not picking up?"

"No. Anything else you have to reveal about that?"

"Well, um..." I cleared my throat.

Ethan was getting impatient. "What, Chris?"

"It could be that she was quite mad when she left. Or

maybe not mad. More like...er, confused. Or..." *Disappointed?* Was that the word I was looking for? "Hurt..."

"My God, what did you say to her?"

"I'm not quite sure, actually. After comforting her, I might have asked her to be my girlfriend." I lowered my chin to my knees again. "And then again, maybe not."

"So you told her that you're in love with her?"

"I'm not exactly sure what I told her"—all the messy things were starting to blur together in my mind—"but I think she knows anyway."

His brow furrowed. "And what did she say?"

My sullen gaze dropped to the square tiles on the floor. "That I'm too much trouble, obviously, and that she'd rather be with you."

"That's bullshit, and you know it." Ethan glared at me in reproach and dialed Sue's number again.

"Why is that bull?"

He growled when he apparently reached her voice mail once more and put the phone back in his pocket. "Because Susan knows I'm not interested."

I raked my hands through my hair, dipping my head back against the wall. "See, that's one thing I really don't get. You two hang out all the time, and she's totally into you. Yet you don't want to date her. Why?"

"First of all, Christian"—gah, I hated it when my family used my full name—"as far as I can see, she's really into *you*, not me."

Did she tell Ethan that? If she did, there was hope for me,

right? *RIGHT?*

"And second, I don't want to date her because..." As he sucked in a lungful of air, I raised one eyebrow, urging him to keep going. Suddenly, he spoke in a rush. "Because I'm not really interested in girls that way."

What. The. Hell? My hands dropped to the floor.

Ethan was gay. Like really and literally into boys.

I mean, that's okay. It's cool. I knew it. But—*what the fricking hell?*

It was so much different to hear it from him after only assuming for so long. Mom's guessing, my guessing...all the evidence I'd gathered... It was true. A breath whizzed out through my teeth. "Wow."

"Now don't act like you haven't known that for a while." His cheeks a light shade of pink, he lowered his face and glared at me from under the sweaty hair falling into his eyes. But what was that at the corners of his mouth? My brother really wanted to smile now, didn't he?

And why not? I smirked. "You had Mom and me puzzling over it for the longest time."

"Yeah, I suppose I should tell her the truth sometime soon, too."

"She will understand, E.T.," I assured him after worry lines replaced his relieved expression. "She loves you, and she doesn't mind."

He nodded, not fully convinced yet.

"Are you going to tell Sue as well?" I asked, to distract him from his fretting about Mom.

"She knows."

"*Since when?*"

"She figured it out somehow after the weekend of your big game."

"That was two weeks ago!"

"Yep."

Whoa. That girl could keep a secret. Then again, I had one to keep now, too. Until Ethan was ready to come out to people outside of this house—and he didn't seem ready to do that just yet—I'd keep my mouth shut. But heck, it meant a lot to me that he'd told me. And after this horrible week, too.

All these years I'd been sure, if anything ever came between my brother and me, it could only be a girl. Seemed like I'd been right from the beginning. Except it had happened under totally unforeseeable circumstances.

Inhaling deeply, I leaned forward and held my fist out across the hallway. "I'm really sorry for being such a shit this week."

After a moment's hesitation, Ethan bumped it. "It's okay, bro."

"So would you tell me what exactly happened last Saturday that led to Sue sleeping in our house?"

"I met her parents...sort of. They had a really bad fight." Ethan rose from the floor and headed into the kitchen. "I swear, it was like *Mom and Dad Reloaded.*" The sound of the coffee machine starting up drifted to me and then his shout, "You want one?"

I picked myself up from the tiles and followed him into the

kitchen. He handed me a cappuccino, then told me how he and Sue had tried to sneak past Susan's fighting parents last weekend and were spotted by them. Apparently Mr. and Mrs. Miller were at a vase-throwing level already. I remembered that from my parents and could imagine how bad it must have been for Sue. It appeared she was ashamed Ethan was put in the middle of such a fight at her house. She'd walked up to them and given them a good piece of her mind.

"It was quite impressive," Ethan said in awe. "You should have seen her. But she felt really bad afterward, and there was a lot of crying involved. She didn't want to go back to her parents that night, so I brought her home with me. And that was that. She was beat when she curled up on my bed, and fell asleep within seconds. Even if I'd actually wanted to do anything with her, she was dead to the world. You really don't need to worry."

He didn't have to look across the table at me so reproachfully now, I already believed him. But it was good to hear his side of the story and realize it corresponded with Sue's version.

Then again, what good was it now? I'd screwed up. No chance to change that.

"So what happened when Sue came here today?" At my brother's demand, I told him my miserable story. He listened carefully, though he tried to call Susan a couple of times in between. Still no answer. "Give her some time. A night to sleep on it," Ethan suggested in the end. "She needs to calm down, and then maybe you two can talk about it again."

"You think?"

"Mm-hm." He nodded. "It's probably just bad timing, what with all the trouble at her house. But I know she likes you. And she'll forgive you, too."

Jeez, I hoped he was right.

That evening, I found myself repeatedly knocking on my brother's door and asking him if Susan had called him back yet. She wasn't speaking to me, so Ethan was all I had—my one connection to Sue. Each time he shook his head, my shoulders drooped a little more. I really wanted to call her, or at least send her a message. After our argument today, however, I didn't dare.

At ten thirty, I checked for the last time. When I knocked on his door, he didn't answer, so I poked my head inside, in case he was asleep. My heart kick-started when, instead, he was on the phone. Ethan looked up and beckoned me with his finger to enter and be quiet.

"Is that her?" I mouthed, sitting upright and anxious on his desk chair. "What's she saying?" Jesus, could he not put her on speakerphone or something?

Obviously a little irritated by my pushing, Ethan turned his back on me and walked to the window. I could only hear his part of the conversation, and it drove me insane to wait.

"Do you want to do something this weekend?" he asked her. Whatever her answer was, it wasn't a *yes*, because he added a moment later, "The offer doesn't have an expiration date." Another short pause and he, thankfully, turned around again, so I could see his face while he spoke to her. But one could read *any*thing into his expression, so maybe that wasn't the best idea after all.

"Can I talk to her?" I hissed while Ethan was silent.

He made a shushing gesture at me, then spoke into the phone again. "Yeah. And hey..." His annoyed eyes rested on me, and he sighed. "Chris says good night."

Okay! That was good. Right?

"Will do. Bye." He hung up and tossed the phone on his bed.

"What did she say?" I fired at him as soon as it was only the two of us again. "Is she all right? Did she talk to her parents? How's she feeling?" I paused for a second, biting my bottom lip. "And did she say anything about me and what happened this afternoon?"

Ethan leaned against the window sill, impatiently folding his arms over his chest. "Are you done now or do you want to shoot questions at me all night?"

"I'm done," I murmured, lowering my head.

"Good." From the sound of it, he was suppressing an amused grin. "She seemed all right to me. They—her parents—had a conversation with her, that's why she didn't answer her phone before. It seems to have gone well."

A long-held breath rushed out with relief as I lifted my head. "Thank God."

"And she didn't particularly mention you or this afternoon, but"—he pressed his lips together briefly—"you might want to keep your phone close by. I think she's going to call you. Or text you." He shook his head. "Whatever."

I jumped out of his chair and raced back to my room, where my phone lay on my nightstand. "Thanks!" I shouted over my shoulder before I closed the door and flopped on my bed, waiting for the damn thing to ring.

It took Sue an endless time to finally text, but when my cell dinged with a new message, my heart thumped in my throat.

Thanks for today.

That's it? Nothing else? I didn't really know what I'd expected, but one or two lines more would have been nice. My thumb hovering over the call button, I pondered whether that was a good idea. It was late, for one, and yet it might have still been *too early* to call her. But this was nothing I could reply to and easily engage her in chat. "You're welcome" was just not enough.

And Ethan hadn't been such a great help, either. She'd sounded all right on the phone—but that could mean anything in this situation. Did her not sobbing into the phone necessarily mean *all right*? What if she was just pretending to be okay and in truth was crying into her pillow? If she was, she wouldn't pick up her phone, that was a given.

In the end, I decided to go with a text. It took me three attempts until I was happy with what I had.

Ethan said you're feeling better. I'd like to make sure of that myself. Mind if I call you?

She replied fast. *Do you really think that's a good idea?*

You bet! If she'd told me in no uncertain words that she didn't want to talk to me tonight, I'd have respected that. But what she said was practically an invitation to call. Right? And so I did, holding my breath while I waited.

Susan picked up on the third ring. As she whispered, "Hey," my tension eased and my heart could relax and beat normally again. From the sound of this one word, I guessed she was in her bed. It was funny how I'd taken to notice such small things about her when we talked.

"Hi."

We were both silent for a long moment after that. Dammit, I missed her.

After a few more seconds, her slightly teasing voice drifted through the line. "I thought you'd say something stupid to make me laugh so you could hear that I'm fine."

Any other night, that would have been my plan. Right now, however, I couldn't think of something funny. Too much had happened, and it wasn't the time for jokes. So the first thing that came to my mind was, "Ethan is gay."

Although I was serious, Sue burst out in wild laughter. "Yeah? So what?"

So what? "You knew," I accused her. She knew, and she hadn't told me.

"Yes, I did." She made it sound like it was the most obvious thing in the world that I had a gay brother. "Didn't you?"

"I assumed." A casual shrug rolled off my shoulders. "Never knew for sure." But since we were all clued in now, there was one last thing to discuss. "He told me today. You know what that means."

"No, what?"

"That you can't have him." *Duh.*

"True."

True? That was her answer? In the dim light, I scrunched my face at the wall opposite my bed. "I'm confused. Today you turned me down because you wanted him."

"No, Chris, I didn't turn you down because of Ethan," she declared in a tone you'd use with a kindergartener. "I said I wanted someone a little more like him. That's all."

"Ah. Safe and boring. I get it now." She would never admit she loved a little adventure, too.

"Ethan isn't boring," she defended my brother, and I got the feeling I was about to get on her bad side again. "We talk a lot. He understands me. We can have fun without me having to worry that he's gushing over the next best girl."

Right. "Because he'd be gushing over the next best guy..."

Shit, where did that come from? I bit my tongue as Susan laughed and scolded me, "Chris! You're impossible."

Hearing her laugh made me smile. "Yeah, I know." To change that would probably require more willpower than I could ever master. "But I think it's cool that he finally told me. And he's going to tell Mom, too. You're good for him in that way."

As if startled by my reasoning, the only sound she made for a moment was her breath in the phone. Finally, she said, "I guess he just needs someone who doesn't judge him for what he feels."

"I don't. He knows that." If Ethan hadn't figured that out before, he knew it now. Our sobering conversation this afternoon was really one of a kind. Then I sighed, thinking of the mess I'd made of Sue and me. "I just wish he'd have confirmed my suspicions a little bit sooner. Like a *week* sooner."

She definitely knew what I meant, but she asked anyway, and with an unmistakable tease in her voice too. "What would have changed?"

Many things. For starters: "I wouldn't have been an ignorant dick. I would have come for another kiss the very next day." And most of all: "I wouldn't have messed us up."

"Us?"

"Well, the *possibility* of us."

Even in her quiet exhale, I could feel her smile. Then she cleared her throat. "Dude...shit happens."

God, yes. I rocked with laughter. Sadly, she wasn't taking my suggestion the way I'd hoped, and that made me uneasy. I really didn't want to completely lose her over a stupid misunderstanding. Hm, maybe a change of plans? "So I guess I'll have to show you."

"Show me what?"

"That I can be safe, boring, funny, a listener, a talker"—in short, everything my brother was—"and all on an *exclusive* basis."

Her answer came after a short hesitation. "In your dreams, Chris."

"Perhaps." But from her giggle, I knew she liked the idea. "Luckily, you'll be there as well tonight." Then I added in a softer voice, "Sleep tight, sweetness."

ANNA KATMORE

Normally, she would have hung up at this point. She never said anything after that, not even to wish me a good night. Only now, she was still breathing into the phone. And for a reason. She wanted to give in. Wanted to give the *us* thing a chance. I knew she did.

So come on, sweetness! It's not that hard. Just say the words.

"You, too," she murmured, followed by the disconnecting click. The girl was just too adorable.

Chuckling to myself, I dropped my phone in my lap. So she hadn't written me off completely. That was all I could ask for.

Chapter 20

"NO, IT'S REALLY just boys, Mom."

Whoa. I stopped dead in the hallway when I heard my brother's quiet words on Sunday morning. Ethan and Mom were in the kitchen, and they were having *the talk*. Not the one about the birds and the bees—this was about boys only.

Not wanting to be an eavesdropper, I decided to skip breakfast and slinked back to my room, where I sat the next hour reading. Heck, this was the first time in ages that I'd picked up a real book. After I'd pulled it from the shelf, I had to blow off the dust of what seemed to be years. It was *Paper Towns* by John Green, a Christmas present from Ethan two years ago. He always gave me books for Christmas, even though he knew I never read them. Well, not until this morning, anyway.

After the first few pages, I started wondering what kind of book this actually was and turned it around to read the text on the back. Had he given me a romance book? *Jesus, Ethan!* We really needed to talk about boy and girl stuff.

I shut the book and put it back between the other dust traps, getting an *Archie* comic from the drawer of my nightstand instead.

A while later, I ventured off to the kitchen because my grumbling stomach was killing me. Mom was there alone, hunched over the counter, thumbing through a cookbook. She looked up at me with a smile.

"Are you okay, Mom?" I asked as I poured myself a glass of OJ and grabbed a doughnut from the box on the counter.

"Sure, why wouldn't I be?"

I shrugged. "Heard you and Ethan talking earlier."

Straightening, she shut the book and swallowed. "Yeah, that. It was...um—"

"Don't say it was unexpected, Mom." I gave her a pointed look, taking a big bite of my breakfast, which sported green icing.

"No, no! That's not what I was going to say." She blushed a little and went to get a glass of water. After a long drink, she put the glass down and leaned against the island. "It's all right," she finally let out on a sigh. "Ethan is a good boy. He can handle this."

"Of course he can." An amused chuckle escaped around my bite. "Just don't make him feel too special. You have *two* awesome kids, you know." In mock sulkiness, I lowered my chin, and she laughed at that. Then she came around to the table and ruffled my hair.

"So, what's for lunch? Find anything in that book?" I

nodded back to the counter.

Mom tilted her head and cleared her throat. "Know what? Maybe we should go out. You never got that steak at the St. James for your victory, and home cooking is overrated anyway."

Going out? Mom was in a good mood. That was a great sign.

On the way back to my room, I informed Ethan of our plans. Then I asked him if he'd heard from Sue this morning and if, by any chance, she was going to come over later today.

Ethan shook his head. "She's busy all weekend. Her dad's moving out, and she's going to help him. I think she won't be home until Sunday evening."

Oh. That was tough. Her parents had dumped the news of their split on her only yesterday, and already her dad was moving out? Hopefully she was all right. She should have told me what was going on last night on the phone.

The weekend dragged on endlessly, and without the prospect of seeing Susan for the entire two days, I couldn't wait to get back to school on Monday. Yeah, shocking, right? Only, she wasn't there in the hallways that morning. Well, of course she had to be there somewhere, but I didn't see her on the way to my first class. Either she was already in her classroom, or she came late. Was it deliberate, to avoid me?

Nah. I was clearly starting to overthink our situation. A little depressed, I headed to history. After second period and on the way to gym, Brady and I ran into Lauren. Not exactly into her, actually, but I spotted her by the lockers and stopped in

ANNA KATMORE

my tracks, shooting an arm out to hold Brady back, too.

"What's up, man?" he asked with a bewildered look.

"Nothing." I just didn't want to interrupt what looked like Wesley with the elephant ears and Lauren arranging to go out. When her warm gaze wandered slightly off and landed on me, she gave me a quick smile. I nodded in approval. She would have plenty of time to tell me how the chat with Wesley went in Spanish. I was actually getting a little excited—not for Lauren, but for Wesley's sake. The quiet guy had no idea what he was in for with that bombshell of a girl. She might be the stuff of his very own high school legends later in life.

Brady and I headed on to the gym, leaving the new dream couple to their smitten selves.

At long last, between third and fourth period, I saw Susan for the first time since Friday afternoon. Her backpack draped over one shoulder, she came shuffling toward me along the wall. My heart lurched to my throat in anticipation of talking to her. Today, she wore that soft green t-shirt, the one she'd had on when we made out in my house. Was it weird that I'd started to develop a liking for this simple piece of clothing?

I stopped, forcing the kids behind me to stream around me. Sue's eyes found mine. They were shy and friendly, blinking tentatively in my direction. Her sweet ponytail swayed with each of her steps. I wanted to skim my fingers through her soft hair once more and draw in that fruity scent of her shampoo.

But she didn't halt. All she actually did was lift her hand and briefly wiggle her fingers my way as she hurried on.

Was that it? My shoulders slumped, and my stomach

dropped to the floor. Did she actually intend to pretend we didn't belong together like ketchup and fries? She gave me a fricking wave, nothing else? I thought we were over our argument and could start a new chapter.

Apparently, I'd been wrong.

Frustrated, I slumped against one of the lockers behind me and banged my head against it, the metallic sound rising over the crowd of students, making some of them look at me sideways. And ouch, that hurt. Rubbing the back of my head with one hand, I pulled out my phone and texted Ethan with the other. *When you see Sue at lunch today, can you invite her over this afternoon?*

His answer arrived before the bell rang. *Will do.*

Good. I really needed a chance to talk to her in person. On the phone was nice, but it never got me nearly as far as when we were in the same room. When we stood face to face, she had no chance to edit. It was as simple as that.

In Spanish, Lauren told me about her date set for Friday with Wesley Elephant-ears, and I was genuinely happy for her. Still, my mind kept wandering off elsewhere. Maybe I shouldn't leave it up to Ethan to invite Sue. I could walk over to the soccer table and ask her myself. That way, she could see how important she was to me. Then again, I didn't want to ruin anything by being too obtrusive. *Gah*, this was such a dilemma.

In the end, I decided to trust Ethan and hope to see Sue that afternoon.

Yeah, total shot in the dark. Ethan was going to see her, all right! She'd invited him to her place, instead. That girl made

ANNA KATMORE

courting her quite difficult.

Irritated and bored to death, I roamed the house after basketball practice, waiting for Ethan to come home. I needed a detailed report of everything she'd said.

As soon as the sound of the front door closing drifted to me, I dashed into the hallway, where my brother was hanging his jacket on the coatrack. Turning around, he gaped when he found me planted in the middle of the hall, blocking his way.

"Hi," he said warily.

"Don't you *hi* me, traitor. How was it?" I demanded, jaw set.

"It was...nice?"

"Nice? That's all?" Dammit, did he want to kill me with his reluctance? "What did you two do all evening? What did she say? Will she come over tomorrow?"

"Umm..." Ethan squeezed past me and rushed to the kitchen. He freaking *fled!*

"What is it?" I snarled as I strode after him and cornered him by the sink.

Hands gripping the counter behind him, he faced me and inhaled slowly. "She actually wants some distance."

"Distance?" My jaw dropped. "She lives at the flipping other side of town. How much more distance can she want?"

Ethan shrugged uncomfortably. "I don't know. She just said some distance would be good for the two of you."

My gaze sank to the floor. "Distance," I repeated flatly, heaving a deep sigh. "She's punishing me, right? For how I screwed up last week."

"Look, I don't think it's—"

"What do you recommend I do now?"

Lips pursed, he mulled over my question for a moment, then suggested in an uncertain voice, "Maybe you should give her the distance she wants?"

"Right." An almost hurt laugh pushed out of my throat. "Or maybe not."

Spinning on my heel, I trudged to my room and slammed the door shut. Susan Miller had a problem with nearness? Fine. Let's get this sorted out. I grabbed my phone and typed a message for her.

Seriously? Distance? How am I supposed to show you all the good sides of me then?

Within two minutes, her answer arrived in my inbox. *You can shine with your absence. ;-)*

A winking smiley face? Did she think this was fun? Then again, maybe she did. So she wasn't punishing me as much as teasing me? Heck, this girl confused me more than complex numbers in math.

Biting the inside of my cheek, I wrote: *And fade out of your mind? Clever girl. Guess what? It's not gonna happen, sweetness.* And hell yeah that was another challenge.

The sad thing was, she didn't reply after that, and staring at the silent phone was driving me crazy. I finished the *Archie* comic I'd started reading on Saturday morning, then I turned off the light and glared at the ceiling.

Hah. Distance. You wish, little Sue.

*

As I swung my legs out of bed the next morning, my mind was set. I was going to get this girl, come hell or high water.

Of course, she once again successfully dodged me all day long. No possibility of an easy conversation, let alone the chance to touch her. Only, when I caught her gaze across the cafeteria at lunch, she sent me a flirtatious smile. Over quite a distance...

I was so sick of being kept away. Seriously, what a mean streak this deceivingly cute girl had in her! This was cruel.

But also exciting, on a deeper level. Hell, I quivered inwardly each time I spotted her somewhere in the school building, and the tingles in my stomach doubled whenever we locked gazes across the hallway. It was a fascinating game of hide-and-seek, and something that made me completely brain dead all day. Thank God I had no tests to take. The possibility I'd fail was about ninety-nine percent.

Oh, shocking surprise, she didn't come to my place again that afternoon. Man, she was one stubborn little thing. The worst part of it all was that *I* was in love with her but Ethan was the one who got to be with her. She never said no when *he* called her.

Hm. Never said no...

I scratched my brow. So what if—

No! No, no, I couldn't do that! Shaking my head, I abandoned the idea that had just sneaked into my mind. But hell, the thought didn't go away. So maybe I could? It was, after all, for a really good reason—and, at the moment, the only way I could think to convince her that I could be just as much her dream guy as Ethan was, if only she gave me a fair chance. Yep, it was worth a shot.

"E.T.!" I yelled as I raced down the hallway, rattled on his door, and stormed inside. He sat on his bed with a car magazine in his lap and gazed at me, utterly perplexed. "I need your help. Now!" God, I knew being a twin would come in handy one day!

"With what?" His voice was more than a little skeptical.

"With winning Sue."

"Uh, I don't think I want to have anything to do with that, thank you." Chuckling, he concentrated on his magazine again.

"Shut up and listen." I planted myself in front of his bed, hands on my hips. "She thinks you're the perfect guy for every girl, right? Well, at least for *her*. Except, we both know that she's deluding herself and really wants a guy like me."

"*Really?*" He tilted his head up once again, one eyebrow arched.

I gave him a broad grin. "Yes."

"Fine." With a mildly intrigued smile, he closed the mag and leaned back against the headboard. "So what, in God's name, can I do for you?"

Heart racing with excitement, I bent forward and braced myself on the mattress, so that we were on eye level. "I want you to ask her out on a date." As he sucked in a breath to interrupt me, I quickly added, "But *I'll* be the one actually going out with her."

His chin dropped a little. "You want to fool her?"

"Not fool, exactly, but...yeah."

Huffing, Ethan tossed the magazine aside and climbed off his bed. "No way! I'm not going to trick her into a date with you." The hardening lines of his face threatened to ruin my brilliant plan. "If you want to go out with Susan, just ask her."

Desperate, I hung my head and said through clenched teeth, "Given the current impasse between us, she would never allow herself to say yes." I straightened and pivoted to keep my eyes on my brother as he paced the room. "I need your help, Ethan."

At the window, he whirled around to me. "You're insane, you know that, right?"

"I'm a genius. She will go on this date completely unaware and unbiased. It's my chance to show her I'm the perfect match for her." I put on a pleading face. "So, will you do it? Please!"

He looked at me hard, crossing his arms over his chest. "I don't think so."

"Aw, come on," I whined. "I'll pay you."

"Not a chance, Chris. Now go away."

Lacing my fingers, I dropped to my knees in the middle of his room and made the most pitiable face in Donovan family history. "Pleeeeaase. You have to help me with this. It's...it's..."

"It's what?" he snarled, with a reprimanding glare.

I shuffled forward on my knees and grabbed the hem of his t-shirt to plead with him. "It's brother code. You can't ignore that."

"Yeah, right. Guess what! It's still *no*." He almost laughed, but he wasn't amused by my begging. Prying my hands loose, he growled, "Go. Away."

Grinding my teeth, I scrambled to my feet and trudged to my room, but I'd never been one to give up. There was one thing in this world that Ethan couldn't say no to. And luckily, I was in possession of that one thing.

My signed basketball sat on my shelf, looking down at me as if to say, "What's more important to you? Me or a girl?" Thinking back to my perfect kiss with little Sue, the answer was easy. Quickly, I grabbed the ball and returned to my brother's room. Ethan pivoted as he heard me enter. I tossed the ball at his chest, and he caught it with a slight *ugh*.

"Want to think about it again?" I asked, dead serious.

To Ethan's credit, he really thought about it. For all of ten seconds. Then his arctic scowl moved from Kobe Bryant's autograph to my face. "What do I have to do for it?"

Okay, he wasn't happy, but he was willing, and that's all I needed. "Call her and ask her out. Nothing more. I'll go on that date, pretending to be you for a while, and when I'm sure she's seen enough of *you* in *me*, I'll tell her the truth."

For an endless moment, he stared back at the ball, deliberating, his bottom lip between his teeth. Finally, he lifted his head, drew in a deep breath, and commanded, "You'll also take the blame for this shit. You'll tell her you stole my phone to call her or that you drugged me or whatever. But you *will* keep me out of this."

I crossed my heart. "You have my word."

His wary gaze on my face, he threw the ball back at me,

fished his phone out of his pocket, and dialed Sue. Seconds later, his expression changed to friendly, and he tore his eyes away from me to look at the ceiling instead. "Hey, Susan, how are you feeling?" A short pause. "Nothing much. I just thought, since you don't want to come play Wii with me anymore, we should go for coffee again. We haven't been to Charlie's in a while." Another silent second of waiting, in which I could only pray she'd agree. "Cool. How about Fri—"

No! Panicking, I shot the basketball at Ethan's chest, and he stumbled backward, dropping the phone. As he bent down to pick it up, he snarled under his breath, "What the hell?"

"Not Friday!" I hissed back. "That's too far away. Tomorrow."

"Sorry," he told Susan, with a hard scowl at me, as he resumed the call. He clenched his teeth. "Some idiot left his basketball in my room... Anyway, how about Wednesday? Would that be good?" He waited, then he shook his head at me.

Dammit, she said no? "Why?" I whispered.

"Can't," he mouthed back.

"Thursday then!"

Ethan narrowed his eyes in irritation. "Okay, how about Thursday?" he suggested, attention back on Sue. "Cool. I'll pick you up at five." They said goodbye, and he put the phone down. Looking like an irate alligator, all teeth, he snapped at me, "There. Happy now?"

A grin spread across my face. "Very."

Chapter 21

"NO. FRICKIN'. WAY!"

"What?" Ethan replied, his grumpy reflection behind me in the mirror. "That's what I'd wear today."

Yeah, maybe *he* would wear it, but the washed-out green t-shirt and pants he'd worn since ninth grade would not leave this house on *me*, especially not for my date with Sue. I pulled the tee over my head, threw it back in his wardrobe, and discarded those sloppy jeans. "Don't you have anything just a little more stylish?"

He folded his arms and leaned one shoulder against the mirror. "I already arranged a date for you. Why do I have to give you my clothes, too?"

"Because she'll notice the difference the second I show up with something from my own closet. I need to play your part well, and therefore I need to dress up like you. *Comprende*?"

Ethan rolled his eyes. "Fine. Take what you need. But if you say one more word about my clothes, I'm going to send

Susan a text and cancel." He pulled a stupid eyebrow up. "*Comprende*?"

Growling, I searched through his wardrobe once more. There had to be *something* I could wear without having to do a walk of shame in a couple of hours. If it wasn't for the disguise, I'd have picked my dark gray button-down shirt. It was my lucky shirt. Unfortunately, Susan had already seen me in it, and she would never believe that Ethan borrowed my clothes.

Twenty minutes later, I walked out of my brother's room dressed in a bland white tee and a jean jacket that felt like it had never been worn. Ethan had kept it in the very back of his wardrobe, like it was an untouchable treasure. If only he'd take it out and put it on sometime, because it did look good. But I was glad he hadn't, because I quite liked it.

As for the pants, Sue wouldn't really notice whether I wore my own or his, so mine it was. But what about shoes?

Ethan's worn-out sneakers lay in the hallway by the door. I slipped into them and tied the laces.

"You're going to wear my shoes, too?" my brother blurted behind me. "Ugh, that's gross."

"Grow some balls," I snarled, heaving a sigh of exasperation as I straightened and walked a few steps up and down the hallway in his footwear, testing its comfort. Hell, if it wasn't for the fact that we were identical twins, I'd say his feet were two sizes bigger than mine. These shoes were so loose from his wearing them for ages that my feet practically swam in them. I kicked them off and decided that no date was worth wearing those.

"What? Is the king not happy with his subject's shoes?" Ethan mocked in a high-pitched voice.

I cast him a smirk over my shoulder. "I'm going to tell Mom to take you shopping this weekend."

All amusement dropped out of his expression. "No!"

Yep, Ethan loved his threadbare clothes. Shopping with Mom and clearing out his wardrobe was a dreaded spectacle that happened once a year.

The warning was effective, and he shut up for the time it took me to style my hair and put on a light spray of Axe. As I came out of the bathroom and found Ethan still standing in the hallway, I held out my hand. "Keys."

His eyes widened. "What?"

I tapped my foot, waiting.

"Take Mom's car. I'm not letting you drive mine. You crashed hers last year."

"It was only the side mirror, smart ass, and I need the Mustang. Sue will get suspicious if *you* show up in somebody else's car." I tilted my head. "So it's either the Mustang or my Kobe Bryant ball. Your call."

Mumbling an unintelligible curse, Ethan went to his room, came back, and reluctantly handed me the keys.

"Thank you," I said, overly polite, and headed out the door.

A Wiz Khalifa song kept me company on the drive to Susan. I hummed along to it, then cut off the radio together with the engine after halting in front of her house. In the front garden, a woman dug around in a bed of petunias. She straightened as I climbed out of the car, and pulled off her dirty gloves. "Hello, Ethan. How nice to see you again."

We shook hands. "Uh...yes. Hi." Dammit, was Ethan on a first-name basis with her, or did he call her Mrs. Miller? Better not address her with any name at all. "Is Susan ready? We have a date."

"Wait a second. I'll call her." She offered me a smile that made her green eyes crinkle. She was a beautiful woman. One couldn't help but notice that Sue was the image of her mother.

Throwing the gloves on the ground, she went into the house. "Susan!" her call echoed to me. "There's someone waiting outside for you, honey!"

"Coming!" That was Susan's voice from somewhere on the upper floor, and my heart started drumming a little harder at the sound. Trying to rein it in, I leaned against the side of Ethan's Mustang and folded my arms.

Show time.

It only took seconds for Sue to skip out the front door. Her blue dress flapped around her knees, a broad black belt accentuating her slim figure. She wore a very short white cardigan cropped just below her breasts. She looked stunning in that outfit.

Sue slowed down as she came toward me across the driveway, almost shy, probably because she'd noticed how I drank her beauty in. Then again, she did check me out, too—and seemed to like what she saw. "Trying to impress somebody today?" she teased.

She definitely looked better than me, so the compliment belonged with her. From the chest pocket of the denim jacket, I pulled out my shades, and with a smirk, I put them on. "Are you?"

"Just every guy in town," she replied saucily, as I opened the car door for her. "Other than you, since that's not working."

Oh, it was working, all right. She just had no idea...yet.

I climbed in the other side and steered the car back onto the street. The inside of the Mustang quickly filled with her fruity scent. It wasn't a long ride to Charlie's, but I liked having her next to me, so I drove extra slowly. "So you were with your dad yesterday? Have a good day?"

"It was awesome!" Sue admitted, hands clasped in her lap. "I had him all to myself the entire time. We cooked and ate grilled chicken, and he even made eggnog for us." Her smile revealed how much better things must have been for her family after only a couple of days.

Genuinely happy for her, I nodded. "I'm glad things are working out for you now."

We arrived at Charlie's moments later and headed inside. Sue claimed a table somewhere in the middle. It was for two, and a thin vase with a yellow tulip stood in the center. I would have held Susan's chair out for her, but she didn't seem interested in me playing the gentleman at all—she just sat down.

I hadn't been to Charlie's in a while, so the face behind the bar was new to me. A guy maybe my age or a bit younger, with dark hair, was wiping the counter, but he lifted his head and nodded in greeting. He tossed the cloth away and made a beeline to our table, smiling at Sue. "A hazelnut latte deluxe for you?"

"What do you think?" Susan replied cheerfully, rolling her eyes in a mocking way. A hazelnut latte deluxe. Was that her favorite? And why did this guy know that? Were they friends? Reading Susan's smile, I tried to figure out just how close they were. In the end, I got sidetracked by said smile and forgot everything else, because it was the prettiest thing I'd seen all day.

"Ethan?"

"Hmmn, what?" I mumbled, hearing my brother's name. Quickly looking at the guy with a notepad in his hand, towering over me, I realized he was certainly waiting for my order.

"What do you want?" he asked, smiling too sweetly. I'd thought he only gave that smile to his female friends, like Susan, but obviously it was a business smile that he offered to all customers.

"Um...a cappuccino. Thanks." Ready to be left alone by the waiter, I turned my attention back to Sue, who watched me with an odd look.

"Whipped cream, no foam, right?"

And now it was starting to get creepy. The waiter was still here, and he knew how I liked my cappuccino. I tilted my head, studying him for a moment. His dark eyes gleamed with a strange warmth as he held my gaze. All of a sudden, I was hit by my own charade. He'd called me Ethan. They must know each other. Of course. And Ethan's favorite—just like mine—

was cappuccino with whipped cream. "Yes," I confirmed.

At last, he disappeared. As soon as we were alone, Susan leaned forward and placed her hand on my forearm, pulling a wry face. "Sweetcakes, flirting doesn't work that way. You have to smile, not scare him off with a stare."

What the freaking hell? *Flirting?* With the boy behind the counter? Was she on drugs?

I opened my mouth but closed it just as quickly. Duh. The gay thing. Ethan. I should have known. Susan seemed to be determined to hook Ethan up with someone. Obviously, she deemed this black-haired guy a suitable match. I bit my tongue and gave her a stiff nod. "Yeah, right."

She leaned closer and actually rubbed my arm now. Her touch was gentle and very welcome, even though her cold fingers gave me a slight tingle of goose bumps where they brushed my naked skin. "Hey, it's cool. I don't mind you using me for cover."

My brows knitted in a frown. "What?"

"Look at you. You're gorgeous, all dressed up." Sue suppressed an excited giggle as she moved her hand up and down in front of me. "Did you really think I wouldn't realize who you truly wanted to impress today? Actually, I knew when you mentioned Charlie's on the phone."

"You did?" Had she figured me out? But how? And then the truth hit me again. Hard. The joke was on me. Susan had no idea she was facing the wrong twin. Dammit, Ethan had a crush on this guy, and she wanted to play matchmaker. That was the only reason for her excitement at the moment, not because she was happy to be here with *me*.

"Yes," she answered, sounding much too happy. "And I'm fine with that. Now relax and show the guy what a great catch you are."

Now that was a compliment I could happily accept, as it went for both me and my brother. The corner of my mouth slipped up in a smirk. "So I'm a great catch, huh?"

"Absolutely."

My grin stayed, even when the waiter came back with our coffees—although it felt more like my mouth cramped and froze in that position. However, if Ethan was really crushing on this guy, it would be quite shitty of me to ruin it for him. After all, he'd been helping me with Sue, too. But it cost me quite a bit of effort to briefly direct my smile at the waiter. Flirting with boys didn't come naturally to me. And it was definitely not something I enjoyed.

After the waiter left again, Susan whispered, full of enthusiasm, "See? That wasn't so bad."

A long, pained breath escaped me. "You actually have no idea."

"Don't worry. It's okay to be nervous. You'll get used to the butterflies." She grinned. "And at some point, you'll love them."

I will? Could it be that she happened to like the butterflies she had with me? On the other hand, what if she didn't feel excited around me any longer? She'd seemed quite relaxed since the moment she came out of her house.

Of course, she had no idea who was wearing Ethan's mask

today.

Hm, with a little luck, I might be able to sound her out about me...

One elbow propped on the table, I leaned forward and rested my chin in my palm, my intrigued gaze fixed on her. My index finger tapped a soft rhythm on my bottom lip. "I don't make you nervous anymore, do I?"

"No, you don't," she told *Ethan* with a soft chuckle.

"Who does?" When she was reluctant to answer, I suggested innocently, "Chris?"

"Well, he does...sometimes." Her suddenly shy gaze dropped to the latte in front of her, which she stirred with a long-stemmed spoon. "I'm working on getting that under control."

Why would she? I liked that I made her nervous, and even more that she admitted it to me. She hadn't denied the chemistry between us, so not all was lost yet. My hopes flaring bright made me blurt out the next thing that came to my mind. "If you still get nervous when you see him, you haven't written him off completely."

Sighing heavily, Sue ripped a sugar packet open and poured the entire contents into her drink. Then she cleared her throat and cut me a quick, scrutinizing glance from under her silky bangs. "Any chance Chris asked you to grill me about him today?"

I swallowed. "Would you be mad if he did?"

"Not at you, of course." She lifted her head, and her serious look returned to me. "It's not your fault."

ANNA KATMORE

Ah, but it *was* mine—only she didn't know. I grimaced. "So you're mad at *him* because of it?"

Leaning back, Susan crossed her arms defiantly, but a smile still tugged at the corners of her mouth. "I won't say another word if you're going to run off to tell him again at the first chance you get—like you did on Monday."

"Okay, I won't tell him." Technically, that wasn't even a lie. *I* wouldn't tell me; she would. Still, a prickling of conscience made me lower my chin. Uncomfortably, I spooned the foam of my cappuccino into my mouth and asked in a quiet tone, "Now tell me why you don't want to give him another chance." If I knew, maybe I could do something about it.

Sue started scooping up some of her latte's foam, too. "That's a difficult thing to explain."

And I looked like a dimwit or what? "When's your curfew?"

"What?"

"Home? When do you have to be there tonight?"

"Um—" She scratched her head. "Nine. Why?"

"That gives me about three hours to make sense of what you're going to tell me." Cocking my head, I mocked her with a tilt of my eyebrows. "I think I can cope."

Now she laughed. "Fine. But you have to promise that you'll never tell anybody about it."

That, I could promise without regret. "I'll keep all the good stuff to myself, I swear!"

She took a sip, putting me on hold with her irritating

attention to her drink. After she licked the foam from her lips, and I nearly offered to do that for her, she put the cup down and began, "The problem is...Chris scares me."

"He does *what*?" I blurted out in utter shock. "Why?"

"You see"—she nervously tugged at her left earlobe—"when I met him, he was this really arrogant...popular...lionized guy."

"Lionized?" Now that was a cute way to put it. I chuckled.

"Yes." She cut me silent with a stern look. "So, I just ignored him, because—duh—I was head over heels for you." She rolled her eyes. "At some point, he decided he wouldn't let me ignore him anymore. I hated myself because he started giving me butterflies and managed to break through my defenses with stupid little things."

"Butterflies? That's sweet." Heck, I knew she loved those tingles in her gut! Everybody loved them. "So what where those little things that brought you around?" Curiosity was torturing me at this point.

"Text messages, mostly." A dreamy expression crossed her face. It was so adorable, I wanted to start playing footsy with her under the table. Except, I was Ethan, and Ethan wouldn't do that. *Get a grip, Donovan.* Still, there was nothing I could do to stop my flattered snicker.

"That's not funny," she scolded me. "I mean, me and the playboy? Come on, that's just not right."

"But you did fall for him." I shrugged to play down my excitement. "That's cool."

"No, it's not cool. Because I kinda *really* did," she whined.

"And Chris is not the guy to take feelings seriously."

Wait! Where the heck had she come up with that kind of crap? What had happened between her and me in the past few weeks, I took very seriously. I had to muster every bit of self-control not to tell her so this minute.

"I let you guys talk me into that stupid date at your house and it was...fun," she confessed, briefly lowering her eyes. When she looked at me again, she said in a small voice, "And then he stole my first kiss."

I choked on the whipped cream in my mouth and coughed under my breath. *Sorry, what?* My hand holding the spoon sank onto the table as I slowly sagged against the backrest of my chair, a stunned breath leaving me. "That was your *first* kiss?"

Lips pressed together, she nodded. "Mm-hm." She also blushed a lovely pink. "I don't know if you've ever kissed anyone. If you have, you know what that first kiss meant to me."

"I think I do." I'd kissed a high two-digit number of girls in my junior and senior years, but I still remembered my first.

"Please, Ethan," she suddenly begged, grabbing my hand with her cool fingers. "Don't tell him that. For Chris, it was probably a godawful kiss, and nothing that he was used to from his other, more experienced girls."

Was she kidding? She was a flipping natural. I made a wry face at her. "Oh, you're so wrong."

She pulled her hands away from mine. "What?"

Shit. I needed to find a way to tell her without giving away my identity. I bit my bottom lip, thinking hard, and decided to just keep acting the part of Ethan. "When Chris told me about that kiss, he said he found it pretty *amazing*. I think you should believe him this one time." Really, I wanted her to trust me on that.

Sue contemplated my words, then rewarded me with the tiniest smile and rosy cheeks. Oh yes, she did like hearing that bit of truth.

"All right, so let me recap," I said, straightening in my chair. "You had a crush on Chris. He gave you your first kiss. You liked it. He still gives you butterflies." One by one, I ticked all these things off on my fingers. That was a lot in my opinion, and to anyone who could have overheard, it must have sounded like she was totally smitten. A very simple conclusion, in fact. Except, Susan didn't go by this reasoning. She wanted *distance*. I leaned forward on the table, staring into her pretty eyes, and tried to figure her out. "What's the problem?"

She was reluctant with an answer, and her voice was low. "The problem is that I sort of take romance quite seriously. I might have been more into Chris than he was into me. I don't want to be his next go-to girl."

First off, sweetness, you can't like me more than I like you. That was not technically possible at this time. And then I said, "Go-to girl...?" My eyebrows dipped together in confusion.

"Yes, you know, what you said about Chris and Lauren the other day. Even though I'm not one of those girls who want to wait until marriage before they...er...sleep with a guy, it doesn't mean I'll give it away to some arrogant womanizer either." She chewed on her lip. "I think the first time should be something special with the guy I love...and not just about a stupid challenge." Avoiding my gaze, she resumed stirring her latte. "But I don't expect you to understand that."

Whoa. That was quite the chunk of information. If she'd known it was me and not Ethan listening to her, she certainly wouldn't have opened up like that. In fact, it was hard to believe she'd really say all that to any guy. I'd been lucky to get the full, unedited version. The only thing bothering me was that she actually thought I wouldn't understand that.

With a soft smile, I reached out and lifted her chin with my finger. "Did you just say that because I'm a guy?"

"Who can tell what's really going on in that head of yours?" She frowned, probably wondering about that for the first time today. Then she fished a strand of hair from her neat ponytail and tauntingly twisted it around her finger.

Uh, a little more credit, please. "It seems you have a completely screwed up view of us guys," I reprimanded. The first time meant as much to us as it did to any girl—especially if it was *their* first time. "Someone should show you one day. And I'm sure, if Chris was the one, he wouldn't mess that moment up for you." As an afterthought, I added, "Believe it or not, I know he's done some serious thinking on that matter the past couple of weeks."

"Chris is thinking about getting in my pants?" She laughed with dry humor. "Why doesn't that surprise me?"

"Oh, come on. Give the guy a break," I pleaded for

myself—but kept playing Ethan's role perfectly. "You know I didn't mean it like that. He's really not that bad."

"What, are you trying to play matchmaker now?" She lifted her brows, then grimaced. "Please don't." And just as fast, she cheered up again. "That's my job, anyway."

"Your job?"

"Yes. I think you brought me here for a reason."

Most definitely, though not what she thought, so I asked her, "And that would be what?"

"Helping you get on with your own romance."

Of course. Me and the waiter, right? Chuckling, I reclined in my chair. "I don't think I have a romance going."

Chin lifted, Susan cast me a cocky smile. "Well, maybe not yet. But with a little push you might just start one today." With a subtle nod, she confirmed my suspicion about the waiter.

Acting more on reflex than out of curiosity, I tracked her gaze to the bar. The black-haired guy had his eyes on our table—on me, particularly. He must have been watching us for a while, but when our gazes met, he quickly looked away. And so did I. Damn, this was weird. I rubbed my neck, feeling uncomfortable now, and whispered to Susan, "He's staring at me, isn't he?"

She cut another brief glance to the bar and grinned. "Well, I don't think he's staring at *me*."

God, the next time, *I* would pick the location for our date.

"Know what?" Susan said a moment later, lighthearted enough to make me start. "I'll just pop to the loo and you go engage Ted in a nice chat. If it works, I'll call Sam to come

ANNA KATMORE

hang out with me."

Ted, uh-huh.

Wait, *what*?

When Sue got to her feet all of a sudden, panic strummed my throat closed. "No!" I hissed with what little air was left in my lungs and clasped her arm. "Don't leave me alone with him."

"Honey, it's okay," she reassured me. "You talked to him for an entire hour a few weeks ago." Amused, she pried my fingers loose from the sleeve of her white cardigan. "He won't eat you."

"You can't know that." My voice was a whiny whisper.

"Relax. I'll be back in a few minutes."

Remember that game from middle school—seven minutes in heaven? Well, this would be my personal seven minutes in *hell*.

Susan patted my shoulder, her look full of encouragement. "Just be yourself, and no one can ever resist you."

When she flitted off to the restrooms, my legs began to shake and my neck cramped from the way I kept my gaze focused strictly on the cup of cappuccino in front of me.

Jeez, was he staring at me again? What if he decided to come over and engage me in a conversation? His pick-up line was probably *Want a sausage to go with your coffee?* Oh God. I shuddered.

My throat suddenly dry and my hands annoyingly shaky, I fished my phone out for self-defense. Of course, it wouldn't help me ward off an infatuated teenage boy, but if I looked really busy here all by myself, Ted might not even come up with the idea of talking to me.

A message from Ethan was in my inbox. *How's the date going? Did Sue buy the charade? How did she react?*

Irritated, I sucked on my front teeth and typed: *She's trying to hook me up with the waiter.*

The message was barely sent when the brush of a whisper stroked the side of my face. "Who are you texting?"

"Whoa!" My heart nearly gave out from shock. I jumped in my seat, jerking around to Sue. "Don't you sneak up on me like that, woman!"

She laughed. "Why? Did you think it was Ted?"

Obviously! I made a grumpy face. "Not funny."

"Okay, sorry. So who are you texting?"

I pressed my lips together and thought about something to say that wasn't a lie again. "My brother."

"Why?"

"He asked how the afternoon was going."

Susan looked a little horrified. "You did not tell him what I said before!"

Too late. I'd already heard it all—firsthand.

Her stricken expression made me smile, because the way she wanted to keep her true feelings from me could only mean one thing: She was far from being over us.

Reaching for my cell in a panic, she commanded, "Give me that phone and let me see!"

"Does the term *privacy of correspondence* ring a bell?" Laughing, I pulled it away quickly and tucked it back into my

ANNA KATMORE

pocket. Then I made a decision. "Drink up, we're leaving."

"We are?" Baffled, she ogled her still half-full hazelnut latte. "Why the rush?"

"Things aren't working the way I'd hoped." She was far too fixed on hooking me up with someone else, when all I wanted was her. We needed more privacy. A place where no potential matches for Ethan would come between Sue and me. Of course, I couldn't tell her exactly that, so I cut a glance at Ted for her benefit and told her, "It wasn't a good idea to bring you for cover." Maybe this way I could make her believe that I—Ethan—would rather talk to Ted alone.

Sue pulled a disappointed face but relented. "Okay. What do you want to do instead? And don't suggest *Mario Kart*. You know I'm not going anywhere near your house right now."

Nowhere near *Chris*, she meant. I rolled my eyes. "I wasn't going to suggest that. Let's just go find another place. There's a nice bar in Pismo Beach." With lots of older people. She wouldn't want Ethan hanging out with one of those guys. "We can grab some food, and they have great music." It was Pismo Beach's answer to Hard Rock Cafe, quite cozy, but still hip.

Susan understood my urge to get out of here when I rose to my feet. While she practically inhaled the rest of her coffee, I tossed a few dollars on the table to pay for both our drinks and even added an extra dollar for Ted.

From the corner of my eye, I saw him walk around the counter, probably to exchange a few more words under the cover of cleaning our table. I was so not ready to do that, so I grabbed Susan's hand, hastily pulling her outside with me.

With an apologetic note in her voice, she shouted, "Bye, Ted!"

"See ya!" his answer drifted after us.

As soon as we were out the door, Susan dug her heels into the asphalt and made me stop rather abruptly. "What the hell, Ethan!"

What was her problem? One eye brow arched, I pivoted to her.

"It's okay if you don't want to sit in there with me," she ranted, pointing one finger back to the door. Her jaw was set, and her eyes gleamed with real anger. "But you could have at least said goodbye to Ted. From his looks, he really could have a thing for you. Why do you want to ruin this?"

Yeah...why? I took a deep breath. Ethan was a great guy—if a little antisocial as of late. Being gay didn't make things any easier for him. And Ted could be E.T.'s very own love story. I sucked in another lungful of air through my nose. Ethan had also arranged this date with Sue for me. He helped me out when I was completely down and lost. Maybe there was a way to return the favor. Today. Right now. Would it hurt to go back inside and talk to Ted?

Drawing in a third deep breath, I bit my lip and cut a glance at the sky. "You're right. I'm an idiot." Determined, I let go of her hand and walked back into the café.

"What are you doing?" she whispered.

Already in the doorway, I shrugged and glanced back over my shoulder. "Giving him my number...I think." Well certainly not mine, but Ethan's.

ANNA KATMORE

Rounding the corner, however, I stopped dead as my nerves began to flutter. Ted had carried our empty cups away and was putting the money into that old-fashioned cash register. He either heard the door close or he felt my stare on him, because he lifted his head and slid a glance over to me.

His eyes were puzzled, waiting. And I did a hell of a job standing here making him guess. Fuck, I should do something. But what? Oh God, this was weird. I had no idea how to approach a guy, even if I was just acting. On the other hand...why act? Susan was waiting outside. She wouldn't hear a word we spoke in here, so I could be myself and just come clean with the waiter, right?

Yep. That sounded a lot better.

Already chilling out, I cleared my throat, and with a friendlier expression than the shocked one I'd been wearing when I came in, I walked toward the counter. Ted slowly closed the cash register and turned to me, looking wary.

Susan and I had been the only patrons this afternoon, so it was certainly okay to speak normal and not whisper this conversation. "Hi," I said with a light voice, holding my hand out over the bar. "I'm Chris Donovan. Ethan Donovan's twin brother."

With surprise in his eyes and more than a little confusion, Ted reached for my hand with what seemed to be a reflex, and not real confidence. "Uh...hey." His grip was shy and light.

A smirk on my lips as the memory of how Susan had given me her number came up in my mind, I tightened my hand around Ted's and pulled his arm toward me across the counter.

"I noticed how you stared at me before," I told him as if it was the most natural thing in the world, and slipped the pen from his chest pocket. With it, I pointed to the door. "Did you see the girl I just walked out with? Sorry, dude, but I'm totally into *her*." I gave him an apologetic look. "However, I know that my brother would kinda like to...um..." Dammit, what was a good term to use? "Hang out with you." Yep, that worked. Opening the felt-tip pen with my teeth, I scribbled Ethan's number on his forearm. Then I let go of his hand, recapped the pen, and held it out to him. "So maybe you'll call him."

Reluctantly, Ted closed his fingers around the pen. All this time, his eyes were fixed on mine, wide with wonder. "Oh...kay," he mumbled, blushing a pink that would have looked sweet on Susan but not on a boy.

I gave him a quick smile and nodded. "Take care."

Heck, that went better than expected. *Great.*

And now back to Sue.

Chapter 22

OUTSIDE CHARLIE'S, SUSAN waited for me with a hanging jaw and an expectant look. "You really gave him your number?" she exclaimed in awe.

"Mm-hm."

Now she started to grin. "Awesome! What did he say?"

I chuckled. "No way. I'm not talking to you about this." It was hard enough to actually go through with it, no need to spill every little detail. Especially because it would ruin our date, which had gone fairly well so far. Sue seemed quite chilled out and happy to be with me. I could totally pull off the Ethan thing, and it wasn't even hard. That should convince her in the end that we were the perfect match.

We walked across the street to the Mustang and climbed in. I didn't dare look back at the café in case Ted was looking at us through one of the huge windowpanes. In fact, it was a great relief to finally leave this place and head somewhere *I* could be Sue's sole focus again, instead of another guy she thought she had to hook me up with.

As we drove out of town, she turned her head to me. "Did you borrow your brother's cologne?" From the corner of my eye, I spotted a smile on her face. "You smell like Chris."

I bit my lip at the pleased sound of her voice and cut her the quickest glance. "Good?"

She nodded once.

A smirk tugged at my lips. "You said the other day that you liked how he smelled. I thought it couldn't hurt to try it." And for her benefit, I added, "You know...for Ted."

"Do you think he'll call you?"

My shoulder jerked in a small shrug. "I don't know." Ted didn't seem like a forward player to me. Equally as shy as Ethan, or maybe even more, he probably needed a few days to work up the courage. Even then, I assessed him as someone who took the careful way. He wouldn't call Ethan.

As we drove on the highway along the ocean and the sun slowly sank into the waves ahead of us, I squinted at the stark orange rays striking the windshield. From my chest pocket, I retrieved my shades and put them on one-handed, then finally said, "A text would be cool."

Susan lowered her head. When I cut another glance at her, I saw how she smiled, expression soft, her eyes on her knees. It must've been a nice memory that brought out that reaction. Hopefully one she shared with me.

The Merry Melody was a place I'd hung out a few times last summer. Tyler liked taking Rebecca out here because, apart from an awesome cuisine, they had a dance floor, and Becks loved to grind against him to the beat. The DJ usually played some nice rock and pop music. Only, today seemed to be a bad choice. "Oldies night," I groaned as I pulled Sue around the twisting couples to a booth in the back.

"What? I like it," she said into my ear, sliding in front of me with a broad grin. "And look at us"—gripping her skirt, she made it sway a little to the music—"we seem to have picked just the right clothes for it, too." Her delighted eyes gleamed in the colorful spotlights.

We sat in a small booth with green upholstery, Susan opposite me. Studying the menu, I said, "I'm hungry. Are you?"

"You always are." Laughing, she stole the laminated card from my hands. After quickly scanning the meals listed, she made a displeased face. Obviously her favorite—kiwi and cream—was not on the menu. "I think I'll go with fries."

Since this was a self-service place, I told Susan to wait while I went to the bar and placed our order. A cheeseburger meal with extra fries and an extra Coke for Sue. Back at our table, I enjoyed my food while Susan nibbled one French fry after the other. Was she not hungry? I licked the ketchup off my fingers and wiped my hands on a napkin. "You're not really a big eater, are you? I noticed when you stayed over for dinner."

She sucked her Coke through the straw and grinned. "I like to save up my quantum of calories for liquor-filled pralines. They're my soft spot."

Pralines, aha. *And I thought I was your soft spot,* I thought, staring at her slowly emptying basket of fries. As I looked up, her scrutinizing gaze was fastened on me. *Crap.* Had I just said that out loud? I shrugged in a nonchalant manner and waggled my brows once, hoping to cover that capital mistake.

Her eyes narrowed to curious slits. Was she starting to figure me out? Man, I was such an idiot, incapable of holding my damn tongue. Since it was far too early in my plan to reveal the truth to Susan, I settled for distraction. A jaunty song started playing, and that gave me an idea.

I reached under the table and pulled gently on the skirt of Susan's blue dress. "Does that swing?"

She laughed. "What?"

As we'd come in, she'd said she liked the oldies music and even pointed out our perfect clothes for a night like this. We could put that to the test. I got up, shrugged out of my jacket, which I tossed back into the booth, and tugged Sue along to where some older couples twisted on the parquet floor. "They're playing your song. Let's dance."

"I—agh..." She tried to hold me back. "Wait!"

Not a chance, sweetness. Her hand in mine, she had no choice but to come with me. On the dance floor, I twirled her around under my arm and pulled her against my chest.

"I can't dance. My knee. You know that," she protested, staring up at me, baffled. "And why is this my song?"

"Don't get your panties in a twist. Just move your hips a little," I teased her with a smirk. Taking advantage of the moment and holding her tighter, I began to sway with her. "And because it's called 'Runaround Sue.'"

It didn't take long for Susan to finally chill out and get into the quick rhythm with me. She laughed into my face as we twirled around the dance floor. With a gentle push, I rolled her a few steps away from me, then twisted, sixties-style, after her. In spite of her still-healing knee, she even did some gentle and smooth moves herself, and it was a pleasure to watch her. Adventurous, that's what she was today. And she'd been absolutely right before. Her dress was perfect for this kind of dancing.

I snapped my fingers to the music for a few beats. When Sue's hot and burning gaze met mine, I crooked my finger, beckoning her to me. Without hesitation, she stretched out her hand. I grabbed on tight, pulling her into me once more. Oh man, the feel of holding her again! It was worth every goddamned lie today.

Susan searched my face in the dim spotlights as if she was looking for something. Like maybe the answer as to why Ethan would suddenly want to be so close to her. For all she knew, the guy in front of her was gay.

The slight flush on her cheeks didn't entirely come from dancing. If I wasn't careful now, she might fall in love with Ethan all over again. That couldn't happen. Then again, judging by her look, she was falling for the guy she was with right now. And whether she knew it or not, that guy was me.

The song ended, but I couldn't care less. We'd slowed our dancing long before. Another oldie started, a love song this time. Shyness in each of her movements now, Susan tried to slip away from me. I didn't let her. Wrapping my arms gently around her body, I adjusted our swaying to the new rhythm of "Stand By Me."

Her enticing scent filled my head. Our flaming gazes locked, I knew she could read my longing clearly in my eyes, but I couldn't help it. It might've confused her, but she didn't break away.

Soon, her delicate hand moved up from my shoulder to the back of my neck for a closer embrace. At the familiar touch of her cold fingers against my warm skin, my eyes fluttered shut for a brief moment. I completely failed at holding back a pleased smile. When I looked a Sue again, there was only one thought on my mind. Kissing her. And nothing in this world could have stopped me from doing it.

I mindlessly started stroking the small of her back, feeling that the skin under her dress was in no way as cold as her hands. Her breathing sped up a tiny bit, just enough to reveal her surprise and pleasure by this new twist of the evening.

Encouraged by her surrender, I moved her other hand to the back of my neck, too, then let my fingers slide down along the side of her arm, which made her shiver again. The couples around us were still dancing, but Susan and I had come to a standstill in the middle of the dance floor. As I was holding her gently against me with both my hands at her back, I lowered my head until our brows touched, all this time capturing her eyes with mine.

Just when I was sure she wanted me to kiss her as much as I wanted to, she said in a hoarse whisper, "Ethan..."

Shit! My brother? He was here? "Where?" I breathed, but

for the life of me, I couldn't make myself look up, much less detach myself from our embrace.

Susan narrowed her eyes just the slightest bit. "What?" she croaked.

What what? I mirrored her frown. Then realization struck me. *Oh damn!* She thought I was—

My heart raced with anxiety. I should have told her the truth already. She should've known who she was going to kiss, but it was too late. Now was *not* the moment.

"Never mind," I whispered and leaned in the last couple of inches, claiming her lips. They tasted a little salty from the fries and a bit like Coke, but a lot like Sue and our first kiss. In fact, they tasted so good, I never wanted to move my mouth from hers again.

Her fingers wandered down the back of my neck, leaving a trail of goose bumps from the cold. It was heavenly torture, making me moan. All of a sudden, she went stiff as a rock in my arms. And I knew why. She'd found the silver chains beneath my shirt.

"Chris—"

No, no, don't break it, sweetness! Refusing to look into her face, which was doubtlessly filled with shock, I reached for her hands and dragged them away from my neck. The moment was too beautiful to ruin with excuses and explanations. When I laced our fingers, she let me, and I moved her hands to the small of her back. "Don't think about it, Sue, just don't," I quietly pleaded, then planted another tender kiss on her mouth.

Susan kissed me back like she'd finally come to embrace each and every single butterfly in her stomach that she'd spoken about earlier. Little, fluttering fellas she had because of me. Leaving her hands where I held them, her fingers tightened around mine, and she lifted herself on tiptoes, her body flush against mine. I kissed her hard, finding and stroking her tongue with my own. She didn't back down. Not once—until the song ended.

Reluctantly detaching her lips from my mouth, she inched back and gazed at me with huge, question-loaded eyes. Only seconds later, the anger finally surfaced, contorting her face. She shoved my hands away from her waist and took a disgusted step backward. The move impaled my heart with the sharpness of a sword. Helplessly, I locked my gaze with hers, my eyes pleading as I took a small step toward her. I reached out my hands in the hopes of explaining.

But Susan didn't give me a chance. "Don't touch me!"

I froze on the spot. "Sue—"

She wouldn't listen. Her eyes starting to glisten, she whirled about and stormed away. Her aim was the exit. I followed, after a rushed detour back to our table, where I'd left Ethan's jacket. When I found her outside, she was pacing the sidewalk, her phone pressed to her ear.

Snatching her wrist, I tried to stop her and make her look at me. "Susan—please let me explain!"

As if touched by acid, she yanked her hand away and snarled, "I don't need your explanation. You're a bloody—" Her eyes jerked away from mine as she spoke hastily into the

ANNA KATMORE

phone. "Dad? Hi. I'm sorry to bother you, but could you pick me up at the"—she turned around and lifted her head to read the huge cursive letters above the door—"Merry Melody. It's a bar across town at..." Frantically, she pivoted, scanning up and down the street, probably for a hint at where exactly we were. The horror inside me grew as I watched her. I didn't want anybody else to pick her up. We needed to talk this out first.

After a moment, she told her dad, "I'm fine. Just a misunderstanding. I need a ride home." Then she hung up and swirled back to me.

"You didn't have to call your dad. I can take you home." Desperation rang in my voice.

Her eyes sharp as glass shards, they could have easily cut cement as she snapped, "Do you honestly think I'll ever get into the same car with you again?" She pointed at me with her phone still clasped in her whitening fingers. "You goddamn liar!"

"Please. It's really not what—"

"—it looks like? Save me that! I'm done with you."

Great. She was going to keep up this game until her father showed up. Anger surging inside me, I clenched my teeth. "Jesus Christ, why won't you let me explain? You gave me no other choice! All the things you loved about Ethan—" Man, how could I make her understand? At a loss, I threw my arms in the air, Ethan's jacket flying. "I had to show you somehow that you can have them with me, too."

Susan went stiff. It seemed her anger had just reached the next level as she asked, a deadly and slow, "Does Ethan know what you did tonight?"

Oh my God. I'd promised to keep him out of this. But telling her now that I drugged my brother to get on his phone would probably make matters worse. I really didn't know what to say.

Hurt beyond words about the truth I didn't voice, Sue closed her eyes, as if wanting to shut me, and everything else that had happened tonight, out of her mind.

Laughter behind me made me aware that someone was coming out of the bar. The woman's laughter died as she and her companion walked past us, casting Sue an understanding look. They probably thought I'd screwed up my girlfriend's evening. And they were absolutely right—minus the girlfriend part.

A few seconds after the couple was gone, Susan glanced up at me again. Our gazes locked, I whispered, "I'm sorry."

Her eyes misted, and she blinked frantically. She was going to cry. Because of me. "I don't believe you." Then her hands fisted at her sides, her cell phone still tightly in one of them, and a muscle ticked in her jaw. Wrath swamped her sorrow once more. A slap was in my future. Even though I clearly would have deserved it, I backed a step away.

My hands lifted helplessly, I pleaded, "What can I say to make it up to you?"

"You've already said enough. I don't care for more of your false words or actions." Not only her cheeks but her entire face turned red with anger. "Go away and leave me alone."

"Sue—" I expelled a breath. "Me not telling you the truth

from the start was a mistake, I realize that now. I was going to tell you before the evening was over, I swear, but first you had to *really* see me. Nothing about this date was fake."

"Apart from your identity!" she exploded in my face. A tremble of shock zoomed through me. She was like a wildcat ready to pounce. There was no escape for me.

Thank goodness, a car stopped at the curb behind her at that moment. She wouldn't kill me with witnesses around, right? An instant later, it became clear that I'd reached the empty bottom of my bottle of luck today, because the man behind the wheel got out, leaving the engine running, and stepped up to Susan. "Hey, sweetheart," he said as he put an arm around her and kissed her forehead. With a wary expression, Susan's father observed the situation and then held a hand out to me. "Ethan."

Shit. He'd met my brother before, so it would only be logical for him to assume Ethan would be the one out with his daughter. I shook his hand firmly, but told him, "No. I'm Chris. Hello, sir."

He scrutinized me with narrowed eyes. "I see." Then he searched Susan's face for answers. "I believe you will explain that on the way?"

"Yes. Let's just leave," she mumbled. Leaving me behind like an abandoned street dog, she looped an arm through her father's and dragged him to the car.

"Good night, Chris," Mr. Miller said to me, friendly but reserved, before he lowered into the driver's seat. Susan was already inside, fumbling with her seatbelt. She didn't look up as they drove away.

The taillights of their car disappeared down the road. My throat clogged tight, I ran my hand trough my hair and looked up at the night sky. So many stars up there. And none of them had brought me luck.

It could have been seconds or minutes that I stood there, gazing into nothing. Some people passed and they might have been gaping at me. I didn't care. My heart felt like it had slipped into a compactor, tight and hurting. Any more pressure, and it might come out a diamond.

I'd messed up *us*. Utterly and completely. Susan would never forgive me.

Since I'd turned off the volume of my phone for the date today, it took a couple of seconds for the vibration in my pocket to register. Hastily, I pulled it out, holding my breath and hoping Susan was coming around from her shock and would let me explain.

My brother's name flashed on the display. Crappy timing. Disappointment lodged like a fat, tarry lump in my chest.

I answered the call with a quiet "hey."

"What the fucking hell?" Ethan blurted into the phone, and I swallowed. "Susan sent me a text. I'm in trouble? Chris, dammit, why am *I* in trouble?"

"I-I don't—" To stop my stuttering, I drew in a mouthful of air. "She found out."

"She found out? Meaning, you didn't *tell* her, like you said you'd do. You let her freaking figure it out *herself*?"

Oh man. I was in deep shit. "Listen, I'm sorry. It didn't go

ANNA KATMORE

as planned. I really wanted to tell her, but..."

"But *what*, Chris? What's so hard about saying, 'I'm not Ethan'? Tell me now, or I swear I'll come after you with Mom's power mower."

Rubbing my eyes with my thumb and forefinger, I pinched the bridge of my nose. "It's not that easy to explain. One thing led to another, and suddenly we were kissing. I would have told her afterward, really. But she figured it out before." I trudged to the Mustang and unlocked the door with the key fob. As I sank into the driver seat, my head tipped backward, and I closed my eyes. "Did you call her?"

There was a short pause on the line as Ethan heaved a calming sigh, but to me it felt endless. "I tried. She turned off her phone. Voice mail."

With stiff fingers, I worked the key into the ignition and finally got the car started, after some cursing. "I'm coming home now. Would you try her again in the meantime?"

"Of course I will," Ethan snarled. "But not for you, dickhead. She's mad at me, and I'm going to set that right. What she'll do with *you*? Well, I don't give a shit." He hung up.

Chapter 23

I'M SORRY, SUE! Please talk to me! After calling her twice that evening and only reaching her voice mail, I'd decided to text her. Then, staring at the ceiling above my bed, I waited as the minutes slipped by, my heart thumping in my throat.

Why didn't she reply?

God. I shut my eyes tight. I knew why. Because I'd screwed up. And not just a little bit, but royally this time.

One more unanswered call and three pleading messages later, I heaved my tired body off the bed and shuffled to Ethan's room. "E.T.?"

He didn't answer my knock.

"Please, just tell me if you've talked to her."

A second ticked by, then a grumpy snarl drifted through the door. "No."

I scratched my head. "No, you didn't talk to her, or no, you're not gonna tell me?"

"No, she didn't answer her phone. Now go away!"

That was clear enough.

My head lowered, I returned to my room. Susan must have thought my brother and I were in cahoots...which we were, somehow. She was going to hate my guts for a long time, that was clear. But it really wasn't Ethan's fault, so she should at least forgive *him*.

Slumping on my bed, I looked at my phone for the six-hundredth time. What a surprise, there were no new messages. My frustration barely stifled, I wrote her another one. *Ethan is innocent. I drugged him the other day and forced him with a gun to his head to set up the date for you and me. Please don't be mad at him.*

No. Fricking. Answer.

It was nearing ten o'clock, and I was starting to go insane. Had I known any of her close friends, I'd have called them and begged for help. The only person that came to mind was Hunter. With very few details, I explained to him what had happened and asked him to speak to Susan. Maybe he could get through her wall of anger and put in a good word for me.

Ryan said he would try and that he'd call me as soon as he got her on the phone. When he didn't call back that night, I knew he'd had no luck either. Tired of staring at a dark screen, beat, and exhausted, I went to sleep.

Friday morning, I ran into Ethan in the kitchen. Pouring a cup of coffee, I shot him a glance, but before I could speak, he snapped, "Don't talk to me again until you set things right with Susan." His hard stare on my face, he took a sip of his orange juice. "I don't care how you do it, but you better hurry up."

I swallowed. The nod I gave him lacked confidence.

Set things right with Sue. Dammit, was I giving the impression I wasn't trying my very best? It wasn't easy to do when she wouldn't answer her phone.

I ran up and down the hall at school three times before my first class, but I couldn't find her anywhere. After history, I dragged my feet to trig. Brady bumped into me. But he wasn't the one responsible for the small rush of hope in my chest. Behind his shoulder, I caught a glimpse of a short girl with choppy black hair and some sort of army pants paired with black Doc Martens. Unless I was mistaken, she was one of Sue's best friends. A couple of books clasped under her arm, she shuffled down the hallway. Heck, what was her name again? Something with an S.

"Sabrina?" I called after her, but she didn't turn around. *Shit.* Was it Sophie? She didn't react to that name either.

"Who are you calling?" Brady demanded, brows drawn in a deep frown.

I grabbed him by the shoulders. "Tony Mitchell's girlfriend. What's her name?"

Confused, he shrugged, shaking his head.

Terrific. I let go of my friend and whistled with my fingers. The shrill noise made half of the school jerk around. They all stared at me in wonder—the tiny black-haired girl, too. "You," I said loud enough for everyone to hear as I pointed my finger at her. "Wait up, please." While the rest resumed walking or doing whatever they were doing before my interruption, she waited, frozen, in the hallway. I told Brady I'd see him later, then strode toward her. *Whoa.* Up close she was even smaller than she looked from a distance. Her brown eyes lifted to mine, and they had to lift a long way.

Licking my lips, I raked a hand through my hair. "Hi. I'm Chris. I'm...er...a friend of Susan's."

Her puzzled expression turned wary. "I know who you are."

Of course she did. She was one of Sue's best friends. Feeling a little embarrassed that I still didn't know her name, I cleared my throat. "Do you know where I can find her?"

"I'm wondering that myself." Arms wrapped around her books, she pressed them to her chest. "She didn't come to school, and her phone is off, too. It's a little strange."

Maybe she wouldn't think it so strange if she heard the whole story of yesterday. Then again, it was weird that Susan was missing school. Had she caught a cold while waiting outside the bar last night, or was she really trying *that* hard to avoid me?

My heart sank as the chance to meet Susan and talk to her between classes, or even at lunch, slipped away. "Uh, okay." It felt like my facial features had been derailed. "If you hear from her, could you tell her that..." Well, what would be a good thing to have this girl pass on to Sue?

She lifted her chin with a curious tilt of her head. "That what?"

"That I'm sorry and I really, *really* need to talk to her."

"You're sorry?" Her jaw dropped in proportion to her eyes widening. "Oh my God, what did you do, Chris Donovan?"

Mute, I sucked my bottom lip between my teeth, holding her inquisitive gaze.

"That bad?" Her face paled as if I'd told her I'd driven over the Easter Bunny on the way to school this morning...which probably wouldn't have been much worse than what I *had* done.

Taking a deep breath through my nose, I nodded.

She blinked her brown eyes a couple of times, never breaking eye contact. When she seemed to have processed the gravity of the situation, she said with a stern look, "Spill."

"Uh, you might want to hear it from Susan herself. I guess she'll tell you as soon as—"

"*Spill!*" she repeated, taking a small but very intimidating step toward me.

Whoa. Cornered by a black-haired kitten. I backed away and crashed into the lockers behind me. Holding her books tight, she waited. We both glanced at the clock in the hallway at the same time. The eight minutes before next period were obviously enough for her to hear the full story. In the end, there was no good reason why she shouldn't hear my version first, so I heaved a tiny sigh and began, "I guess Sue's been telling you everything that's been going on between her and me, right?"

"You bet."

"Okay. So there were some...um...really stupid misunderstandings last week—"

"When you stopped speaking to her after you kissed her," she cut my stammering short. "And then you taunted her with another girl."

I gritted my teeth. "Yes, that." Dammit, Susan had been thorough with her explanations. "Anyway, when we got a chance to sort things out, she kind of told me that she didn't want someone like me as her boyfriend. She wanted a guy more like my brother."

As if she was already guessing part of my silly plan, she pursed her lips. "O...kay?"

"Yeah. And you see, I had this idea to set up a date with her, letting her—"

"Oh my God!" She made a face like that kid in *Home Alone*, when he slapped some of his dad's aftershave on his sensitive skin and then screamed. Only, her scream wasn't one of pain and shock, but of sheer delight. "You went out with her yesterday, didn't you? Not Ethan. That was you!"

Utterly confused as to why she found this so awesome, I nodded. "It wasn't to fool her or make fun of her, I swear. I only wanted to—"

"Get a real second chance and make her see that you're still the man she actually wants." A dreamy sigh escaped her as a smile stretched her heart-shaped lips. "That's so romantic."

"Romantic?" I laughed. "Sue wouldn't agree."

Her smile disappeared. "When did you tell her it was you?"

"I didn't exactly tell her."

"But how...?" Her dark brows formed a small V.

Dragging in a lungful of air, I told her the rest of the story. After that, her expression wasn't one of delight any longer. "Oh, that's bad," she said. "*Really* bad. You shouldn't have waited until after the kiss. I mean, seriously, Chris, are you a beginner?"

"Sorry, what?"

"You had this wonderful plan, and then you messed it all up because you couldn't wait just a couple of minutes to kiss her. This is bull! No girl wants to be kissed if she doesn't know who's bestowing it! I can totally understand why Susan's peeved at you now."

Ah, she hadn't condemned the entire idea—only the bad timing. Maybe I had found an ally in her after all. "Do you think there's a chance I can make this right with Sue?"

"Well, I can try to talk to her, if you want me to. On second thought, I'll talk to her anyway, even if you say no. This is, after all"—she heaved another moony sigh, clutching her book to her chest a little tighter and smiling at the ceiling— "the most romantic thing I've ever heard."

The bell broke up our little chat, wiping the dreamy expression off her face. "Dang, I've gotta go. See you later!" She flittered away before I could ask her to keep me posted—or even for her name.

When Hunter told me in trig that it was *Sam*, I slapped my forehead. "I knew it was something starting with an S." Unfortunately, he didn't have any other news for me. Susan hadn't answered his or his girlfriend's calls yet. "Thanks for trying," I told him as he slipped into his chair and Coach Swanson entered the classroom.

Maybe relying on others wasn't the right way to go about this anyway. I had screwed up, so I had to sort this out. Sitting

ANNA KATMORE

through the rest of the school day was annoying as hell. A thought came to me during lunch break and grew until the final bell. Instead of going home, I would drive to her house. She couldn't send me away if I stood on her doorstep.

Except, when I parked across the street and stared at the door, a small voice in my mind told me that she could very well do just that. Chances were she'd slam the door right in my face. Or shout at me. Or she could simply refuse to open up when she figured out it was me.

A deep sigh slipped out of me. Maybe it was too early to confront her yet. All this shit happened only yesterday. Since she hadn't come to school, maybe she needed a little more time. Maybe after the weekend. She would probably be back on Monday, and we could talk on neutral ground. No doors to smack my face and, if she intended to run from me, I would find a way to make her stay and listen.

Feeling a little encouraged, I started the engine again, eased into the light traffic, and drove home.

With not much homework to do and my activity barometer down below zero, it was a quiet weekend. Ethan was still evading any contact with me, and from Susan's end, there was only silence. If I spent much longer dragging myself through the house like a retired ghost, my mother was going to make me swallow some happy pills. All things considered, I was glad to get back to school on Monday.

Over the weekend, I'd envisioned—a hundred times—the moment Sue and I would meet today. I knew exactly what I was going to say. Every single line of my speech was carefully put together and waiting to be delivered. She had no choice but to listen to me, and once she did, she would understand my reasons.

The crowd of students in the hallway was thicker than ever this morning. Or did it only seem like it because I was trying spot Susan somewhere in the mass? She had her first lesson somewhere in this section of the building, but her honey ponytail was nowhere to be seen.

Rounding the corner, a group of people forced me to a halt. My breath caught in my throat as it became clear that this wasn't just any bunch of students, but ones I knew. Alex Winter's blond girlfriend was there, Nick Frederickson, a girl with long, dark hair and doe eyes, and in the middle of them all, Susan Miller.

A shooting star of excitement hit me as she, too, stopped in her tracks and looked at me. "Hey, Sue," I said in a low, croaky voice, realizing this was my chance. But those two words were the farthest I got. In the blink of an eye, my mind had gone blank as a sheet of printer paper, ruining the moment. Shit, where was that speech? *WHERE WAS THAT SPEECH?*

Her green eyes blazed with a carefully contained fury. "Excuse me. I have to get to my class." Her voice was so arctic it could have snowed right here in the hall. Sidestepping me, she hurried on without giving me a second glance.

The blonde and dark-haired girls followed her quickly. Only Nick stepped up to me and slapped a hand on my shoulder. "Girls, huh?" he said, rolling his eyes in sympathy. "Who can understand them?"

Staring sadly after Sue, I couldn't agree more. And now that she was gone, the speech resurfaced in my mind to mock me.

The problem had been bumping into her like that. My plan had been to find her first and then walk up. Not the other way round. Lunch break would be a better opportunity. I knew exactly where and when we were going to see each other then, and this time, I'd be prepared.

To make sure I was there before she was, I practically ran from Spanish to the cafeteria. As I shoved the swinging door open and stomped inside, very few students were lined up at the food counter and even fewer sitting at their tables. With no thought of grabbing a meal, I headed to my usual place. The door was in good view. It swung open and closed several times as more kids entered. And each time, my heart jumped to my throat.

Alex Winter came in with Sasha Torres. They made a beeline to the fruit section, where they grabbed a handful of grapes and an apple, then they skirted the tables in the room to get to their usual places. They were the first of the soccer bunch to arrive. It would only be moments now...

When the door swung open next, adrenaline spiked my blood. Flanked by Hunter's girlfriend and Sam with the choppy black hair, Susan walked in. None of the three cast a look at this side of the room. While her friends went straight for the buffet, Susan headed to where Alex and Sasha lounged by the windows. As she lowered into a chair, I rose and strode across the room toward her. I didn't intend to waste another minute.

The fewer friends present, the better. Besides, my buddies were filing through the door this moment, and they would only cause another delay if I wasn't gone before they sat down.

Sue picked up a water bottle from the middle of the table and took off the top. She didn't notice me coming. As she lifted the bottle to her lips, taking a small sip, I planted myself in the seat next to her. Grabbing one metal leg of her chair, I pulled her around with the entire damn chair so that she was facing me. Eyes widening in shock, she coughed and nearly spewed water on me. "What the hell, Chris! Are you crazy?"

"We talk," I informed her coldly. "Now."

"No."

"Oh, yes." My knees placed on either side of her legs, she had no chance of escaping. I leaned forward and braced my elbows on my thighs. Three and a half days—that was the maximum amount of time she could take to come to her senses. Now she was going to listen, because I had a lot to say. "You're mad at me, all right. Not answering your phone? Fine. But I'm not going until you hear me out."

Pressing herself against the backrest, she tried to put as much distance between her face and mine as this position allowed. "Didn't you get the message last time? I'm not interested." Deliberately doing something other than looking at me, she screwed the lid back on the water bottle and put it on the table.

One by one, the soccer table started to fill with guys from the team and their girlfriends. Opposite Sue, Ryan lowered into his place. "Hey, Chris," he said, his tone cheerful. "Showing up here? Respect, dude."

I paid him no attention. None of them. This was between Susan and me. Holding her captive with my gaze, I laced my fingers to keep myself from reaching out to her just yet. "I don't buy it. You were interested from the very first minute you challenged me," I stated solemnly. "You were interested when we played soccer together. You were interested when I kissed you. And you were interested when I fucking kissed you again. Don't tell me bullshit and don't brush me off. This is too—"

"Shut up," Sue yelled, her cheeks suddenly redder than I'd ever seen before. Shoving her chair backward, she pushed to her feet. "I told you why it's not going to work with us. That you fooled me last week only proves my point." I stood up, too. Her sharp eyes followed my movements. Yeah, we would continue this conversation eye to eye, even though the majority of my speech was already out. She took a shallow breath, her voice going lethal. "You're so full of yourself, it's disgusting! Now let me go."

"No." Not a chance. Determined to hold her here with me until we'd sorted this out, I placed my hands on her hips. In hindsight, this might have been a mistake. One of many.

"Don't touch me!" she spat. It had been one of the last things she said to me outside the bar on Thursday night, and just like then, her poisonous tone cut me deep.

Yet I couldn't let her go.

Instead, I let hurt and frustration change into anger and snapped back, "You call me full of myself? Don't throw stones while in your little glass house, Sue." I'd had enough of her mood. Denial would get us nowhere. "From the start, you tried to keep me away, simply out of principle. Because I wasn't who you expected to fall in love with. You kept denying your feelings for me, but I have proof of it on my phone. It's in every damn text you sent back to me!"

For an infinitesimal moment, we were only Sue and Chris, two kids who knew that every word of the past ten seconds was the truth. And then a sharp pain exploded on the right half of my face, jerking my head to the side. *What the hell?* I gasped for air as everyone else at the table sucked in a shocked breath.

Sue slapped me.

Somebody let out a compassionate "ouch," but with the ringing in my ear there was no way to tell which of the guys it was. Sam, however, clapped her hand over her mouth in dismay.

This was the first time in my life that a girl had slapped me in the face. The sting of her handprint didn't hurt half as much as the stab to my heart and pride. I gritted my teeth, staring into her equally shocked eyes. Was it a slip? Judging by her look, she might have wanted to take it back.

Sobering quickly, I kept my hands at my sides and said in a severely low tone, "I certainly deserved that one. But I also deserve a second chance, don't you think?"

Sue's eyes misted. "I think I'm done with you. And I told you so already. Now get the hell out of my way."

She reached for her backpack and flung it over her shoulder. This conversation might have been over for her. But not for me. I couldn't accept this outcome. When would her reason finally kick in? I'd made a mistake, all right. Did she intend to make me suffer for it for the rest of my life?

Before she could run away, I reached out and gripped her wrist, pulling her close to me. Her body, so fragile, trembled against mine. Determined, I looked her in the eye and pleaded in a whisper, "Don't run away from me now."

Equally low, but edged with frostiness, she demanded, "Let. Go." Then she yanked her hand free from my grip and stormed out of the cafeteria.

My heart beat way too fast in my chest. Fast and hard. And it hurt.

Should I go after her? Catch her and start this conversation over again? Hesitantly, I tore my gaze away from the door, which still swung back and forth from her exit, and faced the soccer bunch, who'd just gotten a free show. It was Alex Winter's girlfriend who answered my unspoken question. Her sky-blue eyes finding mine, she silently shook her head.

I dragged a heavy breath in through my nose and walked back to my place at the other side of the cafeteria. Since Susan and I hadn't really kept the volume down, more intrigued pairs of eyes followed me all the way.

Back with my friends, Rebecca watched me sit with a pale face. As we locked gazes, I appreciated that she didn't shove some girl wisdom at me in this moment. Brady wasn't quite so considerate. He leaned on the table, folding his arms, and stretched his neck toward me, definitely coming up with some shitty joke. The moment he opened his mouth, however, Becks smacked him on the bicep. "Shut up, Baker," she growled with a frown. Then she rose from her chair and pulled T-Rex up with her. "Let's go get some food." When none of the others made any attempt to go with her, she added in an annoyed voice, "Everyone!"

Brady, Trevor, and the rest moved, too. As they headed off, Becks waited a second and turned to me. "Can I get you something?"

"No, thanks." Hunger was the least of my problems.

Depressed, I let my gaze stray and wander across the room. People had gone back to munching their meals and chatting away the hour that we had for lunch. One person wasn't eating, though. Ethan's concerned eyes were pasted on me. The lump in my throat made breathing painful. I swallowed, holding his gaze for a moment. Then I pressed my lips together and lowered my head.

When everyone came back from the counter a minute later, their trays loaded with spicy-smelling gumbo and fruit, I snatched my backpack and headed out. I needed a walk by myself.

Chapter 24

"SHE ASKS THAT you stop calling or texting her."

My mouth open like a fly trap, I stared at Ethan. His face was as pale as mine felt. He'd lowered himself on the other side of the couch one minute ago and told me that he'd gone to Susan's house after soccer today. The meeting hadn't gone so well. Apparently, Sue understood why he'd helped me in this, but that didn't mean she wanted him back in her life just yet. Or me.

Damn, if he took that crap from her and still started speaking to me again in the same day, I must have looked *really* pathetic at lunch.

At my numb silence, Ethan scratched his neck, then leaned forward, and braced his forearms on his knees, lacing his fingers. "It's too much drama for her right now. She has a lot on her plate with her parents' divorce. Her family is falling apart, and then you and I, who she thought she could rely on, deceived her."

If you looked at it from her side, it was probably natural that she wanted some distance from us—and time to cope with her new family situation. "How long do you think she'll need to come around?"

"I don't know." My brother paused, staring out the window. "Remember how we felt when Dad moved out? We didn't want to see anyone, just be with Mom and try to understand why Dad disappeared. Susan might be struggling the same way. Maybe you should leave her alone until she starts to accept her new situation."

"But we took *months* to come to terms with that!" He couldn't really expect me to wait that long.

With a compassionate look at me, Ethan shrugged. Oh yes, he did indeed expect that.

"No way!" I jumped to my feet, skirted the coffee table, and dashed outside. A fight was not going to be the last conversation I had with Susan for months. I would go to her house and force her to give me a second chance. Well, ask her. Beg her. God, I was pathetic.

A painful sigh escaped me as I sank onto the front step and rubbed my hands over my face. I couldn't go see her. She didn't want that. And I had to respect it.

Elbows braced on my knees, I stared into the street, watching Mrs. Gilbert, our neighbor, teach her four-year-old to ride a bike without training wheels. Life was so easy at age four. If you fell and hurt yourself, your mother put a Band-Aid on the wound and you headed out to play again.

At eighteen, a Band-Aid could no longer cure every wound.

ANNA KATMORE

Life had gotten a little more complicated, and boo-boos lasted longer than three minutes.

Quietly, the door opened and closed behind me. A shadow fell over my face as Ethan came forward, blocking the orange evening sun. He sat down beside me on the concrete step, slowly twisting his new Kobe Bryant ball in his hands. After a moment, he held it out to me.

I tilted my head slightly to his side and nailed him with a questioning look.

Ethan pressed his lips together for a moment, then said, "You can have it back."

"Why?"

"I don't want it."

My frown deepened. "*Why?*"

"Because..." He cut a helpless glance to the sky and lifted his shoulders. "No idea. It just doesn't seem fair to keep it when your plan didn't work in the end."

Tearing my gaze away from him, I hung my head once more. "But that's my problem, not yours."

"No, it's not." A half minute passed in silence while Ethan drew in a lungful of air. "You're my brother, and you always have my back. It feels like a betrayal not to be on your side now." He pushed the basketball upon me once more.

This time, I took it. Planting my feet one step farther up, I placed the ball on my knees, wrapped my arms around it, and rested my chin on top. My words slurred, I mumbled, "Thank you." For being a cool brother, not for the ball.

Okay, also for the ball, but more for the other thing.

Little Madeline Gilbert pedaled on her blue bike past our house for the fourth time since I'd come out here. She was doing it on her own by now, without her mother holding her, but Mrs. Gilbert still ran alongside. Maddie's small upper body moved in sync with each push of her legs, and she squealed with joy, her eyes pasted to the street in front of her. "Watch me, Mommy! I learned it all by myself!"

"Yes, darling. And just look how fast you're going," Mrs. Gilbert panted.

As they were heading toward the end of the street for another turn, I quietly asked Ethan, "So you think I should give her the distance she wants?"

"Perhaps it's the best way. At least for a few days. A week, or two."

I pouted. "And what am I supposed to do in the meantime?"

Ethan laughed, bumping his shoulder against mine. "I don't know. But you can hardly sit here forever." He stood and held out a hand for me.

I didn't want to get up and go on with my life just yet. But Ethan had a point. In the end, I straightened and grabbed his hand. My brother pulled me to my feet, and we walked inside together.

*

Heeding Ethan's advice, I didn't call or text Susan anymore. That didn't mean the urge wasn't there. On the contrary, it felt like a permanent itch in my brain. Nasty and distressful. I couldn't get rid of it. But I couldn't give in to it either, because that might drive her away from me even more.

It got easier after a few days.

Much harder to resist was the urge to stop in the hallway and speak with her whenever we happened to cross paths at school. In those situations, it took everything within me to keep walking and not capture her with a pleading stare. A painful sting of longing lanced my chest each time. It reminded me a lot of the weeks after Amanda Roseman had dumped me. Losing Sue felt like losing my girlfriend all over again.

Maybe because of the really deep sighs that escaped me as I shuffled around at home, my shoulders and the corners of my mouth drooping, my mother realized something was off. One night, she came to my room, poking her head inside after a gentle knock. "Can I come in?"

"Sure." Wondering what she wanted, I switched off the nerds on TV and sat up on my bed.

She crossed the room, lowering onto the edge of the bed, facing me. In her hands, she carried a cup. As she held it out to me and the familiar smell of tea drifted up my nose, an ironic laugh escaped me. It wasn't just any tea, but fricking strawberry-vanilla.

"And what's this for?" I asked and took a small sip, looking into the cup as I drank.

In a soft voice, she said, "Ethan told me everything."

My gaze snapped to her. I lowered the cup, licking my lips. "Everything about..."

"You and Susan." She reached out and rubbed my shin. "Darling, I'm sorry about that. But if you want to talk about it—"

"No, I don't."

"Yeah, I know. I just said *if*—"

"And I said *no*." It wasn't Ethan's job to tell her about my misery. If I'd wanted her to know, I would have told her myself. When she rose to her feet, though, and walked to the door with sad, heavy steps, regret for my abruptness stung me. "Mom?" I said, before she could pull the door closed.

She turned around, fixing those helpless mother-eyes on me.

"Thanks for the tea."

A small smile appeared on her lips. She nodded and left me to my moping self again.

Maybe it wasn't such a bad thing after all that Ethan told her. This way, she didn't have to guess about the reason for my sad face and wouldn't be breathing down my neck at every opportunity.

Yep, having a blabbermouth twin actually had a good side, too.

*

Happy for the tiniest distraction in those final weeks before Winter break, I rushed out of the house after Ethan when he told me to come Christmas shopping for Mom. Apart from this one time in fifth grade, where I got her a pair of fluffy monster slippers and Ethan bought her a fat, grinning garden gnome, we always got her one present from the both of us.

"Have anything in mind?" Ethan asked during the drive to town.

I shrugged. "Gift card?"

"Beauty salon? Gas station? Restaurant?"

Tough choice. "Garden center?" I suggested, scrunching my face. At the moment, she spent more time with her rosebushes than with anything else, so that couldn't really be a mistake.

"Okay." Ethan took a turn onto West Grand Avenue where most of Grover Beach's stores were lined along the road.

My gaze caught on the giant glass shoe outside Cinderella's Jewels & Dreams. It wasn't a big shop, but Mom was known to spend hours in there, just marveling at the many rings and necklaces with pretty little gems. "Or," I said, "we could get her a pair of earrings." Since Dad had moved out, she didn't have anyone who got her jewelry on special occasions. And that was, apparently, something a woman would never buy for herself.

Ethan slammed on the breaks, causing my body to be pressed into my seatbelt. A whoosh of air pushed out of my lungs. As he reversed down the luckily empty road, it was clear he liked my suggestion. Hands on the dashboard, I groaned until he put the Mustang in drive again and steered it into a narrow parking lot right in front of the jeweler.

"Jeez, Ethan! Where the hell did you get your license? The grocery store?"

He smirked as he opened the door. "No scratch, no bump.

Everything's fine." While he had enough space to get out easily, my door would have knocked a dent in the red pickup next to the Mustang if I opened it too far. Squeezing out through a mere crack, I shook my head and gritted my teeth.

Ethan took a moment to check out the jewels in the shop window, then followed me inside. A tiny bell above the door gave us away to the tall man in a gray suit behind the counter. "Good afternoon, gentlemen," he said as he looked up from polishing a watch with a velvet cloth. Somehow, he didn't fit into my memory of this place. There had always been a lively stout woman that swirled around this room whenever Mom forced us to stop in here.

Standing rigid in the middle of the shop, I fixed the guy with narrowed eyes. "Where's Cinderella?"

The man returned my glare with disapproval, put the watch back into the glass case, and adjusted his dark tie. "Mrs. Everbackle is on vacation to see her newly born granddaughter." Behind me, Ethan snorted, clearly amused by the name. I sucked in my cheeks and bit on the insides to keep from laughing, too.

Mr. All-in-Gray put on a friendly smile that was certainly made for difficult customers. "May *I* help you instead?"

Just as he'd mirrored my look before, I now imitated his grin. "You may."

Ethan came forward and explained to him that we were looking for a pair of earrings for our mom. No more than sixty dollars. And she hated the color orange.

"Very well," replied the stiff replacement of Grover Beach's own fairy godmother. Within moments, he'd filled the glass counter between us with all kinds of studs—with and without gems—and a multitude of dangly earrings. Ethan and I examined all of them thoroughly. "If the right ones aren't among these, I can show you some nice pairs of creoles, too," the holiday replacement offered.

"Oh, would you be so kind, please?" Ethan asked.

As the man busied himself in one of the shop windows, I leaned closer to my brother and hissed in his ear, "What the hell are creoles?"

"I have no idea," he whispered back.

A moment later, we found out. They were the most boring, simple gold or silver hoops. Where were the pretty gems? I liked the gems in the other earrings. Mom should get jewelry with actual stones in them. "They have no gems," I pointed out, lifting my brows.

"Yes, sir. That's why we call them creoles."

"Then we don't want creoles," I muttered and let my gaze skate over the colorful ones again.

"How about these?" Ethan picked up a small box with a set of dangling silver feathers, each of which had a tiny, sparkly blue something in them.

"Excellent choice," the shop assistant gushed.

Fifty-nine ninety-nine. "Yep, excellent choice," I agreed with a broad grin. "We'll take them."

"Very well." He put the lid on the box and removed the price sticker. "Do you want me to gift-wrap it for you?"

"Yes," Ethan and I blurted at once. The man snickered and

pulled a small square of Christmas paper from the counter behind him.

While he wrapped Mom's present and Ethan handled paying with the money we'd put together back home, I roamed the shop, glancing at this and that. In a corner, Cinderella—now also known as Mrs. Everbackle—kept a whole selection of small crystal figurines in a locked glass cabinet. Living up to the shop's name, there were all kinds of Disney things. Bambi, Winnie the Pooh, Nemo, all seven dwarves, and Peter Pan's little pixie friend—whatever the hell her name was.

Susan would probably know it. I'd been thinking about getting her a gift for Christmas for a while. But one of those finger-tall figurines cost about two hundred dollars, some even twice as much or more. That busted my entire budget for Christmas presents.

Nose pressed to the glass, I jumped when the shop assistant appeared through the wall of the glass cabinet. "Can I help you with anything else, sir?" he asked in his ever polite tone.

"No. Well, yeah. Maybe."

He arched a graying eyebrow at me.

"I need a gift for a friend."

"A girl?"

"Yes."

"How close a friend is she, if you don't mind my asking?"

I didn't mind, because it meant he was thorough and knew his job. Only, I didn't have an answer to his question. To say I hadn't hoped Sue would have forgiven me by now was a lie. All would be easier if she let me talk to her—and figure out my chances. But as of right now, they might as well be zero. Pressing my lips together, I shrugged.

"I see." He unlocked the cabinet with a key he pulled from his jacket pocket. "Maybe one of these beautiful Swarovski crystal figurines is just right for her then. Girls love them, and the present is noncommittal enough."

I licked my lips, waiting with a wry expression for him to look at me. When he did, I pulled my brows up. "You heard my brother say sixty for the earrings, right?"

He nodded.

"Well, that was between the both of us. *This* one I have to afford on my own."

"Ah, yes." Clearing his throat, he locked the door and slid the key back into his pocket. Then he held out his arm, subtly motioning me away from the expensive section of the store and back to the affordable side.

"Do you have an idea?" Ethan asked me, squatting down as he looked at some watches for men.

"Nope. And I don't even know if it's a good idea at all."

He lifted his head, gazing sternly at my face. "Oh, I think you should get her something. She won't be mad forever, and this way you can show her that she really means something to you."

Ethan was right. Even if Sue didn't let me in now, I wasn't giving up hope that, if nothing more, we could be friends again one day.

My mind was set; a gift it was. And since I didn't have a fortune to spend, the choice was narrowed down to: three necklaces with either a teddy bear, a flower, or a heart pendant, some rings that looked like they were stolen from a crackerjack box, and a bracelet made of seashells. Nothing really appealed to me. But when the man put those things away, my gaze got snagged on a different kind of bracelet in the adjacent shelf in the glass case.

It was made of silver and had some small items clipped to it. A single flip-flop, an open book, a shamrock, and an angel. Excitement gripped me. "Ethan, come here. Look at this!" It was just perfect for Sue.

"I'm sorry, but this won't fit into your financing plan, sir," the salesman said with regret. "The bracelet alone is twenty-five dollars. But it's not complete without any charms, which cost five dollars each."

Hmm. Rubbing my neck, I took a deep breath. So what if there wouldn't be four charms dangling from it in the end, but only one. Or...maybe two? Yes, two should be okay, as a gift and budget-wise, too.

I turned to the man in gray. "Do you have other charms to choose from?"

Grasping that this really was what I'd set my mind on, he nodded, smiled, and went to get a whole tray full of tiny items that could be randomly clipped to the bracelet. There were a million little things—flowers, a sun, horses, cats, a cell phone, pens, a lady bug, birds...the list was endless. I took my time in examining them all.

In the end, I picked three items and laid them on smaller padded board beside the tray. All three of them were things

ANNA KATMORE

that had to do with Susan and me. Things that defined our relationship. A basketball. A strawberry. And a tiny purple butterfly.

"You really want to buy three?" Ethan reasoned in a low voice.

I grimaced. "Actually, I was thinking just one." It was impossible, though, to single out the most meaningful item. Weak-minded, I cast Ethan a hopeful look. "Maybe I can afford two?"

He gave me the final, much-needed nod of encouragement. "Which one goes back?"

A big breath expanded my chest. "I think the butterfly. It will only remind her of the chat we had on that last date, and I don't want her to get angry all over again." Even though I loved the idea of being the one to cause butterflies in her stomach.

"Very well," the tall man said once more and put the bracelet, together with the chosen charms, into a small bag of dark blue velvet. "Shall I wrap this one for you, too?"

I chewed on my lip. "Um, no. Thank you." For some reason, I wanted to do this on my own at home later. Also, I wanted to take another look at the present before actually wrapping it up.

"All right." He put the velvet bag into a small box of stiff cardboard and punched the three prices into the old-fashioned cash register. "With tax, that will be thirty-seven eighty, sir."

As I pulled the money from my wallet, Ethan interrupted me. "Er...wait a moment. Can I—can I, um, add a dangling thingy to that bracelet for Sue, maybe?"

Actually...why not? It looked a little sad with only two items, anyway. "Sure, go ahead and find one."

He started to grin. "I already have." Pointing at the lower section of the tray, he showed the shop assistant which charm he wanted. And I cracked up. It was a tiny Super Mario. He really couldn't have chosen anything better than that.

Ethan paid for his addition while I paid for the rest. Mr. All-in-Gray dropped the small Mario into the bag and handed me the box. "Thank you," he said to us, smiling big again. "I wish you and the ladies a lot of joy from these gifts."

We both said goodbye and left the store, the tiny bell above the door chiming again. As the door fell shut and we could finally breathe air that didn't smell of rich people and diamonds, Ethan cast me a satisfied look. "Hey, that went great, didn't it?"

I nodded and climbed into the car after he unlocked the doors. In truth, this was the first day in a long time that I felt a twinge of happiness return to my chest. Now I couldn't wait for Christmas to come so A) I had a reason to talk to Sue again, and B) I could give her this pretty little present.

Ethan put the key in the ignition, but before he turned it, he hesitated, staring out the windshield, his face turning pale. "Chris?"

"Yes?"

He tilted his head toward me with both eyebrows arched. "Does Mom even have pierced ears?"

Chapter 25

IT WAS ONLY a few more days until Christmas, the night before the last day of school. Music drifted from the speakers in my room. The air outside had gotten chilly in the evening, so I'd closed the windows a while back and settled on my bed, letting my gift for Susan slide around my fingers. I'd done everything she'd demanded—I didn't send her texts, didn't call, and didn't talk to her at school—but she still avoided me at every occasion. Tonight, my last bit of hope that she would forgive me was slipping away.

Tomorrow was the last day we'd see each other before Winter break. The last chance to give her the bracelet. I'd have much preferred to give her the gift on Christmas Day, together with a hug and maybe a little kiss, but it seemed like my wish wasn't going to come true.

Rolling off the bed, the words "very well" rang in my ear, a mockery of the shop assistant's voice. We had wrapping paper and bows in a drawer in the living room. The black cardboard box was elegant, but I wanted it to look like a real Christmas present when I handed it to Sue.

Like a small boy in elementary school, I sat on the floor Indian-style and concentrated hard as I carefully cut a square piece of some blue paper with silver glitter—well, it was almost square. Fine, it wasn't really square. It bore a resemblance to a screwed-up triangle, but with any luck, no one would notice once the ends were stuck together with Scotch tape. Crafts had never been my strength. That was Ethan's thing, and he might have done a hell of a better job than me. Yet, for once in my life, I really wanted to wrap a present myself.

Sadly, it turned out that my visual judgment was worse than expected. The piece of paper wasn't only bell-shaped, it was also three times too big for the small box. After cutting around the corners, taking a bit off here and there, I sealed all edges with Scotch tape until the black cardboard was well wrapped in blue. I held the package in my hand and proudly examined it from all sides.

Okay, maybe there was a bit too much tape, but at least this way the silver glitter wouldn't get brushed off the wrapping paper. Now for the bow.

In the drawer with the paper, there were all kinds of ribbons in different colors. I picked a silver one to go with the glitter and sat back down on the floor. When I'd thought wrapping the box was hard, I certainly had no idea what was coming with the bow. The slim ribbon was kind of stiff and wouldn't stay put. Biting my tongue, I fought with the little monster. In the end, I decided to just add another knot on top of the first and, to be totally sure, a third one, before tying the ribbon into a nice bow.

A shadow fell on the carpet in front of me. Mom stood in the doorway when I lifted my face. Arms folded around her waist, she leaned on the threshold and watched me tinkering on the floor. Even though she undoubtedly had a good idea of who this present was for, she didn't ask me about the situation with Sue. Which was for the best, since there wasn't any change to report.

Our gazes locked in silence, and she sent me a small smile of encouragement. I beamed back, full of pride.

And once Susan saw how much effort I'd put into wrapping this little present so perfectly for her, she might be more inclined to give me a second chance.

*

On the last day before winter break, everyone was in a happy mood. In the morning, as Ethan and I left the house together, a confident smile was pasted on my face, too. The smile started to slip, however, when Susan saw me in the hallway before first period. She changed direction to head down a different corridor. Great. How was I supposed to give her the present when she kept running from me?

Then, at lunch, she appeared really absorbed in conversation with her friends. Ethan subtly shook his head at me from across the cafeteria, which meant "not now." So I remained seated at the table with my friends and tried to put on a cheerful face as Becks hummed all kinds of Christmas songs to get us in the right mood for the holidays. By that time, the gift for Sue felt like it was burning a hole in my pocket.

I kept patting it through my final two classes and thinking of plans to catch Susan after school. Unless I decided to drop the present on her doorstep or toss it through her chimney, it was the last chance I had.

Luckily, Mr. Ellenburgh let us out early. "No use torturing you with Shakespeare when all your brains are in holiday mode already," he joked, closing the book we'd been reading the past couple of weeks.

Backpack shouldered, I rushed outside with only one thought in my mind: hopefully, Sue hadn't had as much luck with her teacher as we just had. Knowing where her house was and that she always walked to school instead of driving or biking, I positioned myself at a strategically good point, not too far away from the entrance of the school, but far enough to catch her alone.

Minutes ticked by. My sneakers pounded on the concrete as I paced up and down, waiting. One by and one, students filed out through the big double doors. With the third rush of people, my pretty girl with glasses and a ponytail walked out. My heart tripped a little in anticipation. Sue waved goodbye to her friends and headed in my direction, her gaze pasted on the pavement. With every step she took, my heart pounded faster. Eventually, she looked up. Her initial happy expression fell the moment she spotted me. And so did my heart. To her credit, she didn't stop walking, even though a slight deceleration was noticeable in her steps. Since it was clear that I'd been waiting for her, she came straight for me. Two feet separated us when she stopped.

I opened my mouth to offer a small "hi," but the word never made it out.

"Don't, Chris! Just don't say anything," Susan said, heaving an exhausted sigh as she clasped the straps of her backpack harder.

I let out my breath in disappointment. That was it? Not even a *hi*—on the last day before Christmas break? Adjusting my schoolbag on my shoulder, I cast a helpless glance at the tree under which we stood, as if the answer to all my problems with this girl was to be found up there. Not even a bird chirped a response. I was on my own.

"It's been so long, Sue." Gaze returning to her, I pinched the bridge of my nose. "I did everything you wanted. I stopped texting you, didn't talk to you in the hallways. What else do you want me to do to convince you to give me another chance?"

"Why do you think I'll ever do that?" Her eyes were hard on me, reproachful, and filled with determination. "Chris, we're done."

My throat twitched, and I made an aching gulp. Was I really the only one clinging to the chance that we could work this out somehow?

Obviously. And for all I knew, she might have already replaced me with a new crush. The thought nagged at me, so I asked in a small voice, "Are you dating somebody?"

Taken aback, Sue crossed her arms over her chest. "No."

Oh, but she should. She was the prettiest girl in the world. I leveled her a look from under my lashes. "Why not?"

"Because I'm not interested in anyone else," she snapped, her brows knitting in a frown. She probably didn't even realize the emphasis she'd put on "*anyone else.*" The two simple words did funny things to my stomach, almost as if I was riding a roller coaster. A little smile of joy escaped me.

Suddenly, her eyes widened with understanding. "I didn't mean it like that."

That's what she said, but was it how she felt? For the moment, I wasn't capable of stopping my hopeful smile from widening. "Are you sure?"

"Yes! Of course," she blurted out. Then her gaze dropped, and she started to rub her temples like this conversation was giving her a headache.

I knew there was no way to keep her here with me all afternoon, so, riding a last rush of hope, my hand slipped into my pocket and I pulled out the wrapped bracelet.

"Can we stop this now? I want to go home," Sue murmured a moment before she looked up at me again. I held the package out for her. Lips pursing, she narrowed her gaze at my outstretched hand. "What's that?"

"Your Christmas present. I was hoping this chat would go differently. Since it didn't, I doubt you'll let me see you for Christmas to put it under your tree myself." My hand hovered in midair, and all Sue did was stare—first at the gift, then at

ANNA KATMORE

my face, for a long time. Other than the occasional blink, she didn't move one muscle. Damn, she wasn't going to even accept the present.

My stomach dropped to my feet, my chest tightening in despair. Precisely nothing had gone according to plan since I met this girl. What in the world had I done to bring this kind of bad luck upon myself? Had I mowed down one of God's angels recently, or what?

"Girl, you're one stubborn little thing," I growled. Done with today and done with hoping, I grabbed Susan's hand and planted the present in her palm. "Merry Christmas." Blowing a frustrated stream of air out through my nose, I spun on my heel and stomped away.

People passed me. Some of them wished me a merry Christmas or happy holidays. Head lowered, I ignored them all and strode across campus to the parking lot, where Ethan was supposed to wait for me. He was sitting in his car, patiently typing away on his phone. When I got in and slammed the door, he put the cell away and turned a beaming face on me. "How did it go?"

"She won't be mad forever, my ass." I rolled my eyes, looking out the window. My voice dropped to a wounded level. "You should have seen her. There's still enough anger in that girl to bust a planet."

"Oh." He paused. "And the present?"

"Probably ended up in a trash can on her way home."

"No, she wouldn't do that." Ethan started the engine and reversed out of the parking spot. "She's still angry at you.

That's a good sign."

The seatbelt in my hand, I stopped in the middle of buckling myself in. "Pardon?" I threw him an annoyed look. "Name just one reason why this is a good sign!"

"Simple." He flicked on the right blinker and turned up the road home. "She isn't speaking to you, and she's still angry. That means she's not over you yet. You still matter to her, that's why she's hurt. Make sense?" Halting at a crosswalk, he let a couple of kids pass in front of the car before driving on. "Now let's say she wasn't angry anymore, but still didn't talk to you. Wouldn't that mean she left you behind and went happily on with her life?"

I gaped at Ethan in silence. Could he be right? I liked to believe so, but that didn't ease the awful ache in my chest. We had made zero progress in this tangled situation. How much longer did I have to endure Sue's silent treatment? It was nerve-wracking...and so, so tiresome. Couldn't we just fast-forward to the end of this fight and the moment she showed up on my doorstep, ready to forgive me?

I knew it was a little late, but this was my last-minute Christmas wish.

*

Needless to say, my Christmas wish did not come true.

On the morning of the 24th, my family decorated the tree together, and we put our presents for each other underneath. When my gaze got stuck on the little package for Mom, I couldn't help but wonder whether Sue had put my gift for her under their tree. And if she unwrapped the bracelet tomorrow when she got up...would she wear it?

I tried to shake off the heart-wrenching thoughts of Sue and went to the kitchen to help Mom prepare a huge turkey for later. Like every year, my grandparents came to celebrate Christmas Eve. It was nice to have some distraction in our house for a while, tell Granny everything about my awesome winning dunk in the last basketball game, and watch Grandpa try to figure out how to play Wii golf with Ethan. They stayed with us long after we'd eaten dinner, and together we sang some Christmas songs in the living room along with Granny playing the flute she always brought for the holiday.

Ethan seemed to be happy. He smiled a lot and told jokes all day. But it didn't escape me that he also glanced at his phone really often. Every time he put it away, even for a minute, his face lost some of the joy of the day.

Strangely enough, I did the same. It would probably require more than a Christmas miracle to make Sue forgive me, but a small voice inside my head urged me to check my phone for messages from her anyway.

Nothing.

After eleven, my grandparents took their leave. They lived in Cambria, fifty miles north of Grover Beach, and Granny was afraid her husband would fall asleep behind the wheel if they didn't hit the road soon. After a round of hugs and goodbye kisses, we saw them off at the door, waving until the taillights had disappeared down the street.

I was the last to walk back inside and locked the door. Then I tugged my cell out of my pocket and checked once more.

"Did she text you?" Ethan's voice surprised me as I stared at the blank screen.

Biting my lip, I shook my head. "You?"

"No." His shoulders lifted in a sad shrug. "Think we should call her?"

That wouldn't be a good idea. Not for me, anyway. "You can if you want. She wouldn't answer the phone if she saw *my* number."

"She probably won't answer for me either."

I sniffed, curling my lips. "Should we drive over there and throw rocks at her window until she comes out?"

Ethan chuckled. "She might open the window, but all we would get is probably a bucket of ice water dumped on us."

Fair point. Never underestimate the anger of a girl. "Then what do we do?"

He made a humming sound of helplessness and walked into the living room, where the Christmas tree still twinkled in multihued decorations. Together, we settled on the couch and stared at the sparkly lights and baubles, mesmerized like little boys on their first Christmas. "We could send her a message," I suggested a few minutes later.

"And what do we say?"

"Hmm..." Contemplating, I put my feet up on the couch and hugged my legs to my chest. With my cheek pillowed on my knees, I fixed him with a stare. "Maybe send her a song?"

Ethan tilted his head to me. "You mean a YouTube link?"

"Yeah. A holiday song. You know, like 'We Wish You a Merry Christmas' or something."

He sucked his bottom lip between his teeth. "Not a bad idea. Do you want to send her the message?"

"No. You do it. But say it's from both of us."

Ethan nodded. He pulled his phone from his back pocket and punched in a message together with a link to the song. After he'd sent it off to Susan, he put the phone down on the coffee table, and we waited.

And waited.

And waited.

Mom came into the living room after a while and said good night. She planted a kiss on each of our foreheads, ruffled our hair, and then smothered a yawn behind her hand as she went off to bed.

We waited some more, my impatient heart pounding "Little Drummer Boy" all this time.

"It's late. She's probably asleep already," Ethan reasoned after a while. He had to be right. It was Christmas. If Susan had read the message, she would have sent something back.

"Yeah," I breathed, my eyes closing slowly. "Maybe tomorrow..."

Judging by the rustle next to me, Ethan was standing up and heading to his room. I couldn't bring my body to move just yet. He was still crossing the threshold when a whistle sounded out, making my head snap up.

He stopped in the doorway, reading something on his

phone.

"Is it from Susan? What did she say?" I blurted, gripping the legs of my jeans with suddenly clammy hands.

After what felt like forever, Ethan lifted his head, and a slow smile curved his lips. He tossed me the phone. Heart drumming wildly once more, I turned it around and read her text. *Merry Christmas to you, too... And to your family.*

The corners of my mouth tilted up. Your family—that included me. She didn't wish me death today, but a merry Christmas. I could have hugged the prickly tree from joy.

Ethan came back to get his phone. He placed a hand on my shoulder, and as I looked up at him, he squeezed, nodding encouragingly. Back at the door, he cast one last glance over his shoulder. "Are you going to stay up?"

"For a while."

"Okay. See you in the morning." He slipped around the corner, and shortly thereafter the sound of the door to his room closing drifted to me.

Heaving a deep sigh, I hugged my knees to my chest again and kept gazing at the beautifully illuminated Christmas tree.

Chapter 26

I'D JUST TURNED on the water in the shower and soaked in the heat when a rattle on the door made me squint into the downpour around me. "What?"

"Wha wha-wha, wha-wha-wha-wha!"

I recognized Ethan's voice over the noise of the running water, but heck if I knew what he was saying. Working up a lather and soaping my body, I shouted, "I'm in the shower! I can't hear you!"

More of his unintelligible blabber sounded through the door.

"I. Can't. Hear. You!" What was his problem? The bathroom would be free in fifteen minutes. He could certainly hold it that long. Shaking my head, I resumed washing off the sweat I'd worked up during a game of basketball with T-Rex and the others at the street court near Brady's house this afternoon.

When I was done, I stepped out of the shower cubicle and

toweled myself dry, then wiped the terry cloth across the fogged-up mirror and started shaving. It was two days after Christmas, and Hunter had asked me to join him for a drink at Charlie's. Apparently his girl was gone for the weekend to visit family, and he was bored as hell.

And I was sick of sitting in my room all day, waiting for a message that never came. The invitation was a welcome distraction. The text Sue had sent Ethan on Christmas Eve had caused my heart to play its own game of jump rope inside my chest. I really thought she'd be ready to talk to me after that. When only silence followed, disappointment had washed away all my hope.

There was going to be a big New Year's party at Ryan's house. He'd invited me a while back, and from what he'd said, it sounded like Sue would be there, too. Last night, I'd made up my mind. Susan Miller had exactly until the end of this year. Until that party. It was in four days. If she hadn't come around by then, I was going to find her in Hunter's house and make her talk, even if it meant I had to throw her over my shoulder, carry her out, and tie her to a tree so she couldn't escape me. Susan didn't have to love me; she didn't even have to like me. But the time of being angry and punishing me with her silence was over, once and for all.

I only had to wait four more days...

Going out tonight would do me good. I needed a change of scenery or I might very well go crazy thinking about her.

Donning a white tee and jeans, I walked out of the bathroom. Whatever Ethan had wanted before, he could tell me

ANNA KATMORE

now. Mom sat alone in the living room, and the kitchen was empty, so I headed for his room.

The doorbell rang, making me change direction. I glanced at my watch. If this was Hunter to pick me up, he was two hours early.

As I opened the door, a breeze wafted around my naked arms, giving me a slight chill after the hot shower. A girl stood on the doorstep. She wore a sunny yellow sweater and her honey-colored hair was tied back into a ponytail. Huge, gummy-bear eyes staring at me made me freeze on the spot.

Three endless seconds ticked by. Was she going to say something?

Was I?

My hand wouldn't let go of the door. In utter shock, I blinked at her. Finally, she said, "Hey."

"Hi." The word was a breath, not even a whisper. Then amazement scrunched up my face. "Why—"

"Ethan," she explained quickly, trampling on my hope that she'd actually come to see me.

I clenched my teeth. "Right."

The sleeves of her sweater were shoved up her forearms, revealing her bare wrists. She wasn't wearing the bracelet. So the text on Christmas didn't mean anything. I wasn't part of her life anymore. But obviously Ethan was. And he hadn't even told me they were talking again, or that she was coming over today. What sick joke was that?

Keeping my crestfallen stare off her, I focused on the daisy next to the word *Welcome* on our doormat, instead. "He's in his room."

Susan ducked inside under my outstretched arm, because I still clasped the door so hard, my knuckles were turning white. Silently, she walked past the kitchen and down the hall to Ethan's room. Watching her go, I closed the door, the word "wait" on the tip of my tongue. As if she'd felt it and wanted to escape, she broke into a run all of a sudden, not even stopping outside my brother's door. Forgoing the courtesy of knocking, her body practically slammed into it, and she stumbled into his room. The door closed quickly. She was out of sight.

Why did she have to torture me so? And why couldn't I just get over her and go on with my life? I rubbed both my hands over my face, growling in frustration. This wasn't fair, goddammit!

With angry strides, I headed to my room and slammed the door shut so hard, the entire house shook with a mini quake. But that wasn't the end of my rage, not by far. Heat built up inside me. Barefooted, I kicked the swivel chair out of the way and wiped my arm across the desk. Books and pens went flying everywhere.

Deep breaths, Chris, I told myself, turning on the spot and pulling helplessly at my hair. *Deep breaths.* But they didn't cool me down. If anything, they hurt. Really, really badly. Nothing could ease the pain inside my chest. Nothing but—

Without another thought, I stomped out of my room, leaving the door open behind me, and walked down to Ethan's. Sue was in there with him, and I was so sick of her ignoring me. This just wasn't right. Thoughts of charging inside and

ANNA KATMORE

yelling at her rolled inside my head. Yes, I made a mistake not telling her about the charade, but, dammit, she was being cruel, treating me as if I had committed the worst crime ever.

What's more, it was killing me, the way she kept me at a distance.

But I couldn't do that.

When two feet separated me from Ethan's door, my hand hovered. And then it sank to my side again. Minutes passed by. I stood rooted in the hallway, staring at the knots in the wooden door, exhausted and hopeless because nothing would happen. Nothing would change. She wouldn't come out and wrap her arms around me like the last time she was in my room. And she wasn't going to gaze at me again with those shy eyes like I was the only one she ever wanted.

Susan Miller was done with me. The sooner I accepted that, the sooner I would feel better. If that was even possible...

A silent tear trailed down my cheek.

Soft steps in the hallway behind me announced her approach even before Mom gently put her arms around me. "Come with me, Chris," she said quietly in my ear. "There's no need to stand here and wait."

I swallowed hard, my head sinking low. Wearily, I gave in as my mother turned me around to face her. As if she were a mirror, my own sorrow reflected in her eyes. *A problem shared is a problem halved,* they say. But that's complete bullshit. A problem shared means making someone you love hurt with you. And that's what was happening here. I didn't like to see my mom aching because of me. But the comfort she gave me when she pulled me into a tender hug was welcome.

Slinging my arms around her, I pressed my forehead into the crook of her neck. In a loving caress, she skimmed her soft hands through my hair and down my back. "Come on, sweetie. I'll make you tea."

"Strawberry-vanilla?" I mumbled and sniffed.

"Of course." An encouraging smile curved the corners of her mouth as she eased back and wiped the tears away from my eyes. With her one arm still around me, she rested the other on my forearm and steered me into the kitchen, where she made me sit at the table. She left me there with a kiss on the top of my head.

Elbows braced on the table and my face buried in my hands, I could hear her putting on the kettle and getting the remnants of our Christmas dessert out of the fridge. The piece of cake she cut for me was clearly a waste since my throat had closed and my stomach rebelled at the thought of eating. When she set the plate and tea in front of me, I leaned back and dragged in a deep breath. My chest still felt too tight to take in all the air that my lungs needed to survive.

Mom sat down across from me with her own tea and took a sip, looking at me over the edge of the cup. When she put it down, she asked in a gentle voice, "Do you want to talk about it now?"

My gaze dropped from hers. With the fork, I started picking at the piece of carrot cake. Three days old, it crumbled more with each poke. Not very appetizing. Then again, not even a Mississippi mud pie, my favorite, would have made me eat today.

Mom cut a small bite off her slice and waited patiently for me to open up as she ate it. Perhaps it was time. Ethan had told her quite a bit, but there was still my side of the story. Filling my lungs with yet another painful breath, I started at the very beginning—when Sue confused me with Ethan for the very first time...

While Mom enjoyed her piece of cake, I kept stabbing at mine. It was pretty damaged by the time I came to the part when Sue had replied to Ethan's text on Christmas Eve. Putting the fork away, I warmed my fingers on the cup of tea and took a small sip.

"Your feelings for Susan sound very similar to what you felt for Amanda," Mom said at the end, speaking slowly and with great concern.

I nodded, blowing out a stream of air through my nose as I put the cup back down. My eyes locked onto the flowery pattern on the porcelain. Apart from Susan, Amanda had been the only person outside family that had ever gotten a Christmas present from me. There were many similarities in my feelings between the two girls. It was how I knew I wasn't just crushing on Susan. My feelings went much, much deeper than that.

"Everything might have started with that stupid challenge, but somewhere along the line things changed." Chin still low, I lifted my gaze to my mother. "Now it hurts to wake up in the morning and not know if I'll get a chance to talk to her all day."

"If she means so much to you, then don't give up." Mom

leaned across the table and rubbed the back of my hand. "She's here. Talk to her *now*, love."

At that precise moment, someone appeared in the kitchen doorway behind Mom. My heart gave out for a second, and my stomach dropped to the floor. Just how long had Sue been standing outside, and how much of this conversation had she heard? I swallowed through a tight throat.

The shocked expression on my face transferred to my mother's. Her chin dropped as she realized just who was standing behind her. She pulled her hand away from mine and jerked around. "Susan! We— I was—"

Yeah, where are you going with that, Mom? Convince Sue that we weren't talking about her? That it's a different girl in the house I want to speak with? My mother must have come to the understanding that she couldn't talk herself—or me—out of this situation, because she stopped her embarrassed stammering and instead greeted Susan with a smile as she rose to her feet.

I remained seated, watching how they shook hands, and Sue mumbled, "Happy holidays." Her gaze, however, was fastened on me. It made breathing hard again. Grinding my molars to keep a steady expression, I glanced down, escaping her gaze.

"Why don't you come in, sweetie?" Mom asked her in a light voice. "Have a cup of tea with us."

Inviting Susan to sit down with us when I was close to a nervous breakdown? Had somebody screwed with my mother's mind recently?

I lifted my chin, fixing Mom with a hard stare that she didn't even notice. Sue, it appeared, however, had other plans than sitting with us and eating cake. As if zapped by my mother's words, she jerked her hand back. "Sorry, but I can't. My mom's waiting for me. I have to go." After a quick, polite smile, as if that would make the lie sound a little more truthful, she spun on her heel and walked away.

Ethan, who'd appeared behind her a second ago, gave me a helpless shrug and dashed after her. They stood out in the hallway, mumbling too low for me to catch. Then the front door opened, and Ethan's sudden shout drifted to us. "Don't forget to call!"

Mom's throat bobbed as she swallowed. She still stood frozen in the middle of the room. Her gaze was pasted on the window behind me. If I got up and peeked out through that window now, I knew I'd see Susan walking to her car and driving off.

I didn't turn around.

Moments later, Ethan sauntered past the door and headed for his room. I jumped to my feet and followed him. Flinging out a hand, I stopped his door from shutting on me. "Why the hell didn't you warn me she was coming over?"

Ethan swirled around. "I did!" Crossing his arms, he gave me a reproachful frown. "But you were in the shower and didn't find it necessary to turn off the water so you could hear me."

"Argh." I banged the back of my head against the doorframe. Rubbing both hands over my face, I moaned.

"Shit."

"Sorry, bro." He sat down in his desk chair and swiveled around to me. "I really tried to tell you."

Still leaning against the doorjamb, I rolled my eyes to the side and then stared at him with a hopeful expression. "How was it?"

"It was awkward."

"Awkward? How?"

"Like she was totally weirded out." He scratched his nape. "Being here made her quite nervous. Also, she refused to let me talk about you. And..."

When he broke off, I arched my brows. "And?" It couldn't be something good he was holding back.

With a deep inhale and exhale, Ethan stalled for time.

"Go on, E.T.! And *what*?"

He lowered his head, only glancing at me sideways. "You know how we talked about you winning her back at Hunter's party?"

He'd helped me plot for hours last night. "Yes?"

"Well...Susan's not going."

"But—it—no..." I shook my head, unable to form a coherent sentence. " *Why?*"

Ethan gave a slight cough. "Apparently, she doesn't want to run into you again."

She was chickening out? I closed my eyes, my pulse racing. What about all my plans to sort this out with her? How could I, if she... A feeling of disorientation came over me. I scrunched up my face and turned, pressing my forehead against the doorframe.

"Chris? Are you all right?"

The wood rubbed against my skin as I shook my head. Nothing was all right. Susan Miller had become my personal tormentor, and she knew how to pull all the right strings to make me suffer. In a swell of frustration, my fist lashed out and knocked into the door.

"Look, maybe—"

"No, Ethan," I cut him off fiercely as I straightened. "Just leave it." I'd had enough. Susan wanted me gone from her life? Fine, she could have it. I gave up. The game was over. She won.

Feeling dizzy and lost, I shuffled to my room. There was quite the mess on the floor from my earlier fit of rage. The only clear spot was my desk chair. I sunk into it and swayed back and forth, my head tipped back. My mind was so full of crap. Thoughts that got me nowhere. It was time to let go and clear my head of all things Susan. She'd been lodged in there long enough.

My throat ached. It hurt on every swallow and every breath. The pain spread down to my chest, my stomach, and into my gut. I felt sick. Really sick. Everything inside me hurt.

My body heavy, as if weighed down with stones, I dragged myself over to my bed, curled up, and pulled the blanket over my head. The entire world could bite my ass today—I wasn't going to come out of here again.

Too bad my phone was stuck in my jeans pocket, because when it started vibrating, I couldn't ignore that. In my own little cave of isolation, the display light felt like an intruder. Ryan was calling. Shit. We had plans.

Pride over misery, I picked up. "Hey."

"Hi. Are you ready? I can pick you up if you need a ride."

"Sorry, dude. Can I take a rain check?" I moaned. "I'm really not in the mood anymore."

He hesitated for a second. "What's up?"

"Nothing." Phone pressed to my ear, I closed my eyes in the already dark cave. "I'm just dying."

"Are you ill?"

"Crushed."

"Girl?"

"Yes."

"Okay, listen," Hunter said insistently. "If you aren't running a fever, you're going to get your ass up right now and get dressed. You're not going to act like a damn wimp and hide in your house."

"Well, thanks for your understanding." A humorless chuckle escaped me. "I remember a good friend sulking in his room for weeks not too long ago when a girl put him through hell. Oh, wait! Could it be that this dude was you?"

"And I remember you calling every other day, trying to make me look forward again. Consider this me returning the favor. Now stop whining. I'll be there in fifteen." Then the bastard hung up on me.

Grinding my molars, I flapped the covers aside and breathed in fresh air. Sometimes even the best of friends had a talent for getting on your nerves. On the other hand, what was

ANNA KATMORE

the point of drowning in misery? The world would keep turning whether or not Sue forgave me. I should roll with the punches and just close that door.

If only my limbs wouldn't feel so lifeless. And my head so heavy. And if basically every muscle in my body could come back from hiatus right about now, that would be awesome, thanks.

The promised fifteen minutes later, Ryan honked outside the house. I'd donned a black hoodie over my t-shirt, and I climbed into his silver-gray Audi, which was a fricking racing car. Cruising around with him was always fun—only, today, it failed to lift my mood.

We headed to Charlie's Café for starters, but it was clear from the beginning that Ryan was going to try to talk me into clubbing later. We would see about that.

Mitchell was waiting tables. He was here every weekend, but I thought even he would get off for Christmas vacation. We bumped fists with him, and I asked, "Man, you're doing a holiday shift?"

"Yep. It pays extra. And I really need the money for a new car." He nodded his head to an open table close to the bar that we could claim. "What can I get you guys?"

"Sprite," I said, and Ryan ordered a Coke. We sat down at the table Tony had pointed out for us—the only empty spot in this place today.

After taking off my hoodie, I draped it over the backrest of my chair. When I turned back, Ryan had propped his elbows on the table and was studying me with eyes that seemed much too nosy this evening. "Trouble with Miller again?"

"Again?" A sarcastic laugh rocked my chest. "I couldn't get out of this shit if I was the wizard of Oz."

"What's the problem? Is she still mad because you fooled her on that date?"

"Yep." I pressed my lips together.

"But that was weeks ago."

Nodding, I sucked in a breath through my nose. "Tell me about it."

All of a sudden, Ryan started to chuckle. "You know what that reminds me of?"

"No. What?"

"Something a friend said to me once. When I had trouble landing Lisa, he told me it's those girls that make you *wait* who are totally worth their salt."

I sent him an irritated look. "Ha. Ha." Did he find it funny shoving my own words down my throat, now, of all times?

"Just saying, dude." He shrugged it off and took his hands off the table as Tony brought our drinks.

I paid for mine immediately, wanting to get out of here fast and be alone again. I didn't want anything slowing me down later, especially not waiting my turn to pay along with about thirty other patrons.

As I took a huge drink of my Sprite, the sour liquid shriveled my stomach. I put the glass down and, from the corner of my eye, saw a familiar black-haired girl in army slacks walk through the door. I lifted my hand in a feeble greeting.

Sam waved back at us, wearing the typical happy grin that I'd spotted on her face from a distance many times. She made a beeline to the counter where Tony was. Because of her short height, she stepped onto the iron bar that was actually made for people to put their feet on when sitting on a bar stool, and heaved herself up by bracing her hands on the countertop. With some effort indeed, she managed to lean across the counter and kiss her boyfriend.

After she jumped back down, she came toward us. "Hi, guys." Her friendly gaze rested on me. "Chris, right?"

I nodded and scooted to the side to make room for her when Ryan asked her to sit down with us.

From her pocket, she pulled a cherry lollipop and unwrapped it. "You two are making faces like us girls do when we're talking about boys." Her words slurred slightly as she put the candy in her mouth, her eyes darting back and forth between us. "So it's either about Lisa or Susan."

I liked the humor of Tony's new girlfriend. And her boldness, too.

"Lisa and I are fine," Ryan stated with an unmistakable rat-your-buddy-out tone and a smirk.

"Okay. Susan, then." Her cheerful gaze fastened on me once more. "Can I help?"

"I don't know." My challenging smile came as an answer to her grin. "Can you make her change her mind?"

"I'm working on that."

The smirk slipped from my face, replaced by a frown. "You are?"

"Oh, of course. You see, I think she got in her own way somehow and just doesn't know how to move from there. It's obvious she wants to be with you."

Yeah, right. "Maybe it's obvious to you, but certainly not to her."

Sam sucked on her lollipop, then rolled it to the side of her cheek. "Aw. Have some faith."

Faith? Who was this girl kidding? "Sue hates me."

"No, she doesn't."

"I'm with the mop of hair on this," Ryan said to me, teasing Sam with a wink. "Miller doesn't hate you."

"Is that so?" Wrapping my fingers around the clammy glass in front of me, I cast Sam a provoking stare. "Did you know that I gave her a Christmas present?"

"Yes."

"Did she open it?"

"No."

"See?"

Sam grimaced. "But that doesn't mean she didn't want to." Her fingers started to fiddle with the wrapper of her lollipop. "She keeps the package in a drawer of her desk. I'm sure sometime soon she's going to take it out and open it." Her gaze suddenly curious, she leaned toward me, biting her lip. "By the way, what's in it?"

Intuitively, I wanted to tell her that I was *not* going to tell her. Her eagerness made me chuckle, though, and in the end, I just thought, *Why not?* "It's a bracelet."

Smitten, her eyes rolled to the ceiling. "Oh, this is

so...romantic."

Yeah, that was a word I'd heard from her before. Only, it didn't matter if *she* thought so. The whole point was I wanted *Sue* to think it. "I really tried to make Susan see how great she and I could work together. Guess what!" Crossing my ankles under the table and leaning forward on my folded arms, I pursed my lips. "It's impossible."

"What? You're giving up?" Sam made a face like someone had run over a bunny in front of her. "But you can't!"

"Oh, rest assured I can. I've tried pretty much everything to make her forgive me, but all she ever does is ignore me."

"If that's your only problem, Susan will be here in about ten minutes. We'll make her sit down, and you can talk to her then."

"She's..." I choked on the spit in my mouth. "She's coming here? Now?"

"Yes."

I cast a reproachful glare at Hunter. With his hands raised in defense, he said quickly, "Dude, I had no idea."

"All right. I'll be gone then." No way would Sue get another chance to brush me off and add more hot coals to my suffering. Grumbling, I half-turned on the chair, pulled my hoodie from the backrest, and downed the rest of my Sprite in one go. Heck, I'd known it would be better to pay for my drink straight away.

Shocked eyes fixed on mine, Sam whined, "You're leaving? No!" Her hands twitched like she wanted to reach out and grab mine, begging me to stay. It was cute...and ridiculous.

"Yep. And I'd appreciate it if you didn't tell Sue I was here in the first place."

"But when will you talk to her?"

A cold laugh escaped me. "Definitely not today."

Sam turned in her seat, and this time she actually did grab my hand, holding me back. "At Ryan's party then? Yes?" she pleaded.

My gaze was fastened on the door. Susan would walk in here any minute, and I really wanted to avoid another unpleasant confrontation. After a short moment of deliberating, I made up my mind and glanced down at Sam, my jaw set. "I don't think so. Tell Susan she can go to the party. I won't." Then I shot Ryan a quick look. "See you."

He nodded silently.

Sam, on the other hand, appeared desperate. "But—but—"

Her hands slipped from mine as I headed away, her stammering ricocheting off my back. She was a really sweet girl and her intentions certainly admirable, but this was my problem. I had to solve it the way I saw fit.

And if it meant I would stay home from Hunter's party so as not to ruin New Year's Eve for Sue, well then...so be it.

Chapter 27

HOW I GOT through the weekend without running amok from the wrenching ache in my chest, I had no idea. But somehow I did, and suddenly it was December 31st. The day of Hunter's party.

All of my friends would be there. Except me. I would be the one sitting at home all by my lonesome, stuffing popcorn in my mouth and watching some Christmassy movie I had no interest in. Oh, joy...

While lamenting in my room this morning, I did something I hadn't done in a while. The comforter wrapped tightly around me and my head still sunk deep in the pillow, I reached for my phone and opened the inbox. Usually, it was empty, because I never kept messages for long. But over the past month and a half, it had filled up with texts from *Ponytail Sue.*

Sitting up and scooting back to lean on the headboard, I read them all again.

It was those messages in which Sue dared to come out of her shell just a little more that coaxed a smile from me—like the night she wrote *Sleep tight, sweetness*, just to tease me by stealing my line. Strangely enough, she was the only one among my female contacts I never rated according to my 1 to 10 scale. If my desire to hold her one more time was any indication, only one number could be considered for Sue. A fricking 100. But rating her would mean putting her on a level with all the other girls in my phone, and that just didn't do it for me.

In fact, all these numbers had lost their purpose the day Susan had let me kiss her. It felt as if I was cheating reading *Lauren 10*, *Tracy 6*, and *Colleen 2* now. *Colleen 2?* Who the fuck was she anyway? I deleted her from my phone. Tracy followed right after, because we hadn't talked in over a year. Keeping her made no sense...as little as keeping all the others I could barely put a face to anymore.

As if on a sudden crusade, I started deleting name after name from my contacts list.

Eileen 6

Tara 3

Jessica 8

A knock on the door made me glance up quickly. Ethan walked inside, already dressed, and from the animated look on his face, he'd already had his coffee this morning. Would it have been asking too much for him to bring me a cup, too?

"Hey," I mumbled and deleted the next bunch of girls from my list. "It's vacation. Why are you up already?"

"I got a call from a very concerned girl thirty minutes ago."

"So?" Lifting my head, I quirked my brows. "Who was it?"

Ethan lowered into my desk chair and started spinning, his gaze on the ceiling. "Samantha Summers. And guess what she asked me?"

"If you're wearing your Garfield boxers today?" I suggested in a sarcastic tone. It could be anything really, heck if I knew. Returning my precious attention to something more important than playing "guess what I'm thinking of," I deleted the *10* behind Lauren and the *5* behind Tiffany.

After a cynical grunt, Ethan informed me, "Sam wanted to know if you'd changed your mind."

"About what?"

"The party."

Oh, that. I vaguely noticed my brother stop spinning and fix me with a hard stare. "Why didn't you tell me you don't want to go?" he complained.

Luisa 5 went, and so did *Sarah 3* and *Audrey 3*. "Because I didn't know you were interested. Also...don't take this personally, but it's none of your business."

"It is my business. Did you forget what we've already talked about? You finally sorting things out with Susan?"

My hand holding the phone dropped to my lap. "No, I didn't forget. Do *you* remember it was you who told me she doesn't want to go because of me?"

Ethan grabbed a pencil from my desk, braced his elbow on the armrest of the chair, and let the pencil twirl around his fingers, back and forth. "She did say that. But the girls will make her go anyway."

"And that's why I won't. I don't want to be blamed again. Not only will I have ruined her entire life with what I did"—frustration tightened my throat—"but the New Year's party, too, if I show my face there."

"I see." Ethan studied me for a couple of seconds. "Don't take this personally, but you're a jackass."

"Yeah, right," I muttered, getting a little pissed now. Ignoring him, I continued the task of cleaning out my phone.

"To hell with it, Chris. You're creeping around the house like the Ghost of Christmas Past, and I'm sick of it. Come to the party with us. Give it one last try with Susan, and if it doesn't work...well, then you can sulk for the entire next year, for all I care."

I'd deleted the last two unimportant names from the list and now thought about a new name for Susan.

"What are you doing over there anyway?" Ethan suddenly rose from the chair, sauntered to the bed, and snagged the phone out of my hands.

"Dammit!" Tossing the comforter aside, I jumped out of bed, hitching up my boxers, not in the mood to start a brawl with my brother. "Give it back," I snapped.

Ethan sat back down and cast me a provoking look. "Ponytail Sue... Gee, is that what you call her?"

"I was just going to change that...*Charlie Brown*," I muttered, grabbing a pair of jeans from my wardrobe and yanking them on. Sitting down on the edge of the bed, I put on a pair of socks and cast Ethan an irritated glare. "Could you please put the phone down and leave my things alone?"

My brother ignored my request and typed something, mumbling, "Are you coming?"

"To the party? No." And if he was so stupid as to just write a message to Susan with my phone, then he better be out of the State of California in the next ten seconds. "Put the damn thing down and get your ass out of my room!"

Ethan looked up, deliberating, while I pulled a sweatshirt over my head. A moment later, he repeated, "Are you coming?" as if it was the first time he'd asked.

"No," I growled.

"Are you coming?"

"No."

"Are you coming?"

Sick of giving the same damn answer time and again, I folded my arms over my chest and arched a brow at him instead.

"I can do this all day, you know," he warned.

"And I can knock your teeth in if you don't stop."

Ethan hesitated a beat, then he started to smirk. "You wouldn't. "

"Oh, I so would!" Reaching out, I snatched the phone out of his hand and shoved it in my back pocket. "Now go away."

"Okay." He rose to this feet and ambled to the door.

Because I was dying for a cup of coffee, I followed him out. Sitting down with my breakfast—black and strong—I leaned across the table to grab the newspaper and skimmed through the sports section. It didn't take long for my dear brother to enter the kitchen, too, and sit down across from me.

Head lowered and eyes on the football scores, I ignored him, but his stare was like spikes in my forehead. "What?" I snarled, when the feeling became too annoying.

Ethan waited for me to look up. Then with one corner of his mouth lifted, he drawled, "Are you coming?"

Jesus Christ! "No!"

"Are you coming?"

"No."

"Are you coming?"

"Shit, E.!" I slammed my palm on the table, the mug jumping almost an inch. "What do I have to do to make you stop so I can drink my coffee and read this goddamn newspaper in peace?"

The second half of his mouth twitched up. "Come to the party."

"Fine! I'm coming! You win, okay? Now leave me the fuck alone!"

With a satisfied hum on his lips, Ethan shoved the chair back and stood. As he left the kitchen, I banged my head on the table. God, what had I agreed to?

It would be a night full of suffering, trying not to stare at Sue. Because, let's face it, she wasn't going to speak to me anyway. Hunter's house was big, but not big enough. Her concept of distance certainly wasn't hanging out in opposite corners of the same room with a handful of party people between us. Even if I wanted to, I couldn't make myself invisible for her.

ANNA KATMORE

And knowing she was there...it would be like the other day when she visited my brother and I couldn't talk to her. Painful shivers trailed down my spine at the memory. No, I really didn't want to experience *that* kind of helplessness again.

Sighing deeply, I lifted my head. With my warm breaths, the damn page of the newspaper had gotten stuck to my forehead. Grunting in annoyance, I ripped it off and scrunched it up into a tiny ball, then threw it against the fridge door. It bounced off and knocked a CD case from Mom's little radio. *Shit.*

The case landed with a clatter on the floor. If it broke, my mother would kill me—or make me buy her a new one. Clenching my teeth, I rose and went to pick it up. It was the Sam Smith album—thankfully, unscathed. As I held it in my hands, squatting beside the island unit, I stared at the picture on the cover. This very CD had been in the player when Ethan had brought Sue home for dinner all those weeks ago. One song was particularly etched in my mind. "Stay With Me."

That night, I'd been able to make Susan eat from my fingers. She'd enjoyed it, and we talked quite a while on the phone afterward. Her flirtatious voice still resonated in my ears.

I straightened and put the CD back in its place, my shoulders drooping. What was different now? Why was getting through to her so much more complicated?

Oh, but of course... Back then, I'd actually had a backbone. I'd known what I wanted and nothing could have stopped me. *No* hadn't been on the list of possible answers back then.

That she was able to keep me at a distance now was my

fault alone. Because I tolerated it. Man, did I have to grow a pair or what?

Ethan was right—it was high time I pulled my shit together and stop lurking around the house like the Bell Witch. Susan could be stubborn as a bull. Proof of that was obvious—she hadn't even opened my Christmas present.

Yeah, I'd made a mistake. But, dammit, I'd apologized a hundred times. At some point, it just had to do.

Tonight, I was going to Hunter's party. And Susan Miller wouldn't get away with brushing me off again.

Filled with new determination, I stomped to the table, picked up my mug, and took a gulp of coffee. Ugh, lukewarm. A grimace marred my face as the liquid slid down my throat. That's what you got for getting carried away during breakfast—a nauseating beverage.

I dumped the rest of the coffee in the sink and then went to find Ethan. He had to help me get a telephone number. Not only would I get my girl back tonight, I would also bring her a little present. And therefore I needed the help of a witchy little girl with black hair.

Ten minutes later, I sat at my desk and punched in the number Ethan had written on a blue Post-it. Saving the number as *Sam (+Mitchell)*, my gaze fixed on another entry in the list, right beneath it. Though I'd changed a lot of names and deleted even more this morning, this one certainly hadn't been among my contacts before.

The number looked familiar. It ended with 1311. *Sue's* number ended with 1311. And then I rocked with laughter.

"Ethan! Seriously?" I yelled, knowing he would hear through my opened door. "*She's the one?*"

"Yeah. Just seemed right to me," he replied from his room, sounding amused.

I shook my head and rubbed the tears from my eyes, calming after the laughing fit. But to tell the truth, he couldn't have picked a better name for Susan. For me, she was *the one*. And tonight, I was going to make her mine, or die trying.

First, there was this call to make, though. I dialed Sam.

"Hello?" she answered with unmistakable curiosity in her voice.

"Hi, this is Chris."

"Chris!" Oh, I could only imagine her stumped face at hearing my name.

"Yeah. Can you talk?" I didn't want to ask her a favor if Sue was with her right now.

"I'm here with Tony, but I can go outside if you want me to," she offered.

"Nah, it's fine. Listen. I need you to do something for me."

"Oh. Okay. What can I help you with?"

I wanted to keep this chat short and come straight to the point. But at Sam's immediate helpfulness, a deep sigh whizzed out of my lungs, and I relaxed into my chair. "First of all, you could tell me how Susan is doing right now?"

"Hm. She's okay, really." Sam hesitated a moment as if considering her words. "I mean, she's coping. The situation with her parents is getting easier. She's laughing more now. But..." Another pause, then she whispered, "I think she misses you."

My heart began to pound like it had been zapped with a defibrillator. The smile tugging at my lips wouldn't stay out of my voice. "Would you say tonight is a good time to talk to her again?"

She snickered. "Does that mean Ethan managed to sway you?"

"By unfair means, yes."

"Wicked! And yes, tonight is perfect. Susan is still a little stubborn, but we have a plan to make her go anyway." I wouldn't have expected anything less from Sam. "So what's that favor you need?"

I blew out a breath. "Did Sue open my present yet?"

"Umm...no. Sorry."

"Did you tell her what's inside?"

"Nope. If she wants to find out, she'll have to look." The determination in Sam's tone was sweet. She was totally on my side. Awesome.

"Good. Where is she keeping it?"

"If she hasn't moved it, it's in a drawer in her room."

"Do you think you'd have a chance today to sneak it out and bring it to the party?"

Excited now, Sam sucked in a breath. "You want to give it to her again?"

"That's the plan, yes."

"Oh my, this is so—"

"Romantic, I know," I cut her off, making her laugh. "So, you think you can do it?"

She hummed into the phone. "I'm not sure. It would be like stealing. I have a weird feeling about this."

Hey, what happened to fricking *romantic*? "Come on, please!" I whined. "This is the last time I'll try my luck with her." Then I remembered that whimpering weakness that had gotten me nowhere in the past and, with more determination, said, "I can't do it alone. I need you."

She sniffed but eventually relented. "Okay. I'll try. But you owe me."

"Whatever you want!"

Instantly, she stated, "A cherry-vanilla sundae."

"All right!" Laughing, I told her, "I'll treat you to as much ice cream as you can eat if this plan works. Do we have a deal?"

"Deal." She chuckled. "See you later."

We hung up, and I let my head tip back, fingers laced behind my neck. A smirk tugged at my lips. The die was rolled. Time to see where it would end up...

Filled with a whole new load of confidence, I grabbed the armrests of my chair and pushed myself up. It was time to thank my brother for changing my mind after all. As I walked into his room, though, I froze on the spot, startled by what I saw.

Leaning against his wardrobe, Ethan sat on the floor, his face pale as chalk. His hand lay loosely beside him, clasping his phone. Shit. Bad news.

I took a wary step forward. "E.?"

His eyes slowly traveled to mine. Other than that, he didn't move a muscle.

Heart beating fast, I strode to him and hunkered down. "What the hell happened?"

The vein in his throat beating rapidly, he held out his phone to me. There was a text open. After checking his face one more time, I read the message that came from an unsaved number. *Hey Ethan. I was wondering if you had any plans for tonight. Maybe we can meet for a New Year's drink. Ted.*

My jaw literally smacked against my chest. Ethan made a small noise in his throat that sounded half like a laugh and half like a panicky gasp.

"But...but...that's actually good, right?" I stammered. "I mean, from what I figured out on that date with Sue, he was really checking me out...well, *you*! He was checking *you* out!" Oh man. "Of course, he thought I was you, so he wasn't really checking *me* out. That would just be wrong. But with you, I mean..." *Damn, could somebody shut me up, please?*

I dropped to my butt.

Ethan seemed so busy concentrating on actually breathing that he probably didn't hear a single word of my blabbering. Inhaling deeply to steady myself, I placed my hands on his knees. "So. A text from Ted. That's cool."

Not yet out of his shock, he whimpered, "I don't even know where he got my number."

"Yeah..." The weight of guilt crept over me, and my eyes rolled to the side. "Me neither."

When Ethan remained silent, I prompted him, "What are you going to do?"

ANNA KATMORE

"I have no idea." My brother's face scrunched up with horror. "Text him back?"

When the initial shock eased out of my nerves, a smile made it to my face. "Yes, that would be a good start."

"Okay." With shaky fingers, he typed a message, repeatedly taking a break to suck in a lungful of bravery. When he looked up with questioning eyes, I supposed he was done but afraid to send it.

"What did you write?" I asked.

A streak of red crossed his cheek and suddenly his voice was defensive. "You're insane if you think I'm going to let you read it."

His shyness was understandable, but in his current state of panic, it was doubtful he'd managed to write something appropriate. Especially because it took him almost four minutes. I arched my brows. "*You're* insane if you think whatever you wrote is cool enough to send to a guy who practically asked you out on New Year's Eve."

His throat bobbed with another swallow. "You're probably right." He handed me the phone and I read, mumbling along, "Hello, Ted. Thank you for the invitation, but sadly it's ill-timed." *Ill-timed? What the hell?* I suppressed a snort and tried to read on with a straight face. "I will be celebrating with my friends tonight and can't cancel on them. Hopefully, you can understand that and maybe we can have that drink some other time. Happy New Year. Ethan." When I was done, I bit the inside of my cheek to keep from grinning. "Well, it's...um...long."

Ethan hung his head. "It's shit!"

I couldn't object. But not all was lost. Tossing the phone in his lap, I crossed my legs and braced my elbows on my knees. "If Susan had asked you to hang out with her tonight, what would you have said to her?"

After a short moment of deliberating, he raised his head and gazed at my face. "I'm going to Hunter's party. Wanna come?"

I cocked my head, casting him an encouraging grin. "Now delete all you have there and write exactly that."

"You think it'll work?"

"I think it's the best chance you have. And he would be a fool to say no."

His chest lifting and falling with a couple of deep inhales, he typed in the new message. And then we waited together. Minutes ticked away in the silent room. My heart beat fast for Ethan. And his probably did twice as fast. Eventually, a quiet whistle jerked us both out of the waiting trance.

While Ethan read it, I demanded through gritted teeth, "What did he say?" The anxiety nearly killed me.

The edges of his mouth tilted up, his joyful smile quickly reaching his eyes. "He said it's cool and he'll meet me there."

I punched the air with my fist. "Yessss!" Then I tipped backward on the floor and let out a relieved breath, arms falling to my sides, spread-eagle.

This should turn out to be an interesting night for both of us.

Chapter 28

NINE THIRTY. I stood in front of my open wardrobe. Where was that stupid tie? I knew I had one. The girls had this funny idea that the New Year's party should be some sort of ball with an exclusive guest list, so it wasn't the usual three-hundred-plus people getting drunk and dancing the night away at Hunter's house. Per the dress code, I had put on black trousers and a white shirt, rolling up the sleeves to my elbows. The tie I finally found went loosely around my neck, but no one was going to make me wear a frickin' coat.

"Are you ready?" Ethan asked from outside my room.

A final glance in the mirror. Agh, still too preppy. Reopening the top button of my shirt, I headed out, kissed my mother goodbye, and followed Ethan to his car.

He was quiet on the drive to Hunter's house, probably a little nervous. Funnily enough, I couldn't say the same about myself. In truth, I hadn't felt this confident and positive since the day Susan and I had been alone in my kitchen for the last time. Who could have known that in the end it all came down to attitude?

As we walked through the door of Ryan's house, an immediate sense of being in a fairy tale struck me in the face. Almost as if somebody had tried to transfer the North Pole into their hall. Stars—or maybe they were supposed to be snowflakes—were cut from white and blue cardboard and hung up all around the place. Crepe paper of the same color scheme wound around the posts of the stairs and a string of lights wound up the handrail. Some plastic reindeer with big, saucer eyes guarded the entrance.

Whoever did this clearly had a weakness for Disney and the winters we never got in California. It couldn't have been Hunter's doing, that was for sure. Probably the girls' idea.

White stuff like heaps of powdered sugar covered a few narrow, high tables and shelves. As we passed, I dipped my finger into the mass and found it was sticky, ill-smelling artificial snow. I wiped my finger clean on my shirt and scanned the place for Ryan.

He was talking to a couple of girls dressed nothing at all like on usual party nights. No tight-ass jeans or the typical LBD. Instead, floor-length ball gowns in bright colors clung to their slim figures.

"Hey," I said to them all, then borrowed Ryan for a moment. "Is Susan here yet?"

"No. She and the girls are still at her place. They're dressing her up, if I got that right. But wait, I'll ask Lisa." He pulled his phone from the pocket of his tuxedo and typed a message. In the meantime, I pivoted and scanned the couples on the dance floor for any familiar faces. Luckily, Tyler was already here. And, it seemed, he'd unwillingly found himself waltzing with Becks to "Winter Wonderland."

"They're on their way now," Hunter informed me.

I turned back to him. "Cool."

"Mitchell said you called Sam today for a favor?"

I pinched a handful of peanuts from the bowl on the table next to us, tossed a couple in my mouth, and nodded. "Mm-hm. I needed something that only she can get me."

He narrowed his eyes at me as if a tiny devil sat on his shoulder, poking him behind the ear. "It's about Miller, right?"

"Yep. You have a problem with that?"

"No problem. Just...be careful with her. I don't want her to run from the party tonight and be mad at me just because whatever's going to happen happened in my house."

His concern was certainly justified. Popping the rest of the peanuts in my mouth, I promised, "No worries. I'll make it right with her and won't get you in trouble for being involved."

At that moment, Lauren—looking really beautiful in a narrow, green satin dress—appeared from the kitchen, hanging on Wes Elephant-ears's arm. "Hi," she greeted me with a bright smile and, without any warning, hooked her other arm through mine, pulling me with them. "Jake and Trevor are trying to talk some girls into dates over there." She nodded her chin back toward the entrance. "I think they need some serious advice about that. Tell 'em that fart jokes aren't what a girl wants to hear, will you?"

"Jeez, are you serious?" Snickering, I shook my head. "Have they been drinking too much?"

"I hope so. Because if those are their usual pick-up lines, someone should have mercy and just shoot them." Then she pulled me a little tighter and spoke in a whisper, only meant for me to hear. "By the way, I knew you wouldn't be showing up in a coat tonight, but you couldn't even tuck your shirt in?"

Turning my head slightly, I winked at her for old times' sake. "Hey, I didn't show up in a tee. Is that nothing?"

Lauren let go of my arm as we arrived at a chest-high table, and Brady was the first to push a drink into my hand. "Finally, the team is complete." He lifted his own beer and raised his voice above all the others in the group. "Here's to an awesome ending of a—" He didn't get to finish, but instead spilled a few drops of beer on his dark gray jacket as Rebecca tackled him, using him as a brake.

"Whoa, dude! A toast and you're not waiting for us?" she scolded him with a reprimanding glare, adjusting her hair and dress after obviously rushing to us from the dance floor. Tyler, right behind her, handed her a glass of sparkling wine. Then we all clinked our glasses and beer bottles together in the middle, and Becks took over the toast. "To great friends and a fantastic last year of high school!"

I took a sip from what turned out to be vodka and grapefruit juice, when someone tapped me on the shoulder. Putting the glass down, I turned around and found a beaming face a foot below my chin. In a baby-pink dress, Sam appeared even more like a little girl than she already did, but to her credit, she looked seriously cute.

"Hi!" I blurted, happy to see her. "Do you have it?"

"Right here." Sam slipped the little package into my hand. "I have to go. Susan's talking to your brother." She cast a quick glance over her shoulder. "She shouldn't see me here with you when she comes back. It would kinda ruin it all, wouldn't it?"

Her conspiratorial whisper made me laugh. "All right. Get back to your friends then. I guess I'll see you later."

Sam nodded. "Good luck."

"Thanks."

Whirling around, she hurried away, her dress flaring in her wake. I slid the present into my pocket, my fingers still wrapped around it.

Laughing along with my friends even though I was only listening to the conversation between Becks and Jake with one ear, my mind strayed off, thinking up a situation for the perfect moment to give Susan the bracelet. She was already here, but I hadn't seen her yet. At the mere thought, my heart pounded in anticipation.

Deliberately slow, I let my gaze skate over the semi-dark room, past some dancing kids and a couple making out in a corner. Nick, Tony, and Sam stood huddled by the stairs. Alex Winter had just joined them with a drink in one hand and his girl, dressed in a sparkling red dress, in the other. And from behind them, a set of striking green eyes stared at me.

My pulse raced in my ears. Unable to remember what I'd just laughed about with my friends, I tilted my head and blinked a couple of times, totally drawn into Susan's spell. Sam unknowingly took a step to the side, revealing Sue's entire form to my view. As if she'd been carved right out of the same fairy-tale book as the whole party, she looked like an ice princess, fitting perfectly into this place. Her light blue satin dress hugged her beautiful chest and fanned out from the waist downward like the one she'd worn on our last date. About the same length as well, it left her stunning legs, clad in strappy, high-heeled sandals, bare for everyone to see. That girl over there was gorgeous, and my heart beat faster with every second I looked at her.

Obviously caught in the same spell as me, Sue, for once, didn't turn and run. On the contrary, she lifted her hand in a shy greeting, the edges of her lips twitching slightly. One side of my mouth tilted up in an answering half-smile. Right then, the space between us seemed to shrink in half.

Gripped by the magic of the moment, I beckoned her over with a subtle nod. Making up with someone usually worked better face to face and not from twenty feet away. Unfortunately, it seemed to be too much for her just yet. Something close to regret shone in her eyes as she slowly shook her head. Then she lowered her gaze and turned to her friends.

Okay. No need to rush this. I could wait.

Moments later, she and Nick walked to the dance floor together, although from the baffled looked on Nick's face it appeared that he'd actually been forced into it. Soon it became clear that Susan was using him as a shield to keep me at a distance. Before tonight, this might have hurt me. But not after the moment we'd just shared. I would give her all the time she needed to relax into this. Well, all the time until midnight, because I did want a New Year's kiss.

Controlling myself, I turned all my attention to my friends around the table. Brady had found Cassidy in the meantime and dragged her over. His arm draped permanently over her shoulders, they were joking and kissing a lot. From what I could see, the two were seriously into each other and started their personal chapter in this crazy book called *The Best Years of My Life Were High School.*

Was it asking too much to want this for myself with Sue?

When a little chill ran down my spine, I realized I'd been caught watching them. Lauren gave me a knowing look from opposite the table. Her fingers were laced with Wesley's, and she seemed to be happier than ever.

Couples were building and staying. Priorities had changed, people had become more important than other things in our lives. It felt like we'd all grown up a little bit more in this final year of high school. Some of us would leave Grover Beach to go to college soon. Some would make new friends and never look back. But there would also be the ones going home on the weekends to see their beloved.

I wanted to be one of those. When I headed off to school at UCLA next fall, I wanted to know that Susan would always be waiting for me and would welcome me with a hug every single Friday of the year. And to make that happen, I had to go find her now.

Finishing my drink, I put the glass in the middle of the table with all the other empty ones and told my friends, "Guys,

I'll see you later."

"Where are you going?" T-Rex demanded as everyone else turned to stare at me.

My gaze moved from him to Lauren, to Becks, and back to him. Then I cracked a smile. "I've gotta find my girl."

With an encouraging nod, Tyler slapped me on the shoulder. "Go get her, bro."

Heading off, I glanced at my watch. It was nearly eleven thirty. Sue wasn't shaking with Nick on the dance floor any longer, but with only eighty or ninety guests tonight, Hunter's house was fairly manageable. It couldn't be too hard to find her.

A handful of people hung out in the kitchen, but not her. Also, most of her friends were missing, too, which struck me as odd. Ryan wouldn't move upstairs to his room with guests in his house, so there was only one place left to look. The pool room.

A lively girl with black hair and a pink dress crashed into me coming out of that very room. Sam giggled and said sorry, but she was in such a hurry to get away that she didn't even recognize me. Tony's hand in hers, she dragged him along. But after a few more steps, she stopped dead and turned around to me. Her face split with a grin. Because the music was too loud to shout, she pointed her finger to the pool room.

I sneaked a quick glance inside and found the whole soccer bunch gathered in there. In the middle, on the pool table, sat Sue. I turned back to Sam and mouthed the word, "Now?"

She nodded with happy enthusiasm and then flitted away

with Mitchell.

All right. It was now or never. And *never* really wasn't an option.

Quietly, I slipped around the corner and stopped in the open door. With my hands in my pockets, I leaned against the doorframe. Ryan's girlfriend, who looked like some sort of Christmas angel in her white silk dress, rubbed Susan's arm, obviously to give her some sort of comfort. "I'm sure it's nothing too bad," she said.

Susan's ironic laughter drifted to me. "Say that again?"

Lisa was the first of them to notice me. The moment she did, her snicker died in her throat, and her face fell. Of course, it only took a second for everyone else to track her gaze and see me standing in the doorway. Susan was the last to turn around.

Her face pale with shock, she didn't get a word out. I pushed away from the doorjamb and slowly walked toward her.

Hard to say what they'd been talking about, but from Hunter's face, this was obviously a bad moment. He and Nick came around the pool table to block my way like Sue's personal guard dogs.

"Hey, buddy," Ryan said, scrunching up his face. "I'm not sure this is the best moment to show up. Susan will come when she's ready."

Seriously? He was still afraid things might blow up and screw him over? *Please...give me a little more credit, Hunter!*

I inhaled a slow breath, cutting Susan a glance to make sure she stayed where she was. Then I cleared my throat and sent Ryan a look between friends, hands still in my pockets. "I get that you want to protect her. From assholes like me. I appreciate it, because you're her friend, and I would do the same." Having said that, here was where I put Susan above our friendship. Lethal cold crept into my voice. "But now get the fuck out of my way, Hunter, and let me talk to my girl."

A silent beat passed between us, everyone in the room obviously holding their breath. I didn't want to fight my friend to get to Susan—but I would. And Ryan understood that. Valuing our friendship as much as I did, he relaxed and chuckled. "All right. Good luck, my friend," he said and clapped a hand on my shoulder. "You'll need it."

I nodded, unclamping my fists in my pockets.

"Come on, everyone," Winter shouted, pulling his girlfriend up from the couch. "Let's give the kids some privacy."

The entire soccer bunch followed him out of the room. From the look on her face and her twitching muscles, Susan wanted to, as well, but I stepped in front of her before she could get off the pool table. One of the others had the decency to shut the door behind them. Good. We were finally alone, and I had Sue right where I wanted her.

Next to her on the table stood a half-empty champagne flute. I moved it out of the way and planted both my hands flat on the green felt on either side of her hips.

"Let me go, Chris," she complained. "I don't want to talk to you."

When I was finally eye to eye with the girl that had me kept at arm's length for weeks? No, I didn't think so. "You're not going anywhere until we've sorted this out. I don't care if you're my friend or my *girl*friend when you leave this room again, but you're going to stop acting like I ruined your life. And you'll stop it right now." Lowering my voice just a dangerous bit, I added, "Are we clear?"

Susan's eyes grew wide with surprise, then they narrowed to angry slits. "You're hardly in a position to give me orders." She slid off the pool table, but with my hands still braced on either side of her, she didn't get far. In the cage of my arms, her body pressed flush to mine and—oh, the pleasure of it!

I didn't budge an inch, only arched one challenging brow. "Am I not?"

For the length of three seconds, she obviously considered her options. They were quite limited. Her face glowing red with rage, she eased herself back onto the table and scooted as far away from me as she could. It didn't matter. I only had to lean forward a couple of inches and our noses would touch.

A sneer crept to my lips. "Good choice."

When she folded her arms over her chest and remained silent—apart from a sulking snort—I went on, "Listen. You had every right to be angry at me. You were right to yell at me, and I even deserved the slap. Though I wish you had chosen a private moment for that." At the mortifying memory, I rubbed my neck, suddenly incapable of holding her gaze. "The guys will never let me live it down."

"You're embarrassed because I slapped you in front of them?" she snapped.

I nodded and lifted my eyes to hers.

A cynical imitation of my former sneer rode her lips. "Good. So you know how I felt when you ratted me out." Her voice rose. "In a full cafeteria!"

Yeah, it probably wasn't the best place to choose to corner her. I'd learned that the hard way. "I'm sorry about that. I didn't think the situation would escalate. I just wanted you to listen and understand."

"You want me to understand? Then why don't you try it first?" She made an effort to calm herself and took a deep breath, speaking on in a more controlled voice, "Can you imagine how it feels to know I told you all those private things about *you* when I thought you were Ethan?"

I frowned. "Why is that such a problem for you? It's not like you told me some weird fantasies you had of me that day."

Whatever it was that I'd just said, it triggered her flush, and this time it was really bad.

"No, I just told you about the most personal moment of my life. My very first kiss, ever. With *you.*"

"And I told you how amazing that was for *me.* So what?"

Her shoulders sunk a little, and her voice grew smaller. "I told you about the butterflies that came with your texts."

Now I had to bite the inside of my cheek to keep from grinning. It was always about the butterflies, wasn't it? "And I've never heard anything sweeter than that, I swear." The truth was, I felt quite special because of it.

I'd thought she'd reached the maximum level of embarrassment before, but obviously, I was wrong. Susan slammed her hands over her face to hide from me as she whined, "And then I practically said I wouldn't sleep with you because you're a womanizer."

Since she couldn't see me, I rolled my eyes. "Yeah, that hurt a little." Then I gently pried her hands away from her face and made her look at me. "But in the end, it only made me fall for you harder. I wanted to be that special guy for you. Still want to be. Sue—" I reached out and stroked her cheek, because if I couldn't feel her right this second, I would die. "For me, you'd never be a simple go-to girl."

"You don't understand." Even though she shook her head and sighed, she didn't slap my hand away. "You were never meant to hear those things. That's just wrong."

So the whole problem wasn't the lying and deceiving, but that she'd told me the truth? I fixed her with a stare of sheer bafflement. "This is what it was all about? You were just feeling embarrassed because you confessed some silly things to me?"

Pouting, she moved her chin away from my touch and scooted a little farther back on the pool table, adding another few inches of annoying distance between us. "You find them silly. To me, they're very serious."

"I know they are," I stated quickly. Heck, I hadn't meant silly in the sense of...yeah, silly. All these things were as important to me as they were to her. I hadn't slept with any other girl since the day we met, nor did I want to look at anyone but her anymore. She was the only one I wanted...in every possible way. Only, she didn't seem to understand that yet. "You actually gave me a great deal to think about," I told her honestly.

She made a wry face and snorted, her doubts quite obvious. Did she really think that was all I wanted? To get her in my bed? I cocked my head, imitating her look of disbelief. "That is *not* what I was thinking about."

"It doesn't matter if it made you think or not," she muttered.

This girl was driving me crazy with her stubbornness. Bracing my weight on the table and my head hanging between my shoulders, I growled through clenched teeth, "Tell me *what* matters, Sue, because I really don't know how to set this right with you."

A silent moment passed. Susan started wringing her hands in her lap. "You tricked me that day. All evening you lied to me, and that left me completely exposed. You know about all my feelings. And I know nothing about yours."

Hands still placed on the table's edge, I lifted my head and frowned at her. "Are you kidding? From the day you walked into our kitchen and let me feed you that kiwi, I couldn't have been more obvious how I felt about you. How very much I wanted *us* to be exclusive. Do you think I lied to you every time I talked to you? Or in all those texts I sent?"

Her lips trembled a little. "Not exactly lying, but you made it clear I was nothing but your next trophy."

"Did I? When?" I straightened and crossed my arms over my chest in self-defense. "When I gave you that hickey and afterward covered it with my bandana for you so no one would ask silly questions? Or when I kissed you while we were alone and didn't mention it to anyone because I thought you

ANNA KATMORE

wouldn't like that? And believe me, that was one helluva kiss I'd have loved to brag about." I remembered how she'd told me—when she thought I was Ethan—that *Chris* would probably think it was a godawful kiss. *Oh so wrong, baby.*

Susan swallowed, and her lips parted, but no word came out.

Again I needed to feel her, assure her with a simple touch, so I reached out and stroked my fingertips over her silky cheek. With our gazes locked, I asked her in a much softer tone, "Or did I treat you like a *trophy* when you let me comfort you after your parents' breakup? Is that really what you think I had in mind?"

Seemingly at the end of her tether, Susan rubbed her hands over her face and moaned sweetly. "I don't know what to think anymore." Well, even if she didn't know, I did. Everything was pointing at one fact. That we had fallen in love with each other. And her denying it wouldn't make it any less true.

Suddenly Sue stiffened, jerking her hands away from her face. Horrified, she stared at her open palms. What she saw there was probably the same thing I saw underneath her lips. A pink smudge from her accidentally rubbing off her lip gloss. Embarrassment turned her cheeks red. As she frantically wiped her chin in the totally wrong place, I couldn't help but chuckle.

I took her hand and moved it away from her face, then I dragged my thumb, deliberately slow, across the tiny stain underneath her bottom lip. Susan sat rigid, staring at me with wide eyes.

"There, all gone," I said, rubbing the smudge that was now

on my finger off on my pants. And with a soft smile, I added, "I like you better without makeup anyway. You're a natural beauty."

Susan lowered her gaze. For some reason, she didn't take compliments very well; they made her bashful. But now was not the moment to be shy. With my knuckle under her chin, I tipped her face up and leaned in a little closer. The mouthwatering smell of her skin got to my head, making me think of only one thing I longed to do in this moment. "And here's a secret," I whispered. "Kissing glossed lips is annoying as hell."

I didn't give her time to retreat but placed a brief kiss on her mouth. Susan drew in a shocked breath. Oh God, was it too much? Foreseeing another slap in the face, I ducked my head and squeezed my eyes shut. Every muscle in my body tensed, bracing for the sting of her hand on my cheek.

It never came. The sound of Sue's giggle made me inch one eye open. "You're not going to slap me?"

Sitting in the same spot instead of leaning away from me, she cracked a sweet smile. "I don't think so, no."

"Good." A relieved breath escaped me, and I straightened, my heart breakdancing with joy. We'd finally made it past the anger. Sue had let me in—but that chaste kiss wasn't enough. I wanted more. Now. And from her burning gaze, maybe she wanted it, too. Filled with longing and unbreakable confidence, a smirk pulled up one side of my mouth. "Can I do it again?"

Her answer shocked me—in the best possible way. Smiling widely, she reached out and wrapped my tie around her fist, pulling me closer to her. Heck, at least the damn thing was good for something tonight.

Going crazy with anticipation, my gaze jumped back and forth between her eyes and her lips. "I believe that means yes," I drawled and ran my thumb slowly over her lips to wipe away the rest of the gloss. When we were going to kiss this time, I wanted to taste the real Sue and not some synthetic goo that ruined the flavor.

Impatience gripped me. With my thumb still at the corner of her lips, I closed the last two inches between us and pressed my mouth on hers. She was soft underneath me, and oh so responsive. Gently, I sucked on her bottom lip, but then our kiss deepened fast. All barriers fell. Still gripping my tie, Susan dragged me closer. A moan of pleasure escaped me as I ran my tongue in slow, delicious circles around hers, teasing every little bit of it. A hunger for her that had been building over weeks broke loose. I wanted to be as close to her as possible, which the gentle kiss didn't even begin to cover.

My hand moved from her heated cheek to the back of her neck. I pulled her against me, claiming her mouth with a fierceness that was new even to me. Susan opened her thighs so her knees no longer pushed against my legs. She let me stand between them and, wrapping her arms around my neck, she held on tight. Her cold fingers on my skin triggered a shiver down my spine, the sensation adding to my pleasure.

I chuckled and, not entirely breaking the kiss, murmured, "We really need to do something about that sometime." Reaching behind my neck, I took her hands in mine to warm them and moved them behind her back. This way, I dragged her closer and lifted her the inch up onto the side of the table. Trapped in my arms, Sue straightened as much as she could to meet each of my hungry kisses. Damn, here was the proof she needed—we were epic together.

Still half-kissing her, I whispered, "Say yes."

Susan's eyes fluttered open. Our foreheads touching, her chest heaved as she struggled to catch her breath. "To what?" she croaked.

I inched back so I could look her straight into her eyes. A tiny smile of hope curved my lips. "Do you want to be my girlfriend?"

Of all the things she could have said and done then, Sue hesitated. Tense with anticipation, I moved her hands to the front and held them tight in her lap. Could she say yes faster, please? Her reluctance was killing me.

To assist her with this apparently hard decision, I started nodding and raised a suggestive eyebrow.

There! A smile. She cracked a smile! That was a good sign, right? She would say yes. Oh please, God, make her say yes. And then, very slowly, Susan began to mirror my nodding.

I swallowed hard and expelled a long breath. "Dammit, girl, you know how to put a guy on the rack, don't you?"

She giggled. "You totally deserved—"

Yeah, whatever. Cupping her face in my hands, I silenced her with another yearning-filled kiss. I'd been waiting too damn long for this, and talking was not on my list of things to do right now.

Susan surrendered utterly and completely. A little late, yes, but here my only Christmas wish was coming true. *Thank you, Santa! I'll have cookies and milk ready for you next year!*

As her thighs pressed against the sides of mine in eagerness, it reminded me of the little package in my pocket, and I broke the kiss. "Since it's official now, we're a couple," I said with a smirk, slipping my hand into my right pocket and fishing out the present, "I guess it's okay to give you this."

Eyes on the little blue package in my hand, Susan's mouth fell open in astonishment. "How did you—" The next instant, she lifted her chin with a knowing laugh and yelled, "*Sam!*"

"I'm sorry!" Samantha yelled through the closed door. And she probably wasn't the only one who'd been holding her breath outside while I'd struggled to put the situation right with Sue. Heck, I should have known...

Laughing, I rolled my eyes to the ceiling. "Guys, go away!"

"Okay!" another girl shouted from the other side of the door. "But don't stay in there for too long. It's almost midnight. We're moving to the garden!"

On that cue, Susan glanced at the clock and asked me in a whisper, "Think we should go with them?" She probably didn't want more of our private conversation to be carried out to the rest of the partygoers.

I intended to take her out to all our friends and wish her a happy New Year on the stroke of midnight. But I also wanted her to be wearing the bracelet at that time. "Open it first," I urged her, putting the package into her hand.

Like a child on Christmas morning, Sue beamed at me and

ripped the bow off the gift. Then she started picking at the Scotch tape from all sides, twisting the little box in her hand like it was a Rubik's Cube.

I frowned at her busy fingers. She was making quite an effort to get into the package, but somehow the fricking little thing managed to stay sealed. "Heck, I'm starting to wonder if the reason you never opened it is actually because you simply couldn't." With a grin on her face and biting her lip, Susan cut me a glance. I grimaced sheepishly. "I did a darn good job with the wrapping, eh?"

"It certainly wouldn't get ripped by accident," she teased.

Maybe I should do it myself. We had, after all, only seven minutes left until midnight. I took the box from her, went behind the bar at the back of the room, and pulled a pocketknife from the top drawer where Hunter usually kept all the utensils to open bottles and corks and stuff. Making quick work of it, I sliced through the wrapping paper, then closed the knife, and put it back. A push of my hip, and the drawer shut.

Walking back to Susan, I took off the blue paper, crumbled it up in my hand, and tucked it into my pocket. Then I held the little box out to her with a broad grin. She opened it and pulled out the velvet bag, then shook her head. Yeah, a little jazzy, but hopefully the content was worth it. She tipped the bag upside down. The bracelet poured into her open palm.

Who could tell what she'd expected, but from the widening of her eyes and her gasp, certainly not this. With a finger, she stroked the tiny basketball.

"That's a reminder of our first unofficial night out

together," I explained in a low voice, "when you tended to my bleeding wound and defended me in front of my mom."

Her finger moved on to the strawberry.

"That's a symbol for the most amazing kiss ever."

Susan glanced up, and I smiled. As she examined the Super Mario next, I rolled my eyes and told her, "That one's from Ethan. He wanted to add something to your present, too."

Boy, she was so silent all this time, it made me uneasy. Did she like it or not? When Sue looked up again, there was a tiny grin on her lips, but she still said nothing. Suddenly she held the bracelet out to me. What the—? Was she giving it back? Knitting my brows, I took it from her and swallowed hard.

I stared at the bracelet, wondering if I should tuck it in my pocket or just toss it on the pool table. Then Susan's forearm appeared next to my open palm. "Help me put it on?" she asked.

Ah, hell yeah! Sighing with relief, I sneaked a glance at her face and smirked before I fastened the silver chain around her wrist. She leaned forward and kissed me on the cheek. "Thank you. It's adorable."

It took a fricking load off my mind as I fastened the thing around her wrist.

While Susan shook her hand, watching the delicate bracelet dangle from her wrist, I checked the time. It was just shy of midnight. The house had become silent in the past five minutes. The music was still on, but no chatter drifted through the door anymore.

"We better join them in the garden, or we're going to miss

the celebration," Susan suggested. As she slid down from the pool table, I held out my hand. Without any hesitation, she put hers in mine. Her fingers were still cold as always, but it didn't matter. I would warm them for her. Tonight. Tomorrow. And every day from now on, as long as she let me.

Chapter 29

AS WE WALKED through the door out into the garden, everyone was counting down the last seconds to midnight. Susan became fidgety. She skipped in front of me, despite the high heels, and pulled me across the lawn. Dammit, girls really knew how to handle those heels, even on grass. Most of the crowd was gathered down by the gazebo. Susan, it seemed, wanted to be with her friends at the strike of twelve. I could understand that. I would have loved to be with Tyler, Becks, and Brady, too, but we were running out of time, and I would certainly not give up a New Year's kiss to go searching for my friends.

As everyone yelled, "*One!*" and party poppers sounded from all sides, I dug my heels in the ground and made Sue stop, twisting her around to me. Falling against my chest, a breath escaped her. I caught her in a gentle embrace and touched my forehead to hers. "Happy New Year, sweetness."

Her eyes fixed on mine, she bit her lip and grinned. "Back

at you, *Dream Guy Material.*"

Oh, she'd finally come to terms with it. I kissed that bottom lip she was biting and then deepened the kiss. Somewhere close by, everyone started singing "Auld Lang Syne." It wasn't the best song in the world, and it was sung off-tune, but sometimes you had to take what you got. Slowly, we started swaying under the starry night, and I told her, "I think we should change that name on your phone again."

She gave me an expectant look. "To what this time?"

Behind her, in the distance, a firework raced up to the sky and burst into a shower of gold and blue sparks. Susan winced at the sudden bang. Distracted from her question, she turned in my arms, leaned back against my chest and, together with the rest of the gang, we watched a series of colorful explosions. Even though the singing had long stopped, I kept swaying my girl, enjoying the nearness that she'd denied me for so many weeks.

Dream Guy Material was all right, but the status had changed tonight. Sue should be reminded of that every time she got a message from me in the future, so I leaned down to the side of her face and whispered in her ear, "To *Boyfriend.*"

She made my favorite sound. The giggle probably meant my proposal was accepted.

Some twenty feet away, I caught a glimpse of my brother. As we locked gazes over the distance, he nodded and smiled, approving of the girl I held in my arms. Obviously, the evening was going quite well for him, too. Ted was in the group of guys around him. Although they both kept their hands safely tucked

ANNA KATMORE

in their pockets, they were turned to each other in a way that left little room for speculation—for those who knew, anyway.

Sue tilted her head back to lean against my shoulder, pulling my attention back to her. "What did *you* save me as in your contacts?"

Why? Was it so unlikely I'd used her real name? Then again, I hadn't, from the very beginning, and she obviously knew me too well. Instead of telling her that she was *the one* for me, I tugged my phone out of my pocket, found her on the contacts list, and showed her.

"Oh my God!" Bursting with laughter, she shook against my chest. "You can't be serious!"

I planted a soft kiss beneath her ear and assured her, "Totally am."

Tucking the phone away again, I made Sue turn back to me, and she wrapped her arms around my neck. "That wasn't your name for me in the beginning, right?" she asked, her gleaming eyes turning skeptical.

"No." I bit down a chuckle. "Not from the beginning."

"So, what did you call me?"

Oh, there were many things I'd called her in my mind. Weird geek, nerd girl, Little Miss Sunshine, snappy kitten, Ponytail Sue, the love of my life... She wouldn't hear any of them. Not tonight, anyway. I shook my head. "Not saying."

"Come on, I want to—" She didn't get to finish that demand, because a bunch of people rushed us then.

"Here they are!" Frederickson shouted, bringing the whole soccer gang with him.

Ryan handed me a champagne flute, and we bumped fists as he mouthed, "Good job." I acknowledged it with a nod and grinned. Then he yelled, "Here's to an epic New Year!"

Susan had gotten her own glass from Lisa. We all raised them to Hunter's toast. Over his shoulder, I spotted T-Rex, Brady, and the others huddled in a group down by the garden swing. When Becky's glance skated over to me, she smiled, slapped Tyler on the shoulder, and pointed in my direction. I toasted them with my glass before finally drinking with the others.

A minute later, Susan lifted to her tiptoes—if that was even possible in already high heels—and craned her neck. Since most of her friends were with us, it wasn't hard to guess who she was looking for. Pointing to her left, where Ethan was still with his friends, I told her, "He's over there." Putting our glasses on one of the tables placed around the garden tonight, I laced our fingers and dragged Sue with me. "Let's go wish him a happy New Year."

Ethan gave me a fist-pound followed by a quick hug. As he released me, he shot Susan a glance and winked.

"So what's the deal?" His gaze returned to me. "Can I hug your girlfriend without you going shark attack on me?"

"Nope."

As I pulled Susan playfully against me, she smacked me on the chest and laughed. "Chris!"

There was no way to hold this kitten tight when she started to wiggle. With a chuckle, I let her go so she could wish Ethan happy New Year, too. Quickly.

Soon the crowd started to move back inside. As we followed, I asked Susan, "When do you have to be home?"

"One thirty."

Oh. That was early. I didn't want to let her go at all tonight, but getting in trouble with my new girlfriend's mother on the first night of our brand new relationship wouldn't be the best start either. "Okay, I can't drive you home because I had a drink or two earlier, but if you like, I can walk you."

"That's not necessary," she replied. "One of the guys can give me a ride."

"But I want to." I put on the sweetest pout I could manage, and it obviously worked.

Leaning into my side as I draped an arm around her, she gave me a small smile. "All right. But we have to leave soon. It's two miles."

I'd rather be alone with her anyway, so that was totally fine with me. We said goodbye to Hunter and the others. Tyler was nowhere in sight, but that was okay. He, Becky, and all the rest would get to know Susan soon enough.

It was good to get out of the house and leave the music and noise behind. A soft breeze wafted around us. It wasn't too cold, but Sue's dress exposed a lot of her skin, and she hadn't worn a coat. Too bad I hadn't brought a jacket that I could have loaned her. When I glanced at her, she didn't look cold or uncomfortable, though.

With our fingers laced, we ambled through the streets to her house. Eventually relaxing after all the stress of the past few weeks, I happily swung our arms between us. The jingle of her new charm bracelet sounded so right in the night.

Some time along the way, she cleared her throat and then said in a low voice, "It's weird, don't you think?"

"What is?"

"This." She held up our joined hands. "You and me, walking here, in the dead of the night...being together."

You and me. I liked the sound of it. "It isn't weird at all." Needing to be closer to her, I let her hand slip away and wrapped my arm around her shoulders. With those high heels on, she was taller than usual, but she still fit perfectly under my arm. I pressed a kiss to her temple.

"It's not?" she murmured in the dark night.

"No." Loving the way she felt and smelled and just everything about her, I pulled her a little tighter against me. "I think it's perfect."

Far too soon, we arrived at her house. Light glowed through the window in an upstairs room. Her mother was probably waiting for her to get home safely.

We stopped in the front yard, and Sue turned to me, expecting a goodnight kiss without hesitation. But I wasn't ready to let her slip away and leave me just yet. What were a few more minutes? We had a lot to catch up on after such a long time apart.

I sat down on the low stone wall hedging the driveway, took her hand, and directed a pleading look up at her. "We could sit here, just for a little while."

Susan grinned as she swayed her hips from side to side, pretending to be contemplating the idea. I tugged at her hand a bit harder. When I drawled the word "pleeeeeaaaase," she rolled her eyes in a sweet manner and sat next to me.

Taking off her shoes, she put her feet up on the wall, too, and wrapped her arms around her legs. Her cheek pillowed on her knees, a happy sigh escaped her as she watched me.

"See anything nice?" I teased her.

"Mm-hm. Very nice, in fact."

"Want to tell me about it?"

"Yeah...nope." A smile on her lips, she blinked innocently.

"Come on, don't be shy." I tickled her side, and she jerked away with a giggle.

"Nuh-uh."

I tickled her again. Susan started laughing, and the sound warmed my stomach. She should never stop laughing when she was with me. With my other hand, I kept coaxing that sweet sound out of her until she choked out a hiccup and squealed away, sliding down from the wall into the grass behind. Following her, I grabbed her ankle, pulled her back and fell on top of her—not accidentally. I stared down into her eyes, which reflected a sky full of stars. Then I kissed her hard.

A small noise above us made Sue stiffen. She pushed at my chest and shot upright. The window on the upper floor opened. Her mom leaned outside, obviously scanning the drive and front yard but not seeing us in the darkness.

"I'm here, Mom," Sue said, audibly straining to keep her voice straight and any giggles out of it.

"Honey, what are you doing outside?"

"Nothing. Chris is with me. We're just...er...sitting here."

"Just sitting here, huh?" I whispered with a smirk. She made a hushing gesture at me, but even in the dark I noticed her cheeks flush and her mouth curve up.

"Oh. Okay," Mrs. Miller said then. "But don't stay out there too long. You'll catch a cold." The curtains fell closed again, and her silhouette disappeared, but the window remained open.

I tried to keep my chuckle quiet as I said, "She doesn't trust me."

Susan snickered. "No one should. You don't play fair."

Oh, that was a low blow. Reaching out with one hand, I placed my knuckle under her chin and tilted her face toward me, planting a chaste kiss on the tip of her nose. "Are you saying that because you lost your heart to me, sweetness?"

"Hah! You wish! Think just because you give me nice presents you already have my heart?" The laugh lines around her mouth deepened, but she fought to keep a straight face.

"What? Are you saying you aren't actually smitten?" I arched a mischievous brow. "You know, I have ways to make you fall for me."

"Confident, are we?" Susan snickered then bit her bottom lip, batting her eyelashes. "You'd never stand a chance in a real challenge."

I leaned in and bit that lip for her. "Game on, little Sue."

One day before college started…

SUE SAT ON my bed, silently watching me packing the rest of my stuff. I hated when she looked at me like that. Moving to L.A. was hard enough, I couldn't handle her tears on top of my own aching heart. But of course, they had to be dealt with. Swallowing the lump in my throat, I zipped my last duffle bag closed, turned around, and leaned against the wall, pressing my lips together.

She sniffed. "Are you ready to go?"

Was I? Most of my things were already in the car my dad had given me for graduation. Ethan and I had a room on campus of UCLA, which he moved into yesterday, and Brady was waiting for me to pick him up at his house in thirty minutes. Yes. I was ready to leave.

But I didn't want to.

Not yet. Susan and I had the most amazing summer together. It was hard to stomach that our time together came to an end today. Of course it was only for a year, because after her final year in high school, Sue would come to L.A., too. And I'd be home every single weekend until then. But still… Seeing her in my t-shirt, that she'd put on after we got out of bed this morning, her lips trembling and her eyes sad, I wanted nothing more than toss my college plans and stay with her. Forever.

Wherever she was, I wanted to be, too.

I still owed her an answer, so after some hard seconds of locking gazes with her, I finally nodded. Another tear trailed down her cheek. I opened my arms, and she shuffled over to hug me. Her arms wrapped around me so tight, I couldn't get air into my lungs anymore. Or maybe that was because of my own sadness overwhelming me.

She sobbed and wiped her eyes on my shoulder then lifted her face with that pleading look of hers that always came with a cute pout. "Can I keep your t-shirt?"

"What?" I laughed softly, surprised.

"I want something that smells of you, so I can sniff it when I'm lonely and pretend that you're still here."

Oh. Cuddling her tight against my chest, I brushed my fingers through her soft hair. "Of course, you can, sweetness." Her hair tickled my nose as I planted a soft kiss on top of her head. "We'll make it. And you'll be fine. It's only a few days, and then I'll be back again for your mom's birthday."

"That's not enough," she whined.

"I know. But I'll come home the weekend afterward, and the weekend after that, and on every weekend until Winter break, I promise."

A deep sigh, then her arms lowered and she stepped back with a brave nod. "Okay. And you call me every day, right?"

"In the morning and in the evening, and if you like, between classes, too."

The sweet pout appeared again on her face. "I like." Then

she trudged out of my room to put on her shoes in the hallway. Ready to follow her, I grabbed my duffle bag, but on the way out, my gaze got caught on a lime green piece of fabric on my bed. Sue's top. I eyed the tee for a moment and then, without another thought, I swiped it. After all, she had mine, so it was only fair to take hers with me. At nights when I missed her, I would need a whiff of her beautiful sent to remind me of our sweet times together.

With the decision made, I stuffed the shirt into my duffle and zipped it close again. Then I went to find her in the hallway and laced our fingers, walking her out to my car.

I'd said goodbye to my mother already in the morning, just before she'd had to leave and meet a client, so at least I didn't have to deal with her tears, too, right now.

The way to Sue's house was short and neither of us spoke a single word. But handling the stick shift was a bit complicated with our hands still intertwined. We got out together in front of her house, and I walked around the car to hug her one last time. From the tight lines in her face, I could see how hard she tried not to cry, but her lips were wet and tasted salty when we kissed.

"I'll call you when I get there," I whispered, then I detached myself from my girlfriend and got back into the car. I knew it was a mistake to look into the rearview mirror, as I drove off, but heck, I couldn't stop myself.

Susan stood on the sidewalk, her arms hanging lifelessly at her sides, her heart-wrenching gaze following me down the road. Why did she have to make this so hard? I squeezed my eyes shut for a second, trying to abandon all memories of us at this very moment, so the goodbye wouldn't be so tough. But I might as well have tried to make this damn car fly to L.A. and would have had as much luck with that.

Ah, what the hell— I slammed on the brakes, reversed, and raced back to Susan's house with squealing tires. Her face when I got out of the car again and swept her into another tight embrace was priceless.

"What in the world are you doing?" She laughed near my ear, her arms tight around my neck. "Brady's waiting for a ride. You should be on your way to him."

I couldn't give two fucks about that right now. "Brady can wait another hour or two. And classes don't start before tomorrow." I swung her around and put her back on her feet, pushing her against the side of my car. "You're the only thing that matters at the moment, and I really don't want to go away. I'm not ready to leave you."

Her eyes grew big with wonder and delight. "So what do you want to do then?"

"Kiss you." I touched my brow against hers. "For all eternity."

Her tears drying, a small smile sneaked to her lips. "Oh, I think I'm fine with that."

And that was when we stopped talking and melted into each other with the longest goodbye kiss of all times...

ANNA KATMORE

Epilogue

"OUCH!" I JERKED my hand back and licked my stinging finger, then wiped it on a dishcloth. All right, the chocolate was ready to go on the cake.

"Chris! Is the tiramisu for table eight ready?" Ethan asked as he passed me on his way to the stove, checking on whatever was cooking there.

"In a minute. Let me just finish this baby off." If I poured the couverture over the chocolate cream cake too fast, there was a chance it wouldn't cool perfectly smooth afterward. And I wasn't doing semi-perfect. Not in my own restaurant.

Teaming up with my brother last summer after I stopped playing pro basketball in order to be home more, was one of the best decisions in my life. That and chasing after Susan Miller (now Donovan) in the first place. Whenever I thought of my wife—and that happened a lot during the day—a smile always tugged at my lips.

The cake was done and ready to go into the cold storage

room for the next couple of hours. On the way back, I cut a square piece of tiramisu, decorated it with three strawberry slices, some mint and cream, and handed it to Ethan, who was sweating it today. Marina, our part-time waitress was ill this week, and my brother helped out in front as much as he could.

Running my hands through my hair, I spun around in the middle of the huge stainless steel kitchen and glanced at the clock above the door. Ten to three. Dammit, I was running late. As soon as Ethan hurried back through the double swing door, two minutes later, I grabbed a fistful of the sleeve of his white chef's jacket and yanked him to me. "When did Will say he'd come?"

My brother opened his mouth, but the answer came from a tall guy walking in through the back door. "I'm here."

"Awesome, man!" I walked over to William Davis, who I'd known since high school and who'd also played basketball in college with me. We bumped fists, then he greeted my brother with a very personal tilt of his eyebrows while his lips were pressed together in the tiniest smile. Ethan never kissed his boyfriend in front of me...which was okay. I never kissed Susan in front of him either.

Now that my replacement had finally arrived, I shrugged out of my chef's coat, hung it on the rack by the door and, with a quick goodbye to the others, slipped out.

"Have fun!" Ethan shouted after me, then he added in an afterthought, "Or whatever is the right thing to say in this situation."

Laughing, I called back, "I'll bring you a scan of the bump.

The doctor said, we could have one this time." Then I pulled my phone out of my jeans pocket and pressed star one.

Susan answered immediately. "Chris?"

"Hi, baby. How are you feeling?"

After a short hesitation, she drawled, "I'm fine." Oh man, I could even hear the eye-roll in her voice. "I just got ready to go. See you in the evening."

"No, wait!" I unlocked my car and slid behind the steering wheel. "I'm on my way."

"Home?" Her voice rose as if this was a big surprise.

"Yes."

"You left the restaurant early?"

"Of course! I told you I don't want you to drive by yourself."

"Chri-is," she growled in frustration. "I'm not an invalid. I can still do things on my own."

"You know what the Dr. Lady said," I argued for what seemed to be the sixtieth time this week. "You have to be careful." Why was she always so stubborn?

"You're being overprotective again."

"So? Deal with it." I slid the key into the ignition, and the engine roared to life. "Now, stay where you are. I'll be home in ten minutes."

After we hung up, I maneuvered out of the parking spot and headed home. Grover Beach was beautiful during Christmas season. Houses were decorated with lights, reindeers and elves stood in everyone's garden, and you could hear the song "Jinglebells Rock" in nearly every shop these days.

As I turned into our drive, Sue came out the door. She must have been waiting by the window again. She always did when she knew I was coming home. And deep within my soul, I hoped she'd never stop doing that.

While she locked the door of our two-story house, I got out of the car and walked up behind her. When she turned around, her gummy-bear eyes lit up with delight. And my heart did a somersault of joy. Was there anything better in the world than coming home to a beautiful girl that loved you even more after seven years of being together? Without a word, I cupped her face in my hands and kissed her. Hard. Because I'd been waiting to do that since I left our house this morning.

Then I inched back and breathed, "Hey, sweetness," running my hands down my wife's alluring body. Reaching her sexy ass, I just couldn't resist pinching her, and she jumped in my arms. "Ah, happy to see me, are you?" I taunted her.

Sue smacked me on the shoulder for the pinch, but her girly strength had never grown into full woman strength, so it was like the brush of a dove, really. *My* dove. With a chuckle, I pressed a kiss on her lips, laced my fingers through hers, and walked her down to the car. Holding the door open for her, I took her hand and helped her in. She rolled her eyes at me. Was I overdoing the protective part? Nope, I didn't think so.

One hand on her headrest and one on the dashboard, I leaned down and kissed her again. "Just being careful."

On the drive to the doctor, Susan went really silent. Her gaze was glued to the side window for most of the ride, but I doubted it was something outside that held her interest for so

ANNA KATMORE

long. Usually, when she fell this quiet, she retreated into a world of her own. Some place inside her head where she hardly ever let me in. It was happening a lot when she read books or edited manuscripts for the publisher she was working for. But right now, it had to be something different.

"What are you thinking about?" I ask her softly, to bring her back to reality as we stopped in front of the doctor's office.

Smiling, she tilted her head. "Nothing. Let's go inside."

It sure wasn't *nothing*, but as long as that particular thought made her as happy, nobody would hear me complain.

Susan reached out to open her door, but I stopped her with a hand on her shoulder. "Wait." I climbed out quickly and rushed around the car to help her out. Sighing heavily, she let me have my way. I smiled apologetically as she got out and then laced our fingers.

On the stainless steel sign next to the door of this yellow bungalow, the words *Alice Tallaware, Dr. med., Gynecologist* were carved in black italic fonts. I'd only been here once in my life. Four weeks ago. When we got Susan's test results. And everything had changed after that.

As soon as we walked inside, the receptionist looked up and greeted us with a big smile from across the frosty glass counter. "Hello, Mrs. Donovan," she said to Sue. "You can go right in. The doctor's waiting for you." Then she turned her beaming face to me and brushed a few strands of hair behind her ear that had slipped out of her black bun. "Mr. Donovan, would you mind signing a card for my nephew? It's his tenth birthday on Saturday and he's one of your biggest fans." She held out a basketball card of myself to me.

"Yes, of course." I signed it, then followed Sue into the doc's office.

"Ah, Susan," the woman with the short chestnut hair and freckles said as she shook my wife's hand. "I see you brought support."

The wry grin on Susan's face when she looked at me was unfair. The girl deserved another pinch in her butt cheek, but it would have to wait until we were out of here again. She laughed, turning back to the doc. "Yeah, he barely lets me go anywhere alone since we left your office the last time."

"Just taking care of the little bump," I murmured in defense, as I shook the doctor's hand. I sure wasn't the only concerned man coming in here. Right?

Dr. Tallaware nodded to a stool next to the examination table. "Please, take a seat, Mr. Donovan."

I did, after helping my wife onto the examination table. She reclined, then took my hand and squeezed, mouthing, "I love you." Yeah, deep down we both knew how much she really liked me taking care of her. And the bump, too. I rubbed over her knuckles with my thumb and sighed.

"All right, let's see how this darling is doing," the doc said while she squeezed a transparent goo from a plastic bottle onto Sue's tummy and ran her ultrasound device over the lower part of her belly. It only took seconds until she obviously found the right spot to zoom in. On the monitor above the ultrasound machine, a picture emerged in various shades of grey.

Sue and I watched in silent anticipation.

Last time we'd been here, all Susan had to do was pee in a cup. The doc had said it was too early to see anything on the screen yet. But today—

I held my breath as the random valleys and hills on the monitor came to life. They moved whenever the doc moved the device on Susan's belly.

"You see, this triangle is the cone of the ultrasound," Doc Tallaware explained, pointing out what she meant on the screen. "Here's your uterus, Susan, and this"—she tilted her head and smiled at us—"is the little Donovan that will soon move in with you."

The little Donovan. Susan's little bump. According to the measurement at the bottom of the screen, it was only the size of a walnut yet, but it made my chest swell with daddy-pride. I tightened my hold on Susan's hand and gave her a smile when she beamed at me.

"Let's see, if we get a surround view of your baby." The doctor pressed the device down a little harder, tilting it this way and that. The picture on the screen changed. Something about it must have made the doc a little nervous, because suddenly her nose was glued to the screen and her brows came together in a frown. I tried to understand what was going on, but all I could see was another walnut inside my wife.

"Is...is that normal, Doc?" I asked, my heart suddenly pounding with fear. Good Lord, it didn't mean that my son was going to have two heads or anything, right?

"Well, it certainly happens more often than you'd think."

What? That a kid was born with two heads? Why the hell

would that make her so cheerful?

"Congratulations, Susan," she said then. "From what we can see here, you're going to have twins."

Twins...

I looked at Susan's face, but her eyes were still focused on the screen, her cheeks going as pale as mine felt. She said something, but the conversation that followed between her and the doctor were like underwater noises, floating past me and out the window.

Twins...

How did *that* happen? What on earth had Susan and I done wrong to produce two?

Sweat started to gather underneath my collar.

Twins...

They would use their identical looks to trick us. My hand slipped away from Susan's. I raked my fingers through my hair, envisioning how they were going to wake up every morning and think: *How can we fool Mommy and Daddy today?*

Twins...

If they took even just a little after me, they would be up to mischief. A lot.

Oh dear, was I really ready for this? Was Sue? I knew she really wanted this child. We both did. But two at once? Frankly, it scared the shit out of me. Closing my eyes, I rubbed my hands over my face. And suddenly an image danced up inside my mind. Two little guys, smiling at me with gummy-bear eyes as warm as Susan's, their hands maybe sticky from a stolen chocolate cake, and their blond hair tousled like mine.

We could paint picture books together. Or I could teach them how to play basketball. Note to self: pave a basketball field in the garden next week.

The two of them would have an awesome childhood, sticking together all the time like Ethan and I had done. They were going to be two cool dudes, twisting the girls in kindergarten around their fingers. Oh damn, wait! Girls? That was bad. I would have to set a few things straight before they could get their necks into the kind of trouble I did with Sue.

Picturing my kids in that kind of mess one day, I was overwhelmed by a flood of sweet and funny memories from my time in high school. And just what would E.T. and Will say when they saw the double walnut on the scan photo tomorrow? Rippling laughter rocked my chest. "Well, Uncle Ethan and William are going to love that," I answered my own question, got up from the stool, and headed out the door. Fresh air, that's what I needed now. A lungful. Or two.

At the car, I pulled out the keys, but instead of unlocking, I just banged my head on the roof.

Twins... Oh boy.

*

"What do you think about Elizabeth and Taylor?"

My eyes flew open, but they took a second to adjust in the dark. "What do you mean?" I asked Susan over my shoulder. The digital clock on my night stand flashed 23:19. Obviously, someone couldn't sleep.

"As names. For the babies," she explained. "I think it would be cool to name them after some celebrities. Maybe, Matt and Damon for boys. Or—huh!" The mattress wobbled, which meant she'd just jerked upright in bed behind me, thrilled by her own genius. "We could name them after book characters. Like Percy and Jackson. Or"—she clapped her hand on my shoulder—"Harry and Potter!"

Was she for real? I switched on the bedside lamp and rolled around, propping up on my elbow. With a stern look at her, I told her slowly and clearly, "We're definitely not going to name one of our kids Potter."

"Okay, then not that." She rolled her eyes, but the excitement stayed. It was there all through the afternoon, dinner, evening, and while we watched her favorite movie: *50 first dates*. "So what would you suggest?"

"Isn't it a bit early to pick out baby names?"

"Hello? You're going to pave a basketball field in our garden tomorrow! I mean, it's not like they'll be playing there any time soon."

"The cement needs to dry."

"How long? Like four and a half years?" She laughed at me, making the bed wobble again, and dropped back onto her pillow, staring happily at the ceiling. "Do you think we'll be good parents?" Her eyes moved to lock with mine. "Do you think they'll love us?"

Scrunching my face, I chuckled. "Not if we call them Potter or Percy."

Susan shoved at my shoulder, but I only leaned down to

kiss her on the lips then I switched off the light again. It didn't take long until she came crawling under my covers and snuggled up against my chest. Sliding my arm behind my head, I wrapped the other around Sue, holding her tight for a moment. "Honestly, I think we'll be pretty awesome parents. And of course our sons will love us!"

"I think you're right," she mumbled, then she paused. "What if they're going to be girls? Would you be disappointed?"

"Are you kidding me?" I brushed my fingers through her hair and planted a kiss on top of her head. "Having two little clones of you would be great." And definitely less trouble than having two clones of myself. But somehow I got the feeling that we wouldn't be so lucky. Donovan genes. They were pure testosterone and obviously they very often came in double packs.

But whatever constellation was growing inside Sue's belly right now, they would be the prettiest and most awesome kids in the world, without a doubt.

Caressing Susan's shoulder under the strap of her top, I softly told her, "I like Felicity and David."

She hummed against my naked chest. "I like them, too."

"See? We're already fantastic parents."

*

I dribbled the ball extra low, making it bounce no higher than a foot above the ground. "Come and get it, buddy. You know how to do it."

When my four-year-old son cut in to steal the basket ball from me with his tiny hands, a wave of pride washed over me. I chased him across the small court, then lifted him up on my shoulders and let him dunk the ball. His squeak of joy as the ball slid through the hoop almost split my ear drums. "Daddy, see! See!"

"Awesome, buddy!" I told him. Spinning on the spot, I held his shins tight while he was stretching out his arms, enjoying the imaginary cheers from an invisible audience around us.

"Chris?" Susan's voice drifted from inside the house and made me stop the rotating. "Where's David?"

"He's here with me! We're playing basketball!" I called back.

Moments later, she appeared through the backdoor. Her warm smile, when she saw David in victory mode on my shoulders, was quickly replaced by a reprimanding one for me. "We should have left ten minutes ago. Can you help Dean tie his shoelaces and find his jacket, please? I still need to do my hair."

My gaze landed on the tiny four-year-old in red flap-trousers, clinging to her hand. His big eyes glassy and his mouth turned down, he looked quite unhappy, but then he always did when we had to drive somewhere. Getting car sick as much as he did wasn't funny.

As soon as I lowered David down, he ran off after the basketball. His shots to the hoop were missing by miles, but that didn't stop him from trying.

I went over to my wife, kissed her on the cheek, and playfully tugged on her ponytail. "Your hair is perfect. Don't change it." Then I leaned in and whispered in her ear, "Anyway, why are we in such a hurry? The baby is out. It's not like it's going to crawl back inside her later today."

Laughing, she pinched me in the side. "No, but I promised Lisa to be there before Ryan's entire family shows up. It'll get really crowded in the hospital then."

"Okay. Go get ready, I'll get the boys in the car." After Sue disappeared inside again, I bent down and started tying Dean's shoes.

"Daddy? Do we get a needle today?"

"Hm?" I looked up at his worried face. "No. Why would you think so?"

"Because Mommy said we're going to the hospital."

Cupping his chubby cheek, I assured him with a smile. "Don't you worry, little man. We're just visiting Auntie Lisa."

"Does *she* have to get a needle?"

"I don't think so."

"She's having a baby girl, right, Daddy?" David cheered as he came barreling toward us, losing the ball somewhere on the way.

"Yes, that's right. And Mommy wants to see the baby. So we're all going," I explained.

A frown pulled Dean's tiny brows together for a second. "But what if the doctors still want to put a needle in my arm?"

Yeah, what did you tell a kid who was traumatized by an

allergy test? I held his sorrowful gaze, feeling his pain inside my own chest as I squeezed his hands and remembered the torture.

"You don't have to be scared, Dean," David said and surprised me when he grabbed his baggy jeans, pulled them higher up to his waist, then laid one arm around his brother's shoulders and looked him solemnly in the eyes. "I will protect you from the doctors."

An instantaneous smile lit up Dean's face. "Will you fight them, if they try to hurt me?"

"Yes. And if you don't puke on me in the car today, you can also have half of my ice cream."

"Ice cream?" I asked with a chuckle, ruffling David's hair. "Who said there was going to be ice cream today?"

He grinned, and all the mischief of my own childhood sparked up in his eyes. "You always buy us ice cream, when we come out of the hospital."

The munchkin had a point, even though it was mostly Susan's and my way of making up for any needles that had previously gone into their arms. But if the rules said ice cream, I should be the last one to object.

"All right, ice cream it is!" I lifted Dean up on my arm and took David by the hand. Together we walked inside, looking for their mom, so we could finally go and see the newest baby in town.

– The *real* End –

Playlist

Sheppard – Let Me Down Easy
(Life is good)

Red Hot Chili Peppers – Snow
(A phone number on his arm)

Kelly Clarkson – Heartbeat Song
(Intrigued by a nerd girl)

Mattafix – Big City Life
(A fight in the changing room)

AURORA – Runaway
(Confused by her care)

Charlie Puth feat. Meghan Trainor – Marvin Gaye
(Eyes in the mirror)

James Bay – Running
(Falling, and falling hard)

Lost Frequencies feat. Janieck Devy – Reality
(Soccer and a hickey)

Ellie Goulding – Love Me Like You Do
(The molten chocolate kiss)

Louisa Wendorff – Blank Space/Style (mash-up)
(A sad week of misunderstandings)

Ed Sheeran – Photograph
(Strawberry vanilla tea)

Die Toten Hosen – Tage wie diese
(Ethan)

Jason Derulo feat. J.Lo & Matoma – Try Me
(Being all she wants)

Pentatonix – Little Drummer Boy
(Waiting for a text on Christmas Eve)

Sleeping At Last – I'm Gonna Be
(Exclusive)

Birdy – Tee Shirt
(Epilogue)

A GROVER BEACH TEAM BOOK

Taming Chloe Summers

BESTSELLING AUTHOR
ANNA KATMORE

CHLOE

Camp sucks.

I should be on a plane to London, heading into an epic second year of college. Instead, I'm stuck on Frog Pond Mountain, tasked with supervising a horde of pubescent teens, all because I had some minor run-ins with the law.

But I came here with a plan: next weekend, I'm escaping from the boondocks and swindling my way back into civilization.

Unfortunately, my brilliant plan B couldn't foresee one tiny detail: Justin Andrews, alpha to the wolves and drool-worthy ghost from my past...

JUSTIN

I can't believe Chloe Summers is going to be my co-counselor at camp this year. We haven't talked in years, and we wouldn't for the rest of our lives if I had anything to do with it.

But I can't get out of this summer job. Since I'm stuck with her for the next few weeks, I might as well use the time to get back at her for what she did all those years ago. I mean, camp is supposed to be fun, right? And this could be fun indeed...

But what if a harmless game unexpectedly turns into something more serious?

Many thanks

First and foremost to all my wonderful readers. The girls and women that pick up my books and send me messages every day, telling me how my stories make their lives so much better, are the real reason for me to sit down at my computer every morning and don't stop writing until late at night. I hope I can make you happy with my books, because you sure make me happy with your beautiful feedbacks.

Hi to my thousand Facebook buddies. Thanks a million times for talking to me, giving me your advice, your opinions, your time, and your love. On so many days, my desk would be a boring place without you!

A shout out to my one and only critique partner, Lyn. You're the very best, and you know that, right? I don't know what more to say, except, I hope that you'll always & forever be around. Hugs! (That one day you actually called was scary, LOL!)

My love goes to my family. I'm sorry that you don't always get an answer from me straight away when you walk into my writing room, but I value your understanding and support more than anything in this world. My home is where you are.

And finally – a huge *thank you* to my very own small group of special people! My beta readers: Barbara, Crystal, Renae, Martha, Shannon, Jessa, Jaime, and Felisha. With your sweet, enthusiastic feedbacks, you always put a big smile on my face.

And then there's Silje... Girl, you know what I want to say to you wouldn't fit on one page. So I won't even try. LOL. Whatever. ;-) Talk later.

Also by Anna Katmore

PLAY WITH ME

RYAN HUNTER

T IS FOR...

DATING TROUBLE

THE TROUBLE WITH DATING SUE

TAMING CHLOE SUMMERS (a spin-off)

*

SUMMER OF MY SECRET ANGEL

*

NEVERLAND

PAN'S REVENGE

ABOUT THE AUTHOR

ANNA KATMORE prefers blue to green, spring to winter, and writing to almost everything else. It helps her escape from a boring world to something with actual adventure and romance, she says. Even when she's not crafting a new story, you'll see her lounging with a book in some quiet spot. She was 17 when she left Vienna to live in the tranquil countryside of Austria, and from there she loves to plan trips with her family to anywhere in the world. Two of her favorite places? Disneyland and the deep dungeons of her creative mind.

For more information, please visit her website at annakatmore.com

Or find her on Facebook: facebook.com/katromance

14914654R00294

Printed in Poland
by Amazon Fulfillment
Poland Sp. z o.o., Wrocław